MW01199817

2/20

Lost Names

A. N. Mouse

This book is, as always, dedicated to a slew of people. Azalea Forrest, my wonderful editor, who persevered to make this book my most polished yet. Ace Layton, Max Steel and Coral Sobschak, all of whom graciously lent me their intellectual property with the trust that I would treat their ideas with respect and love.
And to Heidi Peters. I love you, and happy birthday.

1:

The shadows seemed to stick to him as much as he stuck to them, and the ever-present hum of machinery lulled Yoru into a state of calm contentment. To another thief, that feeling would be a death sentence. To Yoru, it was just a sign that the job was going as planned. There had been thieves since the beginning of time, and he thought that maybe his family had been thieving for about as long. He knew well the measure of night and took solace in all of its oddities. He took solace in his own oddities, too, because life was especially short when you felt called to do dangerous things as a profession.

In the darkness above the guard station, he laid on the maintenance catwalk and closed his eyes, listening to the scattered conversations below. He had a basic grasp of the language, enough to get by. Not enough to wax poetic, but he had other languages to fulfill that particular requirement.

Underneath, they discussed an hourly status update. That was usual. From what he gathered, there was nothing of note occurring. That was true, because he hadn't yet occurred and he did not think that someone would be here with the same intent. There was, by the nature of the world, more things to steal than there were thieves.

He pulled himself up, moving farther away from the guard station and towards their storage areas. It was far too late, or far too early, for any of this place to be very crowded. He thought that perhaps he could have done this job during the day with about the same amount of success, but it wasn't a rush job. Everyone could rest easily, and he would slip in and out with his prize completely unseen.

There were proper lights closer to the ground, but even they were few and far between the farther he got from where the guards had collected. Instead, he was nearing an unusual red glow. Not his target, and he thought that he would pass it by entirely without knowing its source. That wasn't so bad. Work often provided the best inspiration for his written passion and the eerie lights surely would be worth a few words on a page.

And then the screaming started.

That made Yoru stop in his tracks, his head tilted as he tracked the noise. That was not a typical nighttime sound. Buried just under the agony was the sound of crackling electricity, and these two together meant a change of plans. Neither of those things should have been there, and both spelled potential trouble for him if he was unaware of their source.

And, well, someone was screaming. It sounded as though they were in a great deal of pain. It was not something so easily dismissed.

The enchanting light and the disquieting noise seemed to have the same source. Soundlessly, he jumped from one catwalk to another, and when he was close enough he climbed down from the maintenance structure and onto the roof of a lower building. He laid along its sloped surface and peered over the edge. So harsh was the light and so thick were the shadows that he was nearly invisible where he lay.

It was some sort of glass enclosure and the red light seemed to have been a practical measure; the floodlights had been filtered to dampen them. Someone sleeping or working nearby must have complained about the glare. That was not so strange; red was a lot easier on the eyes in the dark. It was what was inside the glass that surprised him.

There was a lone man, shirtless and on his knees. Out of his back protruded all manner of nasty-looking technology. The cycle was easy to spot; things would go quiet for a few moments, and then the electricity would start to crackle and he would start screaming again. At first it was wordless, but soon enough the silence between was filled with weak struggle and breathless pleading for the torment to end.

This did not sit well with Yoru. He had seen much of the darkness in the world, he arguably made his living from it, but this seemed senseless. Barbarity aside, if the lights made problems, surely the screams would as well? There must have been another way.

He moved away from the edge. This would not help him reach his goal, though it brewed at the back of his mind. It hadn't been going on when he entered the facility. But, it went on often enough that they had a setup for it, and that no one seemed to pay it much mind. Interesting.

Yoru dropped down off the side of the building, quiet as a sigh. Ground level was the most dangerous, the most populated, the most well-lit, but the challenge was not more than he could handle. He had the layout memorized, and while he hadn't seen that torture chamber back there —it had been labelled 'organic generator' on the map—the rest of it seemed to line up pretty neatly. A few more corners and he would have his prize.

Usually, he'd be after the data terminal that was to the right. He took a brief detour that way and took a moment to take the plug from his bag and slot it in where it was meant to go. He wasn't here expressly to information drain, but he was sure he could find a buyer for it when he was done. Today, his employers wanted something a little more concrete. Of course, he lived to please.

He was looking for one of the captain's quarters. It was one of the same beige tents that populated the decrepit hangar, only this lucky fellow got one for himself. In it, presumably, was one sleeping body and a very specific firearm.

It had been stolen from a local gangster with sentimental attachments. He'd wanted the man dead, but Yoru wasn't an assassin by trade. He'd settle for his weapon returned, and that was something that Yoru could do. He tried to leave the assassination jobs to the professionals. He was, at best, a hobbyist in that career.

He slipped inside, the darkness therein eagerly devouring him. The messy desk and low bunk weren't a surprise. The fact that it held two bodies, and not one, was. Still, not a problem. Quiet enough for one was quiet enough for two. Yoru stepped in, slipped the gun into his belt and ducked out again, pulling himself away from the shadows with some reluctance. Back into the dim, then.

The screaming had stopped.

Yoru hesitated. Then, instead of leaving as he should have, he doubled back the way he had come. He wanted to see that 'organic generator' again. His stomach sank to think of the reason for the quiet that now enveloped them. Perhaps the map had not been a misnomer at all.

He had to stop short, jumping back into the shadow of a building when he heard footsteps much closer than he expected. He sank back behind a disorganized shelf of supplies and spied through it with little trouble.

They were dragging the man away. Or, he thought it was the same man. He seemed to be unconscious. The machinery that had been fitted to his body was no longer attached to him. Yoru did not get a clear look at his back to see what damage had been wrought.

He should leave, but he didn't. This was a completely avoidable risk, but he reasoned it away tidily enough. His intuition said to go for it, and he would trust that over all common sense. The two people who had apprehended the man then tossed him unceremoniously into a smaller tent. Yoru heard them chatter to each other and watched their backs as they retreated down the narrow alley between constructs.

This time, the tent he ducked into was lantern-lit. He didn't like the light, but ignored it in favour of looking around. The room was entirely empty except the man on the ground and now Yoru saw the awful mess that had

7

become of his back. It had been fitted with some sort of permanent fixtures, right into the flesh, but they seemed badly healed and seeped blood around the edges. The fixtures themselves seemed to leak some sort of terrible, dark fluid.

Yoru bent down. The man could scream and alert everyone around them, but his shaky breathing made it all the more likely that he was on the verge of passing out.

A pair of brown eyes blinked at him under the too-short regulation haircut. Yoru caught the word for 'foreigner', which he was, and then the word for 'help'.

Which, he decided, he also was. Perhaps a bad choice. It would not have been his first.

Yoru took the man's arm and pulled it over his shoulder. He checked his pulse, wanting to make sure he wouldn't be carting around a dead man, but it seemed he was merely exhausted. No sooner had he drawn close to Yoru than he promptly lost consciousness. Maybe for the better. At least he was quiet now. It wouldn't be the first time Yoru had dragged a lifeless body around. It probably wouldn't be the last.

With his two prizes, Yoru made his way out of the base camp just as quietly as he had entered it. No one was any the wiser.

~*~

To some people, Yoru was an idiot. He didn't deny that sometimes he took risks that others viewed as unnecessary. In fact, he was often the first to say so. His saving graces were, of course, his success and his sanity. Whatever he did, he obviously did it well enough to make a career. And, unlike some people he knew, he could still sleep at night.

He traded the gun for payment ahead of schedule and left the job with a flourish and a smile. Then, he took his other acquisition and found themselves a place to lay low, as far away from the pulsating tendrils of the military that Yoru could manage.

And it was a good thing he did, because when the man woke, it was not quietly.

He sat bolt upright in the bed, gasping harshly as though he had run a mile. Or, perhaps as though he had been drowning. That was probably closer to reality. Yoru had been dozing in a chair next to the bed, not quite willing to leave the man alone in case he dropped off in his sleep. Dropped off into death, that was, as he didn't seem to be holding on to life with all that much enthusiasm.

He jumped, frantic and lost, and Yoru was awake in an instant.

8

"Whoa, my friend. You're safe. You're safe." Yoru didn't know enough of his language to get much of an explanation in and he didn't think the man was in any state to listen if he tried.

As for a response, the man gripped the blanket he was under with a hand that went white at the knuckles and began to spout too many questions for Yoru to keep track of. So, Yoru fired back one of his own.

"What's your name?" he tried.

The man was shaking and he curled in on himself, pressing himself back against the corner that framed the bed. He stuttered something about the 'organic generator', Yoru recognized the phrase, and then what seemed to be a string of numbers. An ID of some kind?

Yoru stood and took the man by the shoulders and firmly, calmly, asked him something else.

"What does your mother call you?"

The man looked at him wild-eyed and shocked, but the words seemed to get through to him.

"Dan," he answered weakly.

Yoru released him and sat down again where he had been next to the bed. Then, he smiled.

"Hello, Dan. I'm Yoru," he said. He switched to Omnian after the fact, hoping that the man had picked some up. Most military personnel usually did. "You speak Omni? I'm running out of words."

Dan nodded, and he tried to press his face to his hands when he seemed to realize he only had one.

He looked at the bandaged stump, and then at Yoru.

"My hand...?" he asked.

"You didn't have it when I rescued you. I'm afraid I don't know," Yoru said sympathetically. The wound hadn't looked new, but it had looked a little roughed up, so he had bandaged it regardless. A lot of Dan had looked rough, and Yoru had put both considerable time and effort into cleaning him up and patching what he could.

Dan held the injured arm close to his chest, used his other hand to rub his face. "Where am I? Who are you?" he asked. He sounded tired and there was an edge of panic creeping into his words. He was trying to hold it together. Yoru tried to answer him as reassuringly as he was able.

"I found you in a military encampment not far from here. I wasn't there for you, but you asked me for help and so, here we are." He gestured to the room around them. "It's a safe-house, someplace I trust. I don't know who I stole you from, exactly, but I figured it was better if we kept things low key

9

for a while."

"They won't be happy that I'm gone," Dan said. He seemed comfortable enough using the language, but Yoru could hear where his accent pulled at his words.

"Are you happy that you're gone?" he asked in response.

Dan didn't look at him, and the one hand he had tightened over the bandages of the hand he had lost. Then he nodded.

"How about I make us some tea, and we'll take a look at all those injuries," Yoru said gently.

"What time is it?" Dan did look up at him then. He looked pale and exhausted, and when Yoru stood he laid a hand on Dan's shoulder. It was much more gently than before and Dan seemed to lean in to the contact.

"About 4 a.m." Yoru glanced at the clock. He went to put the kettle on, but noted Dan's wince at his answer.

"That's... You must be tired," he said eventually.

"Nonsense. I'm a thief. We're awake all the time," he said easily.

He made them both some tea. He was careful when he passed it to Dan and rightly so; his hand shook as he tried to take the cup.

"I don't know what to do," Dan said eventually. He seemed to be taking more solace in the heat of the tea than the drink itself. "I've never... I mean... I usually follow the rules," he said.

"There's a first time for everything," Yoru said thoughtfully.

Dan nodded and fell into silence again. There wasn't a lot that could be done, not immediately. The first step was just getting him to talk, about anything at all. The physical recovery certainly couldn't be hurried. Yoru was not a professional, not at this, but he thought that it was going to be a long time before Dan was well again.

He prompted the man to at least drink a little of his tea and he did, without argument. Then Yoru broke the silence in earnest. "Let's take a look at the damage." He nodded towards Dan's various injuries. "I'm sure you'll sleep better once they've been cleaned."

Yoru worked methodically. He was pretty experienced with bandaging people up. That was part of the business as much as the actual thievery was. Dan was compliant, doing whatever Yoru asked without complaint.

"You've had a rough time, haven't you?" Yoru said, mostly to himself. A lot of the bleeding had stopped already but the bruises were huge and dark. As the bleeding slowed, it was clear that the skin around the metal implants was very irritated. He didn't have anything to help that at the moment.

"I was... I made the energy," Dan said shakily. "I made the energy, but

10

I guess they needed a way to channel it. I think. I... I'm a little confused, still. My head hurts," he said.

Without a moment's hesitation, Yoru brushed his fingers through what little was left of Dan's hair. "I'll find you something to take for it, okay?" he offered.

"You're not from here," Dan said. He seemed to have trouble looking at Yoru for very long. He'd glance at him, stare for a moment, and then look away. Yoru let him. That was the least of his worries right now. "Are you from Hino?" Hinomoto, a neighbouring country to Syama. They found themselves currently in the latter, which explained Yoru's lack of proficiency with the language.

"I'm not from anywhere," he said with a smile. Not what Dan meant, but closer to the truth nonetheless. "But I am glad that we crossed paths. How fortuitous."

"For...fortuitous." Dan frowned over the word.

"Lucky," Yoru translated. "It's lucky that I was there, and that you had strength enough to call to me."

"You sound...weird," Dan said. It wasn't spoken with any malice, and he seemed displeased at how rude it sounded to his own ears. Yoru laughed.

"Different accent, remember? And, perhaps, I use big words when little ones will work just fine," Yoru said. "It's not a good habit."

"I like listening to you talk," Dan said. Of course he did. It meant he wasn't alone, and Yoru could not even fathom how much of a problem that would be for the man.

"You're in luck, my friend. I like to talk," Yoru said with a smile. This time, Dan tried to smile back.

Yoru finished his work with the bandages and he was tactful enough not to let Dan see any of the mess he had made. Knowing you were falling apart was not a comforting thought. Dan did not need to see that, not now.

"Let's be adventurous," Yoru said to him. "Do you think you could eat something, if I made it for you?"

Dan hesitated, but then nodded enthusiastically. "I am very hungry."

"Let's take it slow, and see what happens," Yoru said reasonably as he stood again.

This time, Dan glanced at the clock. Behind the curtains, the sun may very well have been rising.

"It is late. We will sleep all day, at this rate," he said worriedly.

"Then we sleep all day," Yoru answered him. "The only rules that you have now, my friend, are the ones you make yourself."

11

A.N. Mouse

2:

Oliver's apartment was meticulously clean for a scavenger. He did have a junk room, but even that was organized and tidy. Three of the walls were shelves and the fourth was a big table with all of his tools. The window was almost permanently grimy, but he had scrubbed it hard until the dirt only stuck in the corners and some sunlight could still come through, whatever rays made it through the smog. He had an old radio he had cobbled together and he used it to catch whatever stations worked that day. He wasn't picky with his music. As long as it was something cheerful, he'd listen to it. He'd sit in his scrap room and clean pieces or tinker on things until they were sell-able. It was probably his favourite part of the job. It was the quietest and safest part, certainly.

Today was not a tinker day. Today was a salvage day. That meant that he was hurrying through the crowded streets of the city, his bag on his back and his head bent low, trying to stay inconspicuous. What he did was technically illegal. At least, it was illegal enough. Arguably, the scrap he worked with was old and discarded and should have been free for the taking. On the other hand, people got killed for a lot less these days and even if he didn't die he was way too poor to even think about the legal system.

Better to be inconspicuous. And he mostly was. He was poor and dirty, the kind of poor that meant he had a job but almost nothing else. As soon as he left his apartment, the dirt and smog seemed to stick to him, and his cloud of hair got all the frizzier in whatever heat there was at ground level. Spectra City was an enormous, disgusting rat's nest of a place with The Dimmet (usually just The Dim) as the centre of it all.

The apartment buildings were huge. The city had something stupid like one hundred million people in it, so the apartment buildings were almost cities unto themselves. Most had different stores and aid centres built right in, although Oliver wouldn't go into them unless his life depended on it because he'd probably leave with something worse than he went in with.

There were other neighbourhoods outside of The Dim that were maybe not less awful but a different kind of awful. The rich kind of bad. Oliver stayed away from those places. Apartments tended to be nicer the higher up they were, and some buildings in those neighbourhoods were incredibly fancy.

How many people to an apartment block in The Dim? Ten thousand? Fifteen thousand? Oliver had no idea. A lot. Too many, usually.

Oliver lived in a dump, to be blunt. He was poor, he lived alone, and honestly, he was surprised some days that his building was still standing. He had put a lot of work into his little unit, and it was tiny and ugly but it was his. And most importantly, he could afford it with his weird-ass job.

Someone tried to pick a fight with a street vendor and Oliver just ducked his head and walked a little faster. He was okay, maybe, in a fight. Against one guy. Depending on how big the guy was. But he was way better at running away. He knew the city very well, or at least this part of it. He knew his building by memory, at least until about halfway up. It was much easier to disappear into the shadows and the dust than it was to try and survive a fight. As long as he was afraid, he was great at running and hiding.

It was when he was comfortable that he got awkward and clumsy again. Oh well. It was a system that worked. He could be awkward in his own house. That's basically what they were for, anyway.

The junk heaps were easy to find once you knew the signs. They were never labelled and no streets led to them. They were just piles of trash, after all. Dark, hidden corners that housed acropolises of old technology. Oliver would find one and then pick it over for anything good to salvage. One pile could last months before he sifted through it enough to be sure that he took everything worthwhile. He had one such pile already discovered and all it took was some winding between a claustrophobic street market and the narrow, dark alleyways between apartment blocks. And he had to keep going down, of course.

That was the thing about cities that got so big. There was always stuff underneath. People just...forgot about stuff. Hell, sometimes they forgot about people. There was certainly once or twice where Oliver was sure he could have just not paid his rent and no one would have noticed. Of course, if he was wrong, he'd be kicked into the street in a heartbeat. There wasn't enough room for everyone already.

He cut through a fallen wall that dropped him down into what looked like an old parking garage under another apartment block. He knew the underside of the building better than the topside. If he got shot down here, he'd have a better chance dragging his ass all the way back to his own block to find help rather than figure out where the aid stations were up top. Better just to not get shot then, because no matter how that story ended, it kind of sucked.

The lighting was basically shit, but he was pretty used to working in that kind of set-up. He had a light in his bag if he needed it, but seeing as that drew more attention, he'd rather not even bother. A lot of the stuff was garbage, but even garbage was useful. He could always use more wire, right? So he dug around, squinted at things in the darkness, cut away parts and pieces that he needed. He'd stop every few minutes, listening. Nothing but rats and roaches in the dark. He was well past being worried about either of them. Hard to be worried about something that was so similar to him, really.

He worked until he got hungry. He could set his watch by his stomach. Actually had before, when it died in the middle of the day and he had to figure out when it was safe to leave. Stay out too late and it wouldn't be the police that killed you.

He had some food in his bag, a little metal lunchbox he had put together out of scrap. There wasn't lots in it, but there was enough.

An alarm on his watch told him when his time was up. It would take too long for him to notice the sun setting. He had learned that the hard way. Oliver silenced the alarm and packed up as quickly as he could, shoving his work into his bag. He got a few good finds, but nothing special. Still, if he could pull that off every day, that would be great. You wouldn't need great days if you didn't have bad ones, right?

He took the open street back. He could have cut through the alleyways, it was faster, but Oliver stayed out of the shadows whenever other people were concerned, and the darkness didn't mean any less people. He wasn't afraid of the dark, he was just afraid of them. People were, without a doubt, the scariest thing in the world.

He didn't stop until the creaking, unsteady elevator finally dropped him off on his floor. Normally he wouldn't even hesitate until his door was locked behind him, but he spotted one of his neighbours struggling to carry her things. Mrs. Ahn had only one arm, two little toddlers and a rapidly ripping bag of food. Oliver scrambled with his own supplies and managed to grab the side of the bag that was trying to succumb to gravity.

"Thank you!" she said, sounding a little harried. One of the kids stumbled and fell, but seeing as they weren't very big it wasn't a long fall. They just blinked up at Oliver and he looked down in time to notice that the kid only had one eye.

He couldn't remember if that was new or not. The scar that was in place of it looked kind of new, but he didn't want to think about that.

"Here, I got it. You get the door—" he managed, trying to take the bag from her without spilling every single one of its contents.

He knew Mrs. Ahn a little. Sometimes he could hear the kids crying

15

through the walls. He was a ways down, so he wasn't sure if it was her kids specifically. It didn't bug him too much. Kids cried. He was sure that some of his machining made noise that was pretty damn annoying, too, but nobody complained to him. It seemed only fair. There had been a Mr. Ahn, at one point. Oliver remembered him. Taller, dark hair. But Oliver hadn't seen him around in a while. Maybe it was just circumstances.

She got her door open, the kid still on their feet ran inside and she bent down to scoop the other one up. With them inside, she came back for her bag. He carefully tried to pass her things to her. She thanked him again, and he went off down the hall towards his own apartment.

The hallways were wide but cluttered with other people's junk. There had been a carpet, once, long before Oliver's time. It still hung on in places but was mostly worn through down to the cement beneath it. His shoes, almost as worn as the floor, made no sound as he walked. There were some more people, either coming or going, and he waved and called out as necessary. He knew a lot of the people on his floor. Other scavengers and junk workers, factory people, cleaners, the list was endless. He tried to stay on good terms with his neighbours. It had helped him out more than once.

There had been a conflict on his floor a couple months ago. Oliver hadn't been in his apartment. But, he had sold one of the guys a hard drive and another one had bought a (minimally scratched) touchscreen from him. When there was a break in the gunfire, they let him through to get back into his house, where he pushed a bookcase full of junk against the door to hold it closed and laid low until he heard the cops come and clear everyone out. Y'know, hours after it had started. He didn't get a lot of sleep that night. Or, to be fair, most of the nights after.

It gave him a good fucking scare.

But nothing that exciting happened now. He unlocked his door (both the key lock, and the two electronic keypads he had installed himself) and closed the door behind him.

Time to get some dinner, and then maybe listen to the radio and clean up some of the salvage he got today. He thought about going to the bar briefly, but decided against it. He was feeling a little raggedy and nervous, and you couldn't pick somebody up if you were drinking just to steady your hand. Nah, he'd take it easy tonight, and maybe go out for a little tomorrow.

The bar was a little drinks n' karaoke place, and sure, it was a little dangerous to get to, but there were ways. Oliver went when he was feeling brave, because he liked it there. It was kind of a hotbed of bad shit, or at least illegal shit, but the people were nice and the music was perfectly terrible.

Today was not a brave day, and that was alright.

He flicked the light on, it stuttered for a minute before it found full brightness, and then he found himself something to eat. The food hadn't gone bad yet. It almost had, but he'd eaten worse.

He turned the radio on, tuned it to something cheerful and was just about to get to work when his phone rang. That was weird.

Oliver's cellphone was an unusual thing. He had built it out of various scrap bits and patched it into the network so he'd have service without having to pay the bill. He couldn't afford one, anyway. It was nothing like those currently on the market. The user interface was hilariously basic (he bought the program off a friend) and it had none of the web capability, visual calling or hard light technology that the new ones did. But it worked. And he could count the amount of people who had his number on one hand. Who could be calling him now?

The caller ID only worked if he had the person in his contacts. That was always fine by him, he didn't want to talk to anyone else. His screen flashed three letters.

DAN.

Oliver smiled and grabbed the phone. "Hey!" he said excitedly. He hurried over and turned the radio off so he could hear his answer.

"Hello?" Not Dan. A woman's voice, inquisitive.

"Hi. Can I help you?" Oliver's tone switched over to something more professional. He tried to hide his disappointment. He hadn't heard from Dan in a while and had just assumed he was busy. He was probably still busy.

"Is this Oliver?" she asked.

Who had his number and didn't know who he was? And who was calling from Dan's number? The whole situation was just so weird. He thought that maybe he had saved the number to his phone wrong, but they had been texting back and forth, too. What the hell?

"Speaking," he said simply.

"This is Selene Violet. Does that name ring any bells?"

Yeah, alarm bells. Still, that seemed rude and he didn't say that out loud. Selene Violet was a name that was thrown around a lot in the media, so it had eventually worked its way into his knowledge.

"You work for Highlight Technology, right?" It took him a while to remember the name. It was written on basically everything, so it should have rolled right off his tongue. Why was the... The... What did she do again? Why was someone from HiTech calling him on Dan's number?

"Yes. I know this must be very strange, so I thank you for your patience. I just thought that it would be best to call and deliver the news myself. I think that so much of humanity is lost to technology today." She spoke very evenly and politely and it did exactly nothing for his confusion. A cold sense of dread gathered in his chest like storm clouds. No matter what this call was about, it could not be anything good.

"What news?" he asked. The words came slowly from his mouth. Something was wrong. Something was really fucking wrong.

"Your friend. Dan? He was recently in my employ. There were only two numbers in his phone. One of them didn't work, and the other led to you. We have no way to contact his family. We don't know his legal name, or even where he was from."

Breathing was suddenly really hard and Oliver thought he might faint.

"What happened?" he asked. Panic had finally started to creep into his voice.

"He's—" Finally, a hesitation, a break in her otherwise pleasant tone. "He passed away. You know, he had some issues. I don't know the details, but I was told that things had not been very kind to him. He seems to have had some sort of...problem. He took his own life."

It didn't feel like a punch to the stomach or anything that solid and sure. Instead, Oliver felt his strength run out of him. The news sank in and he wilted, the sight of his home swimming in his vision.

"What about the others? Do they know?" Oliver wasn't super tight with Dan's friends, but he had met them. They were nice people.

She hesitated and Oliver pressed a hand to his mouth, already knowing what was coming next.

"They... His breakdown must have been awful. They're...no longer with us," she said.

There was nothing. No tears. No real grief. Just shock and emptiness. Oliver was just overwhelmed with it. Not Dan. He had been so nice. Funny and honest. Oliver thought he was doing okay. And his friends! He knew what Selene was implying. He couldn't believe it.

"I'm sorry for having to be the one to bring you this news. I just didn't feel right not telling anyone. You don't have any way to contact his family, do you?" she asked.

Dizzily, he shook his head before he realized she couldn't see it. "No, no I... I don't know where they are," he managed.

"I'm sorry. I... I'd really like to meet with you, if that was alright?" she asked him. The idea sounded bizarre but the weirdness of it barely registered. "I should have liked to tell you in person, and he has a few effects here that should really go to someone. I'm so sorry."

"Yeah, I—Okay." He would go. He didn't know about the others, if they had family to care for them, but there was no one else to mourn Dan or to retrieve his things. He felt he had to. Or at least that he should.

"Do you know where the office is?" she asked. He did. Not right now, though. Right now he didn't know a damn thing.

"Yeah, it's across town, by the…" He gestured aimlessly. "Pharaoh Park," he finally managed to spit out. The skyscraper district. Rich people town.

"Yes. Just walk right in the front door and talk to the front desk. Any time you feel you can, okay?" she said.

"Mhm," he agreed. Whenever he could. Maybe when he could feel his legs again. Oliver drew in a shaking breath. Dan. Gone. His friend. No, worse than that, actually. His acquaintance. They had barely started to be friends. It was all over so fast.

"I'm sorry for your loss. I hope that I will get to see you in person," she said. The end of the call. What else could she say? He was lucky he even got a call, honestly.

"Have…have a good night," he managed. Not what he meant, because that would be stupid and cruel, but she didn't say anything about it. He assumed that she understood his intent. She merely said goodbye and hung up the phone. He heard the call disconnect in his ear, and the arm holding the phone dropped. At some point, he had sunk to the floor and now he sat there with his phone in his lap.

I'll call you when I'm back in town, Dan had said. Oliver remembered how he had smiled when he said it. It looked like he was done waiting for the call.

A.N. Mouse

3:

When Dan slept again it was more akin to falling unconscious than it was to falling asleep. He had managed to eat a little and the bed was warm, so compared to previous experiences, it was heavenly. He was too tired to dream and when he woke up again there was daylight coming through one of the windows. This time there was no panic, but there was a vague sense of confusion while he wondered where he was and how he had gotten there.

Looking around, he saw the bed he lay in, a small kitchen area, the open door to a bathroom. It was a little hole-in-the-wall apartment of some sort. Still, it was clean and the decor was a little tacky, but welcoming.

And then his gaze settled on Yoru, who was sleeping on a blanket on the floor. Then everything came flooding back.

He was…away. Where exactly, he wasn't too sure. But he was away. He shuddered, retreating a little further under the blankets. The window was open and there was a slight breeze. On it, he could hear voices outside, far away. Everything was quiet and calm. He felt no need to try and rise from the bed.

Yoru was awake soon after. He pushed himself up from the ground and Dan watched him stretch. He was taller than Dan by at least a head and almost worryingly lean. That was a little hypocritical, considering Dan's current state. He was definitely underfed. Yoru was just lanky.

It was as the thief was tying back his hair that he turned and saw that Dan was also awake. "Hello, my friend," he greeted him with a smile.

"Hi…" Dan managed back. Yoru hopped to his feet and Dan tried to mimic him by at least sitting up, but even that was hard. It was a lot easier to do it the night before when he was in hysterics.

Yoru was at his side then, helping him sit up and then quickly shoving his pillow into position so he could lean back against it.

"How did you sleep?" Yoru asked him

"Like the dead."

"Looks absolutely right," the other man teased. Dan was sure he was correct. But the food and sleep had started their work. He felt more real. More solid. Yoru made them some breakfast and changed his bandages again. His back ached something fierce.

21

"I have to go out. I'll be back quickly," Yoru told him as he dressed. He seemed to favour black, much like the hair that spilled over his shoulder.

"You're leaving?" And fear, like ice, seemed to grow in his chest. Alone again. Already.

"I won't be gone long." Yoru did up his coat and moved back to Dan's bedside. "Your back needs care that I don't have the supplies for here. And, we could use something more interesting to eat than rice," he admitted with a smile. "Do not be afraid. I won't keep you waiting."

Dan took a deep breath. There were plenty of reasons for this to be silly. On the one hand, Yoru had no reason to desert his things here. On the other, Dan should not have feared being alone so heavily.

But he had no one else. Even this stranger was more reassuring than an empty room.

"I'll be back soon." Yoru laid a hand on his shoulder again and Dan looked up at him. "Be strong for me. You've already come this far."

Hearing that from a stranger should have been weird, or at least over the top. It was a little dramatic, certainly, but Dan was just getting the idea that Yoru liked a little dramatics.

So he swallowed his worry and nodded. Yoru smiled brilliantly at him, nodded back, and ducked out the door.

Of course, the return of the fear was immediate. He sank into the bed, his hand tightening on the covers. He was afraid, and he was tired. He listened to the voices in the wind and tried to let them lull him to sleep. It was fitful and shallow, but he did doze off. His dreams echoed with noises of machines and he could taste electricity on his breath.

He awoke when the door closed and opened his eyes to Yoru once again.

"Just in time, I see..." he said. His gaze was kind and without setting down his bag he went to Dan right away.

Dan wanted to say hello. Instead, what came out was, "I feel sick."

Yoru hooked a foot around his chair to pull it closer and fell into it at Dan's side. "I should expect so. Deep breaths, Dan," he reassured him.

Yoru dropped the bag, took his hand and Dan squeezed it as he tried to do as he said.

"Why are you helping me?" he asked. He laid his head back and took slow, deep breaths. His stomach was trying to crawl up into his mouth but he didn't think his body was sick. His brain was sick, he thought. Dan squeezed his eyes closed for a moment before looking at Yoru again.

"What, I'm going to rescue you and then leave you like this? I don't

22

half ass my rescues," Yoru said gently.

Dan did not know him very well yet but this answer seemed very indicative of Yoru so far. He closed his eyes again and focused on his breath. One thing at a time. Yoru's hand was warm in his own, and after a few minutes of quiet he felt as though he had himself together again. He opened his eyes and managed a weak smile. Yoru smiled back.

"Hello again. Feeling better?" he asked.

"Working on it."

"That's a good start." That smile again. Now that he was settled, Yoru got up and took off his coat finally, hanging it by the door. He sat down again and started going through his bag. "Some more food, medicine to clear up the irritation on your back—" He didn't want to say 'infection'. That was scary. Words were powerful and he was careful. "Oh! And I got you a hat. I know we have some clothes laying around here that you can use, but... Your poor, dear hair..." he mourned.

The hat was knitted and, of course, black. Dan put it on immediately. It was both comfortable and warm, and he grinned at Yoru. "I never had long hair, not like yours. They make us cut it short as soon as we enlist. And I... I guess they had to shave it even lower for the tests—" His smile faltered. Yoru took his hand again.

It was becoming something of a reflex, but Dan didn't mind. The physical contact grounded him. It reminded him of where he was, reminded him to breathe. He was free. He had avoided thinking about that in any sort of concrete terms because the possibilities, the consequences, were just so dizzying.

"Tell me things," Yoru said, drawing his mind back out of where it had started to collapse into itself.

"What?" Dan asked, blinking at him.

"Tell me things. Tell me about the man I, ahem, borrowed from the military," he said mischievously. "I mean, I know your name, and I know you were having a bad time. When I steal something, I usually go in to a job knowing more than that." He laughed.

Dan didn't know where to start. "I... I enlisted right out of school," he said. "My sister wanted to, when she was done." He frowned. "I hope she won't."

"You have a sister?"

"Two. Both younger," Dan explained. "They're... Wait. When is it?"

Yoru checked his watch (he wore it backwards, with the watch face on the inside of his wrist) and told him. Dan noticed that it was just a watch. No fancy interface; it was just a round clock face and hands. He wondered where they still sold them. It was a brief distraction from the impending realization that he may have been putting off.

"Sixteen and eleven," he said when Yoru told him the date. He went to rub his face with his hands, remembered, and rubbed it with just the one of them. "I've been gone a long time. I wonder— My mother probably thinks I'm dead. Oh, shit..." And there it was.

"I haven't called home in...a year." Dan sighed. "A little more than that, I think. I... I can't remember when it started. When I started— You know."

Yoru looked at him patiently, like he was waiting for something. He sighed again, already knowing what it was. "I want to call them."

"You can't," Yoru said, as though it would have surprised either of them. But then it was the thief's turn to sigh. "At least, not yet."

"Not yet? Not ever. If I call them, they'll trace the call and track me down. There's no way I'd be able to even get through to them. If they're half as smart as I think they are, they told my mother I was dead when I lost my hand, there's already been a funeral and she's moved on. Now that I'm missing they'll... I don't know, be watching the phones and the house, thinking that I'll go home. I won't. I won't lead them there."

Yoru let him talk. His even, calm gaze never wavered. When Dan finally stopped to catch his breath, he still waited. He waited until he was sure that Dan was done.

"This is not the freedom you wanted. But it is the freedom you have," he said simply. "Even if you had thought to go back, I had no intention of letting you put your family in danger."

Dan looked at him quickly. He hadn't known enough ahead of time to plan, there was no way. He must have decided that quickly. Very quickly. Well, what did he expect? This guy was a professional.

"Instead, I ask that you hear me out."

He could have said no, but it seemed that his choices right now boiled down to being pointlessly contrarian or at least being polite to the guy who had saved his life, and goddamn it if that wasn't an easy fucking choice.

He nodded.

"I am leaving the country. I have work elsewhere and it's never been my wont to stay in one place too long," Yoru said serenely. When Dan looked at him in confusion, he elaborated. "It isn't my style, as it were. I suggest that you come with me. I honestly do feel that you will be safest across the border. You'll have more freedom, and can start building some semblance of an existence for yourself."

A life. Yeah, he was going to need one of those. But the idea seemed so depressing. So final. He did not answer immediately.

"I guess it's for the best…" he said quietly.

"There is a slight upside," Yoru pointed out. Dan looked up at him again. "You see, I have friends in places. Sneaky places. And they have certain skills, certain ins and outs that are well beyond my ken." And then he smiled. "This is no promise, but… I think I can get you a phone call. More importantly, I can get you the contacts to make that phone call, so that there might be more in the future. I can't give you your family back, my friend. But I can give you something."

And Dan was, for the first time but not the last, utterly surprised and confused by Yoru. This bizarre man who had dragged him from his imprisonment and decided not just to save him, but to be his friend. It had been one whole day. So much was different.

And this wasn't perfect. But when things had been so hopeless, it was something. And it was kind.

Dan smiled at him. "I won't hold you to that," he said. Yoru couldn't promise it to him, but if he knew Yoru (and the man wore his heart on his sleeve, that much was obvious), he would do his best. What more could Dan ask?

"So what's the plan in the meantime?" he said.

Yoru clapped his hands together. "First, lunch," he announced. "But, in the grander scheme of things, we'll still be here a couple of days. You need to be well enough for travel, and I don't want to risk you getting injured or falling ill. After that, I have another safe location for us to head to and we can stay there while I pick up some work. If you feel so inclined, I am sure I can put in a word with some of my associates and find you some yourself."

Yoru took his hand. "And, if not, if you decide that you'd rather go straight, and try to find work in the sunlit world of the lawful, I will help you just as eagerly. I want you to be able to decide these things for yourself."

Dan nearly laughed. He was too tired to laugh, really. It came out as an amused, vaguely aching huff. "I could. But, I think the fear would follow me forever. What if they are mad enough to look across their borders? What if someone slips up? And think of the innocent people I could endanger."

He didn't sigh this time. Instead, Dan nodded. This was not a downfall. This was a good decision. It was just an unorthodox one. "No. I think that working underground would be safest, for me and for everyone. At the very least, if they come to hurt me…The people around me won't be defenceless."

25

"Dan." Yoru leaned forward in his chair. There was no humour in his dark eyes now. He looked at him seriously. "They will not hurt you again. I will not let that happen."

Dan believed him.

~*~

He spent a few more days recuperating. Sleep was a little harder now that he wasn't a total wreck of a human being, but whenever he woke in fright, Yoru was there. He had abandoned his place on the floor when it was made obvious that Dan was waking up at night. It was easier to reassure him from a chair at his bed side. Yoru never seemed to mind.

He ate. He had an actual appetite. He couldn't remember the last time he had wanted to eat anything. Yoru was a talented cook and there were always seconds. They found him some clothes. They were a little big on him, but they were clean and that was something. He finally got rid of the fatigue pants he had been rescued in. They were worn almost to nothing. How long had he been in them, anyway?

And finally, he was well enough to shower. Fuck. It was an amazing experience, both being able to stand on his own two feet and to be warm and clean. He was sure that Yoru spent the whole time listening for him to fall, and though he wavered a little, he never did. He was getting better. He was living. He was alive.

Even breathing was easier now. Yoru helped him bandage his back after he got out of the shower. It still ached, but it wasn't as bad. The sharp pain was gone, as was most of the throbbing and itching. It was manageable.

And...living with one hand was manageable. Different and sometimes difficult, but manageable. Easier with Yoru there, who spoke openly about it and helped him figure out ways around things.

When all else failed, he was there to provide an extra set of hands where Dan's single one simply would not do.

This was not the future Dan had planned on. But he realized one day, as he was flicking through news on the vidscreen that he had borrowed, that he gave up whatever future that was ages ago. He had thought he would join the army to support his family, and then maybe retire and go into engineering like his parents had. Maybe he'd meet somebody, settle down, and make a family of his own.

But that stopped being an option as soon as he was injured. He lost his hand in battle, they jammed who the fuck knew what into his back, and the last year or so of his life was a blur of, well, really terrible shit.

Normal wasn't an option. And Yoru was weird. He was weird and

26

happy and nice. So maybe it was time to try being a little strange, too. Maybe this time things would turn out better.

When it came time for them to leave, he met the day with a real, honest smile. "So, how do we sneak out of a country?"

"I'm so glad you asked," Yoru answered brightly. "We're going by train. We have false papers, and I am sure they will ask us a few questions. You, my greenhorn friend, will say as little as you can."

"I do not have horns," Dan scoffed.

"I am telling them I am going home. My passport is marked as such. You can just tell them that you are coming with me, for a trip," he said.

"What, are we dating?" He laughed.

Yoru shrugged. "Sure. How long, if they ask? Month or two?" He grinned.

It had been a joke, but even if they had merely decided to call themselves friends it would have been just as much of a lie. There just hadn't been enough time. But, maybe there would be.

Dan laughed again. This was not as scary as he had thought. "Sounds good. You managed to get me fake papers that fast?"

Yoru flourished his hands like a magician. "If you're rich, legal is fast. If you're smart, illegal is faster."

Dan pulled on the coat that Yoru had gotten for him, and Yoru helped him tie his shoes. Huh. One more obstacle to work around. He put his hat on his head and together, they stepped out the door. It was a little chilly outside and he took one of the bags that Yoru was carrying and hung it on his back. After all, if he was travelling, he'd have a bag, wouldn't he?

Dan didn't know what town they were in, but it was immediately obvious that it was his country. The language was everywhere around them, the smell of the food from street vendors, even the lay out of the roads were familiar to him. Still in Syama. One of the border cities, clearly.

He drank it all in as they walked. Yoru apparently knew his stuff. Where they had been staying wasn't far from the train. He offered to get them a cab, asked him if he was feeling unwell, but Dan shook his head. He wanted to walk it. He wanted to remember this.

He was never going to come back.

A.N. Mouse

4:

Oliver did not go to work the next day. He also didn't turn on the radio. He looked at it for a long time, seriously considering flipping the switch and filling the silence. In the end, he didn't. He just sat at his workbench and started to clean the things he had brought in the day before. He should have been going out to get more and saved the busywork for a day when the weather stopped him from collecting, but with how his brain was behaving he thought it more likely he'd just wander into traffic.

He just didn't have the energy for salvage. He had slept, sure, but he just felt so tired. And he kept checking his phone, despite the fact that he had no reason to be so fixated with it. Of all the messages he received, none were the one he was looking for.

He knew what he was checking for. He was waiting for a message from Dan, or some sort of sign that yesterday had been a strenuous and convincing hallucination.

Maybe he shouldn't have been so affected. He barely knew Dan. It wasn't as though they had been friends for years or anything like that. But he had been kind of hoping they would be.

It was almost romantic in retrospect, an idea that didn't sit well with Oliver. Had Dan decided not to sleep with him at some point in the future and deemed them only friends, he would have been a little disappointed but ultimately perfectly fine with it. Losing the way he laughed wasn't the same as losing that thing he did with his tongue. But since he hadn't left, merely died, things were different. Friendships took longer to build than it took to have sex, and Oliver had been robbed of that chance.

He could have called Dan an ex without ever having an ex what he was to tell anyone, and that seemed to be the saddest understatement he could think of. An ex-almost friend. An ex-happiness. All Oliver had left was a number in his phone that went straight to voicemail when he called it. Because he tried, of course he had tried. It wasn't even Dan's voice, either, but some robot lady, because Dan hadn't even had the chance to set up his own message. Oliver hated the robot lady deeply. He felt a little bad for how much he hated her.

And then there was how he had died. It was so much easier to think

29

that it had been an accident on the job. A miscalculation. Anything but suicide.

Oliver had held the same knot of wire in his hand for the past hour. He hadn't even looked at it. This wasn't getting him anywhere. Whenever he tried to do something, the thoughts snuck into his head again. He hadn't dealt with this much brain bullshit since he was a teenager.

He was going to get drunk. That wasn't a good answer, but it would do for now. And as dirty as the air outside was, he needed to get out of his apartment. It was a simple decision to make, but it still took him all day to actually make it. Twilight, its deep shadows and multicoloured sky, lit the world outside as he left the building. A dangerous time to be out. Oliver had set aside any semblance of real sadness and settled into being grumpy. Yeah, dangerous. Whatever. He needed a drink.

Oliver didn't even remember how he had found the bar in question. Someone had introduced him to it ages back. There were lots of hidden ways to get around town. The downside was that if you got jumped in one of them, no one would find your body. The upside was that Oliver was quicker and quieter than your average delinquent, juvenile or otherwise. He was an adult delinquent. That was a thing, right?

Too frustrated with himself—and too sad, really—to be scared, Oliver worked his way through the back alleys until he saw the neon sign of the bar. There was one in his own building he could have gone to, but this was his place. It had also been Dan's place.

Maybe he'd find someone to commiserate with.

He shuffled inside and found himself a seat. It was a quiet night. No partying, it seemed. That was okay. He didn't really want to deal with the noise anyway. There were few other patrons, all minding themselves and none with faces that Oliver recognized. The lights in the bar were unsteady and he was certain that there were dangerous job hirings and other illegal trades going on in the flickers of darkness. There always was. It didn't bother him.

"Hey, man. You look like shit." He looked up when he was spoken to. The bartender was an older woman, her hair curled and dyed and frizzy.

"Feel like shit," Oliver answered. "How's your night goin', Suz?"

"Not as bad as yours," she answered. "What can I get you?"

"Something cheap and disgusting," Oliver said. He didn't really care what he was drinking. He just needed to get out of his own head for a while.

She passed him something without a label and when Oliver took a sip, he grimaced. Yeah. That would work.

"You wanna tell me what's got you so sour?" Suzy offered.

No, he didn't. But he probably should. He sighed.

"Lost a friend. Well, no, I mean—" He groaned under his breath. "Do you remember Dan? He was here with a few other people, they hijacked the karaoke for a night a week or so ago," he said.

"I remember," she said. "The skinny one. Yoru brought him in."

He remembered Yoru. Tall, dark haired. Oliver had seen Dan had talking to him that same night.

Oliver nodded. "Yeah. Well, we hooked up, I guess. You know what I'm like." He waved his hand dismissively and took another drink. "Thought he was nice. He said next time he was back in the city, he'd hit me up and we'd pick up where we left off. It seemed pretty legit to me." He shrugged.

"He ghost on you?" Suzy asked him, leaning on her side of the bar.

Oliver shook his head. "Killed himself. I got the call last night."

Now it was Suzy who groaned. "Really? That's fucking terrible. He seemed like a nice kid. And he was a friend of Yoru's, too. I bet he's really fucked up about it." She frowned.

Oliver hesitated. "Do you know... Were they on a job together?" he asked. His drink, disgusting as it was, seemed to be even more bitter now. It was tainted by the looming idea that he might be that phone call. He might be the one to have to tell her the news.

"Yeah. Yoru and I talked a bit. He said that since Dan was new to the scene, they were stuck working together. You know, stuck." She rolled her eyes. "I think Yoru was protective of him, you know?"

Oliver swallowed hard. And then... He decided not to tell her. Let her think that Yoru had wandered off somewhere to work. Or maybe he'd settled down and gotten out of the biz. He wouldn't—couldn't—do that to her. Sometimes, a lie was a blessing.

"Yeah, seemed that way," he said, and took another long drink. The other two had been girls, maybe? If he was remembering right? He was drinking basically paint thinner on an empty stomach so he didn't exactly feel like his thought processes were up to snuff. He finished the bottle she had given him and already doubted his ability to walk straight. Well, he was going to have a hell of a time getting home, wasn't he? Maybe he wouldn't have to worry about that meeting with Violet after all.

He did make it home. He stayed long enough to drink more of whatever it was, and to bitch to Suzy about...well, he wasn't quite sure what he had said. Nothing about the boys. His decision had, in some way, locked those words into his heart. Drunk or not, he couldn't bring them up without choking on them. For now, that was safer.

He woke up with one hell of a hangover and he was surprisingly more productive that day. He threw up, had a shower, got himself some water and turned on the radio. Clumsy and fumbling, he sat on the floor of his junk room and used his knife to cut dirt and garbage out of hinges and joints.

On a good day, he'd be appalled with himself. As it was, with his eyes half open and his newly perpetual frown, he managed not to cut off any of his fingers. He ate when he felt he could. This was progress, he thought. Hungover, uncomfortable progress.

The next day, he sold some shit first thing in the morning (hungover Oliver was way better at texting people back than drunk Oliver) and then made his way across town. It was terrible, mainly seeing as it was full of people and Oliver really wasn't that keen on being so physically intimate with so many strangers at once. It was more than just claustrophobic. Finding any quiet space along the way to collect himself was a blessing.

The building for Highlight Technology was so tall that he couldn't see the top of it from where he stood at the bottom. It was also clean and shiny. As if he needed more reasons to feel really fucking out of place.

Everything about this sucked. But he said he would do it. Now that he was there, he didn't want to, but he was going to. He had said he would. That was serious.

Still frowning, he walked right in the front doors of the building, ignored everyone's strange looks and went up to the desk.

The man behind it was well-dressed and smiling, at least until he saw Oliver. Ha. Suck on it, Mr. Man, Oliver thought. It was kind of fun being a nuisance, sometimes. The man had some of the usual body alterations that people liked to spend their money on, the kinds of changes that were purely aesthetic and thus completely beyond Oliver's comprehension. When he looked at Oliver, his pastel-coloured eyes were only the smallest of those changes.

"Can I help you?" he asked.

"Um, hi. I'm Oliver Muriel, and I'm here to see Selene Violet." He was sure he could have said that more simply, and it only just occurred to him that she probably didn't know his last name anyway. Oh well.

The man looked him over. Oliver knew exactly what was crossing his mind. He was dirty, hairy, and hadn't paid to have his horns removed. They twisted up out of his hair, thick and sharp. They ran in his family, but had he somehow ended up with a more prestigious life, he probably would have had them removed. They weren't pretty or functional for anything. A lot of people had their oddities taken off, or even more of them added. It was something Oliver had never really gotten into.

As it was, they were pretty irrelevant to him, usually.

"Put this card in the elevator. It will take you to her floor. It's single use, so don't get any ideas," he said.

Oliver didn't bother trying to hide when he rolled his eyes. Ideas like what? This place was so uncomfortable that he wouldn't come back if they paid him. Well, maybe if they paid him. He'd do a pretty sizable amount of things for money.

The elevator was crowded, too and this was just as bad as being in the subway, or taking an aircar. Thankfully, the higher up it went the more people filtered out. He was equal parts relieved and apprehensive when he was the only one left and the elevator doors dinged open.

Time to keep his word.

Everything on this floor was even more ridiculous. The floors were dark and polished, the walls brightly and cheerily painted. The lights weren't the dying fluorescents of your standard apartment. Instead, they were sunlight-mimicking, giving everything a cheerful glow. It was weird, basically. And really clean. Oliver felt bad for even breathing in it.

But hey, she had invited him. It was her problem now.

He turned the corner of the hall and stopped short. There, at the little, tidy desk that was in front of him, was the only person that Oliver had seen so far on this floor. A girl (a boy? He was pretty sure it was a boy) with midnight blue hair and big, dark eyes that looked up to him when they heard the sound of his feet.

Something happened. He didn't know what it was. But for a moment, he only stared and was stared at. Part of his brain registered that this boy was very pretty, absurdly pretty, even, but it was a faraway thought. There was something palpable in the air. Something...important.

And then, the boy smiled at Oliver and all at once Oliver felt his blood pressure skyrocket. It broke the effect of whatever had been going on, but really he thought he might pass out. Wow, okay. He was pretty.

"Good morning!" he said. A young man, definitely. Sweetly voiced, but a dude. Cool. Oliver had seen a lot weirder things. Now, if he could fucking untie his tongue and answer, that would be great.

"Uhh..." Fucking come on, was he fifteen again or something? He shook his head. "Hi, I'm here to see Selene Violet." Was she a Miss or a Misses? Should he just use her last name? Her first? This was a particularly unexpected bit of awkwardness.

But it didn't seem to bother the kid. Her secretary, maybe? He dressed like one. And honestly, he probably wasn't that young, but seeing as he was both a little younger and markedly more cheerful than Oliver was, he found himself thinking of him in diminutives. He wasn't a kid, and out of the two of them, he was the one with a real job. As if Oliver needed to have that rubbed in.

He stood up and yeah, Oliver had been right. There was definitely both skirt and heels that slipped into view when he stepped out from behind his desk.

"You're Mr. Oliver, right?" he asked, motioning for Oliver to follow him to the next door.

"Just Oliver," he corrected. The giggle that he earned in response was absolutely saccharine.

"I'll tell her that you're here. Give me just a moment," he said. He stepped behind the next door and disappeared from view. It only gave Oliver a handful of seconds to appreciate how fucking weird his day was so far, but that was easily explained. People with money were strange. He wasn't sure if the process of making money made you crazy, or just having enough of it did the job.

And then the door opened, all black glass, heavy and shiny. The secretary smiled at him. "This way," he said.

Honestly, Oliver would follow him just about anywhere. Call it a failure of character. He was pretty resigned to it.

It was the same nonsensical opulence on the inside, but it was... Squishier. There were comfortable chairs, a couch, a low table. It was much more of a meeting room. It looked almost homey, but in the artificial, magazine-like sense. That seemed a little hilarious to him.

The secretary told him to take a seat, all smiles and glittering sweetness before they were interrupted. An older woman, extremely well-dressed, stepped into the room.

And strangely, as though he had been deflated, the secretary fell silent. A quick glance from Oliver and he seemed almost deadened. That wasn't a comfortable development.

"Thank you for coming. I know the notice was short." And this woman, then, was the one who called him. She sat in the chair that was across from his and he finally got the chance to take a good look at her. She was older, but not old. A regimented skincare routine meant that her wrinkles were minimum and her expressions were still youthful. Her hair was white and tidily kept, twisted up behind her head. "Did you want tea or coffee or anything?" she offered him.

Well, she seemed nice enough.

34

"Coffee would be great," he admitted. He didn't drink it often, couldn't usually splurge for it, but he wasn't about to turn down getting some for free.

She shot a look to the secretary, who had been standing quietly nearby, and he nodded immediately. "Yes, Ms. Violet," he said.

Well, that answered one of his questions, at least.

"Were you...close?" Her tone was sympathetic and her expression showed just how much distaste she had for how she had to breach the topic.

Oliver sighed. "Not really. I mean, to be honest, I barely knew him. But I... I meant to." He hesitated. "I wanted to."

"I'm sorry." She reached over and gently lay her hand over his, where it was on the arm of the chair. The motion came off as natural and comforting and Oliver was not bothered by it. She removed her hand after a moment and continued talking.

"I didn't know any of them very well. I was looking for a team for something I wanted to get done. Something...a little less than legal, I'll admit." She shrugged, frowning faintly. "It's the way business is done these days, unfortunately. I am sure you understand."

Yeah, the rules were only a problem if you got caught, and y'know, if you didn't have more money than was fathomable. He didn't say that, though. He just nodded.

"I posted a job through the usual networks, and Xueying picked it up. Did...did you ever get to meet her?" Ms. Violet asked him.

Oliver hesitated again, and then shook his head. "I don't think so... I knew Dan, and I met Yoru...but that's all," he said honestly.

"The team had two other members, their co-coordinator Xueying and another woman, I don't have her name handy, I'm sorry. It's just slipped my memory." She sighed. "But they picked up the job, and for a while everything seemed to be going well. Just before they could complete it, though..."

She didn't say it. Oliver didn't say it. Their eyes met in a moment of uncomfortable silence.

Yeah. That.

"Guess you need to hire another team," Oliver eventually said, breaking the silence.

Ms. Violet sighed. "There's the problem. It's really hard for people to want to pick up your contracts when word has already gotten out that your last team was—" Another sigh. "That poor man. It wasn't even his fault. He must have been suffering so much."

Pressure welled in Oliver's chest. Nope. He wasn't going to think about it. "So, what's next then?" he asked. Better to pretend he cared about the business than to think about it. Anything was better than thinking about it.

She seemed to sense his apprehension and indulged him in an answer. "Well... I'm not sure, exactly. We keep trying. Maybe the news will die down and people will start picking up the work. We doubled the pay out, so..." She sighed.

It was then that the secretary returned, setting down a tray of coffee on the table closest to them. There was milk and sugar and Oliver took neither. He didn't mind coffee with either one or both, but plain was cheaper and had sort of become his default favourite.

It was hot, but not too hot to drink. The first sip seemed to make him feel a little more solid. Ms. Violet wordlessly drowned her coffee in milk and while she did that Oliver spared a glance to her employee.

He stood silently, eyes unfocused, his hands clasped in front of him. That was suitably uncomfortable to look at. Oliver looked away, back to the woman in front of him.

"Oh, I almost forgot. Hastin, go and get Dan's things. At least, I hope you can make use of them." She pointed the directive at the secretary, who curtsied and left again, before she looked back to Oliver.

"Someone has to," was Oliver's answer. The hardest part of all of this was just finding the words. None of them wanted to come out. But still, maybe it was better that he tried. It was slow going, like learning how to put one foot in front of the other all over again.

It seemed like there was something else she wanted to say, and when she set down her coffee cup it looked as though she finally committed to saying it. "You wouldn't know anyone interested in taking that contract, would you?" This tone was different. More open, more sincere. Less corporate-polite. It took Oliver off-guard.

"I know I look rough, but I'm not that hard," he said quickly, almost defensively.

"Oh, oh no, I didn't mean—" She shook her head. "I was just wondering if you knew anyone. I'd be happy to pay you a recommendation fee. Or even a co-coordinator cheque?" she offered. "If you know anyone in the work, I could pay you to be the relay. I mean, since you had met Dan, I just figured that maybe you crossed paths with those people sometimes and I just hoped, I guess—" She cut herself off and tried to regain her composure.

"I suppose it would make me feel better to do something for you rather than to just hand you his things and tell you to have a good day. That seems so heartless," Ms. Violet said. Perhaps she would have kept talking, but

Oliver looked like he was thinking and she quieted to let him do so.

He did actually know someone. Two someones, even. And he'd be glad to be the one to hook them up with such a sizable paycheck. Rosa and Ame did basically everything, too, so it wasn't likely that the job would be out of their range.

"Yeah, I think I know a team that could do it. I mean, I can't promise anything without knowing what the job is, or talking to them. But I can pass the word along," he said. The idea of him pocketing some of that money didn't upset him, either. Maybe he would stick around for the job if they took it.

Hastin returned, setting down a small cloth bag next to where Oliver sat. He did not say anything before going back to where he had been moments before.

"That's wonderful news. I want to send Hastin here, as well. He has many useful skills, and I think I'll feel more reassured to have a direct line to you and your team," Ms. Violet said. Oliver wasn't going to argue. Any skill Hastin had would be more useful to them than what Oliver could provide. Violet looked over to the young man when she spoke again.

"Hastin, this man is going to be working with us for some time. If not for this assignment, then at least until he passes off his references to us. I expect you to show exemplary obedience." Okay, that was a little strange, but no alarm bells went off in earnest. Hastin worked for her, and when Oliver 'worked' for her, she wanted to make sure that he would listen despite their very obvious differences. That's all, right?

"Yes, Ms. Violet," he said, nodding respectfully to her. That strange, off-looking cast to his eyes hadn't faded. But then he turned to look at Oliver and their eyes locked. There was something alive in there again. Whatever was going on, Ms. Violet seemed blissfully unaware as Oliver watched her drink her coffee out of his peripheral vision.

"Captain. You will have full use of my skills and talents," he said, curtsying again.

Oliver's stomach twisted.

Something was wrong.

A.N. Mouse

5:

The train station was incredibly crowded. Dan held onto Yoru to keep from getting separated on the platform, his hand vice-gripped around Yoru's forearm. Yoru didn't seem to mind, and when he spoke it was quiet and close enough that Dan could hear him over all the noise.

"You doing okay?" he asked. He had switched back to Dan's own language and the shorter man looked at him in surprise.

"Yeah...it's just a lot of people." Once upon a time, a crowd like this wouldn't even have registered. The whole country was jam-packed with people until you went much further north. All the major cities were like this. But today, it unsettled him.

"One step at a time. We're almost there."

Dan kept his head ducked down, pressed close to Yoru's shoulder, and shuffled along behind him. They got onto the train without trouble and Yoru shuttled him into one of the seats by the window. Dan sank down in his chair, barely glancing at the people seated across from them as he pulled up his jacket to tuck his chin against his chest. It was quieter here and for some reason his pulse was absolutely racing.

He was busy just trying to breathe and figure out what was going wrong when Yoru sat down next to him and took his hand, pressing a bottle of water into it. An expensive commodity, certainly, but he didn't waste time remarking on it as he cracked the top and took a drink from it.

"Slowly. It will help with your nerves," Yoru cautioned him.

Dan took a deep breath and tried to do as he suggested, sipping it rather than knocking it back. As people settled in, the train quieted down and he found he could breathe a little easier.

"I don't know what that was about. Crowds never used to bother me," he spoke under his breath, not exactly wanting to advertise his condition. Yoru seemed to understand, and answered without looking over to him.

"Things are different now," he said.

That was incredibly true. Dan sipped his water and watched as the train pulled away from the platform. Once they got moving, he knew that the whole train would pass under a scanner disguised as a structural support. It would pick up both their tickets and their I.D.

Although things were quieter now, he could feel his pulse fluttering at the thought. What if it didn't work? What if they caught him? The idea of being dragged back there filled him with an icy fear that made it hard to breathe. He closed his eyes and laid his head back and, to his great surprise, fell right the hell asleep.

Yoru took his water bottle from him, closing the cap and deciding to let him rest. When the agents came around to check their ID manually and ask the purpose of their trip, he managed to gently slip Dan's ID from the pocket of his coat. Being a thief had its advantages.

Of course, they should have insisted on waking him up, but Yoru hadn't survived as long as he had by following the rules. They had a whole train of people to check! And both of Dan's IDs went through just fine, didn't they? Besides, he was sick, it's probably better if they didn't talk to him.

By and large, people were pleasantly predictable.

He pulled his vidscreen out of his pocket and pulled up the local news. It was always a good idea to have an inkling about the environment you were headed into. Sometimes the news stations lied, but there were trends where you could learn to spot the falsehoods as they were written. He fished in his coat pocket for his headphones to listen to one of the clips, and when he clicked them into place he felt Dan sag down next to him, leaning against his shoulder. A quick glance showed that he was still asleep.

Yoru just smiled and went back to his research.

When Dan awoke some time later it was with his usual panicked start. Yoru put a hand on his shoulder immediately and after a few quiet, confused seconds of glancing around, Dan seemed to realize where he was.

"How long was I out? I—I didn't mean to sleep," he said.

"Shhh," reassuring rather than dismissive. Dan took a deep breath and settled back into his seat.

"Just an hour or two. Nothing to fear," Yoru told him.

"And the checkpoint?" Dan asked.

"Handled," he said. "Hungry? I have some food in my bag."

Dan conceded that he was, and they shared some of the food that Yoru had brought with him. This trend of accidentally sleeping and waking up in a panic was starting to get to him, but Yoru did not seem too concerned. Alternatively, he was worried, but now wasn't the time to draw attention to it.

Instead, Dan asked, "You packed noodles in your bag?" and looked to his friend in astonishment.

Grinning, Yoru nodded. "What else did you think I meant?"

As seemed to be a trend, eating something helped Dan feel a little better. Yoru popped out one of his ear buds and passed it to Dan, and they ate their noodles and watched the news as the train sped them closer to their destination.

When they reached their stop, they grabbed their things and Yoru offered him a hand to help him down the steps. He was stiff and almost fell into him when he tried to get down onto the platform.

"How is your back?" Yoru asked. Dan scrunched up his face.

"Little tense." The crowd here didn't seem to bother him as much. Maybe he was getting more used to it. "Doesn't hurt, exactly, but..."

Yoru nodded. "We've got a ways to go." Now that they were off the train and that the crowd had thinned a little, he switched back to Omnian. Briefly, Dan wondered how many languages he spoke. At least three, right? There must have been one that he grew up speaking.

"Oh, did you end up having to tell them that we were dating?" Dan asked, mostly joking.

"No, actually. They didn't even ask," Yoru said offhandedly. "Didn't ask me to wake you up, either. Overworked security people these days. You'd almost think they had better things to do or something."

"What?" Dan asked, alarmed. "But that's the border. The border of a country at war, even. How was it so easy?"

"The other side is at war," Yoru pointed out. "Most of their focus is on the other borders nearer the war-zone. Everyone over here is more concerned about that side, too, so they don't think there is anything to worry about. They're going to trust their computers. Our paperwork went through so... So did we," he explained.

"That seems really scary." Dan laughed, a hollow, surprised noise. "I can't believe it's that easy."

"Now you know. Don't trust computers for everything," Yoru said graciously. "How are you feeling?"

And it was then that Dan realized where he was and what exactly had happened. This was, if you oversimplified it, running away from home. It was on a stupidly large scale, of course, but here he was.

The country of Vespuchy, usually just shorthanded to The Ves. He'd only ever heard of this place. Seen shows, heard people talk about it, read about it in school. But now he was here.

He stopped short as they walked and looked around. His hand tightened on the strap of his bag and he realized all the signs in the street were a different language. A lot of what he heard was, too. Most of it he didn't understand.

He swore quietly.

Yoru, unfazed, still looked at him for an answer.

"I'm gonna be okay," Dan said, after a moment of hesitation. "I just… There is so much I didn't realize. I had no idea…"

"I think you will have that feeling a lot." Someone bustled behind Yoru and he stepped closer to Dan without missing a beat. "The world is very big. Sometimes even I forget how big, and I stepped out into it willingly."

"I'll be okay," Dan said again, more firmly this time. "Look, I can stand now, right? I can walk and talk and—" He hesitated. What else could he do? "I —I can fight. I was already fighting. I'm going to be fine."

"Yes, you will," Yoru told him with a smile. "I know that, and now you know that, too. Come on, we're going to be late for our dinner date."

Dan couldn't help it. When Yoru smiled, he smiled. He hadn't had any brothers growing up, but somehow he didn't think this was precisely the same.

"We have a dinner date?" he asked, falling into step with his friend. "You mean, a place we are supposed to go to eat or in the literal sense of there being someone for us to meet there?"

"A place we are supposed to go to eat and meet someone to eat with," Yoru said, and all fuzzy feelings aside, Dan had the brief passing thought of strangling him.

He stopped on a street corner and looked around and Dan elbowed him. "Lost already?" he asked, not particularly worried.

"Debating whether to wave down a cab or steal a car…" Yoru mused.

"What?"

He grinned. "I'm kidding. Getting pegged for petty theft would be a grand waste of our time. Here—" And while Dan stood there, mildly flabbergasted, Yoru hailed a taxi for the two of them to duck in to.

"You're going to give me a heart attack," Dan said once they were safely inside.

"Don't be silly. If all that electricity didn't stop your heart, I certainly won't be able to," was the casual reply.

Dan fixated on the windows as they drove, absolutely fascinated by everything he saw. It was, by and large, the same in the way that most big cities were the same. But it was the differences that caught his eye. Next to him, Yoru lounged comfortably. The tidy outer city, not yet rotted by the centre's corruption, passed before his eyes. They were headed further in.

"So, who are we meeting up with? Is this one of those things I should know ahead of time?" Dan eventually asked him.

Yoru straightened up. "Usually, yes. Generally, I'll give you a run-down of what we are doing and who we are doing it with, but this time is an exception to that rule."

"Why's that?"

"Mostly for the fun of it," Yoru said. Dan shot him a look but Yoru held his hands up defensively and continued to explain. "She's both very nice and very safe, I just don't know that I can do her justice. So, in this case, you'll see," he said with a shrug.

Dan wiggled himself down lower into the seat, leaning against Yoru's shoulder as he looked back outside. The city sped past them, indifferent to his thoughts.

Yoru paid the driver—and tipped, Dan noticed. Criminal or not, Yoru wasn't heartless—and he helped Dan out of the car when he stumbled. Okay, maybe he wasn't in fighting shape yet, but he was getting there.

The restaurant was a small one. Dim lights, crowded, but it smelled good. Dan had no idea when he had gotten his appetite back but every time the idea of food was brought up, he always reacted with honest joy. He was almost looking forward to the meal more than meeting Yoru's mysterious friend.

A very pretty woman in a very short skirt showed them to a booth and Yoru sat across from him. He looked at his watch and Dan frowned in thought.

"You can still read that in here?" he asked.

"Yeah." And this time there was something secretive in Yoru's smile. "You haven't noticed?"

Dan blinked at him. "Noticed what?"

Yoru tilted his head and widened his eyes, giving Dan a better look. And then, with that help, Dan did see something.

"Are your eyes...reflective?" he asked.

"Low-light adapted. It's natural, too." He winked at Dan. "Not that I frown on those who buy theirs, but mine is a gift of genetics."

"Along with the rest of you," Dan teased. It was worth it for the absolutely shocked look he earned and this time he was the one to laugh.

"You surprise me," Yoru said. "I appreciate that."

"You always did like a good surprise." And that was a new voice. Dan looked up and saw a stunning woman standing there. He handled it particularly badly by staring, but Yoru leap to his feet.

"Xueying!" Laughing, he wrapped her in his arms and dramatically dipped her down close to the floor. Dan was pretty sure he kissed her, he couldn't see for the table, but then he helped her upright again and she was laughing, too. The patrons of the restaurant continued to brush by them without otherwise glancing at his theatricality.

"You're such a show off," Xueying scolded him. Yoru waved off her words and sat back in his seat.

"Mind if I join you?" she asked Dan, who quickly moved over to make room for her.

"Dan, this is my good friend and associate, Xiao Xueying. Xueying, this is my new friend Dan. No last name, for the moment," he said with a smile.

"Nice to meet you. I trust Yoru's interesting taste in people," Xueying said

"I dunno if I would. He did just pick me up off the floor and bring him home with him," Dan pointed out.

Xueying laughed. "Hey, people drop all kinds of valuable stuff. Yoru knows that better than most."

"So what now… Business?" Dan asked.

Yoru shook his head, but Xueying answered. "No way. We have to eat first. No business until dinner is done. It's tradition."

Dan nodded solemnly. "I think I am going to like this line of work."

They ate together and though Dan wasn't exactly sure what it was that Yoru ordered for them, it was delicious. It tasted like real meat even, and not the fake replacement protein shit they usually passed off as food these days. Also, it was pleasantly spicy. At least to him.

"Wow. They really outdid themselves." Yoru's cheeks were flushed and he took a long drink of his beer. "That's some spicy shit."

"You're weak," Dan pointed at him with his chopsticks. "My mom eats spicier food than this."

"Tell your mom to rescue me. I'm dying. I am aflame."

"You're something, alright," Xueying said. She was suffering, too, but not as obviously. Yoru favoured them both with a wounded look but hadn't stopped eating for even a minute.

"So Dan, honey, you're new to the work?" Xueying asked him. She was very pretty, but her personality was relaxed and approachable. Sitting next to her, Dan felt comfortable and not as intimidated as he expected. Her hair was bright pink and short, and she wore a simple blouse of the same colour.

"Yeah, like, really new." He had no fear of admitting this, not when Yoru was within arm's reach. "So much for the straight and narrow, right?"

"Oh, we have more fun," she said, smiling at him. She was darker skinned than Yoru (and him, at the moment) and he watched as she set her chopsticks down and laid her head back against the wall of the booth.

"Roll me out of here, I am done," she said.

"Hey, if you eat enough shrimp, does your hair get pinker?" Yoru asked her.

Dan looked at him weirdly while Xueying laughed.

"Flamingos. They get their pink colour from the shrimp they eat," he explained to Dan.

"What are flamingos?" he asked.

Xueying finished her drink, Yoru finished his, and with his other hand he pushed the shared plate of food closer to Dan. "I'll show you when we're done here. They're funny birds. Or, they were. I'm not sure if they're still around," he said, thinking. "Anyway, go to town, I'm tapped out."

That was good news, since Dan most certainly wasn't. But, they seemed happy to make small talk until he, too, was fit to burst.

"Okay, so, we've been fed, and adequately lubricated," Yoru gestured with his drink. "Xueying, sunlight of my life, what's the news?"

"I picked up a new contract. Wicked paycheck. Handily, I need a thief," she said.

"Anything for you, darling., he answered easily. He looked like he was going to leave it at that, but thought better of it and looked to Dan. "Usually I'd have a lot more questions, but Xueying and I have a good history. If it's a job she's willing to take, I can assume that I, too, would be willing."

"Yeah, I was wondering if it was usually that easy."

"Work anywhere long enough and you make friends, right?" Xueying explained. "Anyway, the job is for the CEO of HiTech, so you know it's legit. She wants us to steal something from the local records. I figure she has a running total she owes on the operating cost of that huge fucking building and she wants that erased, or something like that. It's a data mission, we just need to get in and get the download. You've done that before." She nodded to Yoru.

"It's much easier than stealing people," he said offhandedly.

"So you're down? And what about your friend?" She looked to Dan.

"He's in training wheels, but he'll be my responsibility," Yoru said. "It's a little big for a first job, so we'll probably pick up a few little ones in the time in between, get his feet wet. That reminds me, actually, what's our time frame?"

"Couple of weeks. Enough time for you guys to get set up in town. I have some more networking to do before it starts in earnest, so I'll keep you posted. Oh, here, I picked up a new burner but you might as well have the number—" She reached her hand out and Yoru pulled his phone from his pocket and handed it to her.

"We have a place to stay, by the way, in case I conveniently forgot to explain that." Yoru cast a glance at Dan as he typed on Xueying's phone.

"Feeling overwhelmed yet?" Xueying asked him. No teasing in her voice, she seemed genuinely concerned.

Dan shook his head and smiled. "Between you two, my only worry is being useful. I am going to do my best." He sounded a little childish to his own ears, a kid telling their parents that he intended to behave at school.

"You'll be fine." Xueying handed Yoru his phone back and she tucked her own back into her pocket again. "In the meantime, I have a charity case of my own to attend to. I'll talk to you shortly, both of you."

Yoru blew her a kiss. "Meal's on me, beautiful. I'll message you later."

"Such a gentleman. Dan, it was nice to meet you," she said as she stood up.

"Yeah, you too," he answered, and he meant it. If this is who he was going to be working with, he thought that things were going to be just fine.

6:

Oliver locked the door to his apartment and walked away without looking back at it. There was no dramatic moment of wondering when he would come home, or what might be different when he got there. Violet had been perfectly accommodating in her explanation; she thought a job like this couldn't take more than a week or two, maybe a little extra with planning, but she wasn't the expert and Oliver would have to wait for a final answer when he talked to his contacts. It wasn't a huge deal to him. She had messaged him the safe house information and he figured he knew how to get there. He did. It was in a nicer apartment block than his house, for sure. He could crash there for a while and work with the two of them no problem, if they decided that was the way it would go.

Then again, it was three of them, not two of them. He had forgotten about Hastin for a moment. That was a feat in itself, as the memory of the man nearly stopped his feet as he walked down the hall.

Okay, maybe 'forgotten' was a lie. Maybe 'put from his mind' was more honest. Thinking of him led to a rise in blood pressure and a slew of incoherent cursing in the back of Oliver's mind. He hadn't actually sat down to organize his thoughts on the matter because damn, did he have a lot of thoughts about it. Maybe Rosa would help him make sense of that. Ame would probably only make it worse.

Oliver didn't waste time doubting that Hastin was worth something. Violet was stupidly rich but he didn't think she was stupidly, well, stupid. The man's appearance was on purpose, probably to give him the illusion of being window dressing. That didn't bother Oliver at all. It was the sudden and obvious personality changes that concerned him.

Oh, he really hoped he wasn't a lunatic. Weird, he could handle. Oliver was weird. But actual crazy was not something he was equipped to deal with. He groaned inwardly and leaned against the wall of the elevator on the way down. It earned him a few strange looks but he ignored them.

He wasn't really worried about the job. He had talked to Rosa about a few of the details and she was pretty sure it would be fine, but even if they decided not to take it he could pick up his part of the pay that Violet had promised him and maybe they'd pass a recommendation for someone else

47

along her way. Easy money. It almost seemed a worse idea if they took the job, where he would probably function as another set of hands or eyes and a general organizer. Oh well. He'd be getting paid to listen to Ame bitch about things. There were worse things to get paid for.

He sandwiched himself into the subway and hopped off when he couldn't take the crowd anymore. Someone had bumped into him and knocked his head back and he might have almost put someone's eye out, so he was done with people for a while and decided to walk the rest of it. It was not a short walk, but the movement would help get his mind off things and maybe he'd be a little less misanthropic when he arrived.

He always felt a little weird being topside in the street, and twice so when it came to entering actual buildings. It was way more likely for him to be digging around under one, or in the narrow alleys around one, than for him to actually step into a different apartment block. He braced himself, but went inside anyways, glancing around for the elevator and was pleasantly surprised when he didn't feel it shake as it rose. He checked the note he wrote himself (saved as a text on his phone because paper was expensive and his phone was garbage) and found both the floor and apartment number he was looking for.

It occurred to him then that he did not have keys. Shit.

He tried the door and found it unlocked.

Okay, then. So much for that problem.

Oliver opened the door and peeked his head inside, and for a moment he was overwhelmingly and unreasonably worried that he had picked the wrong door and was looking into someone else's apartment.

The front door opened to a linoleum square on the floor (faded but otherwise intact), and then a view of a living area. And from where he stood, Oliver could already recognize the back view of the person he saw.

Hastin, pretty as ever, stood by the window.

Oliver stepped in and closed the door behind him but Hastin didn't turn around. Looking around for a moment, Oliver hesitated before taking off his shoes. The carpet actually looked mostly clean and he didn't want to ruin that entirely. This block was on the outer edge of The Dim, and it was nicer than Oliver's own in numerous ways.

He crossed the floor, and when he drew into Hastin's peripheral vision the younger man jumped.

"Oh, goodness." He pressed a hand to his heart, looking to Oliver while being equal parts surprised and sheepish. "I'm so sorry, Captain, I didn't hear you. I was... I was..." He glanced at the window again.

Oliver followed his gaze, but found nothing outside other than a typical high-rise view. Although, these windows were pretty damn clean. That was nice, actually.

After a moment of awkward silence, when Oliver realized that Hastin wasn't going to finish his sentence, he finally spoke.

"It's okay, I didn't mean to scare you."

Hastin smiled at him then, so genuine and open that it actually sparked a pain in Oliver's chest. "I know," was all he said, with a nod.

But then came the problem; what exactly did you talk about with someone who was so... Well, a lot of things, really. There was very clearly something off about him. There were probably several things, honestly. But you couldn't start a conversation with hey, you're a little fucked up, aren't you? Because he might say yes, or worse yet, he might say no and actually mean it. He might have no idea.

"Captain..." Hastin said, saving him from his indecision. "I've never worked with a team before. All of my previous assignments, while successful, were solo efforts. I—" He bit his lip, hesitating for a moment. His eyes were nervous and dark but unflinching, and Oliver was close enough to see the marks left on Hastin's lip by his teeth. "I promise, I'll do my best."

"Oh, honey—" Oliver slipped up before he could catch himself. Probably not ideal to call an adult male that, even a lovely one, and definitely not one he just met. The affectionate appellation had no good use here, and had probably just slipped out because he seemed so young, and spoke so gently.

But instead of being insulted, Hastin looked at him with stars in his eyes and said nothing.

Oliver could have thanked a god, any god, when he heard a knock on the door. He turned just as he heard it open and Ame's voice called out.

"Room service! Someone order something hot?" And there she was, standing in the doorway with Rosa just behind her.

"Who's this cute thing?" Despite the fact that she was even shorter than Hastin, she nearly skipped across the room and slid right up next to him, eyeing him over. Her tail curled around her and, seemingly of its own accord, stroked his arm. Oliver watched him blush, visibly, and then hurry to introduce himself.

"Hello. I'm Hastin," he said.

"Amethyst Orchid," she replied in what was both a name and a description. Oliver thought that she could be called a weirdly-shaped flower, assuming that flower was also kind of murdery.

"You're really pretty," he said, that same amazed tone he had used to speak to Oliver.

"I was gonna say the same thing to you." One hand pushed her plentiful curls away from her face. "You're legal, right, kid? I mean, you look it, but if I am gonna get on that I wanna know what laws I'm breaking."

Hastin swallowed and stuttered. "I—..."

"Holy shit. Ame, can I talk to you for a minute?" Oliver glanced at Rosa, who he hadn't even had the chance to greet yet, and rubbed his forehead with his hand. This was already a train-wreck.

Hastin watched as a frowning Oliver took Ame by the elbow and dragged her into another room. Of course, that left him and Rosa standing together in the silence.

He swallowed. "Hi. I'm Hastin," he said quietly.

Rosa, more than a foot taller than him, grey-eyed and silvery-haired, inclined her head in greeting. "It is nice to meet you. My name is Rosa Silvia." Like Ame, he noticed, she had a tail as well. Hers was not skinny and fuzzy, though. It was long-haired and graceful, like she seemed to be.

He smiled, but it faltered. It was several uncomfortable seconds until he spoke again.

"I feel as though I have done something wrong," Hastin admitted. He looked past her shoulder to where the others had disappeared. He could hear their voices, harsh and quiet, in the other room.

"Don't worry." Rosa set her bag down near her feet and then went to the door to retrieve the others that had been left there. Hastin scurried after her, eager to help. "Ame and Oliver have a long history of arguments. I am sure he just didn't want to to do that in front of you."

The bags were heavy. Still, he did not struggle to move the one he had taken. "Oh. Okay." He set the bag down with the others and then looked at Rosa again.

"May I ask a question?" He sounded unsure of himself but she did not chastise him.

"Is it about my eyes?" she asked.

"Yes, ma'am."

"No ma'am needed. Yes, I'm blind," Rosa said patiently. "I can manage to get around my usual places just fine, but for work I have this thing—" She pointed at the device that sat at her temple. It was no larger than his palm and seemed to sit comfortably there against her skin.

"Oh! What is that?" True to his nature, he sounded curious.

"It's a computer. It uses downloaded blueprints to help me navigate, and I control them with various eye movements. It's also an echolocation device. It operates on a frequency we can't hear, but it gives me updated real time information about my surroundings." It sounded like an explanation that she had given many times but he listened to her raptly.

"Wow!" he said. He rocked back and forth on his feet, thinking about what she said excitedly. "That's amazing."

"Yes, I'm very proud of it."

"You made that?" He nearly bounced in his excitement. It was no wonder to Rosa that Ame had taken to him so quickly. His energy was immediate, much like her own.

"I did. And I've sold a few, also. The one part I can't make is here—" Rosa turned her head, tilting the device so he could see where it connected to her. "—That's the upload where it connects to the optic nerves behind the eye. It's an implant usually used by engineers. But, seeing as I can't currently do brain surgery..."

She was smiling now, but wasn't exactly sure when she had started doing it. Hastin clapped his hands together.

"That's amazing!" he said. "That's so...so... "

"It's cool as fuck, that's what it is." Ame was back and Oliver wasn't far behind. He was still frowning but she seemed to have shrugged it off.

Without missing a beat, she hooked an arm over Hastin's shoulders. "Okay, kid. What's the deal? Mr. Serious I've met before, enough to know that he's in way over his goddamn head—"

"Thanks for pointing that out," was Oliver's sarcastic reply.

"So what's going on? Not every guy I meet looks that good in a skirt and most of them would break their neck in those shoes."

"While you commiserate, I'm going to go set up. I'll need to have some of this stuff working if we're even going to evaluate this job," Rosa said.

Hastin turned to her quickly. "You should probably use one of the bedrooms. Don't worry, this place isn't wired, I already checked. No mics, and no cameras," he said naturally. "But the downside of the living room is—" He pointed to the big window he had been looking out earlier. Even Oliver could follow his train of thought. If someone was going to spy on them, it would be easiest to do so through the big damn opening.

"Work, work, work." Ame rolled her eyes.

"All my clothes look like this," Hastin answered her then. He hadn't shrugged off her arm, but he turned a little to look at her this time while he answered. "Well, I do have shoes without heels, but they're in my bag..."

"You have a set-up under there?" Ame nodded to his skirt. She could feel Oliver getting annoyed and pointedly ignored him. "Like this—" She lifted up her own skirt, showing Hastin the straps she wore underneath that held her pistol and a knife.

"Yeah!" Excited again, Hastin mimicked her movement and pulled his skirt up, too. A glance in Oliver's direction showed him averting his eyes and flushing red, but Ame just laughed.

"See, it's a little different, like this." Shamelessly, Hastin stood there with her and pointed out how his rigging worked a little differently than hers did.

"Your aneurysm aside—" She shot a look at Oliver, "—I'm actually happy to see that yours is a little different than mine, Hastin. Most of the girls I work with tend to swap out for shorts when they get down to it, so I don't get to compare notes often," she said reasonably.

"Wait, how come yours is set up that way—" Dropping his skirt, Hastin bent down to look at her straps a little more closely.

"Honey, think of it this way; I'm a lot squishier than you. I have to wear my straps a little different so they don't rub. Make sense?" Ame explained.

He hiked up his skirt again to look at how his were set up. "Oh. That's an interesting point. I hadn't considered that."

His own discomfort aside, Oliver at least thought it looked as though everyone was getting along well enough to work together. Now, if they decided to take the job, hopefully things would go all the easier for it.

He sighed and pressed a hand to his eyes. In the meantime, he just had to survive Ame's abrasive personality and Hastin's, well... Everything.

He went to help Rosa. He wasn't as technologically attuned as she was, but he wasn't an idiot and could at least follow instructions. Once she was set up, they could do a basic check of resources and contacts and get a vague idea of what the job ahead of them entailed.

By the time they went back into the main living area, Ame had pushed the table and couch aside and both her and Hastin had removed their shoes and were going over her bag of tricks that she had brought with her. He had no idea why they had moved the furniture but Oliver swallowed a string of unsurprised curses and decided not to ask.

On the one hand, it was nice to see Ame taking such interest in someone she was probably going to work with. On the other, Oliver had a sneaking suspicion about why she had that interest in the first place.

Well, it isn't much of a suspicion if she already announced it.

"This kid knows some shit!" she announced. She set down whatever it was she had been toying with (Oliver didn't recognize it at a glance) and spoke again, "This little motherfucker is fast."

"If I wasn't fast, I'd already be dead," Hastin said cheerfully. He seemed unruffled, but brushed his hand over his skirt to tidy it nonetheless.

"You guys all set up?" Ame asked.

"You mean you guys," Oliver corrected. "It's not my system."

Ame rolled her eyes. "Are we all set up, Rosa?" she asked instead.

"Yes," was the answer, accompanied with its own much more understated roll of the eyes.

Their little apartment was exactly that; little, but clean. It had the main area that they were now in and a small kitchen attached to it. Four bedrooms were stuck around the edges. A convenient match, considering that Oliver hadn't fully articulated any plans for the team to Violet. As he had just seen when he was helping Rosa set up, the rooms themselves weren't very large, either. But, altogether, it was a great place to hide.

"Okay, so let's talk in there where we can make a list of what it is exactly that we're getting into." Ame was the one to usher them back the way they had come and Hastin was quick to follow her.

Oliver leaned against the wall as Rosa sat down at her computer. Ame sat on the only bed in the room (the bed was dressed, but was low to the ground and with a thin mattress). Hastin looked around the room once and then sat on the floor.

"Okay, honey, what's the deal?" Ame looked at him. Then, reluctantly, she looked at Oliver. "Or am I asking you that?"

"Well, you don't have to call me honey," Oliver said sourly. "Anyway, he can talk and then I'll talk. He probably knows more about it than I do."

And then, to his surprise, Hastin shook his head. "No, Captain. All I was told was to listen to you."

Ame laughed, but she was the only one.

"Okay, I guess I am going first," Oliver corrected.

"Violet wants something stolen from the local data centre. There's something in their computers that she wants," Oliver said. "A record of some kind. We have the filename, we just need to get in there and get it."

"Pros and cons. Pros is that the systems are consistent and fairly predictable and I should be able to get us in there," Rosa figured immediately. "Cons are that these people have plenty of money to waste on security, so it's not like I can just sit here and work my way into a remote access to steal their stuff."

"There's going to be some legwork first," Ame summarized. "This job is gonna have steps to it. But it's totally possible. I don't see why not."

"And going after something that big has the large and often overlooked bonus of not making us anyone's enemies. It's not like we're personally slighting someone and it is unlikely to turn into a vendetta," Rosa added.

"So...you'll take the job?" Hastin asked.

"Hell yeah, we will," Ame said.

Rosa sighed. "I would have liked to do some more research." She nodded to her computer set-up. "Before we give you a solid yes or no. I just want to cast a net and look for anything that might red flag us."

"Well, now that you have an idea what we're up to, get on it," Ame said with a grin. Oliver didn't bother being insulted on Rosa's behalf. They worked together more often than they didn't. It was clear that Rosa wasn't bothered by Ame's tone.

The chatter, at least, mostly managed to stick to professional things after that. Rosa did some cursory research, but the results were nothing out of the ordinary. "It'll be tricky, but I think we can manage it. And for what she's going to pay us, it's definitely worth the attempt," she said.

Of course, for Oliver, that meant something a little different. If they were going to take the job, then all signs pointed to him throwing his lot in with them.

"Then it's official. We're a team!" Ame announced. She laughed and pointed at Oliver where he stood. "You're stuck with me now, asshole."

7:

Yoru was careful with introducing Dan to the idea of what he did for a living. There was a lot of ground to cover if he was going to feel comfortable taking a larger job, and as much as Dan wanted to be ready, Yoru was more cautious.

"I know how to use a gun. Where do you think you picked me up from?" Dan had joked. "I still have my shooting hand." He gestured with the referred-to extremity and Yoru snatched it out of the air, kissed it, and put it back where he found it. The affectionate action didn't phase Dan, who was used to his mannerisms by now.

"It's not your hand I am worried about, it's your brain," Yoru pointed out. They ate outside, Yoru having bought them some food from one of the vendors. Dan sat at a bench as he poured over his meal but such a simple idea was beyond Yoru, apparently. The taller man was sitting next to him, but was planted on the bench's back rather than its seat.

His words made Dan wilt a little and he looked down guiltily into his food. "I'm... I'm trying, okay?" he said quietly. "I think I'm getting better."

Yoru slid down into place next to him, leaning close so that they could speak quietly. "Dan, it isn't your dedication or resilience I am questioning," Yoru said firmly. "They nearly killed you. My best estimate says they probably actually accomplished it once or twice. Any human being is going to have some problems walking away from that."

Dan looked at him sharply. Stared, even, as though the idea hadn't occurred to him. He swallowed and set his food aside, his appetite going quiet for now.

"Today, we go and shoot some things. Later, I have some other things for us to try. Best case, I am being overprotective and am worried for nothing. Worst case, we have to adjust how we work," he said reasonably. He made no mention of why he was so concerned, of course. They didn't talk about how Dan still woke up in a cold sweat or how sometimes he just seemed to lose his sense of where he was. His coordination often went out the window at the same time, and Yoru had learned to listen for Dan's steps over the sound of his own to ensure that the other man was still on his feet. There was a lot they didn't talk about here, but it was understood. There was a reason that Dan did not argue too vehemently.

"This isn't a legal range, is it?" Dan asked wryly when they arrived. Yoru slid some money across the counter to a man who didn't bother to count it. He just nodded at him and then Dan followed Yoru into the building. It was all plain, crumbling concrete. Clean enough that they kept the graf artists out, but not enough for anyone to bother sweeping.

"Of course not," Yoru answered him easily. "I don't even know that I could find a legal one."

It occurred to Dan then that Yoru was so far off the deep end of legalities that he wouldn't be able to drag himself out even if he wanted to. Then again, he gave no indication of wanting to.

"Here." The table was filled with all kinds of toys. Most of them were things Dan was familiar with, although he noted that a few of them had interesting after-market additions. There was nothing big enough here to be dangerous in the context they were working in, but this was more than enough to get him started.

Yoru handed him a pistol and Dan took it. It had a familiar weight. It didn't feel comforting to hold, not exactly, but it felt natural. Something small to start. He took a deep breath, settled in and took aim.

Time to show off.

Yoru leaned against the wall, watched him with those sharp eyes of his. Dan had to get used to it again. He hadn't been in the field for some time, and on top of that, he was missing the hand he would have usually steadied his shot with. So he rested it on his forearm and felt a little silly...but it worked.

"You're impeccable," Yoru said, watching him. "For someone whose hand shakes when they eat, you sure can shoot."

Dan shot him a look. "Wow, rude."

"It was a compliment. What about the others?"

Dan set down the pistol, now empty, and picked up something else. It all came back to him, not in a flood, but in a trickle. When he needed the information, it was there. As though he had never forgotten it. He thought that maybe 'forgotten' wasn't exactly right, but it felt a little like forgetting.

"You've done a marvellous job. I'm wildly impressed," Yoru said. "I'm a fair shot, but you're something else. You didn't take up sharpshooting while you served?"

Dan shook his head. "The idea of laying around all day waiting for a shot didn't appeal to me. And after that happened, well... I guess I was more useful as a... As a..." Battery, neither of them said.

Instead Yoru just nodded. "Fair. I can't say I would take well to it myself," he admitted.

"So…" Dan set the rifle down and shrugged at Yoru. "Does that mean I pass?"

"It was never about passing." Yoru shook his finger at him. "You know that. What I will say instead is that you've done very well, and I am encouraged. But, there is more for us to try. And then, I am thinking it will be time for dinner." He grinned.

"You think about food a lot," Dan teased him.

"You don't?" Yoru answered. "Life is terrible and dangerous. I value what is good, what is pleasant. Food hurts no one and can be enjoyed by everyone," he said. "I see heavy worth in something so universally indulgent and kind."

"You're weird," Dan simplified.

"That too," Yoru agreed easily.

Dan had no problem following him around. He had come to terms with the idea that, until he was more used to this lifestyle, he'd probably be following Yoru around a lot. It did not seem to bother the thief very much. If anything, Dan's company seemed to please him. Dan found that the system they had in place was similarly enjoyable.

Their next errand looked like some kind of boxing club. Maybe a martial arts studio of some kind? This one Yoru didn't pay to get in, but he did spend a much longer time talking to the girl they met there.

"Hey, cutie," she greeted him. She was short and curvy with a round face and brilliantly purple hair that was spun in tight ringlets. She had a tail that curved up into the air, bright and curious, as she seemed to be.

"Um. Hi," Dan greeted back. He could feel himself blushing a little, and being aware of it only made it that much more uncomfortable.

"Oh, you got yourself an eloquent one here," she said, elbowing Yoru. He laughed.

"Be nice. He's learning. Dan, this is Ame. She's a loudmouth, but she's a darling," he said offhandedly.

"I notice you let her keep her feet," he said. Unlike Xueying, of course, who he hadn't.

Yoru raised his hand. "I can't do that to Ame because she'd put me in the hospital. To be fair, so could Xueying, but she has more patience for my shenanigans."

"If you kiss me, you're going home with me. I ain't got time for any of your teasing," she said, reaching over to tap Yoru on the chest.

"You play for keeps," Dan said with a smile.

"Well, in blocks of eight to twelve hours, I guess," she agreed with a grin.

"Wow, you're committed," Dan mused.

Ame laughed. "Okay, first of all, you boys forget that lesbian sex only stops when you're tired or want snacks. Multiple orgasms are great like that. And, even when boys are involved, I always schedule time for both food and sleep. I don't play at this shit."

"Your friends." Dan pointed at her and looked at Yoru. "Your goddamn friends, though."

"I pick 'em good," Yoru beamed. "C'mon, though, we have some punching to do. Bye, dollface." He blew Ame a kiss.

"See if you can't knock that asshole down a peg or two, eh?" She winked at Dan.

Dirty sunlight trickled through the window and gave everything a dim and sleepy appearance. The whole place was quiet and muffled. If there was anywhere for Dan to try exerting himself, this would be the safest option.

It had been a long time since he had been freely out and about among others. Crowds oscillated between being uninteresting background noise and overwhelmingly incomprehensible. There had to come a day when he could move comfortably in society at large again, right? These thoughts didn't seem to come from anywhere. Perhaps it was how far away everything seemed to feel.

The idea was dizzying, and for a moment he found himself almost separate from the world around him. He felt distant and vague.

Yoru put a hand on his shoulder and Dan snapped back into himself sharply. "S-sorry, I was—"

"Away," Yoru answered softly when Dan was unable to come up with the words. Dan just nodded instead.

"Time to fight," Yoru said lightly. "Take off your shoes and try to kick my ass, pretty boy. Let's see how well your recovery is coming."

Dan took a deep breath, feeling solidity and reality return to his body, and then nodded. He kicked off his shoes and followed Yoru to where some mats had been left out. He squared up against his friend, then he paused.

"It's been awhile since I've done anything like this. And I've never done it with one hand," he noted.

"Better to learn here," Yoru pointed out.

That was a fair statement, and he'd be damned if it didn't feel good to break a sweat again. This was the first real, enjoyable effort he had been able to put forth. Struggling to get out of bed after his rescue was not an accomplishment, not to him. He thought that Yoru would insist otherwise, but he didn't know what Dan was capable of. Or, at least what he had been capable of.

It would have been easier, but Yoru was fucking lightning fast. Dan was not, and he was not used to having only one hand. He had to quickly adapt to using what was left of his arm as a shield rather than using it to strike.

Except, of course, when he saw an opening and struck without thinking about it. He got Yoru right across the cheek with the stump of his forearm and knocked him on his ass.

Yoru fell, laughing. His face was already red where he had been hit and he rubbed at it. "Well, that works," he said.

Dan looked down at his arms, shrugged, and then smiled. Yeah. That worked.

He helped Yoru to his feet and they set at it again. Now that he had struck a blow, Yoru wasn't letting him off easily. His first victory was followed by a string of defeats. Dan hadn't been certain that there were so many ways to get thrown to the ground, but at least he learned something.

And then, just as he was trying to peel his face off the mat, Yoru fell down next to him. They were both out of breath and soaked in sweat, and when Dan looked over to him he saw he was smiling.

"If I'm this tired, you must be twice so," Yoru said. "Let's call it a day. We should probably have a shower before we meet up with Xueying, or she'll never touch me again," he joked.

They sat there together for a while still, though, catching their breath and enjoying the tapering adrenaline.

"Oh, that reminds me... I wanted to ask you," Dan said. He raised his arm as he tried to think of her name. "Ame. So, what, do you not want to sleep with her?" he asked. "I mean, she's pretty obviously down for sleeping with you. And I think she's cute."

"Oh, that's not the case at all," Yoru said. " It's on the to do list, if you'll excuse the pun," he explained. "I'd get on that with enthusiasm, but she's got standards. There's no running off in the morning before breakfast, or cutting out after the act. Unfortunately, I just haven't had the time. Work has been busy. I might make my own schedule, but when there's this many opportunities, you take what you can get. You never know when it will dry up. On top of all that, we're both big travellers and not usually in the same place for long." He shrugged. "So we have a sort of standing invitation. We'll get there."

"Do you want to sleep with all your friends?" Dan asked him. He was joking, but Yoru answered him sincerely.

"Dan, if they're not your friends, why would you sleep with them?" he asked.

Dan had to admit, he had a point.

This time it was Yoru who helped him up. They grabbed the rest of their stuff and headed back to where they were staying. The walk this time was refreshing, but Dan wasn't truly happy until he got cleaned up again. Then, as promised, they had dinner. Dan thought that maybe Yoru had a point about food, too.

"Are you ready for another challenge?" Yoru asked him once they had eaten.

Dan didn't answer right away. He looked at his friend and waited for the rest of it.

"I've tried to, well...pick only safe places for us," he admitted. "But a lot of what I have done, a lot of what I do, can't exist in those spaces."

"We're going somewhere dangerous," Dan surmised.

"Everywhere is dangerous. But some places run on danger. We are going to one of those places. That's where Xueying asked to meet us tonight."

"So that's why the tests today. Those were tests, weren't they?"

Almost guiltily, Yoru squirmed in his seat. "I should hate to see them that way."

Dan shook his head, and this time he reached out to his friend. "No. I prefer that. I also needed to know where I was at in my recovery. And, if you are bringing me with you, it seems I've passed. Your process here was... impeccable."

"You're making fun of me now," Yoru smiled a little. "You aren't upset?"

Dan shook his head. "Not even a little. So, where are we going?"

His friend brightened. "You ever seen a professional underground fight?" he asked.

"That sounds like a bit of a contradiction," Dan noted. It was left as an obvious answer that he hadn't.

"Well, you're in for a show. And here." He dug through one of his bags and handed Dan both a pistol and a holster to carry it. "Not saying that you'll need it, but just in case."

Dan understood. He wore it under his jacket. It was the first place someone would look, but he didn't plan on letting anybody get that close.

Or, so he had hoped. Turned out the place was more than just crowded. It was packed. Yoru slipped between people naturally, but it didn't take Dan long to grab his hand lest he get lost in the shuffle. He suddenly felt a lot better about being armed. It seemed that was commonplace here, and that no one would care to look for it.

They met Xueying without trouble. Even in a crowd, she was easy to find.

"Nice to see you again, stranger." No room for his usual displays, Yoru gave her a quick kiss on the cheek. She turned to greet Dan with her signature genuine warmth and he wondered briefly how she had managed to flourish in such an environment.

"You're looking well," she said.

"Feeling it, too," he answered.

She had found them a spot against the railing. It looked down into something resembling an arena. It was the only empty spot in the place, everywhere else was packed with people. Still, for an arena it wasn't very big, and the walls looked like they were falling apart. Dan had seen plenty of scraps in his time, but he knew that this was going to be a lot more serious.

"So, why are we here, exactly?" he asked under his breath.

"There's someone here I want to hire for our little undertaking," Xueying said. "I've wanted to go after her for a while, but with this job I finally have the financial leverage to catch her eye. You know how it is."

"Well, I'm learning," Dan pointed out. He wasn't about to agree with her, not yet.

"Where did you get that?" Xueying turned to Yoru who was leaning against the railing, sipping a drink he had gotten from somewhere. He just smiled at her.

"I don't know that you should go around stealing people's drinks," Xueying said.

He smiled at her. "You telling me you don't want one?"

With an amused glance, she took the drink out of his hand, stole a swig and then handed it back. He just laughed.

There was some sort of commotion below. Dan leaned over the rail to get a better look and it seemed like they were starting the event. He had never seen a professional fight like this, but judging from the blood that was stained around the concrete and wood barriers, he was going to be in for quite a show.

The announcer was just some slightly intoxicated guy dressed in a beaten-up suit jacket who looked like he hadn't brushed his hair in a month. He held a bottle of something or other in his hand and it didn't take a genius to figure out what it was.

Apparently, the fight was going to be between someone named Mad Dog (how original) and someone named Rusty. Dan already felt lost.

"Which one are we here for?" he asked Xueying quietly.

"Rusty," she said, looking amused. "You'll know her when you see her. Just watch."

So he did. There seemed to be remarkably little preamble to the main event and he watched as two people entered the arena from opposite sides. Both were unarmed, or at least not armed in any way he could see. One was a very large man who seemed very happy to be there.

The other was an incredibly sour looking woman with red hair and deeply tanned skin. She was also incredibly tiny. Xueying was shorter than him by a few inches but if he had to guess, he'd peg Rusty at half a foot shorter than her, at least.

"Oh, this is gonna be a long one," Yoru mused, watching them square off. Dan wanted to ask him how he knew, but once the fight got started any idea of discussing it slipped his mind entirely. It was too fast paced and too engaging for him to try and maintain an intellectual discussion of any sort.

Rusty was the first to draw blood and the whole crowd flinched to see it. Dan pressed a hand to his mouth, but didn't take his eyes away.

"You going to be okay?" Xueying asked him without taking her eyes off of the action.

"Yeah." He took a deep breath. The crowd was very lively and seemed equal parts disgusted and energized by the violence. Dan wasn't sure where he stood on that scale. It was impressive, sure. But there was something visceral about it that got his stomach all twisted up uncomfortably.

Xueying got right into it. She cheered for every blow Rusty landed and winced for every one she received. Yoru, sipping his drink, seemed dispassionate to the whole affair. Still, when Dan spared a glance his way, he saw that Yoru still watched the events unfold with focused eyes.

His prediction was right, though. Dan had no idea how long these events usually lasted, but it went on long after they were both bloody and stumbling. He was sure at any moment they would both collapse. It would have been an underwhelming end to such a drawn out fight, but it seemed nearly a miracle that either of them were able to keep their feet.

When Mad Dog pried one of the wooden boards off the wall, Dan had a sinking feeling overcome him. He was pretty sure he knew what was going to happen. Rusty was bent over, spitting out blood and catching her breath as he prepared to crack her right over the head with it.

He wound up, raising his hands over his head... And Rusty sprung to standing and decked him right in the face while he was unable to protect himself. He fell to the ground and didn't get up.

Next to him, Xueying cheered loudly and enthusiastically. Dan slumped over the railing to try and catch his breath, unaware that he had been so pent up. He felt a hand on his back and didn't even jump. It was Yoru. He didn't have to look to be sure.

"Come on." Xueying elbowed him as he was standing up again. "I got us a meeting with her. Let's go see if we can't convince her to join our little adventure."

"Considering the state she's in now, are we sure that she'll be of use to us?" Yoru asked her quietly.

"Only one way to find out!" Xueying cheered.

A.N. Mouse

8:

Once it was decided that they would be working together, they had to make a plan for how exactly that would happen.

"Okay, but, first thing's first, we don't have any fucking food. If we're going to be using this place as a hub, which I suggest we do because it is free and inconspicuous, we gotta have shit to eat," Ame said.

"Wow, we actually agree on something," Oliver answered dryly.

"Yeah, and we're going to agree that you're not buying the food, because I know you can't cook." And he wanted to be really offended by that, but she was too correct for him to even pretend to have his feelings hurt.

"Ame and I will worry about the food," Rosa said. "Mostly because I know she'll lose the receipts if I send her alone. Any allergies?" Because that was very Rosa to ask. It would have been hilarious and inconvenient to have to halt a job because someone got hives or some shit like that.

"The only thing I am allergic to is her attitude," Oliver answered instead.

Cheerful, possibly oblivious, Hastin shook his head. "None," he answered with a smile. "And while they're gone, I have some files we can look over." He looked to Oliver and despite what Oliver would usually think, the idea of looking over paperwork suddenly seemed much more appealing.

"Sounds fair. You two can tell us what we need to know when we get back and we can start putting this job together," Rosa agreed.

Honestly, complaining aside, Oliver was pretty hungry. It wasn't an unusual feeling, but that didn't make it any more comforting. Instead, once those two had ducked out, he looked to Hastin.

"So, what's in these files, then?" he asked. Maybe work would be a good distraction.

"Well, I figured that if we looked at how Xueying's team had planned to do it, or what information we have from that at least, it might help us build a plan for ourselves," he suggested. Then, a little shyly, he added, "I brought them along for me, mostly, because this job is out of my usual skill set and I wanted to do some research. But I am happy they will be of use."

"You're not the only one a little out of your depth. I think most of the heavy lifting will be those two. We just have to do our best to help them." And his casual animosity with Ame aside, Oliver meant what he said. "That's how teams work, right?"

Hastin's eyes were probably brown but they were very dark. Oliver thought he had read somewhere that black eyes weren't a thing that happened, but then again, all kinds of shit happened now that never used to. Maybe they were black.

Either way, they looked at him in what might have been undiluted adoration. Oliver hastily looked away. Honestly, he didn't think Hastin knew he was doing that.

"Yeah!" he agreed with a smile. "Here, let me move the table back so we can use it…" Without hesitation, Hastin pulled the table back to where it belonged in front of the couch and then excused himself to go get the files. Oliver sat down on the couch and took a deep breath.

Hastin wasn't a bad kid, but he was weird. Oliver just had to remember to keep breathing. Sometimes, he got a little distracted.

"Here." Actual paper files. Oliver had noticed that Hastin did not seem to have any technology on him. No phone, or none he had shown. Didn't have one of those fancy tech watches (didn't Highlight Technology make those? It seemed weird he wouldn't have one). Didn't have a data pad with the files on it, had them on hard copy instead. That was a little weird for a child of a technology giant. To be fair, Oliver didn't mean that in a literal sense. Maybe he was overthinking things.

Paper was expensive, too, after all.

Hastin sat down on the couch, but a little distance away. It was Oliver who moved closer to him so they could look at the files together.

"Here… Xiao Xueying's files…" He set a few sheets of paper down. "She was an ex-idol singer, it says. Picked up espionage as an adult. That's neat."

Another, single sheet of paper. "Oh, not much on this guy. Yoru. No last name. Or maybe that is a last name?" he mused. The sheets had photographs on them. Oliver would have expected headshots, but then again, he thought that getting those would have been a little difficult. It isn't as though any of these people would have had driver's licenses on record, right?

Xueying was very pretty. Oliver recognized her now from the bar.

"Nguyen Han. Rusty, it says. A ring fighter! Wow!" A fair amount of information on her, certainly more than Yoru's little half-page of text. "And…it says Dan. Not much on him either, it looks like. That's weird."

Dan. It looked like the picture was pulled from a security camera, maybe. He was smiling. He was wearing the hat he had been wearing when

Oliver met him, his face turned slightly away from the camera but still clear, still him. He took the sheet from the table and looked at it more closely.

"Captain, are you okay?" Hastin looked at him, concerned. Oliver took a deep breath and set the paper back on the table.

"Yeah, don't mind me, kid," he said. "So, what do we know about all this?" Oliver asked instead.

Hastin thought for a moment. "Spy. Thief. Enforcer, I guess? And I don't know what he did…" He pointed at Dan's sheet. "But what I have here —" He had more papers in the folder and he set them down, "—I started going through it. It looked like their plan was to go through a lot of third parties. Other people who had different pieces of the access path, but hadn't thought to assemble them. I mean, stuff like the access codes would be useful for all kinds of things."

"So…is that a good idea or a bad idea?" Oliver asked.

Hastin giggled. "Well, I mean…we don't look like we're associated with them, right?" he said. "Maybe it would be strange to have someone else try to buy what Xueying's team was just after, though. It might be best if we at least try to make a different approach."

"Well, at least we have something useful to tell the girls when they get back," Oliver noted wryly.

He picked up Dan's page again. It didn't have a lot on it. Guesses about his origination, any ideas about his professional history. Oliver knew a little more than the sheet did. Dan was a beginner in the business, on the run from something. He hadn't said what, and Oliver hadn't asked. Sometimes, you didn't ask.

"Hey…do you mind if I keep this?" Oliver asked him. No sooner were the words out of his mouth than did he start to backtrack. It sounded weirder out loud.

"I mean, I knew him, and I don't have any pictures of him, I just meant—"

Hastin laid his hand on Oliver's knee. "That's okay. I can always get another copy if we need it. There's not a lot on there so I don't think you'll exactly be depriving us of required information."

"Thanks…" he breathed. Oliver stared at the picture a moment longer, then he folded it carefully as to not ruin the photo and slipped it in his pocket.

"He was your friend?" Hastin asked quietly.

Oliver winced. "Yeah," he answered simply. Kind of. Enough.

"You…miss him?" the younger man attempted

Oliver swallowed. This wasn't getting any easier. "Yeah. I mean, I only got to see him once, but we texted a lot, so it's just that something that was common and nice to me is sort of gone now. It's weird, I know."

Hastin opened his mouth to say something and then shut it quickly, frowning.

"What is it?" Oliver prompted.

"Well... I was going to offer to text you, to keep you company...but I don't have a phone. Not really," he said quietly. "So that's no help at all..."

Oliver smiled a little. "Hey, it's not your problem to fix. But it was a nice thought."

Hastin seemed to be thinking hard about something, looking down into his lap instead of up at Oliver. Oliver let him, casting his eyes over the other information they had collected on the table.

"Captain?" Hastin drew his attention back again.

"Yeah?"

"Did you...um..." Hastin started. He hesitated, and Oliver could visibly see him gathering his courage. "Did you want a hug?"

Oliver didn't laugh. He kind of wanted to, seeing as it was a little hilarious, but he didn't. It was clear that Hastin had really tried hard to ask that. It would have been cruel to laugh. Instead, he tried to pick his answer just as carefully.

"You don't need to do that, I'll be okay," Oliver reassured him. "It's kind of you to offer though. I appreciate it."

"I want to help," Hastin said. He looked at Oliver earnestly. "That's why I offered."

Ame was laughing at him somewhere, but frankly Oliver didn't give much of a fuck right now. The more he actually considered it, the more it sounded...nice, actually. And not just because of who was asking, although he supposed that didn't hurt.

"Okay," he said easily. "You make a good point. I think a hug would be good."

He wasn't sure what he expected, but he opened his arms and without any noticeable hesitation, Hastin moved closer on the couch and hugged him. It was immediately very pleasant. Oliver had that perpetual heaviness in his soul, a kind of fog that hadn't dispelled in the wake of his friend's death. A hug wasn't a cure but it was, genuinely, nice.

After a second, Hastin shuddered and Oliver was quick to pull away, holding the younger man at arm's length for a moment. "Hey, hey—" Hastin wasn't looking up at him, and in fact hadn't moved from where Oliver had gently pushed him away. "Are you alright?"

"I've never done that before," Hastin said quietly. "I mean, I've never done that because I wanted to before." But before Oliver could answer, he kept speaking. "They're... I liked it." He looked at Oliver then and smiled shyly. God, he was pretty.

Well if that wasn't a distraction from what he had been feeling, Oliver wasn't sure what was. He hadn't exactly needed confirmation that something was wrong with Hastin but here it was anyway. Still, it never seemed the right time to say anything. Maybe it never would be.

"Well, I like hugs," Oliver said then. "So, if you're ever feeling like you need a hug, you can come to me, okay? And I can't really volunteer Ame for anything, but the same probably goes for her, you can ask." At least Oliver had the excuse of neglect to explain why he was so affectionate as a person. Ame had the excuse of confidence, he guessed. It was a much better excuse.

"Is now an okay time to ask?" Hastin inquired. This time, Oliver did laugh.

"Yeah, c'mere," he invited. Hastin hugged him again. He was smaller across the shoulders and fit well into Oliver's arms. He smelled like something pleasant and floral, but there was a good chance that Oliver had never seen the flowers the scents were derived from.

They sat together there for a moment before returning to their actual task at hand, but Oliver did feel better. Hastin seemed happy, too. That was enough to lift anyone's spirits.

"We have a list of probable locations where they seemed to have picked up some supplies and intel. Depending on who they dealt with, that means we can start looking in those places, too, or maybe that those people won't like us very much," Hastin said. "We know that they tried to go by remote access, and we know it failed," he continued. "That's what all this looks like. Didn't Rosa say something about not wanting to do it that way?"

"I think she did. But I think she's a lot better with computers than Xueying's team," Oliver said thoughtfully. "The sheets don't say anything about them having a technician."

"Rosa's amazing," Hastin said. Oliver didn't have to look at him to know his expression already, but he did anyway and laughed again. It was exactly as he expected, those same starry eyes looking at him again.

"She sure is. I guess if they didn't know they'd need one, it does sound like a better alternative than trying to break right the hell in there," Oliver guessed.

"I know they stole some floor plans, too," Hastin pointed out. "It says that—here." He pulled a page from the stack of paper. "Miss Violet conducted an investigation to try and back track their progress. Didn't find a copy of them, but I assume they must have needed the data for something."

"They must have hit a roadblock," Oliver surmised. "What happened after that?"

"The rest of it says how they were supposed to have a progress meeting with Miss Violet because of how long it took, but before that happened they, um…"

He wondered if ever hearing it would not feel like falling. It certainly felt like he had tripped here, that same sort of shift in his stomach. Oliver swallowed it and nodded. "Yeah."

"I'm sorry your friend was having brain problems," Hastin said quietly.

"Me too." Oliver's smile wasn't a happy one.

Silence, more thoughtful than awkward, fell between them.

"You think there's something wrong with my brain, too," Hastin pointed out.

Hastin wasn't supposed to know that. Oliver had been trying very consistently during their two meetings to be as tactful as possible, and yet… Maybe he had fucked up somewhere.

Still, he wasn't going to lie. The least he could do is be honest. Here, being honest meant being a little more gentle.

"Lots of people have problems upstairs," Oliver explained. He tapped the side of his own head. "Some people are like me, where you get them when you're young, and you learn how to work around them. Nothing you can do, sometimes brains are just uncooperative," he said.

"Dan… I don't know what happened." He sighed. "He was a nice person, a good person, but that doesn't mean that he was okay. Bad things happen to good people all the time. That's not nice, but it's life, and you can't get mad about it. Being mad doesn't help you help anybody else."

Oliver paused to take a deep breath before he continued. "And you… Honey, I don't think you're fucked up." This time, he didn't even think to apologize. "I just… I'm not sure you're on the same page as everybody else. I'm a worrier, so, I worry that it makes you unhappy. I guess I just want everyone to be okay."

Oliver laughed a little at himself. "I mean, that's kind of hard considering what we all do with our lives, but you know what I mean. I'd like that. For you, and for all of us. Even Ame, as much as I bitch about her."

"You're a complicated person," Hastin said quietly.

This time, Oliver laughed for real. "I don't think so. I like food, and

70

sleep, and when people aren't jerks to me. I'm pretty simple."

"You're nice. People aren't nice, Captain," Hastin said. There was a sureness in his voice that Oliver didn't want to know the source of.

"You don't have to call me that, yeah? I'm just Oliver. I'm not even the most useful person on this team," he pointed out.

Hastin smiled. "But you're my Captain, and you're nice. I want to be nice to you, too."

Well, he wasn't going to argue about it. It was kind of cool, actually. And as long as Hastin didn't mind it, he didn't see the harm in it. Besides, if Ame hadn't caught on already, it would drive her crazy when she did.

The door was too quiet for Oliver to have heard it, but this time Hastin did. He jumped to his feet in an instant and it was that movement that made Oliver turn to look at where he was headed. Then, he heard the shouting.

"I am the bag monster! Behold me, and be afraid!" Which is to say, Ame was the first in the door and her arms were full of food.

"Here, let me help you." Hastin was quick to assist. Oliver was a little slower and waited for Rosa to come in before offering his help. What did he care? Ame could probably bench press him. To be fair, Rosa could probably bench press him and Ame.

And wow, he was starving. He knew he was getting a little peckish but seeing the actual food was way harder than he thought it would be.

"Did you two have time to talk shop while we were gone?" Rosa asked.

"Yeah. Nothing groundbreaking," Oliver said. "You were right about the remote access, though. Looks like the other team tried that and couldn't pull it off."

"Well, good to know. I'd hate to avoid the easy way and make our lives miserable for nothing," Rosa said.

"Hey, who said anything about being miserable?" Ame shot back. "Some of us like it the hard way."

"You're literally the worst," was all Oliver had to say to that. Ame's tail flicked dismissively, but Oliver ignored the implied answer.

They got the food organized, but were soon presented with a problem. If they all put it away...Rosa wouldn't know where things were.

"Solution is this. You two kids go argue in the living room. Hastin is going to help me put things away, and we're going to make dinner. That sound good?" Rosa asked.

"I'd be happy to help," Hastin said cheerfully.

71

There were no arguments, mostly because neither Ame nor Oliver had it in them to break his heart like that. Oliver was pretty sure Rosa planned it for exactly that outcome.

As they worked, Ame wandered back into the living room, obediently following Rosa's orders, mostly because it was the room closest to the food. It was there she saw the evidence of their work and she crossed her arms over her chest as she peered down at the paperwork.

"Looks like quite the—Hey, wait," she said. Oliver watched her reach down and pick up one of the I.D. sheets.

"Yoru," she said, holding the paper in her hand. "What is he doing here?"

"Yoru, you mean, Dan's friend?" Oliver asked her, tilting his head. "You know him?"

"Know him? We were tight," Ame said. Agitated, she threw the page back onto the table. Being a sheet of paper, it wasn't exactly a satisfying motion.

"This is bullshit. Why the fuck is he dead?" Ame sighed.

Oliver didn't know the answer to that question.

9:

Xueying traipsed through the crowd of people seemingly without a care. She slid through the throngs with unfaltering steps and smiled picturesquely the entire time. It was like she was from another planet, Dan thought. Yoru too, who seemed to have no trouble navigating through the mass of bodies. Drunk people were never Dan's favourite, and drunk rowdy people even less so. Sure, in his time in the military he had been both drunk and rowdy and usually did those things combined together, but now he felt a little sympathy for the people who had dealt with him.

He kept hold of Yoru and found that it made surviving the tide of people much easier.

Xueying led them towards the back of the building and down a set of stairs that seemed surprisingly solid for how terrible they looked. The crowd was thinner here, the air a little easier to breathe because of it. People looked at them weirdly, though, and Dan got the sneaking suspicion that they probably weren't really supposed to be there.

"Back again, Xueying?" The man waiting to the side of the door was absolutely huge. Dan wasn't sure what purpose that served. This was a place that hosted these awful, brutal fights, right? If he was so tough...why was he guarding the door and not being the guy who made the money? Maybe there was more to the situation that Dan couldn't see, but at the moment it served to make him less on edge than he would have otherwise been.

"Of course. I told you I'd be back," she said sweetly, as though the guy wasn't twice her size and several times her weight. "Can I go in?"

"You're not supposed to," he pointed out.

"Aw, but you want to let me. Besides, you know she wants to see me."

"Rusty doesn't want to see anybody. You know how she is," he said. Then, a little amused, he looked over to Dan and Yoru. "These your muscle? They gonna convince me if I don't let you?"

Yoru was always quick to be a smartass. "If you think Xueying needs our help, you don't know her so well."

"Oh, stop it," Xueying giggled.

"C'mon, Lucas, let me in," she coaxed him. "They won't get mad. I

73

know I'm not gonna tell them about it. And you're not gonna tell them, so who's going to complain?"

Xueying was too charming to be real. Dan was sure it was something Yoru and her shared. Still, he could tell this battle was already over. Lucas's indecision was apparent and that meant that Xueying had won.

"Make it quick," he eventually agreed. She kissed him on the cheek.

"Thanks, Lucas. We'll be fast. I promise," she said.

He let them pass.

The room was simple. It had some chairs, a cot, a table full of medical supplies and alcohol bottles. There was blood here, too. Not enough to be horror-movie spooky. Considering the circumstances, there actually wasn't as much as Dan expected.

Rusty was there. She was bandaging herself up and drinking something from an unmarked bottle. She looked up when they came in and Yoru closed the door behind them.

"You're back." The woman spoke Omnian but had an accent that Dan couldn't place.

"I'm back." And there was something in Xueying's voice that Dan hadn't expected. Yoru didn't seem surprised, though. He hadn't lost that focused look although the fight was long over. Something here was interesting to him.

Xueying took a seat. Yoru pulled a chair out with his foot and offered it to Dan, who shrugged and took it. Yoru didn't sit, though. He leaned against the wall, arms crossed. He looked more thoughtful than intimidating.

"I have a job to offer you, if you want it," Xueying said quietly.

"I have a contract," Rusty answered. She looked to the boys and then back to Xueying.

"Who are they?"

"Just friends," she explained. "They're part of the job, too."

"I told you, I have a contract," Rusty shot back. Xueying never raised her voice, and it wasn't the playfully sweet tone she had used for the doorman. She was quiet and patient in her words, gentle and clear. It made sense, as Rusty's Omnian was clearly in need of practice and Xueying was trying to win her over.

"You only have one fight left, though, don't you?" The inflection meant that it wasn't really a question.

"You've been counting." Rusty looked at her. She seemed perpetually understated, but maybe it was just the context. Getting a rise out of her here wouldn't have helped them.

Xueying smiled. "Yeah, I have. Come on. The one job. If it's no good, you can always come back. The pay is going to be worth it. It's a big job."

Rusty frowned. "If I say no, you'll keep coming," she noted.

Xueying laughed a little, but she shrugged. "You've never sent me away…" she noted. It earned her a narrow-eyed look but no immediate response.

"The fight is next week. Come talk to me before it starts. If you wait until after, they'll be here with another contract for me," Rusty said.

Xueying jumped to her feet excitedly.

"Okay. Okay. We'll be here," she said. That looked like their cue to leave so Dan stood and Yoru followed him to the door.

"Oh, and—" Xueying turned, looking back to Rusty before leaving. "You looked amazing out there. I hope you heal up quick," she said.

She didn't get an answer.

So they had a week. They parted with Xueying and caught the subway back to their temporary neighbourhood. Dan unselfconsciously leaned into Yoru for the entirety of the ride.

"So, what are we going to do with all this time?" Dan asked him.

"Rob some people. Write some poetry. Do whatever I usually do between work," Yoru said easily.

Dan blinked at him. "You write poetry?"

Yoru grinned. "Learn something new every day, don't you," he teased. "Yeah. I like to buy notebooks and write as many pieces as I can, then I leave them in the places I've stayed." He shrugged. "Maybe someone will pick them up and have a nice time."

Dan just blinked at him again. "You're strange."

"Mmm." Yoru leaned back, his eyes going back to the window of the subway, although all it showed him was the swift passage of discoloured concrete walls.

"Tell me one of them," Dan said suddenly. Yoru didn't answer at first so Dan smacked him in the chest with his forearm. Yoru's head tilted back his way and Dan repeated himself. "Tell me one of them."

"What makes you think I remember any of them?" Yoru smiled mischievously.

"Because, knowing you, you remember them all," Dan said. That was to mention nothing of his smart little fucking smile. Yoru only looked too pleased with himself.

He took Dan's shoulders and held him up for a moment while he sat up properly behind him. Then be let his friend fall back against him. Dan endured the manhandling with a roll of his eyes but neither struggled nor complained

"Okay, let's see... Coalescing here, dark eyes, heavy clouds hang low, silence before spring. Flowers that bloom in slow moving horizon light fill me with such warmth."

Yoru beamed at him, proud of himself, and for a moment Dan was speechless.

"You remembered that?" he asked, skeptically.

Yoru's grin widened. "Made it up on the spot, actually. They're haikus. It's a style of poetry from Hinomoto."

All of that went over Dan's head, honestly. He had little understanding of poetry. But still, something seemed off to him.

He narrowed his eyes at Yoru. "That was about me, wasn't it?" he asked.

"If it was, how would you feel?" Yoru asked him with a smile that made something in Dan's chest go tight. This was different than the crowd-panic, or the late night shortness of breath. He crossed his arms and frowned, planting himself against Yoru to try and not be as charmed as he was.

It was a miserable failure.

"Don't be sour with me. I meant it as a compliment," Yoru said gently, his voice low in Dan's ear. His apology was clear in his tone, if not in his words.

"I'm not being sour," Dan said, his frown already hard to keep. "I'm trying not to melt like a goddamn schoolgirl just because you recited poetry for me."

"I can tell you more, if you'd like," Yoru offered gently. "Maybe it would make you feel better if you can say I had to work for it."

Dan tried not to smile and did anyway.

"Okay. Tell me some more."

Yoru did. It was an interesting experience. Yoru was very good, for someone who was reciting poetry off the top of his head. Sometimes he'd laugh and correct himself, and his confidence made Dan smile.

"Is Omnian your second language?" Dan asked him as they got off the subway.

Yoru counted on his fingers. "Fourth? Maybe fifth? I guess it depends on how fluent you'd have to be to count. I can speak some Syaman, right? But I'm not fluent."

Dan just sighed and rolled his eyes again. He hooked his arm through Yoru's this time out of resigned affection rather than need. It was late and the streets were quiet. Maybe he should have been worried.

Yoru walked no slower or smaller for whatever danger might have been hiding.

By the time they got back home, Dan was pleasantly tired and full of feeling. It was a nice change. He didn't know whether to credit the weird emptiness he sometimes felt to the physical or psychological damage he had endured, or even just to homesickness. But, whatever the cause, today it wasn't so bad. He was getting better at these late nights, too.

And, perhaps, he was feeling a little courageous. The full feeling made him feel wonderfully whole. When Yoru sat down, Dan followed him, planting his lap in his friend's own and looking at him expectantly.

"My friend, I'm glad to share my seat, but..." The question was obvious. This was a very Yoru thing to do, but it was not a very Dan thing to do.

"You sleep with your friends, you said," Dan answered cryptically.

Yoru's eyebrows raised but he merely nodded. "Yes, when I'm privileged enough for the honour," he answered slowly.

Dan looped his arms over Yoru's shoulders. He was doing an impressive job at not acting nervous, but really, he was markedly less anxious than the last time he had propositioned someone. He supposed that almost dying might have had some effect on that. "Would you?"

"Is this an invitation?" Yoru asked. In reassurance, he wrapped his arms around Dan's waist. It also helped him feel less like he might fall over.

Dan smiled. "Yeah, it is."

"I'd be glad to. As long as you're sure," he said. He nudged Dan's nose with his own. "I don't want to end up doing something stupid and cruel like breaking your heart or making you feel pressured. You're my friend and that comes first."

"You really know how to make someone want to sleep with you," Dan remarked.

"You mock me," Yoru said, though he did not sound wounded.

"No, I mean it. I mean... I did think twice about this because we both know I'm still kind of messed up but... What's better to know than that you care?" He smiled. "I'm sure."

Yoru smiled and kissed him gently. "Remember that, okay? If you need us to stop, we can stop. No questions asked."

Dan kissed him again then, this one with a little more enthusiasm. "Yeah, I know. I'm not worried. And I'm in no state for a relationship anyway, so there's no worry about that." He laughed.

Yoru was a good kisser, or maybe it had just been a long, long time. Dan hadn't gotten any action since what, high school? Well, before the military. Sure, there had been trips home, weekends out drinking, but his luck had never been great.

It was nice to want and be wanted. And it was nice for it to be by someone so…safe. Young Dan had liked dangerous girls. Hell, he was pretty sure he still did. But this was sweet, in a way.

He shivered when Yoru's hands slipped under his shirt, but the man pushed him back after a moment or two of just getting Dan hot under the collar.

"We can't do this here. It's a chair. We're either going to break it or we're going to die. Or both," Yoru said.

Cheeks flushed, Dan laughed. He got to his feet and took Yoru's hand to help him up, too. The idea of his obituary reading 'weird foreigners die in sex/chair incident' was enough to make him laugh more than was necessary, but he never managed to articulate the headline to Yoru.

Yoru was just glad to hear him laugh.

They stumbled into the bed and it was exactly as much fun as Dan thought it would be.

Yoru pulled him close, his hips against Dan's, and when he murmured Dan's name in his ear, Dan started laughing again.

"Okay, you got off the last time without explaining, but I'm not letting it slip twice," Yoru warned him, smiling. Dan thought that was fair.

"My name," he said.

"Your name?" Yoru asked.

"You've always called me Dan, and I've never corrected you because it makes me smile and usually calms me down." He wasn't laughing anymore. His smile was warm, thinking of how Yoru had helped him so often.

"But it's a nickname. You had asked me what my mom called me. She called me 'Dan' when I was growing up because of an actor we both liked. We'd watch the movies together and she'd cheer with me. Say stuff like, 'he's almost as handsome as you are' and all that stuff." His blush here was from embarrassment, not arousal, and Yoru kissed his cheek.

"That's incredibly adorable," he said. Dan laughed.

"My name is Suparat. Suparat Jirayu. You can still call me Dan, though, I like that, just not, you know…" He looked embarrassed again for a moment.

"Just not in bed," Yoru said with a nod.

Dan nodded, kissing Yoru again. "Yeah, just not here. I mean, I'm in hiding now, right? So it's probably better like this anyway."

"Consider it done, Suparat." And there was something in hearing his name, his real name, that made him shiver. A secret, but not the kind that made you sick. The kind that was warm and soft, that heated him through to his very centre. And the idea that he had shared this secret with Yoru, his friend, only made it better.

"I don't know if I'm strong enough to be on top, by the way," Dan remarked wryly despite the contentment buzzing inside of him. "I probably could, we'd just need to—" He gestured with his handless arm. Anything that meant he didn't have to lean on it.

"I am flexible," Yoru remarked. "In all senses of the word. We'll figure it out."

Dan smiled into the next kiss. He felt tangible, real. Feeling Yoru's hands move over him was an anchor, keeping him in the here and now. He felt better than he had in ages. Even breathing came easily. He knew it was temporary, but he'd take what he could get. It came a little less easily when Yoru's hands got a little more adventurous and Dan found himself moving against his touch.

"You make cute noises," Yoru said, his voice heated and low. Dan shivered, letting his head tilt back so Yoru could kiss down his neck. He fumbled with Dan's belt, undoing it with little trouble before doing the same to his jeans. Dan's hand was mostly busy holding on to him, but even when he pried his fingers away to try and do the same, he found that he wasn't nearly as adept.

"Hold on, I can't—"

"Shhh," Yoru murmured. "I'll worry about my clothes. You just enjoy yourself."

"I didn't proposition you so you would dote on me," Dan answered.

"I know. But life is short and unfair. Let me be kind." And Dan swore under his breath, but he let him. It was so hard to say no when Yoru's hands felt so good.

He did just as he promised, though, undoing his own pants to give Dan access and pausing their fun momentarily to help them both out of their shirts. Dan's was easy for him to pull over his head but fucking Yoru and his stupid buttons meant that Dan had to sit there with utmost impatience until it was removed.

"C'mere." He fell against his friend with an undignified noise but was happy for the return of physical contact.

"Get your damn pants out of my way," Dan muttered. If they weren't so fucking tight he'd be able to push them down lower, but Yoru's bloody fashion sense impeded him.

Yoru laughed, breathless and happy, and did as he asked. Dan pressed his new advantage and enjoyed all the ways he could pull his name from Yoru's lips.

Yoru only let him get away with so much.

"That's enough free reign for you," Yoru teased. He pulled himself from Dan's arms and just smiled at his friend's frown. "Hush now. I'm not leaving," he reassured him.

Yoru pushed himself farther down the bed to where Dan's pants were undone. Without a moment of hesitation, he helped Dan out of them and the underthings underneath and tossed both of them to the floor unceremoniously.

"Oh—" was the sum total of what Dan could say before Yoru made speaking much more difficult for him.

It was clear that Yoru had no shortage of experience. Still, he wore it well and Dan was in no position to complain. Yoru's tongue laved attention on where he craved it most and soon Dan was nothing more than a squirming, quietly swearing wreck.

"H-hey. Yoru, don't tease me like that—" Yoru's hair had come undone but it only gave Dan something to tangle his fingers in as his friend continued.

It did little to stop him, though. Yoru was every bit as thorough and professional here as he was in the field. He didn't relent until Dan had seemingly lost his words entirely. With that said, he didn't really have the breath to warn him but Yoru didn't seem bothered by the mess.

"Well, someone was pent up." Yoru wiped his mouth on the back of his hand, crawling up to lay heavily beside where Dan was. He seemed incredibly satisfied with himself. Dan wanted to be irritated with him but really, he had to agree.

"Rubbing one out in the shower really isn't the same," he said when he had caught his breath a little. He rolled himself closer to Yoru, who flung an arm around him comfortably. He was careful of the damage to Dan's back. Healed as it was, this was still no time to draw attention to it. Perhaps Dan could forget about it for a while.

"Kind of ruins any chance I had of prolonging the fun, though. My love-hate relationship with your mouth just got a lot more complicated." He laughed against his friends collar.

"I guess we'll just have to do it again sometime," Yoru said lightly.

Dan smiled. "Yeah. I'd like that," he said agreeably.

But then he pulled himself away from Yoru and earned himself a frown.

"Where are you going?"

"I should at least return some of the favour," Dan said.

"You don't have to," Yoru reminded him with a pointed look.

"My mom didn't raise me to be selfish," he joked.

Yoru groaned. "Moratorium on discussing both parents and childhood in these circumstances," he said. But when Dan went to move away he tugged him back.

"Besides, I'd like to kiss you, so find another way," he said with a smile.

Dan conceded. "Okay. Well, this hand has to be good for something, right?" he joked.

Yoru didn't argue with him. Dan gave him all the kisses he pleased and though he couldn't match Yoru's level of experience, he was pretty intimately practiced with using his hand for this particular action, so he was sure he could figure it out.

Yoru seemed to be enjoying himself, his dark eyes grew lustful and he murmured Dan's name against his neck.

"Oh, Suparat—" He shivered, getting closer and closer. Dan wanted to memorize the way his name sounded when Yoru said it.

Yoru's hands tightened where they held onto Dan, shuddering as his own quiet release was reached. It wasn't as dramatic as Dan's, but he seemed pleased.

He also made more of a mess.

"We should shower," he said with a sigh.

"In a minute." Dan wiped his hand on the bed. He'd change the sheets once he had gotten cleaned up himself. Not only did they smell like sex now, but he was already in need of a shower thanks to the smoke and other grime from the fight club.

"For now, I just want to lay here," Dan said, happily settling into his spot beside his friend.

"Yeah, me too," Yoru agreed.

They lay in silence for a while, but Yoru always had something to say.

"I didn't rescue you with the intent to sleep with you," he told Dan.

"I didn't even know if we would be friends. I'm glad we are, because you're funny and kind and quick to learn, and I admire all those traits, but we could have just as easily not been." He shrugged. "I'm glad we are, and I'm glad for this, and I'd be glad if the chance turned up again in the future. I just... I don't want you to feel like this is why I decided to pick you up."

"You worry too much," Dan reassured him. He pushed himself up on an elbow to continue talking. The change in position didn't cut off their physical contact; they both needed it too much at the moment. "Two things. One, I was neither attractive nor in any state for this when you grabbed me, so it doesn't seem like it would have been a likely motive."

"Fair."

"Two, I asked you. It wasn't that long ago. You remember that, right?" he teased.

Yoru laughed. "Yes, yes. I just want to make sure. Okay, we should get clean before we accidentally fall asleep," he decided.

As much as Dan was reluctant to move, he agreed.

They got cleaned up, cleaned the bed, and slept. Despite Dan's offer, Yoru took his chair again.

"I'll be less entangled if you need me in the middle of the night," he reasoned. Dan didn't argue. Knowing that Yoru was so nearby was undoubtedly one of the reasons he slept as well as he did.

~*~

They spent the week working. There were a couple of small jobs, well below what Dan thought Yoru was worth, but he took Dan along to see what the experience was like.

Petty theft, cash and valuables. Yoru stayed away from robbing the poor for morals and pragmatism. They had nothing to take. But there were plenty of rich people in the slums, too, and their gains were almost entirely underhanded. Yoru didn't seem to mind taking from them.

They burned away seven days like it was nothing, and by the time the week was out, Dan was feeling pretty good about their prospects. He had even been useful, and that was more reassuring to him than anything.

They made their way back to the fighting club, well ahead of when the crowds would get there. Again, Xueying and her smile were waiting.

"Hey, boys," she said, greeting them both affectionately.

"Hey, Xueying," Dan said, and managed to find his words a little easier this time despite how pretty she was. He was getting better at this.

She led them down again, and this time there was no hulking Lucas waiting outside the door. The place was nearly empty, but Xueying seemed confident that Rusty would be there.

And she was, sitting with her hands in her lap, staring fixedly at the door when they entered.

"Oh my god—" Dan didn't know what Xueying was so upset about. He saw her rush forward, going to Rusty without hesitation.

As his eyes adjusted to the dim light, he saw it. Both of Rusty's hands were heavily bandaged.

"Shit," he cursed. She couldn't fight like that. That was obvious. "What happened?"

"Competition got mad I was wrecking all their fighters," she said slowly. "I got jumped." Her scowl was clear even in the low light.

"I can't win the fight like this, and without another win—"

"You can't fill your contract," Xueying finished.

It clicked for Dan just as Rusty was laying it out. Their last team member was stuck, and for who knew how long.

He swore again, not knowing what else to say.

A.N. Mouse

10:

Oliver hadn't ever roomed with Rosa or Ame before, despite their work history. He didn't think that Rosa would be a bother and he was right. She was pragmatic, and she was a great cook, if their first meal there was any indication. It was Ame who was Oliver's primary concern, and even then she wasn't being as absolutely terrible as he thought she might. The main source of contention were the looks that she often shot him in the middle of conversation. The cause of those looks? None other than Hastin, who seemed blissfully unaware of their silent discussion of him.

Oliver crawled into bed with a head full of questions. How exactly did he expect to be useful here? He was obviously outclassed. Sure, Violet had said that she'd be happy to pay him just for the contact, but since Ame and Rosa had taken the job, he wasn't about to just drop it on them. Besides, that was a lot of fuckin' money and he might be poor as shit, but he couldn't just... walk away with it. He didn't say that out loud. Ame would have laughed for sure. It didn't feel right if he didn't work for it. He wished he wasn't so...so, what? He didn't have a word for it. Boring seemed closest.

And was Hastin really as messed up as he thought, or had Oliver just read too many books? Maybe he was just being emotional. He was worried about the kid, sure, but it wasn't as though Hastin was actually a child, or wasn't capable of taking care of himself. Did he really need Oliver's interference?

He groaned, rolling over and burying his face in his pillow. This wasn't getting him anywhere. He needed to sleep. Eventually, he managed it.

In the end, the first night in the new place was a little weird, but not terrible. The apartment (or, Oliver supposed, it was technically called a 'safe-house' in this context) was sparsely furnished and the lack of his usual mess made everything feel strangely empty. The bed was actually better than the one he owned. It wasn't anything fancy, and you could still feel springs if you really leaned on it, but it was miles above what he was used to sleeping on.

He woke up the next day and stumbled into the living area to try and work through the tangles that had taken over his head. He could have just gotten a haircut, but with these crazy curls it would all go straight up if it wasn't heavy enough. And worse, sometimes parts of it got wound around his horns. So, half awake and already grumpy, Oliver sat down on the couch to try and conquer his hair. Of course, seeing Hastin waltz by him gave Oliver a start and made him give serious consideration to the fact that he might still be dreaming.

He came back with a coffee for Oliver and put it on the table in front of him. Oliver blinked at it, and then looked up to the white-clad boy who sat across from him.

"Good morning?" he tried. He looked at the coffee, and then at Hastin again. He was a little slow to process things when he first woke up. "Thank you?"

"Rosa made coffee," he said, as though her making it somehow explained why he had brought it to Oliver, who took a moment to set his work aside and took a grateful sip. He could stand to be a little more functional.

"Aren't you going to have some?" he asked, noticing that Hastin did not have a cup for himself.

"I wasn't sure if I should. I've never had it before," Hastin told him. He was wearing an oversized, white t-shirt and Oliver fervently hoped there was something underneath it, but it was too long to see from the way he sat in the other chair.

It was the least made-up that Oliver had ever seen him. No make-up, no lace. Hastin tugged his shirt down a little farther over his legs.

"Do you wanna try some of mine? You can see if you like it," Oliver offered.

Hastin smiled at him, every bit just as beautiful without all the extra finery. Then he got up and sat next to Oliver. "Okay, Captain. I'd like that," he said.

Oliver took another drink before he passed it over. It was good coffee, better than what he'd had at Violet's. Probably less expensive, but Rosa was also less of a pretentious socialite.

Hastin took the mug when it was offered to him, took a sip, and then made a face. Oliver laughed.

"It's so bitter!" he said.

"It's for bitter people, honey." Oliver grinned.

"Yeah, like you." Ame was awake, too, apparently. She sat down on Hastin's other side.

"You're not all done up. Too early for that?" she asked. Ame wore nothing more than a bra and an old pair of shorts, but to Hastin's credit his eyes never wandered. Oliver was not as successful. Ame was a pain in the ass, but she was cute. Still, he tried to be respectful, and turned his attention back to his hair as he worked.

"Usually, I have to know what my assignment is before I get dressed, at least on the days where I get to pick what I wear," he said.

Oliver hid his wince behind taking another sip of coffee and Ame spoke up instead.

"Makes sense. Gotta dress for the occasion," Ame agreed.

"Yeah!" Hastin said. And then, with a smile sweet enough to make Oliver's teeth hurt, he turned back to his Captain. "Can I have another try?"

He ignored another one of Ame's looks and passed his drink to the younger man wordlessly. It was a tiny gesture, but simple to extrapolate. Oliver was easy.

"Speaking of, what exactly is the plan for today?" Oliver finally spoke, and looked around for Rosa, who presumably would be the one who knew what was going on.

"Blueprints! We need to know how to get the fuck in there. Ain't that right, kid?" Ame hooked an arm over Hastin's shoulders and pulled him closer to her. He laughed.

"Well, you're the expert," he said.

Rosa was last to join them, but judging from the coffee they were all consuming, she may have been the first to wake. Her headset was left in her room, and she blinked at them serenely as she made her way to the chair that had once housed Hastin's body.

"Good morning. Looks like we survived the night. That's a good sign," she said amicably.

Oliver groaned. "Why is that a good sign? Isn't it a given?"

Rosa shrugged. "If the job was that dangerous, we would know by now."

Coffee in hand, Oliver sighed and his head fell back against the couch. What, were they always at risk of getting murdered in their sleep? He was less in danger in his own slum apartment. This was ridiculous.

"It would have had to have been a fairly taxing assault. Having checked the safe-house when I arrived yesterday, the surrounding population density and the set-up of the building would make it difficult to quietly remove us from the picture," Hastin said. "Especially since at least three of the occupants are not predisposed to going quietly."

"I don't do anything quietly," Ame agreed.

Oliver drained the last of his coffee and looked to Hastin. "I do feel a little better knowing that, honestly." Because all he understood as far as security went was that the world was dangerous and he wasn't. That had kept him alive so far.

"Don't worry, Captain." Hastin nodded at him. "It's my job to check for these things."

"It's like having a guard dog." Ame leaned against his shoulder and Hastin turned his smile to her.

"So, how exactly do we get these blueprints?" Oliver asked Rosa. Immediately he thought of the hard copy kind, the rolled up paper plans that he had seen in old movies. He thought they'd be stored somewhere dusty and disused. Chances are it wasn't going to be that easy.

"They'll be stored in the city planning centre. Getting in there will be tiresome, and getting the file is going to be a headache. I can tell you from experience that they have no idea how to organize themselves. Still, a blueprint will help us figure out what the best access route is for the next step." Rosa seemed assured in her explanation, and Oliver had no reason to question her.

"So, we're headed downtown," Hastin said. "We should probably get a look at the place before we attempt to breach it." Oliver looked at him and Ame used her arm that was still around his shoulder to hit Oliver's arm and get his attention.

"We gotta case the joint, try to keep up," she said. He sighed.

"Breakfast, and then we'll head downtown. We should split up, sets of twos. It'll be less conspicuous than the four of us trying to look in the windows," Rosa said. "Ame, I'd suggest you and Oliver get as close to the place as you can. I'll hook you up with a scanner. I want as much of a physical layout as we can get of that place."

"And that means that you and I are looking for their security measures," Hastin said. "Probably going to try and find a place we can hook up your computer, right?" he asked.

"Yes. For that, we'll probably have to go inside, which is why I want you with me," she said. "If everything goes well, we can get in there today and get it. If not, we'll leave with more information than we started with."

He beamed. "Okay!"

"But we're going to eat first, right?" Oliver asked. "You guys might be able to live off coffee, but I sure as hell can't."

"Believe me, you don't want to see me when I'm hungry," Ame confessed.

They ate and dressed. Next time time Oliver saw Hastin, he was dressed in his usual attire. He stood in the hallway, holding his holster in one hand and knocking on Rosa's door.

"Rosa!" he called. "They must have metal detectors, yes? Do we know if they have anything more advanced?"

"Probably not. They don't exactly expect people to go in and hold the place up. There's probably only basic physical security and more elaborate computer security. That's what cities tend to rely on. I guess it's cheaper to install a program than to remodel a building."

As she explained, Hastin pulled his holster on and did it up, without looking over to Oliver. When he finally did, he smiled.

"I just wanted to know what to pack. I have a few things the detectors won't pick up," he said.

"Do we really think it's going to be that dangerous?" Oliver asked.

"Better over-prepared than under." Rosa opened her door. "You ready yet?"

"Almost." Hastin sing-songed his answer as he wandered off to collect his things.

"Well, he seems cheerful," she noted. Then she nodded to Oliver. "You ready?"

"As I'll ever be." He shrugged. "You got a way for us to keep in touch? Somehow I don't think my phone is the most secure of equipment."

"I've got you covered." She tossed him an earpiece. "You can hide it under that radical power-glam hair of yours."

"Does Ame get one too?" he asked, doing exactly that.

"Nah, those things itch like hell. You can deal with it this time," the other woman said.

They collected the last of their things and Rosa hooked her arm around Hastin's at the door.

"I can't see, remember," she said. Hastin knew that it was not a reminder of her condition. Instead, it was a reminder of the parts they had to play. "You have to pretend to be my guide. That way, we'll look appropriately harmless."

"Okay." He touched her hand with his own. "I'll keep you safe."

"You two should leave first. We'll give it a while and then we'll follow," Ame pointed out. Oliver had little to contribute. Right now, he'd be glad just to listen to instruction. He certainly wasn't a stranger to having people boss him around, but at least he liked these ones and he was getting paid.

"Come on. This way, honey," Rosa said as she led Hastin into the street. He followed where she tugged, despite supposedly being the one who was to lead her.

"You don't have to call me that just because the Captain calls me that," he pointed out to her.

She shook her head. "It seems a fitting nickname and I don't see the harm in it."

"I've never had a nickname before," he said thoughtfully.

"Never?" Rosa asked.

"No." He shook his head. "I mean, sometimes they call me other stuff...but I think 'honey' is my favourite!" And then, with a moment of hesitation, "The Captain and I were talking about how...unusual this job was for us. I think we're both a little worried that we won't be very useful," he confessed to her.

"What's the fear? You are useful now, aren't you?" she said. "The best way to conquer fear is by doing."

Hastin leaned into her shoulder, resting his cheek against it. She could feel him smile. "I think that's a good thing to remember," he said.

They spent the crowded subway ride getting Rosa's visual computer to link up with Oliver's headset. Hastin listened patiently to most of her explanation, but as he was first to admit, most of it was beyond him.

"You'll be able to hear them?" he asked her.

She nodded. "Don't worry, it's taken care of. They can hear me, and you, too, when you're close enough."

"Oh." He looked thoughtful, and then he brightened. "Can you tell them I say hello?" he asked.

Rosa smiled and merely explained that he was close enough for them to hear and they seemed pleased.

Spectra City's downtown area had been moved more times than anyone could count. Historically, most downtowns were near the city's centre, but now that area was all The Dim and the old historical buildings had been devoured by the slums. The new city hub was in a nicer part of town, but it was with some amusement that Rosa noted it probably wouldn't stay that way. As Spectra City grew, so did The Dim, a quiet and complex knot of tumours at the heart of their little world. Soon, the new downtown would be eaten by the same poorly planned zeerust that rotted its old habitat.

Heedless of her thoughts on the matter, Hastin helped her out of the subway all the same. She hadn't picked the boy as her partner for any of Ame's more selfish reasons, or any of Oliver's worried ones. Hastin was simply the best person to play the part. Nothing more solidified that for her than when he held the door for her on their way into the building, and no one said a thing.

A sharp eye caught a few lingering glances on them, but she could assume she knew the reason and that it was benign enough.

"Where are we headed?" he asked her quietly. This floor was busy, but the others would be quieter as people filtered out. Rosa thought for a minute.

"We want to see if they have a public access terminal, preferably one I can use in peace. Barring that, we're looking for a main line. So, construction, or the rooftop," she said.

Hastin nodded, and then he glanced around the room. "Why don't we work from the top down? If someone gets mad and asks us to leave, at least we'll have seen more of the building that way."

Rosa blinked a little, listening to more than just him. "They're outside. Nothing but the usual cameras and the occasional underpaid guy in a uniform," Rosa said. Then she nodded at Hastin's words. "The roof works. Especially if security is going to be that lax all the way up. I'll tell them to come inside. They'll be more use to us watching our backs."

They took the elevator to the top floor. From there it was a matter of trying to find the roof access.

"Those cameras are going to figure us out," Hastin murmured to her.

"We have two options. Either they're live feed and someone is watching us, or they are recordings and we don't have to worry yet. If it's a recording, we can take care of that once I get myself into the system. If it's live, well...you can look pretty and confused, right?"

"I'm sure I can."

"See if you can do that and 'accidentally' get us outside, won't you?" she asked.

Asking Hastin to play the part might have been selling his skills a little short, but Violet didn't give him those clothes for nothing.

It wasn't taxing to tolerate his temporary 'idiocy'. Hastin left her side, tried a few doors that wouldn't budge, and returned to her again. He'd tug her down the hall, wander off, come back. It looked, for all intents and purposes, that her guide had taken them to the wrong floor and was simply confused. As much as his appearance probably helped to pitch the idea, it amused Rosa that of everyone who could appreciate that, she was in the position it least benefited. Eventually, she heard him make a noise of surprised success, and she let him lead her out that door and up some stairs.

"It was open?" she asked under her breath.

"Picked the lock, but don't worry, the camera didn't see," he reassured her. Rosa tried to hide her smile. He sounded so pleased with himself.

The stairs definitely led up to the roof, and after checking in with Ame and Oliver, Rosa told Hastin to open the door. The antenna was immediately visible. Perfect. That would give them a line back down to everything they needed.

Of course, some systems may not have been linked together. Rosa pulled her handheld from her belt and wired herself into the antenna. That was when she frowned.

"Oliver, they don't have their cameras worked into this thing. I need you to find me a line to them." She paused, her head tilted, as she listened. "Yes, I'm aware you have no idea what I'm telling you. Tell Ame, because she will. Yes, Ame has connectors on her," she said.

"He's panicking." Hastin sighed, leaning against the antenna.

Rosa nodded. "A little bit. And then they were arguing. But I think... It sounds quiet now so they're probably doing what I asked."

He nodded, but let her work. The fact that they hadn't been stopped already led Rosa to believe that the videos were kept off-site, but if Ame could get her in, she could take care of that, too.

This was the reality of their work. Sometimes, it wasn't very exciting. She had to figure out where the blueprints were kept, and then she had to figure out what they had named the damn file.

By the time she was done, Hastin had wandered away. He stood near the edge of the building and he tensed when Rosa touched his shoulder.

"Did we get it?" Hastin asked her. His smile was back, as though nothing had happened.

"Yeah. And Ame got us into the cameras, so I can take care of that when we get back. The connectors will let me access it remotely, and I can burn it out when I'm done. You alright?" she asked.

"Yeah..." he said. He looked back out over the edge and she felt him sigh.

"Have you ever wondered what it would be like to fly?" he asked her.

Rosa wasn't the pessimist Oliver was, but the question was still an interesting one for him to ask. She answered honestly. "Not fly like an airplane. I think I'd be worried about hitting a bird," she said. "But weightlessness, yes. That sounds like fun."

"I wish I could fly..." he said, sighing again. "I just... I'm too heavy." He laughed, but it wasn't the sound that she was familiar with.

"Come on. We don't want to worry them." Rosa squeezed his shoulder and he stepped away from the edge and took her arm again.

"Still lots of work to do," He said, leaning against her. She nodded.

A.N. Mouse

11:

They had been to a few different shady places at this point, but Dan thought that the fight club was probably his least favourite of them. It was probably all the people. Even the bars that Yoru had dropped into while picking up or dropping off jobs had never been so crowded. Dan figured they were probably all just about as 'bad' as each other, but this was the only place that really bugged him.

Then again, maybe it was the violence? None of the jobs Yoru had taken were particularly bloody ones. Dan was useful, acting as a second pair of eyes and ears, an extra hand where it was needed. Still, he wished he could do more.

"I can't keep you safe forever, my friend," Yoru told him when he complained. "Let me do so for just a little longer, won't you?"

Well, it was hard to say no to that.

Still, Yoru brought home more than enough for them to get by. They were never for want of food, and Dan just plain old wasn't interested in a lot of stuff. If they were going to travel a lot, he really couldn't own that much, could he? And he just didn't want things the way he used to. Food, a good place to sleep, and his friend. And he'd even put up with the damn fight club, if he had to, because work wasn't always going to be fun and easy, and honestly, Xueying wasn't so bad, either.

That was, of course, assuming she survived her fight and he would still get to be friends with her by the time the night was over.

This time, Yoru didn't bother with finding a spot on the floor above. They got there early and wormed their way into the lower part of the bar, finding a spot right against the edge of the arena. Dan stuck close to Yoru as always, anxious and tense despite Yoru's apparent ease.

"She's going to get herself killed," Dan said, muffled by the way he had his hand plastered to his face.

Yoru hooked his arm around Dan's shoulders so he could speak quietly enough that no one else might hear them over the surrounding noise. "We have to trust her. Every job is dangerous and there is no room for pride. She would not say she could do it if she couldn't."

"And that's it? Aren't you even a little worried about her?" Dan looked over his fingers at him incredulously.

"Terrified," Yoru answered simply. "But what can be done? To be alive is to constantly be afraid and in love. We'll take it one breath at a time, and trust her because we love her."

He threw around that word a lot, and were it anyone else, Dan would think they were shallow or didn't understand what it meant. But, he didn't doubt that Yoru meant every word he said.

Dan leaned back against him and kept his hand tight in his pocket. One breath at a time. Surely if Xueying could do it, he could stand there and support her, at least. Was that really so much to ask?

The space filled further. People got rowdier. Then, the fights started. Both inside, and outside of the ring. Dan paid no attention to the ones going on near him. They were put out quickly, usually by people who didn't have time for those kinds of distractions while they had a real fight to watch. Even if Dan hadn't been told the kind of money that was involved, it would have been pretty obvious.

It did very little to help his nerves.

Xueying wasn't dressed in her usual attire. She had ditched her pink-and-white candy colours for black, and Dan couldn't blame her. Washing blood out of that shit would have been a nightmare. Still, she saw them and flashed a toothy grin. Yoru blew her a kiss.

"How long do you think it will take?" Dan asked him.

"Long enough to make it convincing," Yoru answered. Not exactly what Dan was hoping to hear.

He flinched when the punches started flying. The blood was next. The light was dim, but where it reflected off the blood was overbright and sticky. Dan took a deep breath. Xueying ducked out of the way of a hit and retaliated by knocking him one in the throat. But the blood he saw on the ground was hers and she spit another mouthful as soon as she won herself a second to breathe.

She was a lot smaller than this guy. Faster, but only just. She was doing a lot better than Dan had expected, considering he had kind of expected her to get flattened. She didn't look as tough as Rusty, that much was for sure. And where was Rusty, then? Certainly not anywhere Dan could see.

Xueying took another hit and Dan flinched.

"Tell me if you need to leave." Yoru's voice was low and steady in his ear. Dan shook his head. He wasn't going to make Yoru leave. Not when his friend needed him. He could do it. He could hold on. He pulled his hand out of his pocket and took hold of Yoru's hand where it was gripping his shoulder.

Xueying rallied, and her next kick knocked the man right onto his back.

He had to admire her. She didn't back down, she didn't hesitate. There were no hitches when she moved, she knew exactly where she needed to be and what she needed to do. It was heart-wrenching and Dan felt like he would shake himself apart, but it was beautiful in its own, awful way.

He thought he might have been crushing Yoru's fingers, but the poet said nothing. Dan wished he was stronger, steadier. He hated to see Xueying like this. Was this job really worth it? He had no idea, and he hated that he had no idea.

He'd learn. He'd be useful. One day.

Dan tried to keep his eyes on the fight, tried only to think of how well she was doing and how things would be okay. She hit her opponent in the neck again and when he was struggling to breathe, she kicked him in the head.

This time when he went down, he didn't get back up.

Xueying waited, her hands still raised to fight, until the referee called it over. Dan thought his knees were going to give out in relief and the breath he took then felt like the first one in hours, days, weeks. She was bloody and bruised, but her smile was brilliant. She didn't come over to them. She ducked into the back and Yoru pulled Dan away to follow.

He stumbled along and Rusty found them in the hallway.

"We have to go," she said, stopping them in their tracks.

Dan was going to ask what was going on, but a split second later they were already on their way out the door and Xueying, still bloody, was at their side. Something had gone wrong. Something must have gone wrong. That's why they were running.

Wasn't the whole point of this so that they wouldn't have to run?

Getting through the people was only half the problem. Rusty broke open a lock on one of the back doors when Dan heard someone behind him yell. It was in a language he didn't know, but it was definitely some kind of expletive.

They spilled out into the alley, closed the door, and tried to take a second to regroup.

"This could be rough." Yoru said, catching his breath. "They're gonna come after us in seconds."

"If you get home, can they track you?" Xueying asked him.

Yoru shook his head. "Not these guys. No way. What about you?"

Xueying looked between herself and Rusty, only dimly lit by dying streetlights and vague neon light pollution.

"We'll make it," she said.

"Not if you gotta fight," Yoru said firmly. "Go. Now. We'll buy you some time and then we'll disappear."

Dan thought she would argue. She didn't.

"Rusty, this way," she called, and again, Dan thought Rusty would say something about following a strange woman off into the night but she, too, kept quiet. They ran.

They weren't yet out of sight when the back door burst open and a bunch of heavies fell out of it. Dan felt his pulse jump, but riding on his fear was a weird, jittery kind of excitement. That probably wasn't healthy.

Someone saw the others and shouted, but Yoru didn't let them get far before he jumped on them.

They had guns. Yoru and Dan didn't. But there wasn't really a whole hell of a lot of room for anyone to start shooting, especially since Dan got the same idea Yoru did; it's pretty fucking hard to shoot somebody when they're punching you in the head.

Dan was not elegant, when he fought. He was good, he hadn't lied to Yoru; he was precise and he was efficient and he was a mess to look at. It was everything he had shown Yoru in their practice, and more. Sickly skin split easily under force and soon he was the one spitting blood and wiping it out of his eyes.

Fear clawed at his heart, but so did that same eagerness. He wanted to prove himself.

And for a while, they were doing okay. Then he saw Yoru get knocked down, the man on top of him mercilessly hitting him over and over again. Dan could barely stop to look or he risked the same fate.

Yoru didn't scream or cry for help, and maybe that's what upset Dan the most. His friend. His only friend, really. That weird energy was stronger now, and he could almost feel it rolling through him.

A lucky hit knocked him down, too, and hitting the ground is what finally let it all out.

It felt like grabbing a live wire, but instead of stopping his heart dead, it just sped it up like he was writing a late-night term paper on too much caffeine. He managed a panicked gasp but little else as electricity flooded out of his every pore. It jerked him, his body out of his control for a second that felt far too long. When he collapsed to the ground, his ears were ringing and he heard nothing but the sound of his own rough breaths.

Yoru came to him, the smell of blood and burning thick on the air. Dan couldn't focus his eyes, but he knew it was Yoru. Felt it, the way he could always tell where the man was when he was nearby. He groaned when Yoru helped pull him to his feet and stood there, weak and unsteady. His senses were going haywire. He knew he was hurt, he knew he was bleeding, but he couldn't feel it. He kept his grip tight on his friend, and couldn't feel the blood that had soaked into Yoru's clothes.

They made it, somehow. He didn't remember the trip back, he only focused on holding on to Yoru and trusting that he would get them home. Dan's vision finally settled and he felt like he came back into himself, but it sure as hell wasn't pleasant. Everything ached. Even places he was pretty sure he hadn't been hit. He was shaking, too, he thought, when Yoru helped him to sit on the bed. He watched with dazed eyes as Yoru started pulling off his own bloody clothes to look at the damage, and complied exhaustedly when the thief helped undress him too.

He wasn't too out of it to miss when Yoru pressed a hand to his back and it came away sticky.

"How bad is it?" he asked. He didn't get an answer, he got a kiss on his head and he leaned into it gratefully. That was okay. He wasn't sure he really wanted to know.

Yoru tugged him into the bathroom and sat him on the edge of the tub so he could try and clean him up a little. By the time it was done, Dan felt awake and alive enough to return the favour. Cleaning the blood off let him get a better look at his friend's injuries. He was cut up and bruised, but nothing that wouldn't heal. For how outmatched they had been, they both had gotten away with less than they deserved.

"Don't worry, you're still pretty," he told Yoru with a smile. It earned him a tired laugh.

It was when Yoru was helping him eat some leftovers that his phone went off, and his smile was immediately readable.

"They got back okay, too. Took them a little longer, but they didn't have to pick any fights." And considering the state they were in, Dan was thankful for that.

The four of them were all pretty roughed up. That night, Dan dragged Yoru into bed with him. Too sore and tired to even think about sex, the thought of comfort was the only one on his mind. For the both of them.

Of course, they woke up feeling twice as awful the next day, but suffering was better with company. They only got out of bed to get things to eat, but Yoru did coax him into having a shower. Dan was convinced that showers were magic at this point. Nothing eased what ailed him better, even if what ailed him wasn't always physical.

Yoru felt well enough to sing in the shower, and Dan felt well enough to record some of it on his phone without mentioning it to the other man. It was nice to hear. Much like showers themselves, it helped all the problems he felt that weren't related to their recent beating.

It wasn't until the next day that they talked about what happened.

"Why did we have to book it out of there?" Dan asked him. Yoru was cooking something and already his stomach was anticipating it being delicious.

"Well…" Yoru sighed. "It should have been a pretty easy transaction, right? Rusty had a fight left, but was sabotaged out of doing it. Under the condition that she won, Xueying took up the fight. After all, her winning would have cleared Rusty's contract and guaranteed the people running the fight got the same cash returns they were looking for."

"But that didn't happen."

"Remember how we thought the competition jumped Rusty because she was costing them too much money?" he asked, and Dan nodded. "Turns out we were wrong. That wasn't the competition. That was her own guys. Someone didn't like the idea of her leaving."

Dan groaned, pressing his hands to his face. "Wow. Fucking… Rude."

"I agree." Yoru passed him a bowl and a set of chopsticks and Dan dug in hungrily. The take-out the day before had not compared to Yoru's usual cooking.

"So she's on the run. Or, might be, depending on how many of those people you knocked out versus how many of them died."

It was hard to have an elephant in the room with Yoru. He spoke so easily, so calmly, that almost nothing was a big deal. But Dan had been dreading this, and knew they would have to talk about it eventually.

"I couldn't tell you. It doesn't usually, um, do that," Dan said, frowning a little.

Seconds ticked by in silence before he spoke again. "I didn't hurt you…did I?" he asked hesitantly.

"Never," Yoru answered him. He looked over to him and smiled reassuringly. "Not even the kind of shock you get from a dryer."

Dan breathed an audible sigh of relief and Yoru reached over to put a hand on his shoulder.

"Is that what has been scaring you?" he asked. "You've been very quiet. I assumed it was because you were tired from us getting our asses beaten, but…"

Dan shook his head, and a smile tugged at his lips, the same way it always did when Yoru slipped into more casual phrasing. It just sounded so funny coming from him.

"I'm okay. I just... It's happened before, and I did hurt people. I guess at the time I didn't care who got hurt. It was when, um, you know—"

"Before," Yoru said simply. Dan nodded.

"So, I didn't care who I fried. And then it happened again two nights ago, and I knew you were there, and that I could have hurt you. I'm just really glad I didn't."

"You saved me," Yoru said to him. "We bought time for them to get out of there, and you bought us an escape. I'd be all over the pavement by now if it wasn't for you," he pointed out.

"I just... I'm just glad I could do something. I was really worried that I'd be useless. And even then, I was only useful by accident. What if it hadn't gone off? What if I couldn't make it do that? Or if I had...if I'd hurt you." Dan set his bowl aside and sighed, running his hand through his hair. It was getting long enough that he actually could do that now.

His hand was unsteady, but it calmed when Yoru got up out of his chair and stepped closer to where Dan sat. He took Dan's hand in both of his own.

"Nothing to fear, my friend," he said calmly. "Sometimes, when you plan things, they go well. Beautifully well. And sometimes...they don't. This time, we made it out, and we should be glad." Yoru smiled at him. "No need to make it more complicated than it is. Life is hard enough already, isn't it?"

He didn't fucking need to say that twice. Life was increasingly more difficult and convoluted the more of it Dan experienced. But...he felt a little better. Yoru always seemed to know what he needed.

"How do you do that?" he asked him, when Yoru went back to his own seat and had started eating again.

"Do what?" he asked loftily in response.

"Always know just what to say." Dan, too, felt more like eating again now. The emotional detour had been sudden, but he was glad it was brief.

"Oh...by making a lot of mistakes," Yoru said. His face was still blue with bruises but his smile here was still effortlessly charming. "And by listening. Sometimes to what people don't say."

Dan didn't mind. If Yoru was going to be so adept at interpreting what he couldn't say, it was reassuring more than unnerving. Sometimes words still failed him.

A.N. Mouse

12:

"Captain?" The world's littlest siren song. Oliver looked up to Hastin's dark eyes and was surprised to see the boy unsmiling and with drooping shoulders. When he emoted, it was with his whole body. Oliver, thinking himself kind of dense, was never sad for the extra context.

"Hey, honey. What's wrong?" The trip to get the blueprints had been easy as pie and Oliver had spent the afternoon being pretty cheerful, actually. Rosa had given him something to work on and he had just been laying around, fiddling with it for a while, seeing if he could get it to work. He moved his legs so Hastin could sit down but the younger man didn't move until Oliver actually beckoned him closer.

He put his hand on Hastin's knee and without thinking Hastin covered it with his own. He was paler than Oliver but his features were impossible to place. Oliver's first thought was that maybe his parents were from Hinomoto, if Oliver was going to guess. It certainly wasn't a question Oliver was going to ask. There seemed to be only two possible answers. Hastin, young and with no apparent family, might not know. Or the opposite...he knew exactly, and there was a story there that he probably didn't want to tell.

"I have to leave in the morning," he said, sounding dejected.

Oliver felt his heart sink, too. That was strange. He usually didn't warm up to people so fast. Sure, there had been Dan, but even he had been surprised at himself at the time.

Wait. Was he...lonely? He hadn't even thought of it before.

"What do you mean, you have to leave?" Oliver swallowed, already thinking the worst. "Forever?" he asked.

Hastin was biting his lip and it was already red from where he had been worrying it. "I don't...think so. I think it's just for a day or two. They picked up a contract, and apparently, it can't wait..."

"Wow, they double booked you. How rude," Oliver remarked. But some of the tension in his chest had been relieved. "So you'll be back soon?"

"Yeah!" A flicker of hopefulness in his voice. "I... I think. I just got the message—" He lifted his other hand to show Oliver that he did have one of those fancy watches, HiTech brand and everything. The fact that it was blinking led Oliver to believe that there were probably more messages waiting. "But I haven't read them all."

Looking at it, Hastin sighed. "It doesn't even tell time."

Oliver couldn't help the laugh that burst out of him. "You have a watch that doesn't tell time?"

Hastin smiled a little and Oliver watched as he let it go and it dropped to the floor. He didn't pick it up. "Yeah. It can send and receive messages, but only very basic ones. It's not even a watch, it's a...a..."

"A really tiny mailbox," Oliver answered for him. That earned him a laugh.

"I don't want to go," Hastin said then, suddenly. "I want to stay here."

Oliver turned his hand where it lay so he could hold on to Hastin's, trying to reassure him. "You'll be back soon, right?" He gave his hand a gentle squeeze and received one in return. "Is it the work you don't like?" Oliver asked. That would be kind of a major problem to him, seeing as he wasn't sure what the work was but knew he could be certain it was more hardcore than he was capable of.

"Oh, no... Nothing like that. It's just an assassination. It's nothing like...bad," Hastin said, waving the idea off. "I'm good at it. I'm not worried. It's just—"

And Oliver didn't even have time to process how strange that sentence was because Hastin sighed then and looked at the meagre little room around them with guileless adoration.

"I just like it here. With you," he said. "It's just so...nice."

"Well, then, go so you can come back, right?" Oliver reassured him. "I don't think we're going to get too crazy productive over the next few days, so it's not like you'll miss much. You'll be back before you know it."

Hastin didn't answer right away. He was frowning a little, and before Oliver could ask why, he sighed and then smiled.

"Other people can't possibly be like this every time they have to go someplace. I wasn't like this when I had to leave the unit and come here," he said. He shook his head. "I...don't know what's gotten into me."

Oliver wasn't a really smart guy, he didn't think so anyway. But, he knew some stuff. He sure as fuck knew backtracking when he heard it. Back in the day, when he was scrounging up self-help files from derelict download pages because no one ever cleaned up the internet, he had learned all kinds of things about how people worked in an effort to figure out how to make himself work.

And here he was, watching it in motion, in the way Hastin had come to him, confided in him, diminished his own feelings and then quickly tried to

104

retreat into territory that Oliver could only know in his heart to be toxic. No proof, though. Nothing but the ambulance sirens running in the back of his head.

"It shouldn't really be a problem. I just didn't want it to interfere with our plans. Sorry for being all...you know." He went to stand and Oliver let him, but he didn't let go of Hastin's hand.

"Oh, Captain...?" He tilted his head, curious but not offended.

"It's okay to have those kinds of feelings about things, Hastin," Oliver said. "You don't really wanna go, and heck, we don't really want you to go." He squeezed his hand. "Violet probably wants you to prioritize the contract, right?"

Hastin hesitated, but nodded.

"I want you to prioritize you. When you can. When it can be managed where it won't get you in trouble. And sometimes, that means having complicated feelings about something and talking to someone about it...and that's okay."

Hastin blushed, but the smile he gave Oliver seemed to have immeasurable depth. Something he said had sunk in, he thought. He had been heard. And thank god, because while he knew what he intended to do, he was so shitty with words.

"Thank you, Captain. I... I feel a little better, now," he said. He gave Oliver a long look, as though there was more he wanted to say, but he never did.

When Oliver woke up the next morning, Hastin was already gone. When he went into the kitchen to get himself some coffee, one of Hastin's hairpins was set next to the coffee maker.

Oliver might have been a little slow, but he wasn't an idiot. Someone else hadn't put that there. Hastin had. Whether it was for Oliver or for Ame, or maybe to give Hastin a reason to come back, he didn't know.

But it made him smile. And while he leaned against the counter and sipped his drink, Ame pulled herself into the room and laid her top half on the counter. She was short, and it was a bit of a stretch to get the lot of it on there.

"Dying?" Oliver asked casually.

"Cramps." She groaned.

"Probably a good thing that we're not doing anything important today." Oliver set his mug down. "You need painkillers? I got some."

"Like the normal shit or the heavy shit, because I know you've taken some wild drugs for your cramps, kid." Well, she didn't seem to be that upset.

"That depends... Do you want the normal shit or the heavy shit?" Oliver asked her with a laugh.

He knew her pain. And despite his occasional misgivings with her enthusiasm, Oliver couldn't help but empathize a little. A uterus was no one's friend. He grabbed her the pills she needed from his room, and although he did try to balance them on the back of her head where she was still half-laying, she snatched them up and got herself something to take them with.

Meanwhile, he enjoyed his coffee.

Rosa showed up eventually. She was still in her night clothes but seemed perfectly awake and functional when she also poured herself a cup of coffee and leaned for a moment near where Oliver was still drinking his.

"Sleep in?" He asked her, although the coffee did still taste like the kind she usually made.

"No, I've been up a little while yet. But since we can't exactly do anything big today I..." She gestured to herself without looking down.

"Yeah, why put on pants if we ain't leaving the house. I feel you," Oliver agreed.

"Don't need pants to work. I have to upload those blueprints anyway, so I can see where I'm going when the job comes. And we should probably talk about what comes next when Hastin comes back," she said reasonably.

"He is coming back, right?" Ame had gone to sit down, but looked over to them with a stricken expression that was undoubtedly half because of the pain she was in and half because of the question. "Like, she didn't just give us him to fall in love and then yank him away, right? That would be too cruel."

"Well, that's the long game, isn't it?" Rosa pointed out. "He won't be yours after this job is done."

"Yours?" Oliver asked, looking over to Ame.

"Hey, no, not like that..." She grimaced. "Oliver, really. Tell me he's not the sweetest thing you've ever seen. I'm in no shape to whore it up and I'm feeling emotional." The kitchen was small and the table she was sitting at was just as much so, and she was laying on it with her head on her arms. The rest of her was presumably organized normally below, although Oliver couldn't see it where he stood.

He went and sat across from her and laid a hand on her head. "I'm just a salty, bitter old man. I'll get over it," he said. Old. He was barely thirty. Most days it felt like a lot more.

"He is coming back, though? I don't like the idea of him being there," Ame insisted.

"She's got no reason to keep him when her investment is here with us. If anything, she'll be sending him back specifically to spy on us and make sure we're doing what we say we're doing," Rosa pointed out.

"It has occurred to you that he is basically the world's most obvious plant, right?" she continued. She didn't look at them, but it was implied well enough by her tone that she would have.

"We work, he feeds the information back to Violet, she give him orders on what is and is not okay." Taking a sip of her drink, she let that sink in to the two of them. "And tells him to intervene when necessary."

"So you're saying he's a lot more dangerous than we're acting," Ame surmised.

"Well, I think that goes for most of you guys, honestly," Oliver pointed out. "I mean, you're plenty dangerous, when your insides aren't falling out, and Rosa is just as much."

"Maybe more. Depends on how we're feeling," Ame noted.

"But, I mean, I still treat you guys just the same," Oliver said. "Despite the fact that everyone in the apartment could murder the hell out of me."

"Honey, there ain't no getting the hell out of you," Ame joked.

"My point is just this; yes, he's coming back, and I'll be just as glad for it as you both, and for the same reasons. But we can't guarantee he feels the same way about it, even if he says he does," Rosa said quietly.

"You really think he's playing us?" Ame asked.

Rosa shook her head. "Honestly, no. The vibe I am getting is that Violet went and made herself an assassin out of some poor kid. But we can't assume that. When's the last time someone had a good day when they judged you on your pretty face, eh, Ame?"

"Fair," the woman conceded.

"I think he's sincere," Oliver said with a certainty he felt but absolutely couldn't prove.

"And I think you're right. But we might both be suckers," Rosa said. She went to where they were sitting, found Ame's legs and pushed them out of the way so she could sit down, too.

"We should focus on the work ahead of us. Best case scenario, we're wary for nothing. Worst case, at least we have some warning and maybe we can handle it a little better if the time comes."

"You ain't got eyes but you got twice the brains we've got," Ame said, with the comfort of someone who had been her friend long enough that she could say that.

"More muscle than the both of us, too. Rosa, you're out of our league."

107

"I like you for your personality," she retorted with a smile.

"That's good, because we don't have anything else of value." Oliver rested his elbows on the table and put his head in his hands, not unhappy, but definitely thoughtful.

"Speak for yourself, bitch. My ass is priceless." Ame was going to say something else, but was cut off by one of her own groans.

Rosa got up and decided that now was as good a time as any for some breakfast. Oliver helped, seeing as Ame was basically useless for another good twenty minutes or so until she started being medicated. Oliver didn't mind helping.

"Gimme caffeine," Ame insisted part-way through, stretching out tanned arms and making grabby hands at the machine.

"That gonna make it better, or worse?" Oliver asked her.

"Who cares. I need it for my soul," she insisted. Oliver got it for her.

They collected themselves a little. Maybe it was a symptom of extended exposure, but Oliver was chilling out on the 'Goddamn it, Ame' front. It's not that she was any less...bad. She was still all the terrible influence that Oliver knew her to be. But he guessed sharing a house with her meant he got to see all the other stuff, too.

Like the way she got up, herself, and took Hastin's hair pin from where it had been lying and took it back to the table with her. She leaned her head in her hand and twirled it in her fingers, watching the way the light sparkled off of the fancy pieces on the end. Was it classy or gaudy? Oliver usually wore a tattered, old green hoodie and jeans and could barely keep his hair from strangling him in his sleep, so he had no idea. But it looked nice to him.

"Hey, Rosa... You have those plans uploaded, you said, right? Can I take a look at them? I want to see if I can get started on marking the places where we're gonna have problems." With some coffee and some painkillers in her system, Ame seemed a lot more like her usual self.

"I can pull them up for you when they're done," Rosa said between bites.

"Mind if I clutter up your work space, too?" Oliver asked. "I could stand to learn something. Maybe make myself more useful."

"Actually yeah." Ame pointed at him. "You're a professional sneak thief. I wouldn't mind your opinion."

Well, that's the first time that sentence ever came out of her mouth.

They tossed the dishes in the sink (Oliver knew he'd end up doing them later. Washing dishes was therapeutic) and collected in Rosa's room to go over the plans. While she worked on inputting the information to her headset, Ame and Oliver sat on the floor and scrolled through the layout on a tablet and marked off all the places that they thought would have cameras, or other possible problematic things for them to work around.

"If I was smart, I'd def have a camera here to look around that corner," Ame said, frowning.

"Yeah, but how much credit are we giving them?" Oliver asked sourly. Bitter old man, indeed.

"I don't think they'd have one in both those spots. That seems expensive. We need a colour for Maybe."

"Purple. Definitely." Despite that fact that no one should ever take colour advice from Oliver, Ame agreed with him. It helped that it was her favourite colour.

The three of them worked through their tasks comfortably. It was nicer than Oliver had thought it would be. Sure, Ame cracked a lot of jokes, but he found himself smiling at them even still. He felt a little less out of his element now that he actually had some real insight to offer. It wasn't as if he lacked experience running from goddamn surveillance systems. He knew all about cameras and where people liked to stick them.

It felt good to be useful. But, like Ame, he noticed the difference when their chatting died down and the room was quiet once again. Hastin's absence was palpable.

They got a lot done, at least before the painkillers wore off and Ame helped herself to some more.

"I'll be better tomorrow. I always have one really terrible fuckin' day," she said, laying on the floor of Rosa's room. Oliver debated dragging her back to her own space but was sure the charity would go unappreciated.

The next day was much of the same, although Ame was considerably more active. In lieu of more map work, her and Rosa set to teaching Oliver some self-defence.

"Not that you're useless in fight or anything, but—"

"But I'm pretty fuckin' useless in a fight." Oliver cut Rosa off with a laugh. "I can worm my way out of a bar brawl just fine, but not the kind of stuff you guys get up to."

He was sore when he collapsed onto the couch after dinner. Sore, but happy. He actually did feel like he learned a few things. He was considering going to bed when he heard the front door open and he sat up immediately to look and see who it was.

Hastin locked the door behind him and hadn't yet raised his head from unlacing his boots. When he looked up it was right at Oliver, and he smiled.

Oliver smiled and held out his arms. Hastin kicked off his shoes and hurried right into them.

"Missed you, honey," Oliver said, giving him a squeeze.

"Missed you too, Captain," he said, curled up tightly in Oliver's arms. He let the younger man go and Hastin sat himself happily on the couch next to him. Cheerful as a blue bird on a perch, at least until Oliver saw the bruise that climbed up his collar.

"Hun, what happened?" he asked. The mark went all the way from Hastin's collar to halfway up his neck and was very dark and definitely recent. Who knows how far down it went?

"Oh, I got kicked," he said, waving it off. "It's nothing. There's no internal damage, they said."

Oliver didn't think twice about it, leaning forward to brush his fingers against the darkened skin. Hastin tilted his head back, watching Oliver through his dark eyelashes. Still, he made no motion to stop him or to pull away from the contact.

Realizing what he was doing, Oliver jerked his hand away. Then he sighed, eventually nodding at Hastin's words. No internal damage. Well, he'd take what he could get. But he knew when Hastin wandered off to tell the others he was back that he was only going to face more questions.

"Ame was feeling productive and made jiaozi. The usual ones with, like, pork and cabbage in them? There's some still left in the fridge if you're hungry," Oliver told him before he had gotten too far.

He stood there, looking back over his shoulder at Oliver. "Thank you, Captain," he said, with no indication if he would eat or not. He just seemed to be happy that Oliver had thought of him at all.

Maybe Rosa was right, Oliver thought. Maybe they were all suckers.

13:

Getting healed up this time wasn't so bad. It was all cuts and bruises and they hurt like crazy, but he wasn't upset about it. Dan thought that played a big part in how hard it was to drag himself back to his feet the first time. There was a lot to be upset about.

But not here. Not laying around the apartment with Yoru, teaching each other words in different languages, vid-calling Xueying and Rusty only to hang up when the former started cursing them out about not sharing their food. These things were mundane, but pleasant.

"Tomorrow I think we'll be ready to up and leave. How are you feeling?" When Yoru asked him it was the first sign Dan had been given that they were leaving at all, but he had sort of taken that as the way of things.

"I can handle it," Dan said, stretching his arms above his head, both because he had been sitting still too long and to show that he was all in one piece.

"Xueying has us a spot where the four of us can crash, it'll be easier than trying to coordinate two teams over a distance," Yoru explained. "And maybe we'll get some answers out of her as to what exactly her plan is with this Rusty girl."

Dan tilted his head. "You think she has an ulterior motive? I...didn't think Xueying was like that."

Yoru looked at him in surprise, and then he seemed to come to some sort of an understanding. "No, no, my friend... She definitely does. But don't be upset. 'Ulterior' here is not a synonym for 'malicious'."

Well, that was a relief. Dan didn't want that to have been true of Xueying. He thought she was nice! And honestly, he would have been a little ashamed of himself for being so off the mark had he been wrong.

"You just think she's hiding something," Dan guessed instead.

"Everyone's hiding something." Yoru's grin was cat-like. "I'm just a curious person, that's all."

Dan was still stiff the next day, but nothing was bleeding. Yoru was a little rougher, and while aesthetically his split lip gave his roguish smile a bit of an edge, it really just made Dan worry to see it.

When they had crossed town and found their way into the innocuous little apartment that Xueying had found for them, she fussed over the damage to his face when she kissed him.

"What did I tell you about letting people mess up your pretty face?" she said, scolding him. "It's my favourite part of you."

"Liar," he said, with a confident laugh.

The apartment was two bedrooms that sandwiched a kitchen and a living room, all of which were pretty small. Kind of cramped, but it was in good enough repair. Not like he and Yoru used two rooms anyways.

"I cook, you spill the beans," Yoru said, elbowing his way into the kitchen. "There are things in here for me to cook, right?"

"Yes, yes. We've been staying here since the night we split up, so there should be supplies," Xueying told him.

"Where's Rusty?" Dan asked. He hopped up to sit on the counter, wincing where he caught his shoulder on one of the wall-mounted shelves.

"She's probably still resting. I had to, um, re-set some of her fingers last night." Xueying grimaced. "They weren't braced properly. It wasn't a good time."

Dan's stomach twisted just thinking about it.

"Good, then she won't be upset if we talk about her," Yoru pointed out. He was grabbing things to cook and pointed a wooden spoon at Xueying. "Spill it."

"Spill what."

"Why'd you go and risk your life to spring a cute red-head from her contract?" he asked her. Dan wasn't sure he would have called Rusty 'cute' but she was definitely a red-head. She was a scowly, dark-skinned, red-haired fighter. But, Dan supposed he would be scowly, too with broken fucking hands.

Xueying frowned at him, crossing her arms. "It's a big job, we need the muscle," she said.

"Honey, there's plenty of muscle that would kill to work for you. You know it and I know it," he said, not looking up from what he was working on. "And yet you just had to have that one."

"I didn't have to," Xueying protested. She looked over to Dan. "Help me out here, would you?"

"I have no idea what's going on," Dan admitted. "I have no idea what we're talking about."

"Basically, I'm a five year old and I'm making fun of Xueying for having a crush," Yoru explained shamelessly.

"I do not!" Xueying flushed pink immediately, visibly under the fluorescent kitchen lights. "I'm not some teenager. I don't do crushes."

"Everyone gets crushes. Well, everyone predisposed to romanticism," Yoru said. "That's not a bad thing, Xueying. I just want to know if this is a matter of the heart."

"It's a matter of the wallet, too," she said, still scowling.

"Xueying, Xueying, star in the darkness of my life..." Yoru set his spoon aside and went to her, one hand gently on each of her cheeks when he kissed her. "I am happy you like someone. It's about time. You work too hard," he said. Then, he turned back to his cooking.

She sighed, and when she leaned on the counter-top next to Dan she leaned on him, too.

"I do not work too much," she pouted.

"When's the last time you took a night for yourself?" Yoru asked her.

She thought about it for long enough that he looked over at her with a knowing expression.

"Okay, okay..." She sighed and leaned against Dan a little more. He brushed his fingers through her short hair. It was soft and she closed her eyes at the affection.

"Are we done picking on Xueying now?" Dan asked.

"You're just jealous," Yoru said with a smile.

"Well, a little. Everyone's getting kissed way more than me," Dan pointed out.

"Oh, come here." Xueying reached up to him and tugged his head down closer to her so she could kiss him on the cheek. He laughed, and laughed again when Yoru did the same to the other side of his face.

"Feeling better?" he asked.

"Oh yeah. Way," Dan said agreeably.

They ate together, and Yoru went to bring some to Rusty where she was resting. Dan had even watched him cut the vegetables extra small so she could just drink the whole thing, rather than try and scoop out some of the larger pieces to eat. That would have been hard with no hands.

"How is she?" Xueying asked when he returned.

"Prideful," Yoru said with a smile. "But not unkind."

"Her health?" the woman prompted him again. Yoru laughed.

"She's fine. Resting. Eating. You can check on her yourself if you like," he answered her.

She sighed but shook her head. "Later. We have a job to talk about."

Dan remembered. Food and then work. They had done the former, now it was time for the latter.

"What's on the agenda?" Dan asked.

"We gotta go steal some access codes. And by we, I mean you, loser, and I," Xueying said, pointing at Yoru.

"Talk about jealous," Dan objected.

"Not that you wouldn't be of use to us, but you'd stand out," Xueying said with a frown and a shrug. "You still look like you've been locked in a closet for a year. If we have to go get fancy, there's no way people are going to miss that."

"Why does almost dying gotta impact, like, my whole life," Dan mused sarcastically.

"We'll get you in on the next party," Yoru reassured him. "What's the goal for this one?"

"I've got a lead that one of the attendees holds a set of door passcodes. If we're going to do some B&E, they'd be handy to have. So I figure we get fancied up and go see if we can get them out of him, twist some arms if we've gotta, but if we can avoid it, quiet is probably better."

"Quiet is kind of what we do," Yoru said with a nod. "I'm sure we can pretend to be professionals for a night. You got aliases lined up for us?"

"How do you feel about being a personal assistant to an up and coming technology developer?" she asked him with a grin.

"Do I get a new name? I'm going to need a real one."

"A real one?" Dan asked.

"Yoru is an appellation. My most loved one, but an appellation nonetheless," he confessed.

Dan was almost upset. A fake name? But when he looked to Yoru, Yoru reached for his hand.

"I'm not keeping secrets from you, Dan. Does Xueying not call me the same thing? It's the name everyone uses, and the one that makes me happiest to hear," he explained.

Dan found that a little easier to swallow.

Rusty was up and about the next day and Dan said hello to her, but other than that, he kept his mouth shut. His first instinct was to try and offer her his help, but he didn't think that she would be too appreciative.

They went over the plan again with her that morning. Dan had to admit that he was a little intimidated, but Yoru seemed unbothered.

"We won't be gone for longer than the night," he said. "We'll be back late, or, you know, early. Xueying and I have to go rub elbows with some fancy folks and see if we can't wring some codes out of some drunk corporate associates. Nothing exciting."

"Are you well enough?" Rusty asked, shooting a single, sharp glance at the other woman.

"I'm basically right as rain," Xueying said. "Still bruised, but I can cover that up with some make-up. When in doubt, maybe I can tell them I have a rough boyfriend and they'll feel sorry for me."

Dan laughed, although he felt like he shouldn't. Rusty didn't look pleased.

"Want to make them really uncomfortable? You could tell them it's my fault," Yoru pointed out.

Xueying winced. "Oh, that would be a whole different twist, wouldn't it? I couldn't defame you like that." She laughed.

Dan wasn't sure where they got the clothes (or the ID's, for that matter), but he didn't feel particularly nervous about the whole thing until he saw Yoru braced against the sink in the bathroom, tying his tie with deft, practiced fingers.

Dan found himself a spot in the doorway and leaned there as he mulled over his words. Before he could find them, Yoru spoke.

"Feeling nervous?" he asked.

"How did you guess?"

"You aren't usually of an unhappy disposition." Yoru reached out to him and lifted his chin with a finger. Dan smiled a little begrudgingly.

"There's nothing to fear. I will not be alone and we aren't going to cause any trouble. A few questions, a few well placed implications and Xueying and I will be home safe," Yoru said to him.

"Yeah, but how often have you been out of my sight since we met?"

Yoru turned to him then and he reached out to pull Dan into his arms. He hardly argued and the sigh that slipped from his lips was half indulgence of Yoru's theatrics and half honest contentment.

He felt the fine material of his suit against his cheek and when he breathed deeply he smelled Yoru's cologne in the air.

"I will be out of sight only briefly. If we're being honest here, I'm more worried about you than me."

"And if we're not being honest?" Dan joked.

And that was when Xueying walked by, just in time for Dan to stumble away from Yoru with a mixed look of shock and interest and with a blush burning darkly across his nose.

Whatever Yoru had said, it had definitely earned a reaction.

"What part of that isn't honest?!" he asked, incredulously.

Yoru laughed. "No, no. It's entirely honest. It was just too much of a good chance to pass up."

Later on, past the security of the party, with drinks in hand and coats checked, Xueying leaned against his shoulder to speak quietly to him.

"What did you say to Dan that made him jump like that?" she asked him, smiling. She was stunning here (as far as Yoru was concerned, she was perpetually stunning) and every time she smiled at him he thought his heart might stop. For something so dangerous, it was incredibly enjoyable.

"Oh, nothing important. I whispered a few details about some compromising positions I wouldn't mind seeing him in, that's all," Yoru said easily. She laughed.

"Not that I'd mind seeing you in those same positions, you know."

"Believe me, I know." She winked at him.

A breeze swept over the rooftop and Xueying shivered a little but shook it off. It really was pleasant out, especially as high up as they were. The air did seem suspiciously clean, but a sharp eye revealed that what he had thought were decorative columns for the canopy were actually hiding filters. It was amazing what someone with a design degree and an ounce of imagination could come up with.

Around them milled people of all sorts. At parties like these, outlandish appearances were just a way of showing off that you had more money than you knew what to do with. A woman with a tall construct of hair and shimmery, almost luminescent skin drifted by them. She held the arm of a man with not one tail, but several.

Xueying, in her short, sparkly little dress, barely stood out. Yoru appreciated the artistry of what he saw, the wash of colour and light that surrounded them. But he did think that his friend burned a little brighter than others, if he was being quite honest.

"Do we know where our mark is?" Yoru asked.

"Looks like he just got here." She didn't look at Yoru when she answered, her eyes following a dark-haired man as he stepped out of the lift and onto the rooftop.

"What do we know?"

"He's probably the lowest person in the social hierarchy of this party. Enough pull to have the access codes we want, but not a whole lot else. Doesn't want to leave the party alone, probably will."

"Or, would."

"Plan is to get him to invite me back somewhere a little more quiet. Those codes will let us access the database we need, and it'll be a lot easier to have them than to try and work around not having them." She drained the narrow little glass she had been holding.

"And what, I just rescue you once you have them? That seems a little riskier than I'd like. What if he's a psychopath?"

"Well, I'm not dating him, so he's going to have to find a way to out-crazy me real quick, and let me tell you, it's not gonna work," she said.

He swallowed his smile and instead reached for another drink for her, gently lifting it from a passing motorized tray and passing it to her.

"How about we just drug his drink, you accompany him home and I drive?" he suggested.

"Smart man."

She went. He followed. There was enough going on around them that they were largely lost to the ebb and flow of the party. The music was energetic but largely unremarkable. Yoru had nothing against mass-manufactured pop (especially when it came to music that was made to dance to), but it was just loud enough here to carry and not loud enough for him to really get into it, which seemed like a waste.

"Hi there." Yoru stood far enough away to make it clear he was with her, but that he wasn't talking to her, and Xueying slid right up to talk to their mark unprompted. "I'm Daniella, it's nice to meet you."

"Benjamin." First names only, because neither of their surnames were fancy enough to be bandied around and leveraged for attention. But, getting that out of the way made it easier.

"Quite a show they're putting on tonight, isn't it?" Like talking about the weather, a perfectly safe and bland conversation point.

"A very fine excuse for people with more money than sense to hang around and talk to each other about all the recent things they've purchased."

Yoru could have called every point and turn of their conversation. That one was to open a sense of camaraderie, to paint them as being together outside of the norm of the party. It also had a good helping of unremarkable annoyance for people with more money, which never hurt when trying to win someone over with less.

It was textbook. And the reason it was textbook was because it worked.

"Nick—" Oh, that was him, wasn't it? "—Could you get me another drink?" And then she turned to Benjamin. "Did you want one?"

So he went and got two. One for Xueying, and one for their new friend. It was a bit early to get away with spiking any drinks, but they had all night for things to get interesting.

The first roadblock was how long it took these damn things to get rolling. Yoru was going to need a lot more drunk people if they were going to make an exit properly. Time would solve that problem well, as long as they were patient. The second roadblock was a little more amusing.

Xueying was as lovely as could be. While she was focused on their mark, other people were focused on her. Yoru would tease her about it later, when the job was done, but for now he acted the part of assistant with little trouble and did his best to divert both conversation and personnel away from his partner.

They potentially risked someone remembering her face if she insisted on being so pretty, but Yoru didn't think it would hurt their cause much. Most of these people would end up very drunk and a lot of them had a penchant for harder things than just liquor.

Yoru had never really seen the appeal of drugs as a hobby. But, the fact that the quality of people around them saw something he didn't in the matter meant that they would have an easier time.

A few more drinks into the night and Yoru had no problem slipping a little something into their new friend's glass.

"You're a real treat at parties," Xueying muttered to him under her breath. It was all Yoru could do not to laugh.

"Would you have more fun if I wasn't here?" He asked.

The smile she gave him was pointed. He didn't mind that.

And true to his chemist's formula, it wasn't long before Benjamin started to wilt.

"Feeling tired?" Xueying asked him.

He rubbed his eyes for a moment, but only briefly. He was trying to keep his attention on her. "It must just be stress, it's nothing serious, I'm sure."

"How about we get out of here? My assistant can drive us," she offered.

His smile was enough to know that he wasn't yet feeling bad enough to call off the idea of what might lie ahead.

"Sure. Did you...maybe want to grab some drinks at my place? Might be a little less tense than all...this."

To be fair, he had a point. It looked like a lovely party, if overindulgence and skin were things you looked for in your hobbies. Perhaps, if they weren't working, and if they didn't have two teammates back at home (at least one of whom was) worried about their well-being, they might have done the same. Life was short, after all.

But, work called.

"I'd love to," she said.

So Yoru escorted them downstairs and slid into the front seat of the car while they climbed into the back. The best thing an assistant did was pretend not to exist until they were needed.

The drive wasn't far. This was the nice end of town, so it made sense that he lived relatively nearby. Yoru was a competent driver, as much as he often left that job to other people, and they made it there easily.

He got out, opened the doors for them...and noticed that Benjamin was significantly more affected by the time Xueying helped him out of the car. Alas, whatever he had hoped to share with her would have to be postponed indefinitely. However, provided that he cooperated, that should be the worst of his night.

"Here, let me help you..." He was out of it but not yet entirely useless. He was at the point where, when he leaned on her for support, he thanked her and apologized.

"What apartment is yours? I can at least walk you to your door. Nick, will you get that for us?" she asked him, nodding to the main door of the building. He would have, but it needed a key card to open. Benjamin fumbled his out of his jacket and Yoru took it to do as he was asked. He then pocketed it again when Ben wasn't looking.

He wasn't losing any of his sense. Having him be incoherent wouldn't have helped them. He was just weak, and a little tired. A little sleep and it would work itself right out of his system. Sure, they could have killed him, but that would raise more suspicion than they needed.

So they dragged the poor guy all the way up to his apartment. He pulled out a different key for the door but was unable to get it open. Yoru graciously decided to help him...and took that key, too.

Just in case.

"Guess I'm in no state to really entertain you. Sorry for all the trouble," he said when Xueying helped him into a chair. His apartment was fairly unremarkable. He clearly lived alone, but it wasn't the sty that most bachelor apartments had the reputation of being.

"I wouldn't say that's entirely true," she said, smiling a little. He was slouched over but stable. He probably wouldn't end up on the floor.

And he wasn't too out of it to notice her expression.

"Oh?"

"You could give me your login information for the city datacenter," she said sweetly.

He blinked at her, and then his eyes slid from her to where Yoru was leaning against his door. Effectively blocking the only way out, even if he was able to stand in an attempt to reach it.

"Is this…an interrogation?" he asked her, almost incredulous. Then he groaned. "Oh, god, are you going to kill me?"

"Not if I don't have to," she said. She knelt down so she could look at him a little easier where he was sitting.

"It's nothing personal, and killing you doesn't make our lives any easier. If you give us the information we need, we can just go our separate ways."

"And if I lie?"

"We do kind of know where you live. And have keys to get in," she said. On cue, Yoru pulled both from his pocket.

Benjamin groaned again.

"Same goes if they don't work when we use them, so there won't be much point in changing them or telling your superiors that we have them. Not unless you think you can up and move fast enough, and quietly enough, that we can't track you down," she explained.

He sighed and she reached out and took his hand.

"Oh, it's not so bad. You'll sleep this off and no one even needs to know we were here," she said with a smile. "You won't remember any of this come tomorrow. In fact, you'll probably feel pretty hung over. You might want to call in to work. After all, they don't really pay you enough to worry about this sort of thing, do they?"

In the end, he agreed. Wasn't hard to get him to. Xueying had played this game before, and she got the numbers from him before he was of no use to them. True to her word, he'd wake up the next morning and not remember much of his night before. As pretty as he thought she was, he wouldn't even recognize her if he passed her on the street.

14:

"Where are you coming up with that information?" Rosa asked. Ame was laying on the couch, tapping away at her phone, and she looked up when it was made clear that Rosa was speaking to her.

"I've got a lead. Mr. Target frequents a club I've been to a few times. I know one of the bartenders, so she's giving me the hookups we can use to get in with him. I'm payin' her, of course, but it ain't expensive. It's not like she's gotta dig for it. She says he comes in often enough that she knows most of this shit offhand. I'm just paying her in case something goes sideways and he isn't around to tip her anymore." She laughed.

"So, what do we know?" Oliver asked, wrinkling his nose a little. He knew the answer to the question might not help him out directly, but it was pretty obvious that it was the next one that needed to be asked.

"His name is Sawai. He's got a thing for alcohol and pretty girls. Fairly typical. But he should also have the codes that Rosalina wants for her computer shenanigans."

Hastin immediately looked over to Rosa, wide-eyed. "Is that...?"

"No, she's just being dumb," Rosa said.

That saved Oliver from asking. He was pretty sure her name wasn't short for anything, but hey, what did he know?

"So right now, I'm thinking the plan is that Hastin and I go look cute and load this asshole up with drinks until he gives us the access codes. Should be pretty standard stuff," Ame said. She looked to Hastin, who nodded at her earnestly.

"If you're looking for a pretty girl quota, that's you and Rosa though, isn't it?" Oliver asked skeptically.

Ame jumped up from the couch and went to the chair Hastin sat in, where she proceeded to sit in his lap and drape her arm over his shoulders. "Oliver, fucking tell me to my face that this here is not master bait material," she said, pointing at Hastin.

Rosa made a brief choking noise and pressed a hand to her mouth, muffling her laughter, and Oliver favoured Ame with a scathing look.

"Eh? Right? But you can't tell me I'm wrong. If we want an in on a guy who likes cute girls, Hastin and I are the ticket. Rosa is for classy people. I don't know any of those people."

"I do," the woman in question said nonchalantly.

"Besides, Rosa is also in case we need an ace. Seeing as she's a good room-clearer, if something does go down while we're on assignment, it's easier to have her rescue us than for one of us to try and rescue her."

"I'm convinced. I'm not happy about it, but I'm convinced."

"We'll be okay, sweetie," she said to Hastin.

"I'm not afraid." He smiled.

"I know, hun." Ame leaned her head on his shoulder and her tail flicked contentedly behind her. "I'm really mostly just worried about us getting separated. I mean, at least one of us should wear a comm, but maybe we'll both have to wear one to be safe..."

"Give me just a minute," Hastin said, gently helping Ame off of him. She got up, and instead fell into his chair comfortably when he vacated it. He was back in moments, carrying a long ribbon.

"Whatcha got there?" she asked, sitting up.

"It's a hair ribbon, but I have an idea..." Standing there, he took one end of it and tied it in a neat bow around his neck. Then, taking Ame's hand, he did the same thing with the other end around her wrist.

"Now I won't get lost!" He said, smiling.

"I don't know if that's going to work," Oliver said.

"I think he's onto something," Rosa disagreed. "People are a lot less likely to try and fuck with him if he's stuck with her. And there's a lot of leeway there, it's not like she's not going to be able to use her hand."

Oliver had no adequate argument, so he said nothing.

"I'm am ambidextrous drinker and I don't even need my hands to kill a guy, so—" Ame shrugged.

"Are you sure you're okay with this?" Oliver said, looking to Hastin.

"Oh, Captain," Hastin said with a smile. "It's just some threatening. Everything should be fine."

"No, I mean... Are you okay with this?" He gestured to where the two of them were still tied together.

Hastin laughed. "If I'm going to be on a leash for anyone, I'll be happy as long as it's someone in this room."

As though he would have answered any differently.

"I can wear the comm, then, since my hair is longer and it'll be more hidden. And Ame will never be far, so she doesn't have to wear one."

Ame pointed at her ears, which were uncovered by her short hair. "Yeah, that's a way better idea. I mean, I could hide it in my clothes, but who are we kidding, I'm not going to wear that much."

"So you're after the codes to...what, log in to the system?" Oliver asked.

"Different people's codes give them access to different levels of information. But, once we're in there, it should be easier for me to work around things. Getting a foot in the door is half the problem taken care of," Rosa explained. "So even if his codes are pretty boring, I can probably use them for what we need, in the end. It'll be easier than having me try to work around the system, and honestly, it'll probably take less time."

"Go there, load him up with drinks, make eyes at him, get him to give us the pass he uses to get in. Come home, have a shower to wash the letch off and head to bed."

"Try not to get too much of that letch on the fairy prince, okay," Oliver said sourly.

"Bitter old man," Ame teased him, but Hastin was blinking at him curiously.

"Fairy... prince...?"

"That's you, honey," Ame said. "Probably because you're beautiful and you kill people. Fairies do that."

"Oh, that actually brings up a good question," Hastin said, looking to Ame. "Um... What sort of place are we going? I'm not sure how I'm supposed to look."

Oliver pressed his hands to his face but he needn't have bothered; Ame didn't even look at him.

"Show me what we've got, hun, we'll figure out something that looks the part," she said reasonably.

He had a point, Oliver had to admit. His femme business attire, the classy secretary thing he had going on, was probably not going to blend in very well. And Oliver, who knew exactly nothing about fashion, would not have been any help.

"Well, while they're playing dress up... I'm gonna do some laundry. Rosa, you got anything for me?" Oliver said, standing up with a groan.

"Yeah, thanks," she said. "Let's trade. I'll make some lunch while you're at it."

"Deal."

Oliver liked chores. Like dishes, laundry gave him something tangible, measurable that he could do to contribute. It didn't sound like there was much in the way of problems to overcome with the newest plan. Send the two of them out, sit back and wait as they did some arm twisting, and then welcome them back home with the information.

There was a lot Oliver didn't know. Mostly the specifics. Where was this place? And what, were they just going to extort this guy for information right from the bar? It didn't take him a long time to throw the clothes in and turn it on, but there was enough time for him to whip himself into a flurry of confusion.

So he went back to his room and did some of those practices he had scrounged up. Ways to make his brain a little less busy.

And then, when he felt a little more like he was actually in his own body and plugged in to what was going on, he felt well enough to ask some questions.

"So, where are you guys going, exactly?" he asked, leaning in the doorway of Hastin's room. It was uncomfortably bare. He had his bags, but barely anything had been removed from them. Oliver liked tidiness, but even his own room had some socks laying around and his sweater tossed at the end of his bed and all that. Enough to show that he was there.

"Place called The Dive," Ame said. She was sitting on Hastin's bed and regarding him with a critical eye. Clearly they hadn't decided what would be best to wear yet. "It's exactly what it says on the tin. Well, that's not quite true. It's grungy, sure, but I think that's on purpose. It's a good place to go if you wanna get wrecked and dance, or if you want to disappear. You see CEO's kids there sometimes when they're sick of the high life."

"Rich people pretending to be the poor and hardcore type," Oliver said.

"Yeah. And a few who are. It's one of my digs, so I ain't exactly afraid of it," she said offhandedly. It was followed by, "Hey, kid, take your hair down for a minute, I think that'll do it."

He nodded and undid the braid he was wearing, running his fingers through the navy waves of hair before carelessly tossing it back over his shoulder. "Like that?"

"Yeah! What do you think, Captain?" Ame looked to him with amusement but no real derision. If she was teasing him, she wasn't trying very hard.

"I don't know a good goddamn thing about clothes," he said.

"That's okay, Captain. We're not after a score," Hastin said patiently. "We're after people. Would this work on you?"

"Loaded question," Ame pointed out.

But Oliver wasn't going to let him down. He took a minute to look at Hastin and tried not to let his bias interfere. It was impossible, sure, but he made the effort nonetheless. Ame had dressed him in black; it made him look very pale and elegant. And she was right about the hair.

"Smile?" Oliver asked.

Hastin did, giggling a little as he looked at Oliver.

Somewhere, Oliver felt part of his brain punch out its timecard in resignation.

"If he's got any sense in his head, you'll get him," Oliver said. "Especially if you're standing next to her."

"Wow, rude," Ame said sourly.

"Beautiful things look better in groups," Oliver shot back.

Well, that shut her up.

What should have been an awkward silence was promptly ruined. "I think you'll do great!" Hastin said, turning his smile to Ame. "I know I haven't worked with you yet... But you're so pretty and confident. Anyone would believe you."

He reached for Oliver's hand and took it in both his own. "I know that being in a place like that would probably make you really unhappy, so I'm glad you get to stay home. Don't worry about anything. We'll take care of it!"

"Yeah..." And when Ame looked at Oliver this time, it seemed as though he was forgiven for his earlier comment. "It'll be fine. We'll be back here before you know it."

"Kind of hate sending you two out to deal with those kinds of people, but—" Oliver shrugged. "You're professionals. I know it'll be okay. I'll just feel better when you're back here cracking jokes about the poor asshole you're about to rob."

"Oh, I'll bring the jokes," Ame promised. "You'll be sick of them, just you wait."

~*~

Sawai was your typical salaryman, he thought. In the beginning, he worked too hard and made too little money, and eventually he got tired of the disparity and decided he was only going to do what he was paid for. Which was fair, as far as he was concerned. If he was being honest, however, they paid him quite a lot. It was why he could afford to spend so many nights getting wasted at The Dive. Not enough to even out the stress of the job, maybe, but enough to drink some of that stress away. Sometimes he got lucky, in the literal and metaphorical sense. Lots of cute drunk girls. Richer than him, for sure. Usually more sober than him, too.

The bartenders knew him, kept his drinks coming and didn't complain when he made eyes at the girls to see if they'd do it back. It wasn't like he bothered anyone.

He was the first to notice when they walked in: a curvy, tanned girl with a sassy haircut and a darker-haired damsel tied to her wrist by a ribbon. Well. Two for one, was it?

Sawai wasn't picky. The simple fact of the matter was that girls were pretty, and most girls when they dressed up to go out were attractive. That made his nights easier, for sure. But these two were more than pretty.

"Oh, subtle." Ame swallowed her laugh and spoke under her breath as they stepped inside.

"Eyes on us already. You are very good," Hastin told her, sincerity warm in his voice.

"We'll celebrate later," she said with a smile. "You want a drink, or you not the drinking on the job type?"

"I've never had alcohol," Hastin confessed.

"Probably not a good idea to start tonight," Ame said, leaning into his shoulder.

"Probably not," he agreed.

If they stayed close and hung out near the bar, the music wasn't too loud. He could hear her when she leaned close like that, and it kept them out of the throng of dancers.

The song switched and Ame made a pained noise. "That's my jam. Man, I need to go out dancing. You know how to dance, honey?"

"Mmmm, what do you think?"

"I think that old lady never let you learn how to dance," Ame said. She hooked her arm around his waist and pulled him close. "Well, when we're not working, we're gonna go out, okay? And I'm gonna teach you how. You'll love it. It's fun."

He looked over to the dancefloor, mildly perplexed but very intrigued. "I'd like that." He cast his gaze a little farther, meeting eyes with their target. So he smiled, like the Captain had told him to.

He didn't get a smile back, but the man's mouth dropped open a little. That seemed like a good sign.

"Someone likes you," Ame noted.

"He thinks I'm a girl," Hastin said offhandedly.

"Let's go correct him," she answered mischievously, and tugged him over down the bar towards where their mark sat.

"Hey, mister," she said, hanging comfortably off Hastin. "See something you like?"

On getting a closer look at Hastin, though, he seemed a little skeptical. "I thought I saw two of them, but..."

"Oh, don't be like that—"

Ame felt it. A turn in the air. Something changed. Hastin moved against her, leaning comfortably, tugging on the ribbon he wore and twining it in his fingers.

"You like pretty things, don't you?" he said, in a voice that Ame had never heard before. "Am I not pretty enough?"

Sawai smiled, then. Of course he did. How could he not? Hastin sounded like a cotton-candy daydream come to life.

"It's not that," he said, trying to explain. "I'm more into partiers, you know. The fun type. You just look a little too...civilized, that's all."

"Don't let that scare you." Hastin laughed. Not his usual laugh, either.

"May I?" He turned to Ame to ask it, and to be honest, she had no idea what he was asking, but she was good on the drop and she acted like she did as easily as breathing. She didn't need to know exactly what he was thinking. She knew the type he was playing. She could play.

"Sure, pet..." She tucked his hair behind his ear. "You go ahead."

He reached for one of Sawai's hands, asking with his eyes rather than his words. The man humoured him. Hastin laced their fingers together, dragging the man's touch through his hair, down the material of his dress. That was far enough for the man to get the hint. Those same fingers tugged themselves away from Hastin's and slipped themselves past the hem of his skirt.

"Don't worry, mister. They didn't beat all the fun out of me." And the breathy way he made his words made even Ame's heart race.

"He yours?" Sawai asked her. He was sold. He was sold hard. Hastin was fucking magic.

"Yeah... He's a real treat, isn't he?" Ame said. The fondness she looked at him with was unfaked. That part was easy.

"What's the price?"

And at that, she laughed. Hastin was being awfully affectionate, nuzzling against the side of her neck and making colour rise in her cheeks. It had been awhile since someone was so effective against her.

"For you...nothing. Sounds too good to be true, right?" she asked with a cheeky smile.

"Bet your ass it does."

"I'll bet a lot more than my ass. But here's the thing, mister...my pretty boy here doesn't take a liking to just anyone..." She sighed. A way to catch her breath, or try to. Hastin's lips brushed her skin and that set her right back to square one.

"So, when he sees someone he likes, well...I'm just so happy. I don't mind if you play with him a while..."

"Just him?"

Hastin giggled again. He pulled his arms away from Ame and slid himself all too comfortably into Sawai's lap where he had turned his chair from the bar. Light as a feather, perched there like some unearthly creature. Fairy prince, indeed.

"He wants to play with you, too..." he said, looking to Ame where she stood, still tied to him.

"You'll come play with us, won't you?" Hastin asked her.

One look at Sawai's face sealed it. He was theirs.

"Yeah, honey... I'll play," Ame said, a smile on her lips.

They got Sawai out of the bar. That much wasn't hard. He'd go anywhere they asked. He'd go anywhere Ame asked if she smiled at him wickedly enough. He liked party types, girls who fancied themselves dangerous. The smile looked good on her.

And Hastin, well... He didn't have to do anything. Sawai was so far gone for him that he'd follow the young man's every breath.

Ame kept his attention in the cab. Hastin would have, she knew, but... Oliver had asked for her to keep him free of what she could, and to be honest, she didn't like the idea of him having to play that part. Not more than he already had. He had gotten so little genuine affection, that much was obvious. Seemed a pity to add to it.

"He's just a little shy, out in the open like this," she explained, despite that definitely not having been the case earlier. Sawai was significantly tipsy at this point and well past the point of arguing. "I'll keep you warm until we get there."

They got out at a hotel and swiped Sawai's card to get them a room. Hastin took some of the heat off Ame while she took care of that particular transaction. She never saw him kiss Sawai. He didn't have to.

He had one hand wrapped around the man's loosened tie, his finger pressed to Sawai's lips and their foreheads together. He was murmuring something under his breath. She couldn't hear it from where she was.

Sawai's hands wandered, but never far enough to find the weapons Hastin was wearing. Hastin kept him exactly in line. Played him expertly, until Ame got them a room of their own.

She closed the door behind them. As soon as the lock clicked closed, the air shifted again.

128

She heard a choked noise and turned from the door to see that Hastin had already done half the work. He had his arm locked around the man's neck. The right amount of pressure and he'd strangle him. The boy was quick.

"Well, that's easy," Ame mused, stepping over to where Hastin had him effectively locked up. The hotel was a nice one. She'd rather like to crawl into that fluffy bed that looked so much more comfortable than the one she was staying in. She'd like to take Hastin with her. Not even for sex. So many things were more important than sex.

But no. Another time.

"Okay, Mister Sawai. You have some numbers for me. Spit it out."

"What?!"

"Your job. We need your pass to get inside those computers," Ame said. "Gimme."

"I—I don't—" A subtle shift of Hastin's arm and the man's air was cut off, quick and easy. Ame looked at him, unsure if he knew how far he should go with this. But he wasn't looking at her. He was looking at Sawai as he struggled to breathe. Just as she was about to caution him not to kill their target, he relented.

Sawai gasped in a ragged breath.

"We're not kidding around here. Give me your information," she said, firmly.

He coughed. "It's no use! I can't! I can't!"

"Why can't you?"

"They change the passwords every few days. There's no way to know if it would work by the time you need it," he said. His voice was panicked and it was easy to understand why.

"They're randomly generated. I can't help you. I can't, I can't..."

Well...fuck.

"Randomly generated passcodes. Reassigned every few days. Did they get that?" Ame asked, looking at Hastin.

"They heard."

"Please don't kill me!" Sawai said, terrified. "Please!"

Hastin looked to her now, his question obvious. Did they, or didn't they?

He would. Ame knew that one word from her and Hastin would very carefully and meticulously strangle him to death. She wasn't squeamish about that kind of stuff, not usually... But she didn't really want to see him do it.

"Captain says I should let him go," Hastin said quietly, just loud enough to be heard over Sawai's strained breathing.

"Course he does," Ame said.   "Gimme your comm."

Hastin tilted his head so that Ame could pull the wire from where it was wrapped around his ear without him releasing Sawai.

"Rosa, what do you think?"

"Killing him means a police investigation, even just a cursory one. That's more heat than I want to deal with," she pointed out. Ame relayed what she said out loud as she thought.

"The hospital," Hastin said. Sawai struggled and he took a moment to calmly get him back under control again.

Ame nodded. "Yeah. Beat his ass and put him in the hospital. I'm sure that will be plenty enough warning to keep him from talking."

"We take his wallet, the cops assume we're prostitutes he tried to rip off, we're home free," Hastin said.

"You going to make sure the warning sticks?" Rosa asked in Ame's ear.

"Oh, we'll make sure."

15:

Dan didn't know where exactly Yoru was. He had run out of the little apartment, kissing him on the back of the head as he went by, and said he'd be back later. Usually, he'd explain himself, but he did seem like he was in a hurry. Curious but not upset, Dan figured he'd get the story another time. In the meantime, he cleaned up a little and made something to eat. Everything was really quiet. It wasn't bad, necessarily, but he thought he'd at least see Xueying around.

No luck. Instead, it was Rusty who wandered into the kitchen.

"Want some?" Dan asked her, gesturing to what he was eating. "It's my cooking, not Yoru's, but it's not bad."

"You don't sound confident," she said. She had a hard to read face, dark eyes framed by her straight red hair. Darker than blood red. More of a cherry, Dan thought.

"Have you eaten his food? It's not much of a contest," he answered.

She found a bowl of her own and Dan slid her a pair of chopsticks. Then, he froze.

"Wait…"

Rusty looked at him, and looked at the paper-wrapped sticks. The one-use kind. It made sense, seeing as they weren't hanging around this place for too long. That wasn't why Dan had stopped.

Her fingers were still bandaged.

"Probably a fork," he figured, sheepishly.

"I think so."

She dug one out of the drawer and to Dan's surprise, she sat down across from him at the little square table. The kitchen was hardly a nice one, but it was functional enough and wasn't too cramped with just the two of them.

"How are your hands doing?" he tried again, looking across the table at her.

She didn't look up, shovelling a forkful of rice into her mouth and holding one of her hands out to him across the table. The last three fingers of it were bandaged and braced, but she wiggled the thumb and finger that were free to show they were still usable.

"Healing," she answered.

That was something. At least she had some use of it. The other one looked to be much in the same shape, except he thought she might have had one more finger of use. Broken bones used to take goddamn ages to heal. Thank goodness for modern medicine, Dan thought. Rusty might not have been able to afford it herself, but Xueying sure could.

"I hate being stuck here," Rusty said suddenly.

Dan looked over at her. "Here like…here?" he asked. "Like the job?"

"No. Like… Inside." She looked up at him. "I hate being stuck inside. I want to be useful."

"I feel that," Dan agreed, swallowing another mouthful.

"You still sick?" she asked. That made him stop eating in surprise.

"How'd you know I was sick?"

She looked at him, and used her singular working finger to point at his face.

He sighed.

"No. Or at least, I'm much better than I was," he admitted. "I don't know if this kind of sick goes away."

He hadn't really meant to say that last part. It just sort of…came out. And he immediately regretted how over the top it sounded.

But Rusty just nodded, as though she understood, and thankfully didn't press the question any more than that.

"Did Xueying fill you in on what they're working on? I haven't seen her at all today," Dan asked when he finished eating. Rusty wasn't far behind, and he reached out to take her dishes without really stopping to think about it. She didn't have any hands. She sure as hell wasn't going to be able to clean them.

"The job, yes. Today, no." Rusty frowned (or, he thought she did) and then shook her head. "I don't know where she is today."

"Makes two of us."

Rusty was quiet for a few minutes while he worked. When she spoke it was in that same quick way she had, as though she had already had half the conversation with herself before deciding to let Dan in on it.

"Feel like doing something about it?"

He looked around. He wasn't sure what he was looking for, maybe to see if someone was listening, because this sounded like it was about to get serious. He turned the water off and answered her.

"Something like what?"

"Like going outside," Rusty said, in a tone that made it obvious that

132

'going outside' wasn't half of what she really meant.

"You have something in mind?"

She smiled then. It wasn't a pretty smile, not what he'd usually call 'pretty', anyway. But it had its own charm and mischief to it. To hell with it. It was pretty. It was hers.

"We need computer terminal access. Xueying has codes, but nowhere to put them. We can fix that," she said.

The idea of doing something useful sure appealed to him.

"You think you can?" he asked, nodding to her hands.

"Don't have to punch when I have a gun," she said. "Besides, my legs work just fine."

That surprised a laugh out of him, and then he nodded. "Sure, okay." Maybe he should have been more cautious. Too late now. Besides, Yoru and Xueying trusted her. He could, too.

"Did you have a place in mind?"

"Best one is closest one, probably," Rusty mused. "There's a general access terminal not far from here. You know, the ones for everyone to use? But they lock them at night."

"So rather than try and do it from here, better to do it from somewhere we don't live."

"In case things get bad."

Her Omnian was a little rough, but she managed to get her points across just fine. Dan had no problems understanding her. It wasn't hard to appreciate her efforts. After all, he was pretty good in a conversation, but he was no Yoru. There was always something to learn.

"Is this place far enough away for them not to find us if we screw it up?" Dan asked. It had just occurred to him that 'close' might not be what they needed.

"They would have to go through a lot of people to find us. It's popular, and there are lots of people around here."

Fair enough. "I've gotta ask. I'm, um, still learning."

"Learn by doing," Rusty said. She was headed for the door and Dan watched her work her shoes onto her feet without bothering to use her hands. "Are you coming?" she asked, looking pointedly at him once she was finished.

That seemed to settle it. He hurried to get his shoes on and followed her out the door.

"How exactly are we breaking into this place during the day?" Dan asked her as they walked.

133

"We're not. We're—" She gestured with one bandaged hand. "Looking. Casing. We're casing the place."

Okay. That made more sense. It really wasn't as nearby as he thought, and keeping up with Rusty was a bit of a struggle. He wasn't sluggish, and he even had longer legs than she did, but wow she was quick. He thought it might have been because while he was busy keeping track of her, she wasn't keeping track of him. She just assumed he'd follow. Which was well and fine, because he would, but it did mean he had to work all the harder not to lose her in the crowd.

It was easy to spot the place. Carved out of the lower section of the building, open on three sides with rows and rows of terminals that people could pay to access. And it was busy. These days, everyone had computers in their homes. Phones, vidscreens, smart cookers...basically everything had a way to get online. But that wasn't enough. Cheap household products weren't Certified. If they weren't Certified, you couldn't use them for anything but browsing, basically. Most trustworthy companies wouldn't interact with hardware that wasn't up to spec. Dan wasn't really into business ethics as an area of study, but he knew this for what it was; a way to fleece more money out of people.

They didn't have this system back home, but it had been trying to sneak in. He remembered reading about it. What was so hard about letting people just...have access to stuff? But now wasn't really the time for him to be worrying about it.

"Cameras," she said, looking up in the corners of the room where they were perched. The computers were about five rows deep, and maybe fifteen per row.

"They've got shutters on the windows." Well, not windows. But the places where the walls opened up to become doors. "Metal ones. They've probably got motion sensors on them."

The cameras looked pretty old, and a quick inspection of where the shutters slid down revealed what were probably the very sensors he had been describing. None of this material was new, it looked like. The computers themselves certainly weren't. Make people pay to use them and then make them awful. It was all pressure so people would buy the more expensive household versions.

"I'm no expert, but I'm going to think that if all their hardware is older than I am... We should be able to manage this, I think," Dan mused quietly to Rusty.

"Old things can still ring the alarm on us," she answered.

134

"Speaking of old things... Who runs this place? Is it automated?" Dan asked. She gave him a weird look and he laughed a little. He had been thinking of who would run a place like this, and his first thought was that it would be someone old and wrinkled and white-haired. Maybe when they were young they had more energy and kept the place tidier.

Still, that was a little out of context to Rusty, who only heard the part he said aloud.

"Like, does someone live here, you think? Lots of people who own small shops live in or around them. I don't want to break into this place and then have to deal with someone we weren't expecting."

Rusty's smile was wry, and she chuckled a little. "People don't do that in The Ves. Is that how they do it back in your home?" she asked.

"Gave myself away a little." He laughed. "Yeah, it's really common in Syama."

"Where I grew up, it is the same. Here, they usually lock up and live somewhere else. They're not allowed to live where they work."

As much as Dan would have once strived to follow them, sometimes he really didn't understand laws.

"So, we're not expecting anyone to show up once we crack the lock. Okay. What else?" he asked.

"I don't know. I am a fighter, not a planner. So, what else?" she said, looking at him.

Dan took a breath. Okay, so she wanted him to be the brains of this little endeavour. He could do that. Well, he could try.

"I can probably short out the motion detector. But that leaves the cameras..."

"Could just break them," Rusty said.

"What?" Dan asked, but he figured it out before she could answer it. "Wait, you're saying they probably won't replace them right away, or they probably don't lead to a live-feed because this place is so old and badly managed. Okay. Okay. So...we break the cameras."

"If we work fast, we can break them, and then come back before they are replaced," she pointed out.

"That would be handy. And they might not even notice the motion sensor going down, honestly, unless I melt it right off the wall, which I'll try not to do..."

They were starting to get a plan together, and it felt good.

This didn't seem too hard. Sneak back here, basically melt whatever tech they had monitoring the place, and make sure they could get in and out with ease. After that, it was mostly hoping that the place stayed in disrepair long enough that they didn't have to do it twice.

But even if they did get repaired, they'd have an idea of what they were getting into. They'd know the layout, which means they'd have an idea where they'd put any replacements.

"Do I look like I'm trying to break into this place? I feel like I'm being obvious," Dan joked under his breath to Rusty.

"No one is watching you. No one cares," she answered him. He laughed again.

Dan paused for a moment.

"How much are they not watching?" he asked.

"Very much."

That gave him an idea.

He motioned for Rusty to follow him and he wound his way through the people packed around the computers until he got to where one of the shutters would normally be fashioned. Looking up the wall, he spotted the little contact that would sound the alarm if it was unaligned with its other half. And, it wasn't too far up the wall for him to reach.

"Lemme see," he muttered under his breath.

Dan took a quick glance around, but no one even bothered looking his way. He reached up and tapped the metal faceplate with his finger. He felt the shock more than he saw it, but he knew that whatever was inside of it wasn't going to be working anymore.

"What are you doing?"

"Giving us an entrance," he said.

She looked at it skeptically, but didn't argue.

They went back to the apartment together. You can't exactly break into a place while it's open, and while the idea had occurred to Dan to just do the job during the day, there were a bit too many prying eyes around for that to sound like a good idea. He and Rusty didn't stand out too much. Xueying, on the other hand, actively drew gazes wherever she walked and Yoru wasn't far behind in that effect. They were going to ruin it.

So, breaking in would be better. And with what he had done, it should be easier.

Yoru and Xueying were still missing from the apartment when they got back. Dan texted him, and while he got an answer it was only brief. Still, he said he would be home later that night and his questions could wait until then.

When the sun went down, the streets cleared out quickly. In some neighbourhoods, that wasn't the case. Night time was party time...but not where people were too tired and broke for it. Someone had picked a great spot for their little hideout.

He and Rusty set out again. Dan was actually thankful for the hat Yoru had given him. It wasn't cold out, but he had a shiver he just couldn't shake. His hair was growing back remarkably fast, but it wasn't enough.

They took a different route. It was easier to keep track of Rusty when there wasn't a crowd of people to lose her in. Dan checked the time on his phone and frowned in thought. It wasn't that late yet, and there were still people out and about. Not many, but some. They were going to have to be careful if they wanted to be subtle.

And what if Yoru got back before him? He didn't want to make his friend worry. They'd have to be quick then.

"Here, this is the one I shorted out," Dan said, leaning against the slatted metal door in question.

"It's locked," Rusty noted.

"Probably, yeah. But I think I can break it…" Dan looked at where it was chained closed. "If I break this, and we crack the bottom of the door open, can you squeeze in and take out the cameras?"

"I am smaller than you are," she said, as though that answered it.

"Okay, so, um…cover your eyes for a second," he told her. Wrapping both hands around the chain, he tried to very carefully melt it without burning himself. What actually happened was that electricity sparked between his fingers, the chain snapped in several places and there was a loud bang in accompaniment.

"That…wasn't supposed to happen," he said, glancing around.

Rusty didn't answer. They both waited, listening for more than the sounds of their own breaths in the darkness.

There was nothing.

"Maybe…you didn't ruin everything," she said.

"Maybe not." He certainly hoped that was the case. Then he knelt down and got his fingers under the latch for the wall. He tried to lift it carefully and silently. It wasn't made to be either quick or quiet, and he was relieved when there was enough room for Rusty to squeeze under. He could prop it up as it was and wait for her.

This door would be their access point again next time they needed it, and she'd take out the cameras that needed to go down. At least, that was the plan, and that sounded like what was happening on the other side of the wall.

Rusty popped back out. Dan closed the door again and took the chain from where it was looped and shoved it in his pocket. Ideally, they'd just think they forgot to lock it the night before. Maybe they would think they were robbed. It didn't really matter. The police weren't likely to care. Even if it did get a little heated...they'd hit another place while all the attention was over here. It was perfect.

It was as they were leaving when it finally occurred to Dan. Those computer terminals were capable of making video-calls to anywhere in the world, for the right amount. He could have called his mom. They could have traced the call, sure, but even Rusty had said it would be hard to sift them out of all the people in the area. It would have jeopardized his freedom and their job...but he could have done it. He could have seen her face and heard her voice again. He could have told her that her son was still alive. Alive and more well than he had any right to be.

But it hadn't even crossed his mind.

16:

"So...a password generator. What does that mean?" Oliver asked. Ame and Hastin were back at the apartment, still dressed up and sitting in the living room with the other two.

"Means we're fucked. A little bit," Ame said.

"A little," Rosa answered. "What it actually means is that we have to get that code. I need a copy of the code that generates the passwords so that I can either generate them here, or use it to work backwards and decode them on-site."

"So...we have to go steal you a code?" Oliver said.

"Like, some code," Ame said.

"Rosa will have to come with us," Hastin corrected him gently. "None of us are as adept with computers as she is, and I doubt we would be able to get her what she needs alone."

"I could use the air," Rosa agreed.

"As far as setbacks go, we've had worse," Ame said reasonably. She had undone the ribbon that tied her to Hastin but sat with her arm over his shoulders. "We wasted a single night and no one got hurt. Worse things have happened." She was out a few dollars from bribing the bartender, but hey, at least she knew she could work with them again.

"You did so well." Hastin sighed, smiling a little, and rested his head on Ame's shoulder. "Working with you is so nice."

She reached over and stroked his hair. "You're world-class too, darling. You guys heard him, right? Seeing it was even better."

They decided that they'd talk about the new job in the morning. It was frustrating to Oliver, but he took solace in the fact that Ame and Rosa didn't seem too put out. If they weren't bothered, he didn't need to be bothered, right? Everyone had come back safe, and that had been his main worry.

Hearing Hastin over the comm had been a little...unnerving. But he seemed to be just fine now.

The next day, over breakfast, they got down to business.

"We can target any one of the branches we need to. Seeing as the generator has to be compatible with all of them, it shouldn't matter who we rob."

"Not the one closest to us, then," Ame said with a nod.

"This is going to be very messy." Hastin sat at the kitchen table next to Rosa and without a coffee of his own. Sometimes Rosa would pass hers over to him and he'd take a sip, but right now he was looking at the table as though it was a map and was frowning.

"We should try to work fast, but that means we won't have a lot of prep time and we're going to have to adapt as we go. The best plan is probably to break in a back door, see if we can't short out security and get in and out before they respond," he said.

"We knew the job was going to be dangerous. We wouldn't have said yes if we hadn't considered it," Ame reassured him.

He still frowned. "I don't want you to have to be in danger."

"Hastin." Rosa, this time. "It's your job, and our job. We're all professionals here. It's part of the work." He sank down against her shoulder, and she leaned her head on top of his for a moment.

"I wouldn't be so quick to give myself so much credit," Oliver pointed out.

"That's because I don't really think you should come," Rosa agreed. "No offence, just don't want to see you get shot."

"You really think he should stay home?" Ame asked. "I mean, we could use the extra eyes, and the three of us are pretty capable. I don't think it'll be a real disaster."

She looked to Hastin, and Rosa tilted her head in a way to indicate that she was listening. He was the only other professional at the table who hadn't given an opinion about it.

"Captain, I... I'm really not sure," he said.

"I don't want to be the only one left behind," Oliver said matter-of-factly. "I know I'm not good at the same stuff you guys are, but I'm an extra set of eyes and willing hands. I'm sure I can find some way to be useful." And that was really the big sticking point. He didn't really want to go. He wasn't a thief, and he wasn't exactly their level. But he didn't want to be useless, and he didn't want them to come back with stories of how he could have helped.

Hastin sighed. "It probably would be better if you came than if you didn't, really..."

"Then it's settled. I'll come along, and that way if you need me at least I'm there, and I'm not the reason we all get fucked over."

"What else are we going to need?" Hastin asked.

"I'll have a toolkit with me. I just have to pack it and see what things I

140

think I'm going to have to bring. And we're going to need some kind of firepower. Probably not lots, just enough to keep people off of us if it gets messy."

"That's fine. I'm sure the three of us have it covered," he said. Then, with a look to Oliver. "You should probably take one, too."

Oliver grimaced. "I don't want to, but you're right. And I can shoot. I'm no ace, but I've done it. It just...leaves a bad taste in my mouth."

Hastin shot him a quick look that he almost missed, but the younger man said nothing so Oliver let it go.

"We're also going to need make-up. If those cameras have facial recognition software, we have to fuck it up somehow. But I've done that before."

"Me too." Hastin nodded to Ame. "We can work on that together."

"I can start laying out a map and a plan if you guys want to start getting stuff ready." Rosa drained the last of her coffee. "I can get us a way to and from the building set up ahead of time, and can at least start a little of the planning for what we might find inside."

Most of the day was spent in preparation. Oliver was used to sneaking around and really, he was feeling better about this job than the last one. Hastin, true to his word, supplied him with a handgun and a bit of ammunition.

"Please be careful. I don't want you to get hurt." He spoke in a way that left Oliver feeling touched rather than offended.

"This is just in case of an emergency. Ideally, we'll be in and out before people can get much shooting done. Even if things get a little wild, the three of you are good at what you do," Oliver told him. "I'm nervous because I'm just an anxious person by nature," he admitted with a bit of a smile. "But if this is going to happen, you guys are the safest people for me to be with."

"I'll take care of you," Hastin promised him.

"I know you will," Oliver said in reply, with every feeling that he was right.

They set out well after dark. Late, at a time when Oliver would have much preferred to be asleep. He was hardly about the nightlife, but fear of what was to come kept him awake and alert.

Rosa had gotten them transportation there. An unmarked, dark car with a partition between the back and the driver. Oliver didn't much feel like talking; the oppressive darkness killed any desire he might have usually had to make noise, but Ame and Hastin and Rosa talked quietly and calmly among each other for the duration of the ride.

Hastin leaned against his shoulder but he never pressed Oliver to talk. He was just there, warm and steady, a little funny looking in the camera-scrambling make-up that Ame had given him, but still cute.

They slid out of the car in the alleyway behind a row of skyscrapers. One of a million similar alleys that could be found all around the city, and with some of the same video cameras. Ame shot it out without any dramatics on her part.

"Will that really help?" Oliver asked her, still waiting for his heart to settle after the noise of the shot.

"They don't send someone down for any old shot out camera. The police are strapped enough as it is. They might have a private security force and they'll be a little faster, but that wasn't their camera. It was theirs—" She pointed to the building the camera was attached to. "It could still be used to ID us after the fact, but I doubt they're going to tell these guys we're coming."

There was a fence that cut them off from the back door but he watched as Hastin pulled himself up it, cut the barbed wire and dropped himself down the other side where he quickly picked the plain metal lock that held it closed. The gate swung open and they filed inside.

Oliver thought his nerves were going to fry his whole brain, but at the moment, everything seemed to be going to plan.

"Electronic lock, just like you thought," Hastin said, looking at the door.

"I came prepared," said Rosa. She pulled something from her belt, found an access point and plugged herself in to get to work. For a moment, Oliver wondered why a lock like that would even have one, but he supposed even electronic locks needed to be maintained.

They waited quietly while she worked, not wanting to distract her, but the light flicked from red to green and they were good to go.

"As soon as we open this door and take out those cameras, we're going to be on a timer," Hastin said quietly.

"Well, I'm going to have to be fast, and you're going to have to keep us alive," Rosa said. "That simple."

She counted them down. Ame and Hastin were the first ones indoors and Oliver heard the shooting before his foot even hit tile. Taking out the cameras again. Now people would know they were there.

The three of them ran and Oliver just did his best to keep up. Every hall it was the same thing; Ame and Hastin first, cameras down, he and Rosa following. He hadn't even touched his gun and was increasingly thankful that it looked like he wouldn't have to.

Rosa found a computer to jack into and she worked quickly to wire herself up. When she was connected, she could start working on finding and copying what they needed. Of course, she wasn't supposed to be copying it, and it didn't want to let her, but she'd work around that.

"Hanging in there, Captain?" Not Hastin but Ame, grinning at him mischievously. She liked the adrenaline.

"Trying."

"You look a little green."

"Feel a little green," he admitted, but not without amusement.

"I try to take lots of deep breaths when the nerves bother me too much." Hastin laid a hand on his arm but didn't look away from the hallway he was scanning with his eyes. He and Ame were at the door of the room they were holed up in and he seemed so at ease. Ame's confident grin seemed chosen to spite the situation that might otherwise unnerve her. Hastin didn't seem either nervous or confident. He just was. But judging from his words, it hadn't always been that way.

Oliver took his advice.

"Found it. Just gotta fight with it for a minute and we'll be good to go," Rosa said.

Ame was looking at her watch. "We probably don't have a whole minute. They should be dropping on us any—"

A gunshot rang out, missing her, and she ducked into the room. "Wow, I'm fuckin' good."

Hastin took a breath and Oliver watched him press his back to the door frame and lean out of it. Another shot rang out when he squeezed the trigger and he pulled himself back into the room. "One down. Not sure how many they brought."

"More than one," Ame said, laughing wildly.

"Anything I can do to speed this up?" Oliver asked Rosa where she was working.

"Not unless you're a computer."

He flinched when more shots rang out, but Rosa didn't.

"How are we looking out there?" she asked them.

"Holding them off. They're only on the one side for now, but I expect they'll end up in the other hallway soon. How long until we can make a break for it?" Ame asked her.

"Soon...soon..." Rosa said distractedly.

"Soon better be now, we're going to be locked in," she said. Hastin wasn't complaining, he wasn't taking the time to.

"Got it." Rosa disconnected herself in a flash. "Make an exit for us, we're gone."

"On it." Hastin was the first out into the hall, walking backwards as he fired down at the other end, calmly and unfailingly. He heard the feet behind him before he backed into the opening of the adjoining hallway, and as Ame picked up where he left off, he turned his attention to cleaning their way ahead.

Oliver and Rosa waited until Ame gave them the all clear to move out into the hall with her. With the way Ame and Hastin were working, it seemed unlikely he would have to use his gun, and he just hoped that was the case.

Hastin cleared the way to the next corner and they inched their way towards the exit. One hallway, one doorway at a time. It was a nerve-wracking creep to the exit, and even when they got out they still had to get away. Rosa had her tech tucked away and Oliver saw her flex the fingers of the metal-plated arm cover she wore. Her tail flicked, tense, and she seemed ready to pounce.

What had Ame mentioned of Rosa being a room-clearer? Either way, that claw-thing looked nasty. Still, they'd have to get close enough for her to use it, and he hoped they wouldn't get the chance.

They rounded another corner. Oliver almost slipped in blood. None of theirs. Someone the others had pegged, bleeding out in their retreat. He wasn't squeamish about blood, but now wasn't the time to be losing his feet.

Rosa grabbed him and yanked him upright and they kept moving.

"When we get out there, we have to turn and run and they are going to have the advantage of being able to pick us off from the door," Hastin pointed out.

'They' being the private security. Oliver hadn't gotten a clear look at them, but they didn't really look like any cops he had seen. It would explain the lack of trying to get them to stand down. Cops at least usually shouted at you a little before they killed you. These guys didn't bother.

"We need something to get them off our backs so we can get out of here."

"I think I got it," Ame said. She ducked behind the wall and reloaded her gun as Hastin kept shooting. "One of them has some grenades strapped to that bulletproof vest that keeps getting in my fucking way. I can probably hit one and blow a big hole in this joint."

"You're going to have to be able to hit that on the run," Rosa said. "Can you do that?"

"If I can't, Hastin can. You're wicked with that little gun, aren't you, babe?"

"I can get it," he said. There was a delay in his voice when he talked, always half a second behind when Oliver expected to hear him. Careful of his answers and how they'd affect his work. Oliver wasn't sure that was the only thing he was being careful about.

"Okay. We run for the exit, you two make sure you drop it down behind us," Rosa said. She flexed her gloved hand. "I'll take care of anyone in front of us."

They ran for it. It wasn't far, and Oliver wondered if they were really going to have time to hit the shot they needed before they got out. He could hear the people behind them.

And then he tripped, just as Hastin's shot hit its mark, and things started coming down all around him.

He'd never seen an explosion so close before. To be fair, he didn't see this one either; he felt it. The fall knocked the wind out of him and pain flared where he hit the floor. He heard the explosion—more than one, whatever Hastin hit must have set off the others near it—and he didn't feel exploded, but as he was pushing himself to his feet he did feel the piece of ceiling that fell on him.

The shooting had stopped, but it had stopped because the side of the building was blown out and collapsing. The building material might have been fireproof but it sure as hell wasn't grenade proof and the mess was coming down all around them.

Hastin saw Oliver go down and his feet stopped moving. Ame shoved him out of the collapsing area and he fell, too. Scraped and cut, but not really hurt.

Rosa was neither frozen nor afraid. She ran to where Oliver had fallen, hefted the concrete off of him and dragged him to his feet. He couldn't stand, his eyes fluttering and rolling back as he tried. There was blood in his hair.

Ame was pulling Hastin up, too and by then there were more gunshots. He had one arm hooked over her shoulder and pulled himself closer to her to pivot so he could shoot over her. He stumbled as they moved, his knee flaring in sudden pain, but she held him up and he kept shooting. His aim didn't waver and the gunshots soon stopped.

Ame and Rosa dragged the two of them out, piling them both into another unmarked car. Whereas before they had been comfortable enough to sit in the dark, they hit the light immediately on entering to check on their injuries.

Hastin was bruised and cut up. Ame had a few marks, but nothing serious.

Oliver was bleeding from a cut on his head, and he lolled against Rosa's side, unresponsive.

17:

"I leave you alone for one night and look at the trouble you get into," Yoru teased Dan as he cooked.

"Trouble!" Dan said, sounding offended. "For two cripples, we did great."

"Neither of you are crippled," Yoru said patiently. "You, my friend, have a long term injury. Rusty is a few fingers short of a pair of hands. Neither of you are incapable. As you've proven."

"Does this mean you'll make this spicier than last time?" Rusty asked, raising an eyebrow at him.

It surprised a laugh out of Dan, who was pretty sure that was the first almost-joke he had heard her make, but Yoru was as gracious as ever.

"Anything your heart desires, honey," he said, with a smile that easily disarmed her pride.

Dan laughed at that, too.

"Why does he do that?" she asked him, hissing the words quietly as he went back to cooking.

"Couldn't tell you. It's just how he is," Dan said. What use did a thief had for being so...whatever he was, Dan didn't know. But it sure made being his friend into one hell of a ride.

"So, you said you got us an entrance to the terminal. What's the deal?" Yoru said. He turned and leaned against the counter, looking at the two of them. With no living area to speak of, the kitchen was just where they collected when they didn't want to hide in one of the two adjacent bedrooms.

"Cracked the lock, took out one? Of the cameras—" Dan looked to Rusty who held up two fingers, "Two. Two cameras. And killed the motion sensor on the one door," he said.

"What a laundry list," Yoru said, that same warm smile.

"I feel like I'm being condescended to," Dan said, not being entirely serious.

"Am I not allowed to be proud of you?" Yoru teased. "Look, what could be better for me to hear than the two of you getting bored and deciding to do something productive? That's wonderful! For us as a group and for both of you individually. I couldn't be happier."

147

"You're like...a strange dad," Rusty said, scowling at him with an expression that was only partly sour.

Dan coughed but Yoru beamed. "Am I a hot dad, though?" he asked, laughing.

Rusty didn't answer him but Dan thought he saw her smile, just a little. While they were eating, Xueying reappeared from wherever she had been hiding to eat with them.

"So what, we go do all the hard work and as soon as there's food, you show back up?" Dan teased her.

"Basically," Xueying agreed. She later explained that she had been working on some logistical stuff for the job, but it was all handled. It was no more or less than Dan had expected, really, though Yoru still hadn't offered much in the way of explanation for his own vanishing act.

"I'm actually thinking of going back to that terminal tonight," Xueying said. "I'd like to take a peek around at the security myself and see if we can't make our lives even easier. What do you guys think?"

"Dan and I are busy," Yoru said casually, guiding a helping of food into his mouth and not looking up from what he was eating. Dan wasn't shy about the look he shot him.

"What do you mean, we're busy?" he asked.

"The kind of busy where we keep our clothes on, probably," Yoru added, but smiled. "I've got some news, that's all. They can go work and I can get you caught up."

Judging from his lackadaisical response, it was good news. Dan elbowed him, also smiling, and kept eating. He'd wait and see what Yoru had up his sleeve.

"That leaves us to go cause some trouble. You in?" Xueying asked Rusty.

"I am supposed to let you go alone?" Rusty questioned.

"You don't have to come. It's not like this is official business or anything," Xueying reminded her. "I'm just being nosy. I want to see what you have been up to."

"I better be there to show you, then," Rusty reasoned.

That seemed to settle it. They'd split up for the night, but at least this time everyone would know where the others were.

"Maybe you shouldn't run off," Xueying said to Rusty as they headed to the computer terminal. "If you had gotten hurt, we wouldn't have been able to find you."

"I wasn't stupid enough to go alone," Rusty said to her.

148

It was sort of nice to walk in the dark together. The air wasn't exactly fresh, but it was fresher and it was quiet and calm. It was good to see Rusty on her feet and doing things, and nice to hear about her talking to other people besides Xueying.

"You've been getting along with Dan," she noted.

"He's okay. The other one is obnoxious."

Xueying laughed. "A little bit. He does it on purpose to try and make people smile."

Rusty frowned, but she nodded. "He is amusing."

It wasn't a far jaunt to the building and Rusty showed Xueying where they had broken the lock and worked the bottom slat open.

"They'll replace that eventually, I think, but I'm a fair lockpick so we should be okay when they do..." She held the metal plate up and Rusty worked her way inside, only to return the favour so that Xueying could do the same.

"Those two cameras are gone," she said, pointing to the wall. There was a faint emergency light and although Xueying carried a flashlight, she didn't want to risk a sign on the other cameras, not yet.

"What about the motion sensor? Didn't someone mention one?"

"Here." Rusty pointed it out to her. "It would have gone off when we started pulling on the metal to get it open, but it is broken. Dan did... something."

"Yeah, he does that, apparently," Xueying said. "He's got something going on with him. I'm not really sure the whole story there."

"Your friend didn't tell you?"

"For someone who likes to talk so much, he loves his secrets." She sighed. "Do you think you can get to that camera without it seeing you?" Xueying asked Rusty, looking over to one higher up on the wall.

"I'm not much of a climber. I can lift you," she said simply. "This way, we'll go around it."

They worked their way around, hugging the wall as to hide in the shadows and not be seen by the camera. Like Rusty had said, she had no trouble lifting Xueying up so she could get to the wires behind the camera.

"What are you doing?"

"Giving us a line in. While I was out, I picked up a leech for us. Now we'll be able to see what the camera sees. That way we'll know if they set up anything new before we come back."

Rusty helped her down again and Xueying stumbled when her feet hit the ground, grabbing Rusty's bandage-wrapped hand to steady herself.

"Whoops. There we go—" She got her footing again and then

149

stopped for a moment, looking at Rusty's hands; the one she was holding and the one she wasn't.

"How have they been doing?"

"Well enough to lift you up," Rusty noted.

"We can probably take the braces off tomorrow, if they're feeling okay," Xueying said hopefully.

"We could probably do it tonight, but—" Rusty shrugged.

"I just don't want to push it. You're already healing way faster than we thought," she said with a smile. "We don't want to hurt them again."

"You never told me what that medicine cost," Rusty pointed out.

"It's part of the job. They hurt you because you were coming with us, so..." It was Xueying's turn to shrug.

"Better for me to run now, then. They would have stabbed me in the back eventually," she said.

"Well, we can't do that because we need you, so at least you know you're safe with us," Xueying said as she surveyed the room again, looking for other possible precautions they could take.

"Is that the only reason I can trust you?"

"Somehow I didn't think appealing to your emotions was going to work," the pink-haired woman said with a wry smile.

"You want me to trust you because you like me," Rusty guessed as they worked their way out of the building again. Xueying didn't answer until she too pulled herself under the door and stood up to dust herself off.

"I wouldn't have offered you the job if I didn't like you," she said.

"I haven't had a chance to do my job since then."

"You will," Xueying reassured her. "There's no such thing as a violence-free job down here. It's just a matter of time."

Xueying's hand brushed Rusty's as they walked.

"We'll take them off tonight?" she said. When their hands brushed again she hooked her fingers through Rusty's. "If they're achey, we can always put them back on, right?"

Rusty glance down to where their fingers were linked, but she didn't pull her hand away. "I can live with that," she said.

They walked together, quiet in the dark. When they got back, true to her word, Xueying helped Rusty unwind the bandages from her fingers.

~*~

When Rusty and Xueying went on their adventure, Dan turned to Yoru as soon as he heard the door close. "What's the deal?" he asked. His tone was sharp, but not upset.

"Cutting right to the chase, I see," Yoru teased him. As Dan had done many times before, he hopped up to sit on the counter while he talked to his friend.

"Hey, you've kept me in the dark for way too long."

Yoru regained his seriousness and he looked to Dan. "Do you remember the promise I didn't make to you?"

And Dan did. Immediately, he remembered as though it had been moments ago and not weeks.

"The phone call," he said calmly.

"I got it." Yoru smiled at him. Not his show-off smile. A sincere one, a little one. "That's where I disappeared to. And I'm sorry to have run off on you like I did. You know I hate doing that."

"I'm not a little kid," Dan told him gently. "I don't need to be babysat. You didn't abandon me," he reminded him. Yoru seemed a little reassured at that.

"I went to go talk to a few tech-savvy friends of mine, and whenever we're ready, they can set us up with a line to make the call right from my own vidscreen. There's a couple of rules but...we should be able to make to make it happen without any big trouble."

Dan took a deep breath that ended up being a little shakier than he had originally planned.

"What are the rules?"

"We have about a half an hour. If someone is trying to track us, it'll take them about that long to try and do it. As long as we've hung up before then, we should be off the hook."

"How sure are you about that time?" Dan asked. He frowned a little. "I really, really don't want to lead this trouble back to them."

"My best lady said she couldn't do it in half an hour. That means whoever they have will take longer. Half an hour is our cut off, to keep both us and them safe," Yoru said.

"I can do that. Half an hour is plenty of time to tell her I'm not dead." He nodded. "But you look like there's something more than that."

"It's a smaller thing, but something I think you might need to consider," Yoru said.

"What's that?"

"She might not answer the phone," Yoru said. "Not out of any malice, there's lots of reasons people miss calls, but I don't want you to be heartbroken if it doesn't work the first time," he explained.

Dan sighed in relief. He thought it had been something more serious than that. "That's not something I had thought of, actually," he said. "You're right, there's a good chance I would have gotten really...over-worked about it." It wasn't exactly the word he was looking for, but Yoru didn't look confused, so he continued. "If it doesn't work...I'll just try again, right?"

"If it does work, you can try again, too," Yoru said with a grin. "It's not like this is the last phone call you get to make. We just have to take the time to set them up. I just..." It was his turn to sigh. "I know it's going to be rough even if it goes perfectly. I just don't want you to have to worry about anything that doesn't actually need to be worried about."

That was an understatement. Dan wasn't sure he was in any position to even begin thinking about all the issues he had or would have about this call. Maybe it was better not to get too much into the icky details. He wasn't even sure that it would help it. It might just be better to face the problem at hand.

"I think...I've got some issues," he said, with a little laugh. "And maybe I always will. But I want to do it, and I think I can. But you're right, it's gonna be a hell of a night."

"For sure."

"Would you, um—" Dan ran a hand through his short, dark hair and looked up at Yoru, a little embarrassed. "Would you stay with me for the call?"

"Are you sure?" Yoru said. "I had thought that you might need your space for something like this. I don't want you to feel overwhelmed."

Dan nodded. "You know, I thought that for a second but...I really don't want to do this alone."

"I would never make you."

A smile tugged on Dan's lips. "I know. So, you'll stay, then?"

"Right by your side," Yoru reassured him. "The whole time."

Dan nodded. "Okay. Then I think I can do it. I know I can...although we should probably do it sometime soon before I lose my nerve."

Yoru laughed, then. "What about tomorrow night? I am sure I can talk the others into going out for a little while and leaving us to it. We don't need tons of time, and I'm sure they'd understand."

"Yeah, sorry, you have to not be in the house while Dan is an emotional wreck, thank you," Dan joked.

"Something like that," Yoru said, giggling.

"Tomorrow night. Wow. Okay." Another deep breath. "And no need to get worked up in case it's for nothing. I don't think I can manage that."

"Then get worked up," was Yoru's sensible reply. "You don't need to be useful for the next twenty-or-so hours."

"I don't know if I even could be."

Yoru waved away his concern. "Look, we have time. You're not delaying us, or somehow impeding the job. It's going to be okay."

Dan nodded.

"Okay. Okay. Yeah. I can do this."

Over breakfast the next morning, Yoru broke the news to them.

"Kicking you kids out tonight for like an hour," he said nonchalantly.

"Oh?" Xueying asked. "Like this is your safe-house."

"I know, right? The attitude on me," he agreed. "But I gotta. It's not for long. An hour is tons of time. Go get drinks, go out for dinner, whatever your beautiful hearts desire, my Xueying. But I need an hour."

"And Dan?"

"I need Dan, too," he added. "Go to the arcade or something. Celebrate the fact that Rusty has fingers now."

"I had them before."

"If they're not working, are they still fingers?" he asked, nonsensically. She looked at him with that deadpan way she had and he kept talking. "It really isn't that big of a deal. I'm sure if you guys have work to do we can work around it. It would just be...a little easier," he explained.

Xueying looked to Dan, who had been suspiciously silent. "Dan, what do you think?"

He sighed. "I... Well..." He sighed again."It would make my life a little easier. I'm sorry for making things complicated. It's not that big of a deal but like... I'm sure you guys don't want to have to hear it," he said, without ever explaining what it was.

It didn't cross his mind to elaborate, and perhaps in respect for how uncomfortable he felt, neither of them asked for clarification.

Xueying reached over and gave his arm a squeeze and then nodded. "It's okay. I'm sure we can give you the time you need. An hour, you said?"

"That should be it."

"Not a problem. We can kill an hour, right, Rusty?" she asked.

"Is that an invitation to spend that hour with you?" Rusty answered.

Xueying might have blushed just faintly. "Um, yeah. That's exactly what it is."

That seemed to settle it. Dan's stress skyrocketed through the day but the others mostly let him be. Yoru made sure he ate, and sometimes pressed a cup of tea into his hands to see if he couldn't calm down for a couple minutes.

"I don't think he is okay," Rusty said bluntly to Yoru when he was pouring another drink for his friend.

"No, he isn't. Are you?" he asked, matter-of-factly.

She looked at him, and Yoru met her eyes without flinching.

"Maybe...not so much."

"Maybe all of us not so much," he answered calmly. "We're allowed to not be okay, Rusty. All of us. Especially if the worst it taxes the team is that he wants some quiet before doing something hard. Surely you've been there."

She glanced around the room quickly. No one in the kitchen but them.

"Before fights, sometimes," she said. "The quiet, it... It can be nice. It helps me feel ready."

"He faces the same daunting prospects," Yoru told her. "But some problems are not so easily forced into submission as some people are."

"Some people aren't so easy, either," she pointed out.

He laughed, then, and with a teacup in each hand he leaned over and pressed a brief kiss to the point of her shoulder. "See, you understand."

18:

They dragged Oliver into the house and while Ame laid him down and started cleaning him up, Rosa was on the phone with a friend of theirs to come by and give him a look. It wasn't the worst injury Ame had seen. It bled a lot, but most head wounds did. Oliver was pretty out of it but not too bad. He'd talk if Ame talked to him and pressured him to answer. He sat up on his own as she cleaned him up, held bandages in place where she pressed his hand to them. He wasn't so far gone as to be useless.

But he was in pain, and he was tired. He slept. They woke him up when the doctor came by and the result was reassuring; the cut wasn't bad, and he'd heal up just fine with the bandages Ame had on him. That was a relief to her. She'd stitched a head before, but wasn't exactly looking forward to a repeat performance. On the other hand, the doctor said that the concussion meant it was going to take a couple of days before he was back up to speed.

"The problem with concussions isn't that they kill you. They accumulate." The doctor leaned in the bedroom door with her arms crossed as she talked to Rosa. "He'll be fine in a week, but he can't keep getting hit in the head or that won't happen. He's going to sleep a lot, but get whatever food and water in him you can."

"So, basically, he's a houseplant for a few days," Ame surmised.

"He'll actually be a houseplant if it keeps happening," she said. "Let him sleep, he needs it. If he's not on his feet in three or four days, call me. Don't let him work for at least a week."

They agreed and paid her. She left. Oliver had fallen asleep quickly after that. At least now they knew it was safe to leave him that way.

In all of this, Hastin said nothing. Did nothing. He sat on the floor of Oliver's room, his back to the corner, his huge eyes fixated on where Oliver lay in his bed.

With no time to worry over him until the doctor left, Ame and Rosa let him be for the first little while. He just sat there, his knees pulled up in front of him with his arms resting over top, his hands tight where they held each other. He waited there, unmoving and unspeaking from the minute they got Oliver into the room. Ame hadn't needed his help with the first aid, seeing as Oliver was able to do that part on his own, so no one had called on him. He barely blinked, not reacting when the stranger came or when she left, not getting up when Ame threw out the armful of bloody bandages they had already ruined while she was getting a proper one tied where it needed to be.

And the first time Rosa called to him, trying to coax him into the bathroom to clean up his cuts, he didn't answer.

Ame came to him then, some blood still streaked on her hands when she knelt down in front of him. "Come on, honey. Let's get you cleaned up. You must be tired."

He didn't look at her at first. It took a long second for him to pull his eyes from Oliver's bed to where she was in front of him, and when he did he merely blinked for a minute, as if confused to see her.

"Come on." She held her hand out to him. "You're all cut up. We have to take care of them."

He took her hand and she pulled him to his feet. He moved easily, lightly, on autopilot. As though the pain of his injuries didn't exist. As though the ache in his joints from the way he sat had disappeared. He didn't stumble when she tugged him forward, his feet crossing the floor to the bedroom door. He stepped through it.

And then, all at once, he pulled his hand from hers, turning and running back to Oliver's bedside. The tears were sudden and overwhelming. He fell to his knees next to the bed, his arms folded on top of it, and he cried. Awful, ragged sobs that tore their way out of his chest as tears flooded down his face.

For a moment, Ame didn't react. The breakdown had been so sudden and so severe that she couldn't immediately process what was going on.

But he sounded like he was in so much pain. It didn't take her long to snap back to her senses.

"Oh, babe, no…" She got to him just as Rosa stuck her head in the door as well.

"Is he—?"

Ame cut her off before she could finish, shaking her head. She wrapped her arms around Hastin's shoulders to try and pull him off the bed and into her lap. It wasn't exactly an easy task, but she managed it. He collapsed against her, still crying.

Rosa sat down next to Ame. Hastin didn't stir when she did, his hands pressed to his face as he drew from a seemingly endless well of tears.

Ame, sitting there with her arm around him, could clearly remember the last time she had cried. It was from a cute movie, and Rosa had made fun

156

of her for it, but she wasn't that embarrassed.

She didn't think that the circumstances had probably been the same for him. This was the same boy who had so casually and calmly offered to murder their informant and who had no problems scoping out their apartment or showing Ame what was up his skirt.

All of these thoughts went by very quick before she decided on one simple thing. Her night wasn't done yet.

"It's okay, babe, it's okay... Shhh..." She kissed his forehead and brushed her fingers through his hair.

Glancing at the bed she saw Oliver stir, so she leaned her head to talk to Rosa. "Hey, can you...?"

"On it."

Rosa got up and Ame let her go to Oliver, where she would undoubtedly explain to him that despite the noise, everything was actually under control and he should go back to sleep.

That let her keep her attention on Hastin.

"You're safe, you're safe... We're here, okay? I'm here..."

Eventually the tears stopped but the sobbing didn't. She took him by the hands and walked him through his breathing. "Here, with me, like this..."

Rosa stayed with them. When the hysterics stopped, she was the one to get the first aid kit so they could clean him up.

He looked shell-shocked, almost. Red-eyed and stricken, tear stains on his cheeks and neck, patches of colour flared in his cheeks. That same sort of stunned, pained looked in his eyes.

"You want a drink, honey? I can get you one."

But he shook his head, his hands tightening in hers, pulling her closer so he could press his face into her shoulder.

"Okay... I'm not going anywhere..."

But she did trade spots with Rosa. The taller woman didn't seem to mind when it was her turn for Hastin to lean on her so Ame could clean him up. The injuries weren't serious, a few cuts and scrapes, but if you didn't clean them then Ame knew they would get all sticky and gross and that was the worst.

Rosa rested her head on his, and it was in her arms that his eyes finally flickered closed. Not asleep, not from the way his hands kept tightening and releasing. But finally, finally quiet. Rosa's hand rubbed his shoulder, reassuring him in what way she could.

"I was supposed to protect him..." he said eventually. His voice was rough and he coughed when he spoke. "I told him... I told him I would keep

157

him safe... I... I..."

"And how many people did you kill that were trying to kill him?" Rosa asked him quietly.

But Hastin shook his head. "No, no... I... I fucked up... I was the one who... I brought it all down."

"You closed the path," Rosa said.

Ame gave a snort of quiet laughter. "If I remember right, someone fell on his stupid fucking face and almost died. Darling, oh, love, that isn't your fault." Smiling a little, Ame took his hand in hers. "When he wakes up, I'm going to make fun of him for almost getting killed because he doesn't know how to walk."

Hastin pouted at her. She didn't think it was on purpose. "No..."

"We asked you to shut it down. You did," Rosa said simply. "It was an accident. There's always the threat of something unforeseen on a job. Especially a job like this where we were in a hurry."

Hastin sat up a little, but he didn't move from where he was next to Rosa and neither did he take his hand from Ame now that she had picked it up. "It can't. It can't. If that happened before I'd... They'd..."

Rosa felt rather than saw the breath lock up in his chest again but Ame pressed her hand over his heart. "Breathe now, babe, come on..."

He did. He pressed his hand over hers and breathed in and out, in and out until it came a little easier again. "I... I don't even care what they'd do," he said then, bitterness in his voice and in the scowl on his lips. "I don't care. But he..." He glanced over to the bed.

"He will be fine. You heard what Zaila said. It's a concussion. He just needs to sleep. You've had a concussion before at some point, I'm sure," Ame pointed out.

"Oh... I don't know. I've been hit in the head before," Hastin said quietly. "But, um, sometimes I don't go out after. And sometimes I do pass out, but it's for like...days. I think the IV keeps me under, but..." He shook his head. There was an edge to him, still. Sometimes, he'd blink and more tears would roll down his cheeks, but he didn't seem to be really, truly crying anymore.

"Okay, well, I've definitely been concussed," Ame said. "And you get like, nauseated, like your stomach gets all fucked up because your eyes don't work. And you're really tired. It's just sucky. But it'll go away in a few days. He just needs rest."

Hastin sighed. It was followed by the first, real, steady deep breath and he leaned back against Rosa again. Comfortably, she put her arm around him.

"I... I'm really sorry for...all that," he said.

"It sounded like you needed it," Rosa said. Her tone was warmer than the words it held. "Sometimes, in this work, I think we all need it."

"I just... I was really upset, that I made a mistake and that I made him get hurt... Um..." Hastin looked down at his hands. "I mean... I know we're supposed to be a team and work together, but I... I'm a little more invested than that. I think I have to be honest... I probably would have reacted like that for either of you, too..."

"You're allowed to care about people! Fucking hell." Ame laughed. "You have to, in this job. If you don't care about people, it makes you crazy, baby. You gotta have feelings. People look at this work and they think that you have to be cold and no, no, that's not how this shit works."

"It's a hard life. You have to take care of yourself. That means making friends," Rosa said. "And sometimes, it means crying your eyes out."

Hastin nodded and his eyes slipped closed again. Rosa's breathing was deep and even and calming. Ame still held his hand. Nearby, his Captain slept. Healing.

There was an ache in his chest, but it wasn't all-consuming. Not anymore. Like a bruise, tender to the touch. No longer the jagged pain of a knife wound.

It was quieter and gentler, and it was going to be okay.

"Do you...think it would be okay if I stayed in here tonight?" Hastin asked them, sitting up.

"I was going to do it, so I am sure it would be okay if you did," Rosa said.

He nodded. "You should rest. Not only did you just do the same work we did, but...both of you took care of us after all of it. I'll stay with him. In case he needs anything, or if he gets sick, like you said, Ame."

"I'll get you a bucket. And you'll drink some water," She said, firmly. "Do that for me, and you can stay in here."

He smiled at her and nodded eagerly. "Yes! I will!"

Rosa convinced him to change into something more comfortable, and true to her word Ame made him drink a big glass of water.

"When you cry out your whole soul like that, you need to drink water after. It really dehydrates you," she said.

"Do I have a soul?" he asked her, curiously.

"Oh, probably. I think most people do," she said.

He nodded, taking her word for it as he drank.

Hastin took his spot at Oliver's bedside again, but this time there were no tears. He laid his arms on the blanket and rested his head on them, watching his Captain where he slept.

"You going to be okay? I can get you a chair," Rosa offered.

"No, it's okay," Hastin said. "Goodnight, Rosa!"

Rosa went to bed. She really was tired, and hadn't been looking forward to staying up if it had turned out she had to. The sleep was welcome, and she woke up the next morning feeling significantly better. When she pulled herself out of bed to make coffee, she was surprised to meet Hastin in the kitchen. She recognized him by the sound of his steps, and when he spoke it was in a hushed, early morning voice.

"Good morning!"

"Good morning to you, too, sunshine," she said, a little wryly. He sounded much better than the day before.

She went through her usual routine of setting up the coffee maker, and she had the very specific suspicion that Hastin was trying to get up the will to say something. Eventually, she was proven right.

"I really wanted to thank you for yesterday. For taking care of me," he said. "Could...I give you a hug?"

Rosa had been thanked for a lot of things in a lot of ways, but this one made her smile, "Sure," she said, opening her arms.

He hugged her tightly, his head resting against her shoulder. Rather than let him go, she stood with him and leaned comfortably against the counter until the coffee maker went off.

"You want some of your own coffee this time?" she asked.

"Okay. And maybe I'll share it with the Captain when he wakes up," Hastin said cheerfully.

Rosa poured them both some and before long, roused from her slumber by the smell of caffeine, Ame joined them. Hastin hugged her, too.

"Oh, any time, kid. And next time we watch a kids movie together and I end up a crying wreck, you can take care of me," she said.

He agreed to that with enthusiasm.

Hastin waited on Oliver every moment he could. The first day wasn't very exciting. Oliver sat up a little and had some water. Later, he managed to eat something and keep it down.

"Honestly, I'm a little impressed with myself," he joked, lying back against his pillow. "But as long as I keep my eyes closed, it isn't so bad."

"I can be your eyes until they work again," Hastin said gently, sitting at the edge of his bed.

160

"Too bad you can't be my feet, or maybe I wouldn't be in this situation." Oliver managed a bit of a smile. "What a jackass I am. I can't believe falling on my face almost got me killed."

"You're safe..." Like Ame had done for him, Hastin pressed a hand to Oliver's cheek. "Everything is okay now."

And that night, like the night before it, Hastin slept at the side of his bed. Oliver slept with his hand on Hastin's arm.

The next day, true to his word, Hastin was Oliver's eyes to help him into the shower and back to bed. Anything he wanted, Hastin was quick to get for him.

"You're too good to me, hun," he said, when Hastin returned to his side with more food.

"I don't think that's a thing that can happen, Captain," he replied.

"Your knees have got to be killing you from sleeping on them all the time," he pointed out. "I think the worst of it has passed. You don't have to keep doing that."

"I feel bad for what happened. And..." He hesitated. "I know I hate recovering in bed alone."

Oliver made a noise of agreement, and then he tried to sit up and start moving things around in his bed. Lightly panicked and more than a little curious, Hastin quickly stopped him.

"No, Captain, you're not supposed—What are you doing?"

"Moving my pillows..." He took the ones he was lying on and shoved them over to the far side of the bed, where he resumed lying on them.

"There. Now there's room for both of us, if you go get your pillow from your bed." He laid down again, feeling victorious. The moving wasn't so bad, but the head turning back and forth hadn't been a real great time. He was going to need a few minutes.

When he heard nothing in reply, though, he cracked his eyes open to see Hastin sitting there, wringing his hands and looking at him.

"What's wrong, kid?" he asked.

"Are you sure?" Hastin frowned and Oliver watched as he made himself stop fidgeting. "I mean...it's your bed..."

"It's a little squished, but we can both fit. It's gotta beat losing the feeling in your legs every night," Oliver pointed out.

"You mean it?"

Oliver closed his eyes but smiled, and reached out to touch Hastin's arm. "Yes. I do. I'd be happy for the company. You're right. Recovering alone is terrible."

Hastin slept on his bed for the next few nights. He didn't take any of Oliver's blankets, despite the other man's offer, and though it did get a little cold sometimes, he was happier to sleep there than anywhere else in the world.

19:

Rusty and Xueying did decide to go to the arcade.

"Look, I didn't have a childhood, and Rusty has hands that work now, so fucking right we're going to the arcade," Xueying said. "I'm an adult, I can do what I want."

Were he feeling more himself, Dan was sure he would have asked her to elaborate. As it was, he was sufficiently distracted that he barely heard what she said. Neither was he in any position to argue with her about what sort of things adults did or didn't do. Really, in some ways...he almost wished he could go, too, instead of doing what he had to do.

"This job has not been an incredibly fun one," Yoru pointed out. "I will not be sad to hear that you two had a good night."

"And you two?" Rusty asked.

"We will have a night of some kind, I'm sure." But that was all he would say of it.

They left, and the sudden silence of the apartment seemed deafening.

Dan sat on Yoru's bed in their room, his back against the wall, the other man's vidscreen in his hand. The bed had been tidily made, unlike Dan's that was across from it. The single window in the room let in dull, muted moonlight that was burned out into nothing by the bright bulb on the ceiling. Yoru sat down next to him.

"So?"

Dan didn't answer immediately. "I... I'm going to call her. And there's a couple of less than stellar possibilities. The number could be wrong, maybe they've changed it, or she could not answer me," he said. He almost sounded as if he was reciting it. Reminding himself that other possibilities were out there.

"And if those happen?"

"Then I'll call her back. Or I'll find the number. But I have to remember that tonight doesn't make or break anything. There will be other times."

"Right." Yoru leaned against his shoulder. "Are you ready?" he asked.

Dan laughed, but it was mostly just air. "No. Not at all. But I'm going to do it."

He didn't immediately. He held the phone in his hand for a few moments more, taking deep breaths and just trying to calm his heart in his chest. How long had it been? He wasn't certain of the last day he remembered, and he wasn't sure of the last time he had called home. Looking back, he had lost more than a year, but...how much more? That was where things started to get a little fuzzy.

He didn't remember when he had lost his hand, either. There was a lot still missing, but maybe those pieces didn't mean as much as the pieces he was making now.

Dan took a deep breath and looked over at his friend. "Here goes nothing, right?" he asked. He handed the vidscreen to Yoru, not trusting himself to hold it.

Yoru's smile was reassuring, as it always was. Either tonight was going to be nothing or it was going to be, well, everything. But at least Dan didn't have to do it alone.

He nodded, and Dan hit the call button.

In the unbelievably tense seconds that followed, he grabbed Yoru's hand and squeezed it tight. He had tried to prepare himself for the wait but nothing had prepared him for how little he seemed to be able to breathe or how his vision narrowed to just the vidscreen, as though there was nothing else in the world.

And then, the call picked up. Dan's grip tightened, but Yoru's hand that held the screen was unwavering. The woman on the other end was young, dark-haired and tired-looking. She had an inherent pleasantness to her already, Yoru thought. The same kind he felt from Dan.

"Malee!" he said. His image loaded, his voice called out, and the girl at the other end nearly dropped the screen she was carrying.

She swore. So did he. Then, he started crying, and she started screaming for her mother.

Dan let go of Yoru's hand. It was red where he had been gripping it, but his friend said nothing. A flurry of activity on the screen and another face came into view. Older than Malee. Older than Dan. He pressed a hand to his mouth, sobbing a word through his fingers that Yoru could still understand.

Mom.

"It's me, Mom. It's me. I'm here..." He coughed, trying to string a coherent sentence together. His mother was crying, too.

"Dan! Oh, god. Where are you? Where are you? They told us you died. The army, they told us—"

"I ran away," Dan said. Then he shook his head. "No, no, I was rescued. My friend, he rescued me." He pointed at Yoru. "Mom, we don't have a lot of time. I don't have long. God, I miss you... I miss you so much..."

"Where are you? Are you safe? What happened?" Yoru could follow along the conversation well enough. He knew enough Syaman to figure most of it out. Deciphering it from the crying, now, that was the real challenge.

"I can't tell you." Dan shook his head. "I can't tell you where I am. I'm still running. I... I might always be running."

"No!" Her turn to shake her head. "No, you have to come home! You have to come home. You can't—"

Her plaintive cries were cut off by another voice. A girl's voice. There was some reshuffling and now the video showed them three faces. Three women, all black-haired and brown eyed like Dan.

Dan hiccuped sadly when he saw the third face. "Hey, Preeda, hey... Missed you, kid, I've missed you all so much, I—"

Yoru wrapped his arm around Dan's shoulder as he cried. They were tears of relief and of fear. It worked, it worked, but would it work again? And when? And how could he stand to be so far from home?

Dan's breaths were shaking and he tried to compose himself a little before he spoke again.

"I can't come home, Mom. They're still looking for me," he said. He was a little slower now, a little more coherent. "And if I take too long to talk, they're going to trace my call and we'll both be in trouble... But I'm okay." He nodded, as if trying to convince them and himself.

"I'm free now. I have a place to sleep, I have a job. I..." He faltered. "I think about you all the time. Please, please tell me you're okay. I've been so worried..."

"Take a deep breath, okay?" Yoru murmured, quiet enough that the mic wouldn't pick it up. "Take your time, we still have plenty left..."

"Who are you?" the older of the girls, the one Dan had called Malee, asked.

And, using the best words he knew, Yoru answered. "My name is Yoru. Dan asked me if I'd stay with him for the call. I'm very honoured to meet all of you." He bowed his head. "I wish the circumstances were kinder."

"He's my friend," Dan said. Yoru looked shy, as though upset he had said anything, and Dan kept talking. "No, I want you to meet them. Yoru, Malee and Preeda are my sisters. Preeda can beat me up and Malee is smarter than I am..."

A small, aching smile on his lips. It was mirrored on theirs.

165

"He's more organized than me," Malee said. "And he's better behaved than Preeda." The younger sister started to argue, but it didn't last.

Yoru smiled. It was hard not to.

"My mother, Naiyana."

"Yennie is fine," she said, and he could see the tears falling from her eyes when she tried to smile for him. "You're a friend of my son? He's never been good at making friends..."

"He's my closest," Yoru said. "And there's more of us! Yennie, I promise you on my heart, he isn't alone out here."

Dan leaned against Yoru. It was easier to breathe there. "I still have some time. And I can always call again! I'm not sure when, but I will. I'm here. I'm... I'm still here..."

He rubbed at his eyes with his hands...or, his hand, and Yoru saw his mother's expression fall.

"Oh, Dan...your hand... What happened?"

He shook his head. "I don't know. I remember calling you from the camp. And then we went on patrol, and for a few days everything was fine. And then... I don't know. Everything gets really messed up. I was... Something was really wrong. When I woke up, I was very sick and hurt, and it was gone. Yoru rescued me, Mom. He pulled me out of there and took care of me."

His mother didn't answer. Preeda did.

"Dan! He's like... He's one of those princes from the books you used to read me!" she said.

Dan's laugh was embarrassed but blessedly unburdened. "He is. He is, though!" And this was so much easier to talk about. Blush rose in Dan's cheeks but it was colour, real colour in his pale face and his mother was glad to see it.

"Does that make you the princess?" Malee asked.

Dan answered without hesitation. "Yes. I was the princess and he rescued me. And I rewarded him with..."

"Your unfailingly pleasant company."

"Your friend is very well-spoken, Dan," Yennie said warmly.

"He cooks good, too. He's keeping me well fed," Dan said. "But enough of that. Tell me how you're doing. I've missed so much."

This was easier. The words came more freely and Dan could blink the tears out of his eyes to actually see them, his family.

"I decided not to join the army," Malee said. "I...guess that's a good thing, now. I'm back in school, and so is Preeda."

"When I'm done with school, I'm gonna come find you and we're going to go on adventures together!" Preeda insisted.

"That's still a long time away," Yennie told her daughter gently.

"Maybe by then…all this will have blown over. We can always hope," Dan said. "It sure as hell can't get much worse."

"Don't invite it to," Yennie cautioned him. "Bad luck will enter your life however it can. Do not give it reason to follow you."

Dan nodded, acquiescence to his mother's advice. "Maybe…maybe one day I will see you again. No. I know I will. I don't know when it will be, but one day I'll find a way to come home."

"We're just so happy you are alive," Yennie said.

"There was a funeral, and all kinds of people showed up," Malee told them.

"I guess since I died in the field they gave me a traditional showing," Dan said bitterly. "To hell with them. Bill them for my burial when I'm actually dead, the traitors."

"Hopefully it will be a while before that yet," Yennie told him gently.

Realizing what he had said, and to who, Dan nodded. "Yes, of course. I just… How could they do that? And who else have they done it to? I can't believe it…"

"All countries at war act like lives are nothing to them," Yennie said. "They take our young people and bring home caskets. I think it will be that way forever…"

"Wait, I can't tell anyone at school that you're alive?" Preeda said. "Because they'll get mad, right?"

Dan nodded. "Yeah. I'm still dead, okay? Shh. Our secret." He smiled at her.

"You're a ghost!"

"Don't talk about ghosts like that." Yennie brushed her fingers through Preeda's hair.

"Does this mean you can't play cello anymore?" Malee was frowning. "You can't do that with one hand."

Dan shrugged. "I don't have room for a cello right now. We move around too much. Maybe I can get it replaced with a bow. That would work."

"We could do that," Yoru told him, with a look that led Dan to believe he was being entirely serious.

This was nice. Knowing he couldn't go home was painful but this, just sitting here and talking… It lifted a huge weight from his shoulders.

"The time," Yoru pointed out to him quietly and Dan nodded, although his heart sank.

"I have to go," he told them.

167

"When can you call us again?" his mother asked.

"When can you see us?" Preeda added.

"I'm not sure." He swallowed hard and all at once, the tears started again. No sobs or coughing this time. He couldn't think to spare the time for it. Every second was too precious.

"I will call you again. I will. And if you don't answer, I'll just call back until I catch you at home. Don't worry about me. I'm okay. I'm going to be okay."

"Yoru." Yennie looked to him.

"Yes, ma'am," he answered.

"Thank you for saving my son. And...take care of him, please. For us." The three faces were squeezed together in the frame and he saw her put her arms around her daughters. "For all of us."

"I will."

"Suparat, I love you. I love you so much," she said. His sisters echoed the sentiment. They had started crying again, too.

"I love you, too. Be safe. Please, be safe."

It took all the strength he had to hang up. When he did, Yoru dropped the vidscreen and Dan pulled himself into Yoru's chest. He wasn't crying as hard this time, and not for the same reasons. It was the sheer amount of relief working its way out of his body.

They were alive. He was alive. He was loved.

And he wasn't alone. Not only was he here, buried in Yoru's arms where there was nowhere safer for him, but they knew that. They knew he was alive and in good care. The idea that they could have been worried about him or mourning him was just too much. But he could breathe a little easier now.

Or, he could when the tears finally quieted.

He shuddered, just laying against his friend and taking some time to catch his breath.

"That was rough..." he said, sounding exhausted.

"It was. But you did it!" Yoru brushed his fingers through Dan's hair. "How do you feel?"

"Can I say awful, and still feel better than I did?"

"Oh, certainly." Yoru nodded despite Dan not looking at him. "I think that's a perfectly reasonable answer, all things considered."

"Okay, then that's my answer. Because I feel like shit. But I also feel pretty great. I...might have to go throw up," he said suddenly.

"Probably from all the nerves." Yoru rubbed his back. "Lay with me until you decide you can't."

It didn't take much convincing, that was for sure.

"They seem like wonderful people," Yoru said into the quiet of the room.

"My sisters used to bother the heck out of me when I was growing up..." He sighed. "I guess siblings do that. But they really are great. I meant what I said. Preeda is a tough kid and Malee is brilliant. Sure, sometimes they ate the last of the leftovers or snooped through my room but... They're my sisters. And I do miss them."

"Your mother is very beautiful. You look a lot like her."

"Are you calling me pretty?" Dan asked, his cheeks marked up from crying and red around his eyes.

"Always, darling."

Yoru got him out of bed and into the shower. Dan was reluctant to move, but as soon as he stepped under the water he was thankful. He was definitely several levels of disgusting after all the crying he had done, and a shower made him feel a lot better.

And, for the first time, he could think of his family and smile. He scrubbed his fingers through his hair and found his mind wandering to the past, not to torment his fears or his guilt, but to think of happier memories. Doing homework in the kitchen with his sisters and his mom. Helping with groceries. Running around with Preeda on his back at the park.

Out of the shower, he threw some clean clothes on and found Yoru in their room again. He lounged against him and wasn't sad when the taller man started idly playing with his hair.

"What's it like to have sisters?" he asked.

Dan shrugged. "I can't really compare it to anything. I don't have any brothers, and I don't know what it would be like to grow up alone. Usually, I wanted to kill them. But as soon as someone else said something about them, that was too far. And they're both younger than me, so I guess I was pretty protective of them... We were a real handful for my mom, I'll tell you that."

"You were a bad kid?"

"Not...bad. But I was a kid. There were a lot of times I caused more trouble than was absolutely necessary." Dan laughed. "After my dad died, though, I really tried to settle down. I think that was where we fought the most, because I tried to get them to settle down, too, but they were younger and didn't really understand. They didn't mean it, though. They were kids! And we got along most of the time."

He felt Yoru sigh under him. "It sounds...different. But nice," he said.

"I mean, I can see how they bothered you, but to have your mother and your sisters… That sounds truly like a gift."

Dan nodded. "Yeah, some people end up with shitty families, but not me. That's why all of this was so rough, I guess. Because I love them, and I know they loved me, so I knew they must have been unhappy…"

He sat up then and looked at Yoru. "Thank you. I don't know what you had to do to get me that call, but I can't ever tell you how much it meant to me. Yoru…thank you."

"Your happiness thanks me enough," Yoru reassured him. "It always does."

20:

As the days passed, Oliver started being more and more independent. True to their word, they weren't exactly going to let him out of the house for that entire week, but that didn't mean they had to stay in, too.

A few days after he was up and walking around, Rosa sat Ame and Hastin down. "I have a job for you kids," she said. "Especially since you like working together so much." Not that anyone could really complain about that. In this business you just didn't always get chances to work with people who you liked. It was good to take them when you could.

"It's the best!" Hastin said.

Ame nodded. "Heck yeah. What do you need, lady? We'll get it for you."

"I need you to get this—" Rosa held up a memory card in between her fingers, "—into one of the computers at the data centre."

"Wait, if we're breaking in there now, don't you think we should all go?" Ame asked. She narrowed her eyes and looked at Rosa skeptically.

Rosa shook her head. "This isn't the end of the job. I need information on how their systems work. I just need you to slip this in. Any one of the computers should do it, as I should be able to look into the whole system from there. It's not powerful enough to extract what we need, I don't have a program that can do that on the fly without me there, but it can do some surveillance and broadcast it back to me."

"Sounds like something we can do," Ame said.

Hastin nodded. "That place isn't open to the public, but I do think we could slip in there during the day." He paused, thinking. " If we're quiet and can move fast enough, they might not even notice we're breaking the rules. Especially since we're not after anything specific."

"So, what... Business casual, look like we work there, see if we can't get to a computer and get the fuck out? Is that the deal?" Ame asked.

"Sounds like. Considering that I don't even need you to steal anything, it shouldn't be that hard." Rosa smiled. "So, how about it?"

"Well, fuck. I'll get dressed and we can go now," Ame said, pushing herself up from her seat.

"I'll get a comm from you?" Hastin asked Rosa brightly. "I know they drive Ame a little crazy to wear them."

She was more than happy to set him up.

They got dressed and headed out together, much like anyone else on a commute to work. It was still early, and Ame happily leaned on Hastin in the subway, squished between a thousand people all headed to the same kinds of places.

She thought, briefly, how much she would hate to have a day job.

It was a lot more natural to hook her arm through Hastin's as they walked, but that wouldn't really do much to lend credence to their costume so she didn't. She walked close to him, her mind mostly on how much she wanted another helping of breakfast as they climbed the steps up the building's front. They just couldn't ditch stone facade fronts in exchange for fucking escalators, at least not on the 'official' buildings. Someone had a love for tacky old architecture.

Okay, so Ame was a little grumpy. No real reason, she thought, just one of those days where an extra cup of coffee or a few extra minutes in bed would have been nice. Alternatively, her new favourite treatment was cozying up to Hastin.

They better get this job done, then, if she intended to pursue that.

"Watch a movie with me when we're done this bullshit?" she asked him under her breath.

Hastin's disinterested gaze almost threw her off, but he leaned a little closer to her and didn't bother disguising his voice. "I'd really like that a lot."

She had to try hard to hide her smile.

This also gave her a good chance to look around the building they'd later be breaking into and she wasn't going to waste that chance. She mentally marked how their predictions of the blueprints differed from actual security placements. Maybe it would help them figure out problems with their predictions through the rest of the establishment. After all, later on they'd be trying to get into places they really shouldn't be, and that job was going to take a lot longer. But this should help.

She followed the click of Hastin's heels across the tiled floor and found it fairly easy to keep a disinterested look on her face. Her tail was curled up under her skirt. It wasn't the kind of augmentation her secretary-esque persona would probably have. Corporate life bored her. Surely there were people doing the white-collar version of what they did. The kinds of professional thieves and scoundrels who kept their hands clean.

But where was the fun in that?

They needed a computer that was hooked up to the main system, but not one of the terminals that everyone would use. The card had to be left in there if it was going to work. Ame wondered briefly how much protection Rosa had taken to make sure that the disc couldn't be traced back to them, but it was more curiosity than suspicion. Ame wasn't the one with the technical knowledge so she had no way of figuring out what steps she might have taken.

But it was Rosa. She wasn't an idiot. It was going to work because everything she made worked.

"We should see if we can't get into those back offices," Hastin said under his breath. "Rather than go higher up in the building. Disable the alarm at the back door and just sneak out."

Made sense to Ame. Half the job of breaking rules in broad daylight was confidence and she had enough of that to spare. If you looked like you were supposed to be somewhere…people largely left you alone.

The key was to keep walking and to look like you knew where you were going. They wanted a floor-level office with maybe an open door, but definitely no one in it. They could deal with a locked door, but if it was already unlocked, that would be golden.

And if all the offices didn't have frosted fucking windows, that would have been great, too.

Oh well, they'd make do.

Hastin tried a door. Locked. He remedied that swiftly as Ame crossed her arms with feigned impatience. She recognized the hand motions. Pretending to have lost his keys, with his hands in the way of the camera. Sometimes the simplest tricks really did age the best.

He popped the lock and opened the door and when they stepped in, they closed it behind themselves.

The room was largely empty. A computer, a desk, a lamp. Either it was an unassigned office, or whoever used it was severely lacking in personality. Ame didn't know which one was more likely.

But it didn't have a camera in it, and when she hit the power button for the computer it started up soundlessly.

"Let's pop this thing in and be gone," she said, at least handling the first of those steps herself.

They left the office moments later and locked the door behind themselves. Whoever actually used it would have a key, but it might buy them a little more time of being able to snoop around their systems. It would at least deter people from randomly wandering in there and wondering why the computer was on.

173

Frosted windows or not, Ame had turned the computer screen off. They didn't need any nosy janitors wondering why the light was.

Now it was just a matter of getting the hell out of there. Once upon a time, businesses had to mark their exits. Ame supposed that was still technically true, but who the hell followed safety laws anymore? Not the city, that was for sure. Besides, when the fires started, it usually wasn't these buildings going down. No, the residences went up way easier.

They knew they had found a back door when it was alarmed, though. They had kept those, at least.

"Think you got it?" Hastin asked her.

"I gotta do something to earn my paycheck," Ame answered.

Alarm systems and her had a history, and this one didn't look entirely that complicated. The handy thing about suit jackets were that they made it so easy to carry tools with you, and she kept her back to the camera that might have been able to catch part of their location.

Suspicious, but not enough to have anyone running with their guns out.

"Just about got it," she said, and for a minute she was sure she had. And then she cut something and there was a sound sort of like a sigh from the overhead vents. She stopped, gave it a weird look, and kept working.

Until Hastin grabbed her arm and dragged her to the floor. "Knock-out gas. It's scentless. It must be so they can catch someone when they fuck with the alarms. But it's light, we'll have a few extra seconds down here," he explained in a rush. His eyes were looking up, as though he could pick out the colourless contaminant in the air. "Is the alarm offline enough for us to get out?"

She nodded. "Yeah, at least the sound is. I'm not sure if it will still ding the computer, but the gas might have done that anyway. Let's get the fuck out and let them deal with it."

They did, running outside through the door, mixing with the crowd before the door even fell closed behind them. Ame felt a little woozy but it was nothing bad. Now that they were out, she hung off of Hastin's arm without consequence.

"How did you know about the gas?" she asked him.

"I've been gassed a lot," he said, with a bit of a laugh. "You can't smell it or see it, but it has a different...texture, almost? And it takes longer to affect me than it used to, so I usually can see it coming."

"Huh."

She tucked that particular knowledge away for later. When they got back to the apartment, she had something different in mind.

"Hey, I still want to watch that movie with you, but will you come talk to me for a little before we do?" she asked Hastin.

He blinked those dark eyes at her. "Oh, yeah. Of course."

She sat him in the living room. And then she collected Rosa and Oliver.

"What's up? I should really be monitoring that program you set up for me," Rosa pointed out.

"I know, I know. And you can go back to it in just a minute. I don't think you like, have to be here for this. But Oliver does, and I thought maybe you'd want to see the start of it," Ame explained.

Oliver, looking particularly put on the spot, glanced at Ame with some discomfort.

"What's...going on, exactly?"

"We need to talk about Hastin." She stood with her hands on her hips, looking at the three of them. "Honestly, Oliver, I thought you'd be the one doing this, but—"

He rubbed at the back of his head. "Well, I thought about it, but, I mean, I didn't—"

"Didn't want to make it seem like it bothered us. Yeah, I get it," Ame said. "But by not saying anything, we make it sound like we don't notice or we don't care, and that's not cool."

Hastin, who had been listening, looked between the three of them in some confusion.

"Am I...in trouble?" he asked, looking concerned. "Did I do something wrong?"

"No, baby, no..." Ame shook her head. "You're fine. In fact, you're wonderful. Can you tell them what you told me about the gas?"

Hastin was fidgeting with his hands, looking down at them when he spoke. "So, the alarm system was wired into the vents. I guess they've had a break in before and wanted to catch anyone who might mess around with them... But Ame, you haven't worked with something like that, right? So she set it off accidentally. I knew what kind of gas it was, and we got a few extra seconds because the gas is really light and takes time to come down, and I pulled us closer to the floor..." He looked up at her. "Is that what you meant?"

"Yeah. You really saved our butts," Ame said. "Can you tell them what you told me, about how you learned that?"

"... Because... I've been gassed a lot...?" Hastin said. He looked between them again. "Usually when I'm being...uncooperative, I guess?"

"...Wow..." Oliver had pressed his hands to his face.

"Stop freaking out and sit with him—" Ame shoved Oliver's shoulder. "You can't direct this discussion, but I can, and it's going to be uncomfortable as shit, so get over there."

Oliver did. He stumbled to his feet and went to sit next to Hastin on the couch. Rather than fall against him as Hastin normally did, he sat there tense and unhappy until Oliver took his hands.

"Hey, honey, no... You're not in trouble, okay," he said quietly. "We're not upset with you. We care about you, and that's why we're worried when we hear about stuff like that."

"I don't want to cause any trouble," Hastin said. "I... It's kind of funny, actually. I don't get worried like this when I'm with them. I guess because, really, even if they do get upset with me... What else can they do?" He laughed a little, a high, unsteady sound. "But I... I really don't want to make anyone upset. I'm just really happy to be here and you're all so nice to me..."

Oliver put an arm over his shoulder and finally Hastin relaxed into him. "We know, hun, we know. We like you. And that's why we're worried about you."

"Hastin... Nothing you've done is wrong. What worries us is that someone has very obviously done wrong to you," Rosa said.

"I know," he said, shocking Oliver. "Or, I mean, I know they have. I figured that much out." He laughed a little at himself.

"You can talk to us about that stuff, you know," Ame said. "We're not going to get mad at you. We might get a little mad at them, but not at you."

Hastin squeezed Oliver's hand. "I... I never know what to say. I usually don't know I've said anything wrong until I see the way you guys look at me, and then I figure I said something that's not good."

"We're going to do that," Rosa pointed out. "Not because we're upset with you, but because it's usually a shock."

"When we were talking about how Oliver fucked himself up and you were blaming yourself for it—" Oliver looked at Ame sharply and she ignored him, "—you talked about what might happen if you did that back home and like... Okay, I wasn't surprised, but that's fucked up."

"That's not my home," Hastin said.

Ame laughed, then. She was the only one, but she did. "Good, fuck those guys. But you get what I'm saying. You can tell us what's going on. We'll listen."

"I... Well, I don't always know what happens," Hastin said. "I told you. They like to knock me out if I'm fighting too much. Sometimes I just wake up in

176

my room, but other times I wake up in the medical centre."

"What d'you end up there for?" Ame asked.

"Well, sometimes it's because I get hurt during training. That happens a lot. Why I end up there after they knock me out? I don't know. I'm usually out cold for most of it." He laughed.

"And, let me guess, things get rough when you screw something up?" Ame asked.

Hastin swallowed, then he nodded. "...Yeah."

"As someone who's been in the business since I could shoot, that's bullshit, basically," she answered. "They don't have to do that."

Hastin faltered a little. "I...don't think I learn as well as you do, maybe."

Ame frowned and shook her head. "That can't be true. I've worked with you. I know that's not how it works."

He hesitated then, looking as though he was going to ask something, but as they waited, nothing came.

"What is it?" Oliver prompted him gently.

"Some of the stuff that's happened, I... I don't understand why," he said. He looked at all of them. "There's been so much pain and so much... everything. Why? I don't understand. Just to turn me into this?" He looked down at himself. "What is this? What am I?"

"Those aren't things other people can answer for you," Oliver said. He understood immediately what Hastin was asking. Not about his clothes or his long hair or his pretty face. More than that. What was he? A person? Or something else?

"You have to understand... Some of what they did was almost certainly just to fuck with you," Rosa explained plainly. "To make sure you behaved, or to make you question yourself and your worth. That's how people like that work. They want to control you."

"I'm very good at playing pretend..." Hastin said slowly.

And then, with just as much caution in his voice and a quietly emerging twist of viciousness, Hastin kept speaking. "You know... They've spent a lot of time and money turning me inside out for their own purposes. And I know the prices they charge for my work... I wonder if I misbehave enough if I can run up a tab. It's the only thing they care about anyway."

"I mean, hit those motherfuckers where it hurts, but not at your own expense, babe," Ame said.

"We just want you to be safe." Oliver hugged Hastin tight to him.

A.N. Mouse

21:

"So, are we going to try and wrap this thing up tonight, then?" Yoru asked them.

"Already? Seems hardly worth the effort to spring me," Rusty said, casting her eyes over to Xueying.

"Well, maybe you can take the next job with me, then," she offered with a shrug.

"So that's a yes to my question, hm?" Yoru continued.

Xueying nodded. "We'll see. I figure we'll hook ourselves up tonight and try to get the information she wants. It should work; we have the information we need to get in there and we have access to a certified network, so it should be fine. If it works, I'll give her a call tomorrow and we'll turn it in ahead of time. We get paid, and we move on with our lives. If it doesn't, well, we'll have to figure something else out. But it should work."

"I guess this is why you plan for more time, because who knows, right?" Dan asked.

"That's precisely it." Yoru nodded. They were gathered in the kitchen, as it was the only real space the four of them could fit. "There are countless things that can set you back. It's best to overestimate. People will complain, but hey, they can hire someone else. There's no shortage of work. If they want it done right, well...then they can call us."

No excess of humility there. It made Dan smile. Maybe it was a little prideful of Yoru to say so, but it came off as more matter-of-fact than boasting.

It would be kind of nice to wrap the job up. Not that he wanted to say goodbye to Xueying and Rusty, but it would be nice to have a real contract under his belt. The downside was, as Rusty had pointed out, that they didn't feel particularly useful, but there would be other jobs. And he knew that even if they finished this one now, he'd see the two of them again.

"Does this mean this is the last time we have dinner together?" Dan asked, looking around.

Yoru shook his head. "Nonsense. If the job goes well, that will be tomorrow night, and I'll make something special. Just you wait."

That in itself was a reason to want to be done. Dan had no idea what

179

he planned to cook, but he was already looking forward to it.

They got ready and for the first time, all four of them left together. It felt fun, almost. Dan thought of wandering the streets late at night with his friends on weekends, before all of this had happened. No curfew and no worries. The gun on his hip did little to shatter the illusion. He felt happy, certainly happier than he had been in some time. Xueying offered him her arm and he took it with a grin as they walked. The world around them was dark and quiet.

He heard a laugh from behind him and he turned his head to see that Yoru had mimicked their action. More than that, Rusty had conceded to hook her arm through his. She was much smaller than he was, but seemed comfortable enough.

Yoru met his eyes, their happiness twinkling in the night, brighter or somehow more endearing than the streetlights they passed. Dan's fondness for him was as warm as the air around them. And not just for him.

He felt now, really, as though he had friends again. When could he have once said that?

It must have been years. He thought he had them in the army. Hadn't he fought and bled next to those people? Should they not have been the closest to him? Weren't those bonds, those mythic, fire-forged chains supposed to be stronger, closer than even family?

But he hadn't felt like this since he had been home. Maybe he really could be okay out here in the big world.

It was a strange thought, but in the hazy orange light of the streets, Xueying's gentle perfume on the air and the sounds of their chatter around him, he felt like it might have been true.

Even if they were going to steal some stuff. That meant little to Dan, now. So what if they were? They'd get paid and move on.

They made their way to the terminal building and this time the lot of them managed to work their way inside. Yoru even managed to look graceful doing it, somehow. Dan said nothing of it, lest he have to listen to Yoru crow about it. Another time, certainly.

"Let's see if those passwords get us where we need to be," Yoru said, as Xueying was plugging things into the terminal. Some of the devices Dan recognized as portable memory. Obviously somewhere to store the data that their employer was after.

"So, what, are we just waiting around to see if you can do the thing?" he asked her.

"Yes. And on the off chance that I fuck everything up and set them after us, I'm going to need the back-up."

"Is that an option?" Rusty asked.

"It's always an option," Yoru answered her wryly.

Soon, the cursing started.

"Oh, that point already?" Yoru asked jovially.

Xueying hit the side of the terminal with her fist, a quick vent of frustration. "They changed the passwords on us. We waited too long."

Dan looked over her shoulder where she was working and he tilted his head at the error message.

"Actually.... I think they didn't change the passwords. It says 'passwords not updated', which is like the error message I'd get when my key would time out back on the base. I think we're outdated."

"Whatever it is, these passwords aren't fucking working. I think things are going to get messy."

"In the physical or the mechanical sense?" Yoru asked her.

Xueying, still typing, retried the keys she had been given and sighed with the same frustration Dan could feel coming from her typing fingers.

"The physical sense. The mechanical sense is basically dead at this point. I don't think we're going to get anywhere with this."

"Well, ain't that a sonofabitch," Yoru said mildly. "Not to fret. We'll find another way."

"All that time, though," Dan said. "What a waste."

"These things happen," Xueying said, disconnecting herself from the computer. "I should have seen it coming... But live and learn. Assuming we live."

Dan heard the click of Yoru's gun cocking. "Oh, we will," he said lightly.

No sooner than he made his lofty remark then did they hear the wheels roll up outside. Someone's business was about to get shot up. Dan felt a little bad about it, but considering the other option was to roll over and die, well, it wasn't a very hard choice.

"So, what's the escape plan? Split up again?" he asked.

Xueying shook her head. "Not this time. We have a pretty good defence set up here. We should try and force them back and head out together. We'll stand a better chance if we're all there."

He nodded. Dan had no problem taking orders.

"They're going to try and break in. Get those metal sheets out of the way and see if they can't trap us here," Rusty pointed out.

"Yeah, I know." Xueying had her own gun in hand and slid near to one of the walls in question. "So the plan is, don't let them get close enough. Use the gaps to your advantage."

"And don't get hit through them," Yoru pointed out.

"If they can hit me through that gap, they might deserve it," Rusty noted.

"It's no time to play fair," he countered.

They took a spot, two to a corner, looking out the gaps in the metal slats. Two cars. Eight people? Ten? They piled out into the night and the first thing one of them did was take out the streetlights that would have helped Dan get a headcount. Smart.

Dan waited. One of the hardest things he had learned was patience. More than once he had been trapped and low on bullets. Patience. Make it count.

Xueying, sharing his view space, was faster on the drop than he was and her shot either took someone out or gave them a really bad day, judging from the noise it made.

That was a good start. Bullets dinged off of the old steel siding and Dan was concerned that a few less lucky shots might just punch right through it. Right now they were safe, but for how long?

He saw his chance. Someone moving behind one of the cars, not quite low enough. He took a deep breath and took the shot. Either they ducked or they went down, but it disappeared and another one did not reappear in its place.

Slowly, slowly. But they were going to have to be faster if they were going to make any progress.

It was Yoru that had the idea. He moved himself from the corner he had been aiming out of, and looked instead through the bottom of the metal barrier.

"Hey, Dan..." he whispered.

"Yeah?"

"That car on the left. The back windows. There's someone there."

"I can't see them. Are you sure?"

"I can see their feet but no knees. They're not below the window. Take it out."

Yoru could see that? In how dark it was and how narrow the opening was?

Dan trusted him. He took the shot. Something hit the ground.

"That's it, then, you're our eyes," Xueying decided. "Call the shots. Tell us where to go."

So he did. Yoru's eyes were sharp and his directions were clear and concise. Whoever was after them probably had low-light or night vision tech, that would make the most sense, but they didn't have the same abundance of cover or communication. Their next shot punched through the metal siding, however, and those inside scrambled to make themselves scarce.

"Okay, that's not a good sign," Rusty voiced what they were all thinking.

"Now what?"

"Now we give them a door." Xueying took aim and shot out the track that held the one steel door in place. The idea was pretty clear. By giving them an entrance, it made it less likely that they would get flanked.

The emergency light behind them did give them a little to work with. Dan did the same thing he had before; took his time and measured his shots. They had the advantage: the rows of computer terminals were good cover and a lot more flexible than the two cars that the others had to hide behind.

He was worried for a moment that the snap of gunshots and the burn of bullets through the air would make him useless. That the reminders would be too much, and he'd fall back into himself again. But no, not here.

He was precise and calm. Not every shot hit its mark, but none went wild.

"One of them has grenades on his belt. We have to run before he gets the bright idea to use them," Yoru said.

Rusty was the one to figure out how. She turned, shot the lock off the back door and kicked it open. "Before they come around the building."

"We don't know where that leads," Dan noted.

"Somewhere with less bullets," Rusty shot back.

Fair.

They ran into the hall. It was some kind of maintenance corridor. Dusty, full of wires. A fire hazard waiting to happen. "This is not an improvement!" Dan called.

Xueying, ahead of them, shot out the lock on the door that led outside. They spilled out into the alley and Dan had a sharp feeling of deja vu. Except this time, he had a gun in his hand and a whole second to react. He used it to whirl around, stick his hand back in the doorway and grab the metal shelving that was nearby. He electrocuted it.

The electricity jumped back down the hall. It didn't feel like it was strong enough to kill somebody, he hadn't the time to build up the charge, but judging from the noises in the dark they didn't have a good time.

"That should buy us a little bit," he said proudly.

"You're pretty handy with that," Xueying said, catching her breath.

"Well, it has to have some kind of upside," Yoru said. "But this is a discussion best left for later."

He didn't need to say it twice. They needed to clear out, and fast. It took half a second for them to holster their weapons before they did exactly that. It was only when they were out of danger that someone finally noticed.

"You're bleeding!" Xueying hit Yoru on the shoulder, above the wound, and looked at him in surprise. "How long have you been bleeding?"

"Since I was shot," he answered calmly.

Dan looked over to see what the fuss was. There was a cut on Yoru's arm where a bullet had grazed him, bleeding into his dark shirt. One of his hands was also covered in it, presumably where he had been putting pressure on the injury.

It didn't look bad, but even a gunshot wound like that wasn't to be taken lightly.

They nearly fell into the apartment, the four of them pressed together and exhausted. Yoru winced, covering the cut again as he found himself a spot at the kitchen table.

"It needs to be stitched or you're going to have one heck of an ugly scar," Xueying pointed out.

"It'll give me character," he said airily.

"You're already a character," Rusty pointed out.

"I can stitch it," Dan said. "I heard the hell she gave you about your split lip. Imagine how upset Xueying would be if you had a scar like that."

Xueying laughed. Yoru smiled.

"Alright, alright. I will try to sit still for you," he said.

It was a slow process, getting it cleaned up and stitched together. Dan's stomach wasn't super happy about his decision, but his will won out. It wasn't the blood that unsettled him, he thought. It was whenever Yoru winced or tensed. He hated the idea of having hurt him. But then Yoru would let out a breath and remind Dan that he was okay and tell him to keep going, so he did.

"Is that it? No one else is hurt?" Xueying asked, looking around.

"Better me than you," Yoru said, to no one in particular.

The rest of them were scrape-free, which was a relief. But, they were also unsuccessful, and Dan could see how much it dampened their mood. Xueying especially. Dan could understand that; she was the leader of their little operation and most of what they had done had been under her direction. Her frustration was easy to understand.

Dan bandaged Yoru's arm and collected all the bloodied materials from the table. Blood was one of those things that seemed to get everywhere when you weren't looking. It only reinforced that idea when Rusty motioned to him that he had gotten some of Yoru's blood on his cheek. He wiped it off.

"So...now what?" It felt like he was always the one asking that, always a little more behind or out of the loop than the others. He just had to hope he'd learn. Maybe it was the tiredness making him second-guess himself. The waning adrenaline had left him exhausted.

Yoru smiled at him and he felt his spirits lift a little.

"Well, we need a new plan. Probably something a little more direct. It probably won't be nearly as quiet, either."

"I'll have the next step hashed out for us soon," Xueying said. "I'm going to have a shower and sleep off this salt, and then we'll see what I come up with."

A shower sounded like a great idea.

They got washed up. Yoru put plastic wrap over his bandages with Dan's help, much to Rusty's amusement.

"That is a good trick," she noted.

"I've been cut up a few times before," Yoru told her. "I've learned a few things."

He went to get cleaned up and Dan sat down with the others. Xueying was flicking through videos on the vidscreen and scowling.

"Bastards. Look at this." She showed Dan was she was looking at.

The building they had just broken into was on fire, and the news were there.

"Why'd they burn it down? What the fuck?" he asked, confused.

Xueying frowned, reading the updates that were scrolling in next to the picture. "They're guessing it was an electrical fire—" Dan looked shocked and she looked over to him.

"I don't think it was you. They could be lying."

He thought of all the dust in the back hall, the open wood frames and the dry air.

"Are you sure?" Dan asked her. "Because I'm not. That place looked ripe for a fire and when I stuck my hand in..."

"Dust explodes," Rusty said.

They both looked at her.

"If your...whatever you did, if it did that, we would have seen it explode. Dust explodes. Or at least, it burns very fast. We would have known."

He took a shaking breath. Had he done that? They were both right. They could have been lying, and maybe what Rusty had said was true. They didn't exactly run out the door and never look back. They had regrouped there...but was it for long enough?

When they had all gone to bed, he mentioned it to Yoru. He could see the man's silhouette lying in the darkness. A lithe shadow, as much a part of the darkness as the deep corners themselves. But, he was a welcome sight.

"Either you did, or you didn't. What was lost is lost, and without proof, there is no use in feeling guilty. You have to ask yourself... Will feeling guilty over this improve you as a person?"

"Does it ever?"

"Well, yes. When you do a wrong, and you feel bad, you try not to do it again. But here... You took no malicious action that wasn't for your own defence or the defence of your team. I don't see how feeling guilty will improve your actions in the future."

It wasn't an easy answer, but if he had wanted an easy answer, he wouldn't have asked Yoru.

22:

The work might have been slow, but Oliver wasn't really complaining. The company was stellar and they were making progress. The little 'intervention' with Hastin had been a bit…stressful, but he had to admit that Ame was right. Ignoring the issue certainly wasn't getting them anywhere. Oliver had wanted to give the idea that it wasn't a big deal, but she had a point. The last thing they wanted was for Hastin to feel like they didn't care.

"I'd never think that, Captain," Hastin told him. "You do all kinds of things that show me you care about me. You feed me and you hug me, and you say nice things to me. You wouldn't do that if you didn't care about me," he said, as though it was obvious.

Honestly, Oliver thought it would be harder than that. He didn't mind that Hastin's idea of bliss seemed to be laying with his head on Oliver's lap while he read, or sitting and playing with Ame's hair while she told him stories. He was easy to please because he had so little, and he appreciated everything they did.

But Oliver was the anxious type. It couldn't really be that easy, could it? He knew there would have to be a point where he really had to dig his heels in. Hastin had at least twenty years of serious abuse on the table. It was not going to be that simple. It would not be solved by him sitting at Rosa's feet while she worked at her computer, quiet and happy as could be.

Surprisingly, or maybe not surprisingly at all, the first hurdle wasn't from Hastin. It was when they got a message from Violet asking for a meeting and a status update.

"What, like a phone call?" Ame asked.

"No. She wants a meeting," Hastin explained quietly. "She asked if the team would meet her in her office. She doesn't expect the job to be completed, but she said she would like to discuss our progress with us."

"Guess we can't tell her to go fuck herself," Ame mused.

"Not 'til we get paid," Rosa added.

"What kind of time does this lady have?" Oliver sighed. "Doesn't she have a job and a family? She can't just let us work."

"Just a job, no family," Hastin pointed out.

"None?" Ame asked.

"Well, she has a son. But he's away at school enough that sometimes she forgets she has one," he noted lightly.

"This doesn't make me want to talk to her any more." Rosa sighed.

"Then we go and we say hello, what's up, we have to get back to work," Oliver said. "I mean, I don't want to go, but let's get it over with. There's no reason to try and put it off, especially when we're going to have actual work to do."

Hastin smiled at him, but for the first time there was a waver in it. An uncertainty. "This is why you're the captain," he said. His voice was warm and adoring. It was also nervous.

Well, for someone who had been so confident in his decision, Oliver certainly didn't feel that way anymore.

They packed up all the things they'd need for the day. Rosa had organized a brief report of what they had done and a very vague outline of future plans.

"Not that we don't know what we're doing, but she doesn't need to know. It's actually probably better for everyone if she doesn't know." The less people who knew the specifics, the less people they had to worry about getting in the way. One less person who could screw them over. Best to keep that list as small as possible, in whatever ways they could.

Oliver tried to look presentable, and was a little jealous of both Ame and Rosa. If they looked rough, they looked the part of their job. Sure, neither of them actually looked that bad, but Rosa was nearly a head taller than Oliver and strong across the shoulders, and Ame looked like some kind of glitzpunk monstrosity but with the kind of smile that meant you'd never say it to her face.

Oliver was...Oliver. And both of their tails looked a lot nicer than his horns did.

Hastin, of course, almost made up for it. He tied his hair back (he seemed to wear it down around the house a lot, now) and dressed in his usual way, which was with more grace and tact than Oliver could articulate, let alone emulate.

He was quiet for most of the trip over there. When they arrived, he showed them in and no one stopped him. Either they had been told that they were coming, or they simply knew not to question Hastin. He opened the doors for them and led them around the back of the front desk to a set of service elevators, where he keyed in the code to take them to the top.

"Babe, you okay?" Ame finally asked.

"We're here together," Hastin told her. "I don't know how I could be more okay."

It made Oliver wonder exactly how Hastin was when he had to come back alone.

Violet was waiting for them in the same meeting room that Oliver had first met her in. She wasn't alone. She sat on the same couch and beside her stood a tall, muscular-looking man dressed in dull colours, especially when compared to the room and to Violet herself.

She smiled to see them. He didn't.

Both Ame and Rosa managed to get smiles of their own, personable-looking ones, even. Oliver managed an awkward half-effort. Hastin, dead-eyed and silent, did nothing.

"It's very good of you to come here, especially on short notice," she said to them. "It wasn't imperative, but I was hoping to get an update, and I really do prefer face to face discussions. I find there's a lot less miscommunication that way."

"We don't mind. With the progress we've made, we're actually at the perfect spot for an update," Rosa said. Thank god for that. She was the consummate professional.

"That's wonderful news. Oh, I suppose we should be introduced. I'm sure you know who I am, but this is Donovan Helmer. He is my head of security and Hastin's mentor," she said.

"We were just finishing up," he explained. "You're earlier than we expected. That's a good sign."

"Didn't want to keep you waiting," Ame said simply.

Oliver introduced them. He felt he sort of had to. Not just because he was the one who took the job, but because he had to say something. He knew the feeling of being stuck in a room of people with more commanding personalities than he had. He knew it acutely, in fact. And if he was going to be heard, he would have to make it happen.

Already the idea exhausted him.

"I'll leave you to your update. Hastin," Donovan spoke to Oliver and then addressed the younger man without looking at him.

Ame's hand tightened and for a second Oliver didn't know what was going on until those empty, dark eyes turned to him. Oh, shit. Donovan was calling him away. Why?

"Hold on a minute. Hastin is part of our team. He should be here for this, shouldn't he?" Oliver said, more sharply than he intended. All eyes snapped to him. "He's part of our team for this job, so I don't see why he shouldn't be," he said. It came off way more natural and calm than he felt.

189

"Is he still required?" Violet asked him. Everything sunk into place for Oliver at that moment. He knew what this was. What it really was. A show of force. Why was she laying the pressure on them? Were they taking too long? Or, maybe they weren't the ones she intended to pressure.

"I had thought by now he'd be of no use to you," she said.

"We still need him for the rest of the job," Oliver said cautiously. "I mean, I know he's yours and we have to give him back if you need him—" Rather, he didn't quite realize that until the words came out of his mouth, but that was a horror to consider for another day. "But he's super useful. Things would go a lot faster if we got to keep him around."

Not a lie. Hastin was very good. But what she was trying to do was twist someone. Oliver just wasn't sure who yet. Was this her trying to remind them of their deadlines and the money they were costing?

Or was this purely for Hastin's benefit?

'Benefit'. Ha. Good one.

Of course, Violet treated it like it was nothing. "Oh, of course. That's good news, actually. I was worried he'd be useless."

She turned and smiled at Donovan. "It looks like the new schedule will have to wait. From what we discussed, I can't see the delay causing too many problems."

"It's no trouble," he said easily. "As you said, I'm glad he's coming in handy." He ran a hand through his short, blond hair. "I'll be heading out then. Let us know when you're done with him and we'll arrange transport back here. It's nothing you should have to worry about."

"No problem," Oliver said. He could hear the strain in his voice. Could they? But Donovan waved carelessly as he left and stepped out of the room as though it was nothing. The tension didn't drop. Of course it didn't. The cause of it was sitting right there, across from him. Violet.

"Sorry for complicating your plans," Rosa said, cutting in where Oliver's words failed him. "Hastin's skills have been great to have. We could hire someone to replace him, but finding someone like that would take a while."

"Oh, no. It really is no trouble. I'm actually very pleased. Hastin's never been one for team work, so I was concerned how well it would go. I asked you to take him on in the hopes that he'd be of use, so this is good news to me," she said, smiling pleasantly.

Either she was lying or she was painfully, awfully inconsiderate. Oliver didn't know which was worse and he didn't really care to find out.

The rest of the meeting was more uneventful. Hastin brought them coffees and they sat and talked over their results with Violet while he waited silently nearby. Oliver did his best not to look over to him.

He wasn't sure the rules about a situation like this. What he did know was that worrying over Hastin was exploitable. Sure, Oliver had no idea how that shit worked for rich people, but he knew having feelings was asking to get hurt. So for now, he pretended he didn't.

He was worried Ame might not get the memo, but she seemed perfectly comfortable and he didn't see her look over to Hastin even once. It took him a minute, but Oliver realized he had no reason to be concerned. After all, she did have more experience than he did.

"It sounds like you are making good progress. I'm wholeheartedly reassured," Violet said. Of course she was pleased, all of her money was paying off. Oliver tasted something bitter in his mouth. He still wasn't sure what it was they were after. The file names meant nothing to him, and Rosa hadn't said anything about them when he showed her.

There were a lot of unanswered questions. They made him nervous, but also unexpectedly angry. There was something going on here. He could feel it.

"And his behaviour has been fine?" Violet asked, all innocence in her question. 'Honest' concern as to how her property had conducted itself.

Was she trying to convince them? Or maybe she assumed they felt the same way?

"Well, he's better behaved than any of us," Ame noted. A perfect non-answer, matched with a laugh. "Nothing to worry about. He's useful and he doesn't get in the way. And it saves us the out-of-pocket of hiring someone to fill the spot, right?"

"I do suppose it is a little easier," Violet said, matching Ame's smile with one of her own.

That seemed to be the end of it. The three of them rose to leave and Rosa held out her arm. "Hastin?" she called. Like calling a dog. But she could get away with it, Oliver realized. Hastin went and hooked his arm through hers wordlessly so that he might help her navigate the room and the rest of the building.

"We'll keep you updated. We're on track for being done right on time," Ame told Violet.

Then they were dismissed.

Hastin didn't seem to snap out of it until they stepped back in their own apartment. The whole ride back he was still distant and vacant-eyed. They didn't pressure him too much. He stayed on Rosa's arm and kept his head down. Rosa was protective of him, and seeing that did a little to make Oliver feel better.

He looked at you if you called his name, but Oliver did his best not to. Something in his chest went cold when Hastin looked at him like that. Like something in him died every time he did it.

As soon as they stepped inside their home and closed the door, he slipped his arm from Rosa's and buried himself against Oliver's chest. Oliver held him tight, and while both Ame and Rosa took off their shoes and got out of the way, he didn't move from where he stood for several minutes while Hastin seemed to come back into himself.

"Sorry…" he said, with a weak, embarrassed smile. "I… You know," he said, biting his lip. Oliver did know. He didn't understand, not entirely, but he knew. "And then the, um, the cameras. I think the cameras made me a little… weird. The ones in the subway look like the ones in my room. I guess they just kind of…yeah…"

Oliver hugged him again. This time it wasn't Hastin pulling him close. Oliver wrapped his arms around him because just saying you're safe didn't seem to be enough.

"Hey… I put some tea on. You guys want some?" Ame put her hand on Hastin's shoulder.

It was Oliver who nodded, though. "Yeah, I think we could use some… And we should try and figure out what just happened with that fucking trainwreck we just went through…"

It was definitely the weirdest tragedy Oliver had ever endured. No one had died. No one got hurt. So why were they all so fucked up?

He sat next to Rosa at the table. Hastin was curled against Ame's side, sipping tea that she had made for him. His eyes slipped closed as Oliver watched him. Deep, measured breaths. Trying to come back down. Oliver had definitely been there. He had a handle on his anxiety now, but that wasn't always the case.

So when he spoke, it wasn't to Hastin. Let the poor kid rest. He addressed the other two.

"We wanna talk about why she was putting the gears on us?"

"Usually, I'd suspect that she just wants us to hurry up, and that might be the case…but I don't think that's all of it," Ame said, frowning as she sipped her tea. She looked tired. Their short façade had worn on her, too.

"That wasn't the whole reason. He's the reason." Rosa pointed at Hastin. "Either the reminder was for us, or for him."

Hastin opened his eyes just as Ame put her arm around him. Then he sighed.

"She wanted to test us," he said quietly. "I expect she answered a few questions with that meeting."

"Like what?" Oliver asked.

"Do you like me?" Hastin asked, not looking at him. "I'm supposed to be likeable. Am I useful to you? Enough that you'll insist I come back? I'm supposed to be useful." Hastin leaned his elbows on the table and took another sip of his tea. "How far are we on the job? Right about now was where things started going sideways for Xueying's team. Some of it likely was about the job. But Rosa's right. I wouldn't be surprised if most of that meeting was my fault."

"Okay, but her being a creep isn't your fault, babe," Ame pointed out. He didn't answer.

It wasn't his fault, but he was the reason Violet was bothering them, now, wasn't he? Oliver didn't have to ask to know what he was thinking about.

"You know that discussion brought up something else, too, right?" Rosa asked.

Oliver and Ame looked at her. Neither of them had the answer on hand.

"When this job is done, we will have to give him back. We've kind of... forgotten about that," she pointed out.

Ame's arm tightened where it was around him, pulling him close to her protectively, or selfishly. Oliver didn't know or care which one.

"You can't be serious." She looked at Oliver.

Oliver swallowed and looked between the three of them. Slowly, Hastin opened his eyes and looked right back at him. He already knew, he knew what Oliver felt in his heart and was struggling to express. He couldn't do it.

"I...I don't want to say it out loud," Oliver said. "I can't."

"I can," Hastin said. He set his tea cup on the table. "You don't have much of a choice, Captain. I have to go back."

It sounded like a cold shower felt. Not the kind that woke you up, but the kind that soaked your clothes and weighed you down with the sheer dread of it.

"We do not want you to go back," Ame insisted.

"I'd put you in too much danger to stay," Hastin said. "If something happened to you just because I was that selfish... I don't think I could handle it."

Selfish. Because it was selfish of him to want his freedom, or at least that's how he felt. Oliver thought he might be sick. This was too much. It was all too much.

"We are not there yet," Rosa said. "I see no reason to dread an ending that isn't guaranteed."

And that wasn't what Oliver expected her to say. Oliver thought she was the one who would have pointed out that they knew that in the beginning, that none of this was new, that they should have been prepared for it. That Hastin didn't deserve to go back, but they didn't have any choice and that was that.

Instead, Rosa said to wait. Oliver wasn't sure if he could.

"Besides..." Hastin looked at them and smiled again. That same unsteady expression. He was trying. "I mean... I never thought I'd be sitting at a table with people who...who wanted to keep me." He bit his lip again. "It's..really nice. Even it it's just for now."

23:

No one was particularly chipper the next morning. Yoru cooked, shirtless, and with no regard to the still-healing injury on his arm. Xueying kissed his bandages as she went by him, running a hand through her short hair. There wasn't much for it. Sometimes things just didn't go the way they were planned. Dan sat at the table and didn't feel as put out as he thought he might. So it didn't work? They'd try again. Rusty sat next to him and he moved over to make room for her.

The only sound was the radio, softly playing some sort of jazz. Undoubtedly it was Yoru's doing.

He was also the one to break the silence. "I was the one who lost the most blood, so why am I the most awake?"

"You're not allowed to joke about being shot," Dan said.

"But then I've lost half of my material," Yoru said, sounding offended.

"I'm sure you have some more interesting injuries to talk about," Rusty pointed out to him.

He winked at her. "Not in polite company, I don't."

That at least earned a smile from her.

The day looked like it would be a quiet one. It wouldn't be a terrible idea to take a day off to regroup and lick their wounds, as it were. After they ate, Yoru sat in the kitchen, an empty notebook and a pen in his hand. Dan immediately knew what he was doing and left him to it, undisturbed. It made him smile to think of it, though. He wondered if Yoru would tell him any of them, when he was finished.

Partway through the day, Xueying knocked on the kitchen wall to get their attention and they both looked up to her.

"Put some clothes on. We gotta go," she said. She didn't sound particularly panicked, though.

"Where do we gotta go?" Yoru mimicked back to her.

"Employer wants a meeting. She sure picked a hell of a time," she called back.

"That's rough." He sighed and slid out of his chair. "You sure I should put clothes on? She might be happier to see us if I didn't."

"If I was banking on that, I'd go topless," Xueying shot back.

195

Dan, laughing, got dressed next to Yoru without a moment of hesitation. Where he would have once been shy, he was now only too comfortable. It was hard to be shy around the person who was at your side for every nightmare and who cleaned up any of the disgusting blood and whatever it was from his implants.

Yoru dressed and tied his hair back, his long-sleeved shirt covering his wound as though it was never even there. They met the others outside, both of them already dressed.

Xueying was twirling car keys on her fingers, but where she had gotten them from, Dan wasn't sure. "So, this isn't going to be a great time," she said as they headed downstairs towards where the car was parked.

"No, but we're not out of time yet. We tell her we hit a snag, but we're not down. I mean, she could try and yank the contract, but I don't think she's going to. Snags happen. She might be mad, but she'll get over it., Yoru reassured her.

"We can't be the first thieves she's worked with," Rusty pointed out. She had tied her long hair into its usual two braids and flicked one over her shoulder disdainfully.

"Probably not, no. And we won't be the first to have a hiccup. Nor will we be the last," Yoru said. He opened the door that led out to the street and stood there patiently as the three of them filed out.

"To be honest...she doesn't know we fucked up yesterday," Dan pointed out. "She's got no way to know. I mean, tell her, sure, but there's no reason for us to go in there dreading it."

"I mean, she could have gotten our pictures off the camera, but I'm pretty sure we were missed by most of them. We certainly weren't caught by anyone who's a friend of the target," Xueying said.

"And that still doesn't mean she knows what happened," Rusty added.

The keys seemed to belong to a little white car. Clean, cute, without any frills. Rusty slid into the back without waiting to be told, and Dan took the other side. It made sense; Yoru was taller than he was and would have a harder time fitting.

It was kind of nice to at least have the car to insulate them from the crush of the city. It was cool and quiet while the streets outside teemed with people. It was, all in all, a little easier on Dan's mind.

"Really, you guys should see who we're working for anyway. It's just good practice," Xueying said. "So let's not make this any more than it is. Just an update. And then we'll get back to work."

196

She clicked the radio on. Pop played. Dan smiled. He had a soft spot for pop tunes. They were light and fun. They had kept his head up in the army and gave him something to sing with his sisters at home. Xueying apparently had a fondness for them, too, as she tapped her fingers on the steering wheel as she drove.

The traffic was awful, but it always was. The multilayered streets had done a little to help alleviate that, so at least the packed roads usually moved consistently. It didn't take them too long to get to where they were headed. Highlight Technology. A skyscraper in the posh area of town. Leaning back in his seat, staring idly out the window as they drove, Dan could see all the signs of money just out wandering around. The suits, the phones, the aesthetic modifications. Yoru's pretty eyes would fit in just fine, although they were probably too subtle for these people to appreciate.

Dan's own modifications? He sure as hell didn't appreciate them, honestly.

He actually wasn't sure if they conveyed any benefits. He had no real way of knowing. It wasn't like he could go back and test it out from before he had them. Not that what he thought of them mattered: they weren't going anywhere.

The building was rife with security, not that Dan was surprised. She ran the place, didn't she? Anyone who hired thieves had to learn to anticipate them. It certainly looked like the kind of place that would be a headache to rob. Xueying did most of the talking and he was happy to let her. As hands-off as he could be seemed a good default to strive for, seeing as it wasn't his gig and he was absolutely not the most knowledgeable person in the room. He wasn't out to impress anyone.

And that was way more thought than Rusty gave to it, who stood there with her arms crossed and matched it with an expression that made it clear that she wasn't there to answer questions. She was way better at this game than he was.

They'd let the eloquent two do the talking. Make life easier for everyone.

The secretary at the front directed them where to go. She had feathers that grew from her temples in lovely opalescent colours, and when she pointed them towards the elevator, Dan saw more of them around her wrist. Pretty, but they looked kind of uncomfortable.

It was less crowded in here than on the street, and it was much less so once they entered the elevator. The very top floor. At least it moved quick, and it didn't have windows, so Dan never quite had to get used to how high it was. He wasn't afraid of heights specifically, but everything was scary after a point, wasn't it?

Like how he didn't particularly have a fear of insects, but when he walked into spider webs he still did the 'get it off!' dance. It was, to him, just one of those facts of life.

The elevator opened to a hallway. It was long and over-polished, with an empty desk at the end. Xueying's shoes clicked on the floor. A clean, precise sound. None of the others wore shoes that were capable of making such an impression.

They reached the desk, and just as Dan was wondering how to alert anyone of their presence, the door behind the desk opened.

An older woman, white haired and smiling, stepped out. Oh, cameras. She must have been watching them arrive.

"Xueying, so good to see you. And your team as well. How wonderful. Come along, there are better places for us to talk," she said, beckoning them into the back room.

They followed her, and Dan was briefly preoccupied taking in the new scenery. Couches, a coffee table, the same shining, polished floor. Everything in this room probably cost more than he had made in his whole life.

It had a way of making you feel reduced as a person.

"Go on, find a seat," she encouraged.

Xueying did, and then pointed out something just as Dan realized it, too.

"And your...associate?" she asked, looking to the tall, blond man who was also sitting there.

"Donovan Helman. He's actually unrelated to our little meeting. We were nearly done," their employer explained.

"We'd be happy to wait outside," Yoru said. "We don't mean to impose."

"Nonsense. I called you here," she said, nodded. "We were just finishing up. Donovan, I have all the paperwork from the tests, correct? Is there anything else we need to go over?"

"Nothing pressing. When you read through them, you'll notice I've made some changes to the training schedule. I didn't think the other version was challenging enough," he said.

"I trust your expertise. We'll meet again in a few days. You can let me know how those changes work out," she said.

He stood, then, and nodded. "I'm sorry for taking up your time. You know how it is," he apologized.

"No problem." Xueying smiled at him in that way she had, the one that made you actually believe that it wasn't a problem.

He excused himself, and the meeting seemed to get started for real.

"Well, it is nice to meet your team," she said, looking pleased. "I'm sure you know me, but I'm Selene Violet. I negotiated your contract with Xueying."

Xueying introduced each of them in turn, and at least Violet seemed pleased by her choices.

"It always seems more tangible to me when I meet with people in person. I know that email and vidcalls are so much quicker, but I think I just remember things better in person and feel more organized that way."

"It's no problem on our end. We had planned to take today to regroup and set out the next phase of planning, so your timing is eminently convenient," Yoru said.

"How lucky for us." Violet smiled.

She certainly seemed nice enough. But she was definitely dealing with a room of people with very illegal backgrounds who she had hired for very illegal things, so it wasn't hard for Dan to figure out that her persona was probably largely a lie.

He didn't mind that, at least her fake persona was nice. She could have been creating the illusion that she was a bitch. That would have been a lot more annoying, honestly.

"And how is progress going? I haven't heard much in the way of news, but I know that is to be expected in a job like this," she said lightly.

"We hit a bit of a snag, but nothing serious," Xueying said. "With a little creative planning, we'll be back on track in no time. We should have no reason to change our agreed-upon end date."

Violet nodded. "Oh, these things happen. But, I'm certainly impressed. Someone of less skill might have asked for an extension."

"I don't think we will need it. Plans are already in motion to compensate for the hang-up. It will be taken care of soon," Xueying replied.

"Brilliant," Violet said, clapping her hands together. "You know, I've always thought I was a good judge of character. I was so impressed when we met by how down to earth you were. I'm happy to see it working in both of our favours."

Dan rubbed at his nose. Not because he was itching, but because it stopped him from pulling a face at Violet's words. The part about Xueying being down to earth was true, as was the part about it being helpful. She wasn't prideful or blustery, which would have made getting any real business done a pain in the neck.

But that wasn't why Violet liked her, if Violet actually liked her at all.

At least Dan was learning, though. This was a master class in how tactless people could be, especially people who were used to having all the power. Trickier than the army, where there was just as much bullshit, but the people pulling it had all the power and never bothered with hiding it.

Here, Violet still needed them, so she had to at least make an attempt at being careful. Rusty met his eyes, just the briefest second, but it was enough for him to know that she felt the same way.

It occurred to him that, with the other two taking care of negotiations, he and Rusty looked like they were the muscle. It was a little flattering, actually.

"The next update you get from us should be the call to say everything is taken care of," Xueying said.

"There's a few things still to do—" Like most of the job, Yoru didn't say, but Dan knew, "—but we'll have it wrapped up just as expected."

"Of course. All in time," she said amiably. "I supposed I had better let you get back to it, then. No point keeping you here while my curiosity gets in the way."

"It isn't a problem." Yoru was just as good at this game as Xueying. "But I'm sure we'll be glad to get back to work."

That was that, then.

They found their way back to the car and the air tasted like relief as they drove away.

"Well, she ain't happy, but she's not mad, yet," Yoru noted.

"Does she know that everything she says tastes like lies?" Dan asked incredulously.

"Oh, probably. But why does she care? Everyone has to play along whether she is lying or not."

He had a point.

"Besides, we didn't have to stretch the truth at all. I already do have a new plan in the works, and we'll be getting started soon. I actually don't think we'll have much of a headache coming up. We just have to be a little more... direct."

Dan believed her. One of the problems with Xueying was that she wasn't Violet; he actually supposed he would have no idea if she was lying to them. She was believable from the start, and that was a gift, true, but not one that he was immune to.

Maybe Yoru was. Maybe he wasn't. The man in question had his head

200

back, his fingers tapping along to the music as though nothing was amiss. If he wasn't worried, then Dan wouldn't be, either.

He dreaded the day that he would have to see Yoru worried.

"We getting to work today then, or...?" Dan asked Xueying when they were back at the apartment.

"Nah, tomorrow. We're all tired, and despite how he's acting, one of us does have a bullet wound to mind," she said.

"I'm fine!" Yoru called from the other room. Xueying rolled her eyes.

"We're just going to lay low for the night. Our day off even got messed up, there's no reason to make it worse." She laughed.

Dan didn't mind. His back was acting up again and while he was doing some stretches to alleviate it, Yoru gently bullied him into having a shower.

"The hot water always helps," he reminded Dan. "Go on. It's not like the rest of us are using it." He nudged him.

Dan rolled one of his shoulders, winced, and then agreed. If they were going to get rolling tomorrow, he wanted to be a little more useful than this.

He cranked the hot water to as hot as he could stand it and stood with his back under it. The shower was a little cramped to stretch in, but he tried. If he really thought about it, he could feel the spots where his skin met the metal. The sensation was heightened when he realized that the metal held heat better than his skin did, and he could feel all the places it pressed into his flesh. It made his stomach turn to think about it too much.

He washed himself off. He took consolation in the fact that he wasn't scrubbing dried blood off of himself. It used to be all the time that he'd step in the shower and watch rust-coloured water swirling down the drain. He still felt some wear, but it was better than before.

He dried off and went back to their room. Without saying anything, Yoru turned where he sat and extended his hands to Dan, beckoning him closer. When he sat, the other man started rubbing his shoulders.

"You don't have to do that," Dan protested half-heartedly.

"Shh, I'm thinking of poems. It gives me something to do with my hands."

That didn't give him a lot of room to argue. And, true to his word, every once in awhile Yoru would stop and scribble something down in his book. Dan didn't turn to try and read it. If Yoru wanted him to know, he'd tell him.

"Are you really going to leave that book here?" Dan asked. "It seems like such a shame after you put all that work into it."

"They're all my ideas. They're not lost," Yoru pointed out. "But they also don't serve me anymore. They'll stay here so they can be of use to someone else. I don't miss them when I leave. It is the way of things."

Lost Names

24:

"We're going out," Ame said.

"What? You're going out?" Oliver asked, looking up from his dinner. Well, second dinner. Everyone else had already finished eating. He had still been hungry.

"No. We. Us. All of us," Ame said.

Oliver blinked at her.

"Today was shit. We need to get some air and relax. We're going out," she insisted.

Oliver thought about arguing. He didn't like the feeling of slacking off when there was work to be done...but what could they really do tonight? Really? What were they going to get done?

Maybe they did need a little air.

He sighed, and then he nodded. "Okay. That sounds like a good idea," he agreed. "What's the plan, go someplace to grab a few drinks?"

She nodded. "I got a place in mind. Finish eating, c'mon. I'm gonna put some make-up on and tell the others."

Oliver ate and washed up. The more he thought about it, the more the idea of a night out sounded appealing. Ame was right. They could use some free time. The idea of having people to spend time with was kind of nice, actually.

And then he realized just exactly who he was drinking with. Ame he wasn't worried about. Sure, she was a party girl, but between him and Rosa he was sure they could handle her.

No, it was the other one that concerned him.

"Hey, honey?" He found Hastin in the living room, already waiting for the others to be ready.

"Yes, Captain?"

"Are you sure you're okay if we go do this?" he asked.

Hastin looked at him and tilted his head in confusion. "...Yes? I'm... I'm actually really looking forward to it," he admitted. "Ame says it will be nice for us to get out a little. And she said...she wants to teach me how to dance!"

Hesitation and confusion gave way to honest happiness and he seemed excited. If Oliver wasn't sold already, that would have sealed the deal. It was too hard to even pretend he could say 'no' now.

"Okay." Oliver nodded. "I just wanted to make sure that you were alright. I know you've been through a lot today and didn't know if adding something new on top of that was a good idea."

Hastin shook his head. "I'm looking forward to trying something new. And you'll be there. I'll be okay!"

He had dressed down from his usual clothes. He was still classier than he had any reason to be, classier by miles, but at least he looked a little more comfortable. The other two joined them shortly after. Rosa, like Oliver, dressed for comfort. Besides, it wasn't hard to impress when you were a tall, buff, white haired lady with a goddamn luxurious fox tail.

"We all ready?" Oliver asked.

Ame nodded. "And I have a cab number on speed dial from my phone when we all inevitably end up wasted."

"I'm not planning on drinking that much," Rosa said.

Ame laughed. "You've said that before. Let's go!"

She hailed them a cab to get there and Oliver recognized the address immediately. The Tint. It always came back to that, didn't it? Oliver didn't think that Ame was out to get him or anything that dramatic. It was populated by people like her. Of course it was where she wanted to go drink. It was her crowd!

And maybe he should learn to associate the place with something other than black-out misery drinking. That might be a good idea.

Ame sat in the front seat and Hastin sat in between Oliver and Rosa. He held Oliver's hand but leaned over to look out of Rosa's window as they drove.

"Everything looks so nice at night time," he said. "You can't tell how dirty everything is."

Oliver laughed.

Back in the day, someone would have carded Hastin. Oliver thought about that as they walked into the bar. Maybe in some places they still did. No one here was going to care, though, and any ID Hastin carried was almost certainly fake anyway.

"'Kay, what are we drinking?" Ame asked.

"Beer," Oliver said. "Whatever they have that's dark." Better than what he had last time. The drinks here could be great. He just hadn't been looking for that, last time.

"Rum and coke," Rosa said simply.

"I don't know!" Hastin announced.

Ame laughed. "I'll get you something sweet, kid. Back in a sec."

Better to have one person squish to the bar than the three of them. Besides, if Ame was buying this round, Oliver wasn't going to complain.

Ame came back with drinks fairly quickly. She had both a drink and a shot and she sat down at their table and downed the latter before sipping on the former. "Oh, don't look at me like that. I have to get a head start on you guys or I'll never even get tipsy."

"What's this?" Hastin was looking at the glass she brought him with curiosity. It was very green.

"Grasshopper. Tastes like mint and chocolate. Shit is delicious," Ame said. "Try it. If you don't like that one, I'll drink it, and we'll get you something else to try," she offered.

He took a sip and nodded eagerly. "It's really good!"

"I always think they taste like ice cream," she said.

"I've never had ice cream," he told her. "But if it tastes like this, it's wonderful!"

He drained it fairly quickly, much to Oliver's amusement.
"Be careful. That stuff is alcoholic. You don't want to over do it," he cautioned Hastin. "Take your time. If you start to feel funny, we'll get you some water."

"I'm okay, Captain," Hastin reassured him. "Besides, it is really good."

Rosa bought him his next drink. It smelled like cinnamon, and he drank it with the same curiosity.

"Mine are all delicious but...yours don't taste as good, do they?" he asked.

"Eh, that depends. I like beer, it's more savoury, and sugar isn't always nice to me," Oliver explained. "Beer is nice, but it's usually something you grow to like. Same with what Rosa is drinking."

"Here, try it." She offered him a sip, he took it and looked at her thoughtfully.

"It's sweet, but not as much as the stuff I had," he said.

"Yeah, that bitterness is the rum. Some people like the balance. And Ame is drinking... What are you drinking?" Oliver asked her.

"Eugh, something terrible. But once I get tipsy I can drink cute shit with Hastin." She elbowed him playfully. "I just gotta get there first."

"Why do you want to get tipsy?" he asked her.

She shrugged. "Sometimes it's nice to indulge in letting your guard down a little. Sometimes that shit gets you killed, but here that seems pretty unlikely. People do all kinds of dumb shit to unwind. Getting a little toasted sometimes doesn't seem so bad."

He nodded, listening to her intently and rather quickly downing the next drink he had been given.

There was music playing, some kind of pop/dance nonsense that Oliver would have never put on himself. Now that he had to listen to it, though, he had to admit that it was kind of infectious. He rocked a little in his seat, sipped his beer and chatted with the others. He had to admit that this was pretty nice.

The song switched and Ame jumped out of her seat. "'Kay, this one is my fuckin' jam. Hastin, let's go!"

She pulled on his arm but he was slow to move. "But, if this is your favourite song, I'm going to slow you down..." he said.

"Bullshit. You'll catch on fast." She tugged him out of the booth to where some people were already dancing. There weren't tons of them, it wasn't a very busy place, but there was enough. Oliver didn't doubt for an instant that Ame would have gotten up and danced even if they were the only ones. He was sure she had done it before.

It was easy enough to see them where Ame started dancing, and it was just as easy to see that she was having a good time.

Her guess was right on the mark. Hastin was a natural.

"I'm not really surprised. Fighting and dancing use a lot of the same muscle control," Rosa pointed out when Oliver mentioned it. All of the noise made her tech a little buggy in here, especially with all the human movement, but it gave her a solid enough idea where the chairs and walls were, so she kept it on.

"No wonder I can't do either." Oliver laughed.

It was nice to laugh and drink and listen to music, good or bad as it might be, with friends.

Ame and Hastin were only on their feet for a song or two before they came back, fresh drinks in hand. He had something else to try, and he sipped at it as they sat down.

"So, how was it?" Oliver asked him, feeling oddly parental.

"It was great! I love dancing! And I really like music," he said cheerfully.

"Don't get any at home?" Rosa guessed.

He nodded at her as he drank.

"This isn't even the good stuff. Wait 'til tomorrow. I'll show you what I listen to." Oliver was joking but he should have seen it coming. Those eyes. Those fucking eyes. Looking at Oliver like what he said would make Hastin the happiest in the world.

And for all Oliver knew, the look was sincere. Maybe it would.

"I'd love that! Rosa, will you show me what you listen to?" he asked her.

"Sure. Maybe you'll find something you like," she said.

Hastin wiggled in his seat, pleased as punch as he finished another drink. "These are really good. Captain, can I try what you have?" he asked.

"You won't like it," Oliver offered, handing him the glass.

Hastin took a sip, but he didn't make a face. "It's different. It's definitely not as sweet as what Ame has been getting me," he said thoughtfully as he passed it back to Oliver. "But you said you're not so fond of sweets, so it's definitely more you," he said with a smile.

Oliver was not nearly drunk enough to justify how strongly that smile affected him.

"Come on, let's go dance some more. It's not a good night unless you work up a sweat," Ame said, taking Hastin's hand.

Eagerly, of course, he went with her.

"How many drinks has he had?" Rosa asked.

"Four? I think," Oliver said as he sat down with another beer.

"We're going to have one drunk little bird on our hands," she noted calmly.

Oliver laughed and shrugged. Yeah, they were. But let the boy drink. He could go home and sleep it off. It wasn't going to do him any real harm. He wasn't alone. And, even drunk, Oliver couldn't imagine Hastin defenceless. No, let him have his fun. He deserved it.

It would be back to work soon enough. And that meant the clock would start winding down.

That thought made Oliver drink just a little faster.

"Captain, will you come dance with me?" Hastin asked him when they stopped to get another drink. His cheeks were flushed pink and Oliver made a mental note to remind him to drink some water before they went to bed.

"I can't dance, honey. Maybe Rosa will go with you?" he said.

"But I couldn't dance! Ame taught me and now I can. Maybe Ame can teach you."

Oliver laughed. "No one can teach me. I'm impossible."

Hastin didn't pester him, and Rosa did go with them for a little bit to dance. She wasn't as much of a partier as Ame, but she looked like she had fun. Hastin fit comfortably against her, and dancing with him was easy. She fell back into her seat and grabbed herself a water when she did.

"They make me feel old," Rosa said, laughing.

208

"I'll drink to that." Oliver tapped his beer against her glass of water and laughed, too.

Hastin loved dancing, and part of the reason he loved dancing was because it was nice to be so close to someone he liked so much. Ame was fun, and dancing with her was great! Knowing that Rosa and Oliver were nearby made it even better.

And sure, Ame wouldn't really hesitate to call herself easy. She was easy. She liked boys and girls. She liked Hastin, even if she didn't understand him.

She understood him even less when he stopped dancing, his arms around her still, and pressed his forehead against hers.

"Would you kiss me, Ame?" he asked her.

"Would I or will I?" she asked him in return.

He smiled. It was shy, maybe a little mischievous, and utterly charming.

"Both."

"You want me to kiss you, honey?"

"I've never kissed anybody nice before. But I think kissing you would be really nice," he said.

Ame smiled, and she nudged her nose against his. "You drunk, honey?"

"A little," he admitted honestly. "But I'm not being silly. I mean it."

"Tell me you're sure." Ame was smiling, though. She believed him. She was a little drunk, too, but not enough to have lost all her sense. A kiss wasn't going to hurt him.

He was a sweet, pretty thing. If he wanted a kiss, she'd be happy to give him one.

"I'm sure!" he said, giggling.

She did kiss him then, swept him right off his feet, her lips on his. His hands were on her shoulders, holding her close when he lost his feet. He started to laugh and then she did, too, but that hardly stopped either of them. He tasted of sweet alcohol and an even harder to place sweetness of being, and he moved against her with natural, honest desire. She leaned forward too far and fell to the ground, landing on her knees. It barely hurt, she had already been leaning too far forward to have far left to go. So she laughed more, and so did he.

She kissed him right down to the dance floor, her arms wrapped around him and their legs in a tangle from how they landed, breathless and laughing and happy.

209

"That as good as you imagined it, baby?" she asked him.
Hastin, laying under her, nodded and beamed. "Better!"
He kissed her again. Briefly, softly. A quick 'thank you'.
Then she gracelessly clambered to her feet and offered him a hand up to do the same, which he took.
She hooked her arm around his waist and pulled him in close to kiss his cheek and he leaned against her comfortably. They headed back to their table together.
"Honey, you're all dusty," Oliver said, looking him over.
Hastin nodded, but smiled. "It will wash off, Captain."
"I'd say that you're as dirty on the outside as I am on the inside...but you're still coming up short," Ame said.
"I know junk piles that are cleaner than your mind, Ame," Oliver teased her.
Oliver was oddly pleased by what he had seen. He hadn't heard them speaking, but he saw it happen. He saw them talk, and he saw them kiss. And he saw Ame do absolutely nothing else. Here was Hastin, drunk, eager to please, perfectly exploitable.
And she kissed him silly and brought him back to the table.
He said nothing of it. But he smiled at her when she looked to him.
They had a few more drinks, and Ame and Hastin danced some more. Oliver was a little tipsy by the time they were done but nothing serious. Rosa, too, was a little unsteady.
Ame and Hastin were a little more than that.
"Captain," Hastin said. He fell into his seat and immediately snuggled in close to Oliver, who let him do exactly that.
"You drunk, honey?"
"Oh, yes," he answered, nodding against Oliver's shoulder.
"Ame?" Oliver looked to her.
"Wrecked, Captain," she said, laughing.
"Mission success?" Rosa asked.
"I'd call it a success," Oliver agreed. "Let's go the fuck home."
He finished his beer and called them a cab.
They waited for it outside, where Hastin stood there visibly pouting until Oliver put his arm around him. "What's wrong, honey?"
"I don't know who I want to hug more," he said, looking up at him. "I don't have enough arms."
"Oh. That is a problem," Oliver agreed, trying not to laugh too hard.
"Problem solved, though. You're here now," Hastin said agreeably and

wrapped his arms around Oliver.

They sat in the back of the cab, all four of them. They put Hastin on Rosa's lap rather than be apart. Something was different now. Oliver could feel it. Not bad, just different. Hastin snuggled happily against Rosa's shoulder. Ame held her hand, with her own head resting on Oliver's shoulder.

Something was definitely different.

While Oliver was unlocking the door, Hastin had found his way to Ame again. Not enough arms to hug everyone at once, but he had become a master of dividing his time and affection, at least while drunk.

"Remember, babe, you're supposed to have a shower and get all that dust off you," Oliver told him.

Hastin groaned. He nuzzled Oliver's shoulder sleepily now that they were inside. "Ame says I'm going to wake up with a hangover. I'll shower then. It'll feel great!" He sounded half amused and half resigned.

Oliver ran his fingers though Hastin's hair. "Okay, okay... But you should drink some water before bed. It will make you feel less terrible tomorrow. You're young. You'll bounce back."

"I don't know how old I am," Hastin said, although he didn't seem to dwell on it. "I will drink some water, Captain," he added then.

Oliver got him some and stayed with him in the kitchen while he drank it.

"Guess who is also covered in fucking dust and didn't notice," Ame announced, wandering through the kitchen in her underwear.

"I guess Ame," Hastin answered.

"Bingo, babe." When he finished his water she took the glass, refilled it, and drank it herself. "That floor is awful."

"You should shower," Hastin said smartly. Oliver snickered.

"Yeah, yeah. I will. I gotta wash all this fucking make-up off, too. Makeup is bullshit, by the way. I'm so fuckin' cute. Why do I wear makeup?"

"I could not tell you," Oliver answered diplomatically.

"'Kay. I'm gonna go scrub this gross off me. Night, bitches." She kissed Hastin on the cheek, her hand trailing over Oliver's chest as she passed them both.

"Bedtime for me, too." Hastin nodded at him and rubbed his eyes. "I'm very sleepy."

"Okay. Take some more water to bed with you, though," Oliver insisted.

"I will."

Hastin refilled his water glass, and he leaned in to kiss Oliver on the cheek.

"Goodnight, Captain."

Lost Names

25:

Xueying sat at the kitchen table, her vidscreen laying flat on its surface as she flicked through the pictures it projected above itself. The visualization of it and going through the motions helped her to feel more organized.

Paper would have worked, too, but one of these things was on hand and the other was a little harder to find.

"How are those plans coming?" Yoru asked her.

She sighed. "I was looking for a way that wasn't straight up breaking and entering, but now it looks like we're probably going to have to do it that way." She frowned and looked over to him. "I mean, we have you, so it's not terrible, but I really was hoping to go the way of remote access. It doesn't look we'll be able to manage it without a technician, and even then, I can't imagine what they'd need to even get started."

"Finding someone who can do the job would take too much time in itself," Yoru agreed.

"What we don't have is a computer tech. What we do have is a master thief."

"You're too kind."

"You're going to need blueprints."

"They'd be handy," he admitted idly. He leaned close to her, one hand taking a lock of her hair between his fingers and toyed with it. A smile was faint on her lips, but she didn't pull away or otherwise chide him.

"So we have to steal them, too."

"We're going to need uniforms and key cards," he pointed out.

"Yeah... Can I leave that to you and Dan?" She looked over to him. "If you can get them for us, Rusty and I can sneak in and get the plans ourselves. Easier than trying to get four so the lot of us can go."

"Yeah, and a group of four is going to stand out for sure," he agreed. "That makes sense to me. Are you sure you don't want me on both teams? Not that I doubt you, just thought I'd offer."

Xueying shook her head. "It's the same team composition. One person to do the sneaking, one person as backup in case things get hard. We'll be okay."

He nodded.

"I can get to work on those things today. Uniforms and access cards. Shouldn't be too hard. People leave their shit lying around all the time."

"Keep in mind, we'll have to be fast. Chances are they can cancel cards when they're reported stolen. In the meantime, I'm going to look at secondary entrances, because I bet the computers know who is clocked in and who isn't, and as many of those checkpoints as we can skip, we're gonna."

"So what are the cards for, then?"

"We'll need them to get into that computer, I'm sure."

"Unless it's also time-locked."

She blinked at him. "Well, shit."

He shook his head. "We can get the cards today, pay someone to do the override for us tonight, and you can use them tomorrow before they're reported missing."

"There's a reason you're the professional."

"Hey, you're a spy, technically. Not usually a thief. There's some intricacies you are going to miss out on," he said comfortingly.

"Yeah, usually I'm let in the front door." She laughed.

"It's easier when you work in just information. That's what you're used to. Tangible objects are such a headache."

He smiled at her and she laughed. It helped her feel better about the whole thing. The real charm of stealing information was that you didn't have to smuggle it. All you had to do was get in and get out alive, and she was good at that.

There were a lot of overlapping skills, but not all of them.

"'Kay. Dan and I are going to cut out and get busy. We'll keep you posted. See if you can get ahold of a tech for us? I can't imagine the job will be that hard for them." Hiring them for a few weeks of work? A pain in the neck. But something like this should be easy.

"Already on it. I'll let you know how it goes."

He kissed her cheek and went to collect Dan. Time to get to work again.

"So we're going to go rob some people?" Dan asked him.

Yoru shrugged. "Really, I plan to pickpocket two of them, and then stick my hand in someone's window and steal their laundry. Hardly glamorous, but I mean, it'll work."

"Then what am I here for?" Dan asked him, incredulous.

"What if I get punched?"

"You can punch people, I've seen you do it."

"I can't do it while I'm getting punched, Dan."

Dan laughed.

They caught a ride across town and Yoru was quiet, but when Dan asked him why he just said he was 'weighing possibilities' and Dan left him to it. When they got out into the sunlight again, Yoru swept his eyes across the concrete plaza skeptically.

"What are you looking for?" Dan asked.

"People getting off work." He looked at his watch and then at the building. "Stay here for just a minute. If you see me getting beat up, then you can come help."

"'Kay," Dan said, trying not to laugh too hard.

Yoru had no problem moving through the flow of people. Dan tried to spot what he was after, wondering if he could pick up on the same clues Yoru did. Still, if he was just looking to pick a few pockets, it probably was better that he worked alone. The two of them would just give someone more chances to remember them.

He expected to see Yoru trip, to stumble, his shoulder clip that of his target to turn them the way he needed to make the lift, but it never happened. Dan leaned against an ugly poured-concrete statue and waited, glancing up when he could to watch, but he saw nothing of the sort.

Maybe he was thinking too much like the stereotype. Dan had never been robbed, nor had he tried to rob someone else (okay, well, now he had, buildings and such, but not a person directly). He tried to watch more closely, but by then Yoru was already on his way back to where Dan was waiting.

"Did you get it?" he asked, incredulously.

Yoru grinned and tapped his jacket pocket.

"You're something else..."

"Next is the clothes, and they're going to be a little harder. But I picked up something that might help us." Yoru pulled something from his pocket.

"A dry cleaner tab?" Dan asked.

Yoru nodded. "It's also a wash and fold laundromat. Maybe we'll get lucky and someone else will use it, too. Or maybe we'll just have to follow some employees home and rob them the usual way. We'll see. I'm going to call Rusty and have her check it out for us. In the meantime, we're going to look for somebody to follow home."

"Might be a while before another shift change," Dan noted.

Yoru nodded. "Yup. The cards were the easy part. People are so careless with their ID."

"Says the master thief."

"You and Xueying with the flattery today." He gave a low whistle.

"Hey, maybe sometimes it's nice to try and make you feel the way you make other people feel," Dan said.

Yoru laughed a little, his cheeks flushing, and Dan was immediately pleased. "We should probably see if we have to break into some people's houses," he said, turning their attention back to work.

Dan let him. He was just happy to have made him smile.

The phone call to Rusty wasn't a complete waste. They waited and kept an eye out for employees while she went to search the shop they had suggested. While she did that, Yoru sent the information from the cards he had stolen to Xueying so she could get to work on getting them in the system.

"Like cogs in a machine," Dan noted.

"Teamwork."

Rusty's search turned up one uniform. "I have it. I pretended not to speak Omni and that I had lost my slip."

"That worked?" Dan asked, shocked.

"Do I look like someone you want to fight with?" she asked.

He had to admit, that changed things.

"So we have one. That's not quite enough," Yoru said quietly.

"Time to break into some poor sucker's house?" Dan asked.

"Sounds like. And I've got just the sucker in mind." Yoru motioned for Dan to follow him and he did. They walked, casually, in the direction of the subway, and it was some time before Dan asked where they were headed.

"Guy in the blue coat," Yoru said.

"You sure?"

Yoru nodded. "I saw him through the window earlier while I was picking pockets. And, he's short. Kind of handy for our tiny lady friends."

Well, they were both on the smaller side, so Dan had to admit that he had a point.

"So...we're just tailing him?"

"Yup. Kind of a bonus to living in a fucking big city is that there's too much noise and too many people to really think anyone is going the same place as you." Yoru shrugged.

He looked at the guy ahead of them and frowned a little. "Actually, we might not even need to follow him the whole way there..."

"Why's that?"

"When he turned, you can see he isn't wearing his uniform under his coat anymore. That means it's probably in the bag he's carrying."

217

Dan snorted in laughter. "You're going to jump him?"

"Fucking right I'm going to jump him."

"Yoru, you're a delinquent." Dan was trying not to laugh at any real volume, lest they draw attention to themselves, but the idea was hilarious.

"You're not going to tell my mother?" Yoru winked at him.

They slipped into the same subway car. Dan kept an eye on the man in the blue jacket while Yoru pretended to sleep against his shoulder in a way where he could still recite poetry under his breath. This definitely made Dan feel more useful, and he sat comfortably with his arm over Yoru's shoulders and tried not to react to what he heard whispered in his ear.

"Time to go." He nudged Yoru 'awake' and the two of them slipped from the subway car. The sky was just starting to darken, but the streets were nowhere near empty enough for them to get this guy alone.

"I'm gonna have to go bother him," Yoru said.

"I can do it," Dan offered.

Yoru shrugged. "Think you can?" And then, he shrugged again. "I mean, it's a pretty low risk one. If he puts up too much fuss I'll jump in and help. Meet you back at the subway? We'll catch the other line home."

"Sounds good." And then Dan grinned at him. "Now I get to be a delinquent. Don't tell my mom."

Yoru laughed, clapping a hand over his mouth to muffle the sound when Dan took off at a run. He sprinted ahead of him, heading straight for the back of the man they had been following.

Yoru watched as he crashed into him, grabbing the strap of the bag with his hand. The man fell, but also grabbed his bag as he went down.

Dan kicked him off, stumbled, and kept running.

The man was pulling himself to his feet, brushing himself off and cursing by the time Yoru was close. He didn't seem seriously hurt, just mad. Yoru kept his head down, and headed towards the nearest subway entrance.

Dan took a little while to show. He had run farther than he had to, just to make sure he was really free of it. But, the man seemed in no hurry to chase after someone for what Dan had taken, and he slipped into the waiting area completely unnoticed.

Yoru appeared at his elbow, silently enough that Dan jumped when he saw him.

"Feeling a little high strung?"

"Blame the adrenaline," Dan said with a laugh.

Dan adjusted the bag on his shoulder and the two of them took the next subway back to their own neighbourhood. Quick and easy.

"Okay, but we're washing this before I wear it, right?" Xueying said, looking in the bag Dan had lifted.

"I mean, we have time. You're not going until tomorrow night right?" he said. "That's plenty of time for some laundry."

"Good, because this guy smells like feet, apparently."

"Maybe he was just feet," Yoru suggested. "It could have been a clever disguise."

She went to hit his shoulder and Yoru moved sharply, making sure her jab connected closer to his elbow. Immediately she looked at him.

"Shit, I forgot. I'm sorry," she said.

"Crisis averted, nothing to fear," he reassured her.

Dan volunteered to get the uniform clean for Xueying. He didn't mind it. Apparently, he wasn't doing it right because Rusty came in and took over where he was scrubbing it clean in the bathtub.

"I've cleaned clothes by hand before," he said. "I know how to do it."

"You said you were done. It still has soap in it," she pointed out.

"Okay, maybe I wasn't done." Dan laughed sheepishly.

"The washing machine at home used to break all the time," she said as she rinsed the shirt out under the water. "We always ended up with soapy clothes and had to go outside and rinse them down. Pain in the ass."

"I bet." As she finished rinsing pieces, he took them and wrung them out, getting as much water out as he could before he hung them to dry.

They'd get in the way a little, but what could you do? They were dry by the time Xueying and Rusty needed them.

"How do we look?" Xueying asked.

"Definitely not like you're going to rob a datacenter," Yoru said with a smile.

"Good, that's kinda the point." Rusty matched his smile with one of her own. Dan had thought her so expressionless when they met, but it seemed as though she had warmed up to them.

"You want us here or there with you?" Yoru asked Xueying.

"Here. We'll have comms, but we don't want to have to worry about getting the four of us out of there," she said. "Just us should be plenty. All I'm doing is plugging into a computer and getting those prints. Once we're in, it should be fine."

"Should," Dan said.

She shrugged. "What else have we got?"

Of course, he had no answer.

They set out, and Yoru and Dan shared the mic that went to their earpieces. Not that they had anything relevant to say, but that hardly stopped them.

"They are so talkative," Rusty muttered.

"I just think they're antsy from being left behind," Xueying told her with a smile. "Being on the sidelines is always terrible."

The same building. The same absurd façade. The same steps. They climbed them without any sign of hurry. Rusty grabbed the door for Xueying, and they flashed their cards over the security reader. Both of them got through.

"Well, at least we know they work," Dan's voice in Xueying's ear.

People didn't even glance at them as they went by. They had garnered more attention wearing their uniforms on the subway than they did wandering around in them here.

"I guess, once you get passed the front doors and now that we look the part…no one really cares," Xueying mused.

By now, the building was closed to the public and on top of that, their cards got them access to hallways and offices that the public didn't see.

Accessing it via an office's personal computer would be a headache. But the storage centre underground? That would be much simpler.

The access elevators were a little rickety. Xueying seemed unbothered, but Rusty spoke up as she leaned against one of the walls. "Be just our luck for this thing to drop us," she said.

"Just gotta hope that luck likes us a little more than she likes the other guys."

Rusty didn't seem like she was holding out much hope for that.

"There, see, we're fine," Xueying said as they hit the ground floor.

Data storage towers in huge rows. Perfect.

"Does anyone clean this place?" Rusty looked around in disgust. "Computers are supposed to be…delicate, right? It's so dusty down here."

Xueying shrugged. "People are probably supposed to clean it. But who cares these days? Every day kind of feels like the end of the world so I guess people just…stop trying, after a while."

"Getting a little heavy there, darling," Yoru's voice in her ear. "But I won't tell you that you're wrong."

"I'll be surprised if they work well enough for us to jack what we need," Rusty said. Practical, as always.

"Can you imagine the state of panic if the data centre went down?" Yoru laughed in her ear again. "Then again, Xueying's probably right. I actually don't know if a lot of people would even notice…"

"Cut the poetics, I have to figure this out." Rusty hushed him as she was walking down the rows of servers. Labels, handwritten, ancient and yellow and neglected, curled away from where they had once been neatly taped.

"This one." She tapped the one she stood in front of. Technology and decay. The whole city. Maybe the whole world. She was sure Yoru would have something to say about it. She didn't ask him.

Xueying was the one with the handheld that could dig out what they needed from the mess and copy it over. Not even taking it, really, just copying it. That would be enough.

"I think I'm going to need to scrub out my lungs from all this dust," she said, tucking the computer back inside of her uniform as they took the elevator up into the world again.

They ditched the clothes in the dark of a back alley, tossing them in a garbage bin. It was chilly to wander the dark in only what they wore underneath, but Rusty wrapped an arm around Xueying and they hurried home.

26:

Oliver was not hungover the next day. He actually felt pretty good as he stretched out in his bed. He felt happier than he had since...well, he wasn't sure, exactly. But the house was quiet and memories of the night before rolled leisurely through his dozy, sleep-fogged brain as he slowly worked his way towards full wakefulness. It was pleasant to be so lazy.

He had a song stuck in his head, he realized. One of those atrociously catchy pop tunes that they had played at the bar. He didn't even know the words to it. With a groan, he pushed himself up and out of bed. He needed a shower. And then, if the song persisted, he'd put on one of his own to drive it out. Battle of the Earworms.

But stumbling to the bathroom left him with a strange problem; the door was cracked, the light inside was off, but it sounded as though the shower was running.

Oliver blinked at the door, waiting for the solution to present itself. When it didn't, he pressed his hand to the wood and pushed it open slowly. Then he flicked on the light.

It snapped on, and the person in the shower let out a gasp of surprise. The door was frosted glass but Oliver could see enough to know who it was; they were far too short to be Rosa, and too pale to be Ame. By the time his eyes found the blur of distinctly navy hair, Hastin had stumbled and fallen onto the shower floor, knocking over bottles of assorted bath products in the process.

"I'm sorry!" Oliver flailed and hit the light again, turning it off. He could still see some of the smudge that was his teammate, but what little details he had seen were now entirely lost.

"Are you okay?" he asked, a little panicky. Hastin was picking himself up, so at least it seemed like he was alright.

"It's okay, Captain!" he said, sounding a little unsteady. Oliver couldn't really blame him. He must have given him quite a start, and then with the fall...but he seemed to be steady on his feet once he got to them.

"Why are you showering with the light off, honey?" Oliver frowned, a little concerned.

"My head hurts."

Oh. Hangover. Oliver had escaped without one. There was no way Hastin was going to be so lucky.

"I'm sorry for scaring you, babe. How about I go grab you some painkillers? You can take them when you get out, okay?" Oliver tried to keep any wayward laughter from his voice. It was a little funny, but he was concerned about Hastin first and foremost.

"Okay, Captain!" A hand, sticking up above the door, pale fingers flashing him the okay sign.

Oliver went to collect some for him. He thought about leaving them in the bathroom for Hastin but reconsidered when he realized that he didn't want to startle him again. So he got himself some coffee and hung out in the living room until he heard the water turn off and saw Hastin shuffle back to his room.

Oliver followed and very gently knocked on his door. "Hey, honey. I have your pills and some water. Can I come in?"

"Yes, Captain." He sounded cheerful enough, at least.

His room was dark, too. He wore the same plain white shirt he always slept in, and it was no more modest here than before. Oliver found that to be less of a problem for him as time went on. Hastin was beautiful, but it wasn't the distraction it once was. These days, it was different things that drew Oliver's eyes. The way the young man currently had his towel still on his head, for example, looking up at Oliver with a slightly red-eyed smile from under it. He looked a little tired, but he didn't seem too hard done by.

Oliver was still blushing. Hastin still had an effect on him, of course. But he wasn't as tongue tied as he once was.

"How are you feeling?" he asked, sitting next to Hastin on his bed.

"Head hurts. My stomach was a little upset, but weirdly, showering helped. It's still a little topsy-turvy, but I'm okay." As he spoke, Oliver pressed the pills into his hand and passed him the glass of water. Then, now with free hands, he reached one up and brushed an errant lock of damp hair out of Hastin's face.

Hastin leaned into his touch and looked down at the pills in his hand. "These are good pills, right, Captain?" he asked Oliver.

"Yes." Oliver squeezed his shoulder. "They'll help you with your headache. They might upset your stomach again, though, so maybe we can try and get you something to eat?"

Hastin took the pills with no trace of hesitation. In fact, he drained the whole glass of water rather quickly.

"Okay. I'll go get something to eat. And maybe...get dressed, too. For real, I mean." He laughed a little.

"Hey, for your first night out drinking, you are recovering really well. I half expected to find you being sick this morning," Oliver told him. And then, affectionately, "I'm glad you're not."

"Me too!"

When he came out into the living room later, he was dressed as he said, and his damp hair was tied back into a braid. He was stocking-less, and rubbing his arms with his hands as he went into the kitchen to get something to eat. He was still doing it when he came back with some food on his plate, although it was a one-handed gesture at that point.

"Honey, you cold?" Oliver asked him, looking up.

He smiled, a little embarrassed. "Yeah."

"Lemme help." Oliver hopped up from his seat and went to his room to grab his sweater. Something fell out of the pocket when he did. It looked like a memory card, no bigger than his thumbnail.

Frowning, he tossed it on his bed. He'd figure that out later. When he gave Hastin his sweater, the younger man pulled it eagerly around his shoulders and then hugged himself tightly.

"Thank you, Captain."

"No problem, kid."

Rosa was the next to show her face. Oliver passed by her as she headed for the shower and he was headed back to his room to look at that memory card. He didn't remember having one in his pocket, and he really hadn't drank that much, so he was curious to see what he had misplaced.

He popped it into a reader and was surprised when it only had one file on it. A video file, with his name.

He didn't remember making a file like that. He didn't remember the last time he recorded something and had no idea why he would name it after himself, of all things. So, of course, he hit 'play' and sat himself back to rediscover whatever it was that he had forgotten.

Except it wasn't his own face that showed up on the screen. It wasn't his face, his apartment, or even a place he recognized.

But it was someone he recognized. He had seen her, once. And he had seen her picture.

Xueying looked back at him from the video screen. Same pink pixie-cut. Same movie-star eyes. He had never heard her speak before, but he had heard her sing, and when she spoke it was immediately her voice as he knew it would be.

"Oliver. Hello, I guess." He had seen her smile before. She had been smiling while she sang. She barely managed the hint of one here.

"I don't know if you'll get this. I don't even know if I'll send it out, but..." She sighed. "I'm giving this card to a friend of mine at The Tint. If we don't come back, he said he'd get it to you. Maybe I'll end up re-watching this myself and laugh..."

Her tone made it clear that she didn't think she would. A cold fog settled over Oliver's heart. That heavy, nebulous feeling of dread. This was the phone call all over again. Except this time, it wasn't a stranger calling to tell him about the death of a friend.

No, the stranger was right here, in front of him. And she had known about her own death.

"I didn't want to drag you into this, but I did a little digging. You're far enough out of the business that I don't think she'd bother connecting you with us. You should be safe. But I want you to know. Someone has to know. Someone has to warn everyone."

It was as though the world around him fell away. He could feel it, like she was right there in front of him. His one reference of her was that narrow window when he watched her sing. Other than that, she had spent the night hanging out at the other end of the bar. But she had seemed happy.

There was something deeply troubling her now. Something that made his heart ache.

"I think we're being played," she told him. "This woman, Selene Violet, I don't know what she's after...but I think this whole thing is bad news. I mean, I've taken some pretty rough jobs before but...I've never felt like this. If I turn up dead, someone fucked me over," she said sharply. "And if they turn up dead...if something happens to Rusty and Yoru and Dan, it's because someone made it happen. We're not here to get killed. I wouldn't pull my friends into a job I thought would kill them. I..."

She pressed her hands to her face. The sound quality was kind of shit, and the video was just grainy enough to notice. She might have said something, or maybe she cursed. Oliver couldn't be sure. When she looked up, her eyes were glassy.

"Look, Oliver... I know you didn't ask to be part of this shit. But I can't risk handing this over to someone closer. You're about as far to the outside as someone like me can get."

A bitter laugh. Oliver's own eyes threatened to blur. He blinked the tears away.

"Just take this file to someone good. It's loaded with proof. I learned that trick from a friend of mine back in the day." Xueying smiled at him. "Just...

get the word out. I don't want anyone else getting burned. I could be wrong. This is all just a gut feeling... She'd be stupid to fuck something like this up. If we get out, you might never see this..."

She sighed then, and looked at him with an unspeakable sadness in her eyes. "I don't know if we're going to get out."

That was it. It wasn't a long video. Few minutes, max. Way smaller than the file size should have been. Of course, she had stuffed it with other things. Rosa would know how to pull it apart.

But Oliver's thoughts weren't on that. It processed those things almost mechanically, in some quiet, distant part of his brain that didn't feel anything. But once it hit that end point, it stopped.

Oliver didn't cry. He thought he would, but the tears never really came. He fell back onto his bed, staring up to the blank, off-white of the ceiling.

They had been set up. Dan hadn't done it. It wasn't suicide. It was murder.

But what did his heart care? Dan was still gone. And Xueying, well...he didn't know her. But she had been alive once, too. Not that long ago. And she had looked to Oliver with hope.

Well, she had looked to Oliver with something. There had been no hope in
her eyes in the video. Just anguish. Anguish, and maybe something else that he couldn't quite name. A sense of finality that he didn't have a word for.

You might never see this, she said, but she hadn't believed that even when she said it.

An overwhelming sense of loneliness threatened to drown him. What was he going to do? What could he do?

But that was what broke it. Years of work to win a gruelling, struggling mastery over his own anxiety meant that those thoughts now had a quick and solid answer.

The answer was, of course, that he wasn't dealing with this alone. To think that was irresponsible and inaccurate. It also meant that he wasn't in charge of solving the whole problem by himself. No, he had a team, and keeping this from them was both inconsiderate and dangerous.

And while he hated the idea of showing it to them, hated to be the one to bring their whole job, all their hard work and their preparation and desires to a screeching halt, the fact that he was responsible for them made it impossible to avoid.

This changed everything. In fact, it more than changed it, it made a ruin of it.

He had no more than shown his face in the living room than was Hastin on his feet, worry on his face. Ame and Rosa weren't far behind, looking to him with concern.

"I got something you guys gotta see," he said, and that was all he could really say about it.

So he sat down on the carpet and the three of them sat behind him on the couch and looked over his shoulder. The same grainy video. Xueying's same heavy words. And from behind him, silence.

The same silence pervaded once the clip ended. Watching it a second time had been no easier on Oliver. He had never felt so relieved and so disgusted simultaneously before.

It was Rosa who broke the silence. "I need to get my hands on that file. I need to see what we're getting into here."

"To fucking hell, apparently," Ame said. "This whole job is a bust if this shit is true, and I don't know about you guys but I believe the dead girl. People don't just do this shit for fun."

"Here." Oliver clicked the memory card from its holder and passed it to Rosa. "I don't know what's there, but I don't think she's lying, either."

"No, I believe her, and that's what has me worried. I just want to know precisely what kind of fucked we are." Rosa may not have seen what they had seen, but she had heard it, and that was enough. There was no lie in Xueying's voice. That kind of despair wasn't easily faked.

"So, what do we do? Violet screwed over the other team and what... had them killed? Is that what we're getting at here?" Ame ran her hand through her hair, scowling. "So it doesn't matter if we finish this job or not, she's going to try and screw us. That's what this means, isn't it?"

"Looks like..." Weirdly, Oliver's despondency was tempered a little by the fact that at least he wasn't alone in this. He felt entirely at a loss. Of all the things that could go wrong, this wasn't one he had seen coming. "I should have known... I should have figured it out..."

"Figured out what? That she's a fucking psycho? What person in their right mind screws over their own hires? Even if they fucked up, you kick their ass to the street and hire someone to do it right. You can't just go around killing them or no one will want to work for you! It's a rule."

"That's why she lied." Oliver pressed a hand to his face. "The suicide. Dan's. That's why she lied. She's been lying this whole time. Of course she did."

"That's low," Rosa said, the disgust clear in her voice.

Hastin had said nothing. Oliver looked back at him, but he was staring at the space that had been occupied by the video.

Ame looked over to him, too. Rosa didn't have to, of course, but it was clear her attention had shifted all the same.

Hastin said nothing.

"Kinda makes sense why she stuck the assassin on our team now, doesn't it?" Ame said quietly.

Hastin flinched. He still didn't speak.

"Hastin..." Oliver laid a hand on his knee but Hastin jumped, pulling himself away and pressed his hands to his face, curling in on himself like a dead flower.

"I don't know if that's what I'd panic about," Rosa commented dryly. "I mean, yes, it's incredibly underhanded of her...but it's not like she gave him a choice." The bitterness in her voice, though, made it all too clear that she agreed with Ame's deduction.

Hastin stood up quickly. He stepped over where Oliver had been sitting at his feet, but still kept his hands to his face. When he sat down again, it was almost as though his legs had given out. Oliver winced.

"Hastin..." But he didn't look when Oliver called him. That seemed more strange than anything. Hastin jumped to obey him. This should have been better, but it wasn't.

With a shuddering sigh, Hastin finally removed his hands. He looked stricken, and though he looked in their direction, Oliver almost felt as though he was being looked through.

When he pulled a gun from under his skirt without even looking down, Oliver jumped. He felt Ame tense, but wasn't sure why she bothered. What was she going to do? Even if she had bothered to wear a weapon while they were lounging around, she wouldn't be fast enough.

Rosa didn't move. She was completely still. Watching. Maybe waiting. Between her and Ame, Hastin would have been short work. He was good, but no one was that good.

But no one had expected him to sit down in front of them and pull a gun, either.

And no one expected him to set it on the carpet, with the handle at Oliver's feet.

"There's nothing I can do," Hastin said. The ache in his voice was terrible to hear, but at least when he looked at Oliver now, he looked right at him. "Ame's right. That's why she put me here. She never told me, but I knew... I knew..."

He pushed the gun with his hand until the grip bumped Oliver's foot. "It's too dangerous. I can't prove that I'm safe. There's no way—" A crack in his voice and he took a shaking breath.

"You have to run. You have to get away from her. It's safer if you kill me now."

27:

Rusty and Xueying made it back to their hideout, a little shivery but otherwise unharmed. Yoru was quick to supply them with tea, and Dan found a spare blanket for them to wrap themselves in. Or, that was the idea. It was a little small for the both of them, so Rusty gave it to Xueying. She bundled herself in it, looking surprisingly regal for a woman in a blanket with a mug in her hand.

"Could've worn more layers," Dan pointed out to them.

"Wouldn't fit under the uniforms." Xueying sipped her tea, but she didn't seem sour about the whole affair. "But hey, it worked. We have the blueprints and we didn't die. 'A' Plus."

"'A' Minus,." Rusty corrected. "I'm freezing."

"If I may—" Yoru again to the rescue. Where Rusty stood with her arm wrapped around herself, Yoru gestured to her with both of his.

She hesitated, frowning, and then went over to him. Like a snake that was equal parts languid and smug, he wrapped his arms around her. His smile was entirely serene, and he leaned his head against hers lightly.

"I was skeptical but…" she started, "You're really warm."

"Happy to provide my services," he said easily.

Once they had returned to a more comfortable state, Xueying's mind was back on the job. "What's next?"

"We need to see what kind of a break-in we're going to pull," Yoru said. "We need details on the building's security."

"Except we can't go in during the day. This place isn't open to the public at all," she said. "We could try to fake some references to get in there while they're open, but it almost seems better if we just do a soft break-in first… "

"We fuck up and they crack down on security," Dan said.

Xueying frowned, but nodded. "Yeah. Better not fuck up, then. Working around that would be a real serious headache."

Dan frowned. "There's no way to prep a backup plan ahead of time?"

"Not if we don't know what they're going to do when they crank up their security," Rusty said.

"Not gonna lie, I am concerned."

"You better be less concerned, because you're coming with me," Xueying told him.

He looked at her. "For real?"

"For real." She nodded. "I can get us in, but if we trip anything, I'm going to need someone to help me get out. That's you. You did a fantastic job at the computer centre. You're a heck of a shot, and you were quick with the plans." Her original plan had been to take Yoru, and to be honest, that was still the strongest idea. But, Dan had proven himself, and she wanted to give him another chance.

He had been a little distracted at the time with getting out of there, and then later with getting Yoru's injury taken care of... But he had done rather well, hadn't he? It was nice to be noticed, especially by someone like Xueying who was a professional. Of course, Yoru regularly reminded him that he was doing well, and Dan did not think he was lying. But this was different.

"Okay," he said, looking a little more sure of himself. "Let's go breaking and entering. It sounds like fun."

"You and Xueying will read all the information you get back to Rusty and I, and we'll record it. When we're going in for the job itself, the four of us will have a plethora more of information to work with."

"Just reconnaissance. Nothing we can't handle," Xueying agreed.

Dan thought for a moment, his arms crossed. "You know... I kind of wish I had been a worse kid sometimes. Maybe I'd have more experience with this stuff."

"Never too late to be a kid," Yoru reminded him.

Dan laughed.

They took a day to rest, and to look at the information that they had for the building. Entrances, exits, known security, the streets and alleys that would take them in and out. Dan had a good memory, and he felt confident going over these things. Plus, Xueying was incredibly clever. If he forgot, he knew she wouldn't.

And, of course, having the blueprints would help.

The building's size was a testament to how out of place it was. Sure, it was a major data centre, and was relied on by the city itself for much of its infrastructure needs...but it was small, and squished between two much larger towers. The only investing that ever went into Spectra was corporate. Why waste tax dollars on things they actually needed? Eventually, a company would privatize it and build their own.

Sure, Dan knew that. But it seemed that every corner of this job reminded him over and over again in ways he never would have realized.

231

When it got dark, they packed everything they thought they would need and made sure their comms worked before they stepped out the door. Of course the comms worked. How else would Yoru soliloquize at them as they crossed town?

"You're insufferable," Xueying muttered, but she had a smile on her lips that wouldn't quite fade.

Still, the chatter wasn't bad. They didn't need to be on high alert yet anyway, and Yoru had a way of making Dan feel like this was any other adventure. True, they hadn't had many of those to speak of yet, which made what Yoru did all the more impressive. He made this feel natural and comfortable.

Dan had remembered co-op classes in high school that had made him more nervous than this.

He mostly didn't want to fuck up anything for Xueying. She was nice, and he knew her years of experience left him in the dust. Still, he wasn't going to close that gap by lying around, was he? She had been kind enough to reassure him. It was time to show her that she was right.

They took the subway. Dan noticed a lot of that. It made sense. There were cameras, sure, but once you knew where they were they were easy to give trouble to. They ran on the same schedule, and they ran if they were full or not. There were always enough people on the platforms to cause trouble; even at the latest hours of the night, some people had no better place to sleep.

"You're going to run out of material eventually," Dan noted quietly as they stepped into the street.

"You insult me," Yoru replied lightly.

Still, that seemed enough of a hint, and there was nothing more from him as they looked around in the dark.

"We have to get to those cameras," Xueying said, gesturing to the ones they had previously discussed. "If we stick close to the side of this building, we'll be out of the range of those ones over there..."

Dan nodded. They had already figured out the cameras they needed to disable. Now it was just a matter of getting close enough to them to do it.

Dan didn't think he had ever really taken the time to appreciate darkness as much as he found he did now. There was a freeing sense of anonymity in the shadows. He could see why Yoru felt so at home in them.

He boosted Xueying up to wrap a leech onto one of the cameras, and then did it again on the other side of the alley for the same reason. While they weren't really worried about them, it would give them some breathing room to work. With that done, they turned their attention to the back door of the building. It was looming and dark, seeing as it was long closed for the day.

"The door is going to be alarmed, that much is obvious. You have more toys for that?" he asked Xueying.

"In a manner of speaking..." Gadgets were great. There was a piece of tech out there for everything your average petty criminal could want. She pulled something from her belt, something metal, and wedged it in the crack of the door. Carefully, she moved it along the edge of the door until the red light on the other end went off.

"There's a contact device on the other side of the door. Probably a motion detector, to let them know when the door is open. Fry it for me?" she asked Dan nonchalantly.

"What?"

"Why not?" she said, and shrugged. "I mean, that's what I'm going to do, anyway. I just thought I might as well ask you."

Dan shrugged and switched her spots, holding onto the device. "It doesn't freak you out?" he asked.

"Nah. I mean, sure, it's weird, but like...everything is weird." She sighed. He had to agree with her there.

Then he paused. "If I use this thing, I'm going to wreck it. Do we have a piece of metal I could jam in there instead?" he asked her.

She went digging. There was enough thrown away in the alley that it only took her seconds to find something suitable. He pulled the tester out and traded her for the scrap metal, which he unceremoniously wedged in its place.

"You sure this will work?" he asked her.

She nodded. "If I wasn't, I wouldn't be asking, right?"

Fair. He nodded back at her and took a deep breath before holding on tight to the hunk of metal that stuck out of the door. He could actually feel where it hit the contacts on the other side. That seemed a little strange. Still, it was more interesting than unpleasant. Just as Xueying suggested, he focused until he felt the other side of the metal melting.

"Mmm... I'm making a mess. I didn't see that coming..."

"Better get that door open before it cools itself closed," she said. Good point. The melted metal wasn't exactly going to make it easy to get in there if they waited.

He cracked the door open. No alarm. He grinned. Looks like he had done just fine.

"That's a start. You got something for the camera on the inside?"

"You're not asthmatic, right?" she asked, handing him a smoke bomb.

Sure, it would show up on camera, but considering how little light there was, well...it sure wouldn't show up much. Besides, it meant they wouldn't show up, either.

Dan waited until the hallway was full of smoke before he pulled the door open again and they both slipped inside. It was even darker inside than out. The hallway had no windows, and the closed door let in none of the scant light from the alley.

"There's gotta be a camera pointed at this door," Xueying said. "Help me find it."

"Got it." It was habit that had him confirm verbally rather than to nod. In the darkness, she may not have seen him. Sure, his work experience might have been different, but there was some overlap.

With the door closed, and the smoke that was now rolling through the hall, it made it as hard for them to find anything as it did for them to be found. He half expected it to be hard to breathe but there didn't seem to be any such trouble, and he spotted the camera before she did.

"Xueying, it's here. C'mon." Too high for him to reach, though. She was pretty easy to lift, and he hefted her up so that she could wire another leech onto it.

"Okay. So, we're in. I think that's the hardest part." She crossed her arms, thinking.

"What, really?"

"Well yeah. From here, we should be able to use blind spots to get around more easily. And, it's going to be too dark for their motion detectors to work."

Dan frowned. "Too dark? You think they used to have emergency lights?"

She nodded. "Yeah. That's what that is." She pointed to a square panel in the wall up by where the camera was. "They would have helped the cameras, too. Which also means it's very unlikely that they have infra or anything like that."

But Dan was still looking up to where she had pointed.

"Wow... Everything in this city really is garbage," he mused.

"It's not like that where you grew up?"

He shrugged. "I wasn't breaking into places where I grew up."

"Remind me—" Yoru's voice in his ear. "—next time we get a chance, we'll go home and rob some people."

Dan laughed, but pressed a hand to his mouth to keep it quiet.

Home. Hearing him say it like that was only strange in how natural it sounded.

For now, he and Xueying were basically playing 'spot the camera before it spots you', and they were doing pretty well at it. Once they had as many of them wired up as they could, it would make getting back in much easier.

As they worked, Dan scanned every room they entered. "Would any of these computers work? What are we looking for?"

Xueying looked at them. "I'm not sure. I'd start with these when we come back. I'm not an expert at these things, but I'm pretty okay. If I can't get it from here, there's probably an easier access point."

"And that's using the code generator that you bought?"

Xueying nodded. "Yeah, assuming it works. If not, I have some doors to go knock down. But, that's tomorrow's worry. For today, we just make sure this place is safe to get in and out, for us at least."

Neither of them had thought anything about chatting. They talked to each other, and made remarks to Yoru and Rusty, who made the appropriate notes or joked at their expense. Dan was firmly convinced by now that Xueying had been right. The hardest part had been not tripping the contact on the back door.

Until someone flicked the lights on, shouted something Dan didn't catch, and started shooting.

He didn't even have time to swear. Yoru must have heard the gunshots because he was asking Dan what happened, but he didn't have the chance to think of a response. He ducked behind a wall, trying to find cover until his eyes adjusted. Live security. Of course. It made sense, now that the lights were on and they were being shot at.

Xueying had the same idea. He saw her hiding, ducked down behind a table, pulling her gun out of her belt. He did the same. He really didn't want to shoot these guys. That was going to end up causing them a lot more mess than they needed for a job like this. Or maybe they were screwed anyway. The cameras couldn't get them, but these guys might be able to.

When she fired back, the shots she took were aimed noticeably lower than he thought would be appropriate. He took that as advice, and tried to do the same.

"Dan, Dan, you gotta tell me—"

"Pinned down. Two hostiles," Dan snapped. "Might be more. Working on it."

That would have to do for now.

The lights helped him get a better idea of the room he was working with. The two people shooting at them were ducked behind the door, having been driven back when Xueying started returning fire. There was nothing outstanding about the room, and the computers they would have once used to try and access the stored data were now certainly garbage. They were going to need a different room to use as an access point.

There was a flash in his brain. A moment where he couldn't place himself. Was he in Spectra City? Or was he on patrol? Where was his squad? Where was he? When was he?

Pain tried to pull him back. Burning. He had been hit, grazed along the back of his arm. He ducked behind the table again, short of breath and blinking distortions out of his eyes.

Without his help, Xueying was losing her attempt to keep them out of the room. She shot out the window, looking to make an exit for them. The pain from his injury actually wasn't that bad, it was the shock, and whatever fresh hell his brain was putting him through.

It felt like a film reel, rolling backwards and then jumping ahead, trying to find its place. He was disoriented and though she shouted for him, he barely heard it.

Xueying was out the window and looked back to see the security guards in the room, one of them yanking Dan to his feet and the other moving to the window. She didn't give him the chance to fire at her again and made herself scarce, heart hammering.

"We're fucked," she said, knowing Yoru would hear her.

"We're already on our way. What's going on?" Rusty's voice answered her instead.

"Live security. Turned the fucking lights on and started shooting. They've got Dan. Don't think they're going to shoot him, seeing as they have no idea who we are."

"Make sure they don't leave the premises. We're minutes away," Yoru then, terse and short. Pointedly unlike him. And the building was so fucking big that there was little she could do to make sure of that. She didn't think they were going to shoot Dan. She had run off, so Dan being alive was their best bet at actually getting the cops to investigate.

To be fair, that probably also meant that they wouldn't leave, and would wait for the cops to come to them. Xueying was a patient person, but waiting for the others to show up while she paced the alleyway was stomach-turningly awful.

At the very least, she didn't have to worry about being startled. She knew Yoru's footsteps by the sound. Already, she felt more calm just to see them.

"They're inside, but cops are probably on the way," she said. "I don't know how much time we have."

Yoru shook his head. "Doesn't matter, we still have to go. Dan's not answering when we call out, so they either have his headset or it was broken, or, you know—"

"He's unconscious," Rusty finished. Rather than the alternative, of course.

Yoru was scowling, and Xueying shot a look of concern to Rusty. It was all the time they spared before they went inside.

28:

"Hold on a fucking second."

Oliver almost didn't believe that those words came from his mouth. Not that he was a stranger to cursing, but the force with which he said them seemed highly unlike him.

He nudged the gun away from himself with a single finger, too uncomfortable to touch it more than that. Then he crawled across the floor to where Hastin sat and opened his arms.

"Come here."

It wasn't a request.

Hastin did as he was ordered, pressing himself against Oliver's chest where the other man hugged him tightly. "Hastin. Look. We're fucked. No matter what kind of files she's got hiding in there, Xueying is dead, and that makes it pretty obvious what happened. That means we're not going to do this job. It also means that you're not going back."

"Captain—"

"No," Oliver said firmly. "I've hated the idea ever since you got here. She's not taking you back."

Hastin quieted, and Oliver looked over to the couch, ready to face any argument.

None came.

"We might be already fucked, all of us," Ame said. "If this place is bugged, the three of us are dead and I don't even want to think about—"

Oliver shut her up with a sharp look, and tightened his arms around Hastin.

"If this place is bugged. If. Didn't we check that when we got here?" Ame said instead.

Rosa sighed. "No, we didn't, because—"

"Because I said I had already checked...." Hastin's voice was muffled, but not quieted so much that they couldn't hear him.

"Then that settles it." Rosa stood up.

"Settles what?" Oliver asked, suspicious.

"I'm going to do a bug sweep. If the apartment is clear, then..."

"Then he's telling the truth," Ame finished. She got to her feet, too.

"I'll help."

Oliver and Hastin didn't move. The two of them went room to room, with handheld machines that Oliver could only guess at the purpose of. Did they look for things transmitting signals? Or maybe they tried to track something else about the bugs that Oliver couldn't understand? Trying to puzzle it out seemed like a waste of time.

He sat on the carpeted floor, one arm around Hastin's middle while the other rubbed his back. Oliver could feel the lines of his dress under the sweater he wore. "I don't give a damn what they find..." he said, muttering the words against Hastin's hair. There was an edge to his voice that surprised even him. "You're not going back."

The apartment wasn't very big. The four small rooms, the main living area and the kitchen. It took them minutes to go through them. When they did, they returned to the living room in silence.

Ame sat down next to Hastin and Oliver. After a moment of waiting, Rosa sat, too.

"We found nothing. No bugs," Rosa said. "Violet's got enough money to make some pretty fancy shit, but nothing I can't find. The house is clear."

"Baby..." Ame put her hand on Hastin's shoulder. "We wanted to believe you. But this job is a bitch, you know that."

Hastin raised his head. That stricken look didn't seem to have left him, but he nodded. "I know, I know..." he said, so quiet she could barely hear him. "I just want you to be safe. It's not... I mean, I'm not...."

"Hastin." Rosa's turn to speak up. Her voice was level and calm. Of all of them, she was the hardest to shake and it seems that the situation hadn't managed that yet. She took Hastin's hands when he looked to her.

"Trust is built by these kinds of things. Even if you had tried to tell us in the beginning that this job would go sour, there wouldn't have been any proof. Now we have proof of that, and that you were telling the truth about the bugs. It's one thing for us to like you. It's an entirely different thing for us to trust you."

He slumped down against Oliver, who just held him close.

"I'm going to open up that file and see what kind of trouble we're looking at," Rosa said, getting to her feet.

"In which case, I'll make us something to eat. We can't plan on empty stomachs." Ame stood up, too.

But she didn't go to the kitchen at first. She went to her room and came back with a vidscreen. It was much newer, and much shinier, than any scrap one Oliver had put together. She knelt down and handed it to him.

"There's a bunch of movies I've got saved on there. Tons, actually. Not sure what you like, but I thought maybe you guys—" she nodded to Hastin, "could watch something together. Maybe…decompress a little."

Probably a good idea. Oliver knew how to handle anxiety, and he had a couple tricks for managing his depression. He did not know, at a glance, what was going on with Hastin. What he did know was that he wasn't about to let the boy deal with it alone.

"Lay with me and watch a movie?" Oliver nuzzled against Hastin's hair.

"Okay, Captain…"

Oliver had a fondness for kid's movies. Ame did too, apparently. And pornography, although the two lists were markedly separate. He went to tug Hastin over to the couch, but the younger man was slow to react.

"Hastin?"

"Mm?"

"You wanna talk about it?" Oliver asked him.

He shook his head, and when Oliver laid down and made room for him, he found himself room on the couch and pressed his face against Oliver's chest again. Oliver eschewed the movie, found a list of music labelled 'sleep' and tapped it on. He set the vidscreen aside, and used his hands instead to play with Hastin's hair.

He knew that he liked it when he was stressed out, although Oliver reasoned that 'stressed' didn't begin to describe how he must have been feeling. Still, with how Hastin seemed to be clinging to affection, it seemed to be a safe bet.

For a while, everything seemed to be okay. At one point, Hastin shuddered really hard and Oliver froze, worried he had done something wrong.

But when Hastin raised his head, there was finally some semblance of clarity in his eyes.

"I'm sorry, Captain, I just—" he tried to explain, but ran out of words before he got anywhere with it.

Oliver shook his head. Hastin sighed and laid back down.

"Don't be sorry, hun. You know, um…" It was his turn to sigh. "When I was younger, I used to get really anxious about stuff. Like, it was really bad. I'd, like…have these breakdowns where I couldn't breathe, or I couldn't stop shaking. It was really miserable. I cried all the time."

Hastin shifted, laying his chin on his hand so he could look up at Oliver as he spoke.

240

"I don't cry a lot," he said. He sounded thoughtful, not insulting. "The last time I cried...was when you were hurt, Captain. But I can't remember before that..."

Oliver smiled, brushing his fingers over Hastin's cheek. "I still cry a lot. But, I do a lot better day to day, too. I work on it, and I'm pretty okay most of the time. I just thought, you know..."

Hastin smiled. It was weak, but it was there. "You want to make me feel better for what happened..."

Oliver nodded. "It's okay to not be okay."

Hastin took a deep breath. "I just... I've never been that scared before. When I saw that video, I just... Something happened. I froze up. It was so hard to move... I..."

This pause was unlike the others. Hastin hesitated, but kept trying. Oliver waited.

"I've never had anything to lose before. It... It never really mattered what they did to me. How much can you take away from someone who doesn't have anything?"

"Oh, baby..."

"I was so scared. And I'm still scared. But...less. I guess I just forgot what it felt like..." Hastin closed his eyes and took another deep breath. "It's hard to be scared when you're here."

Ame came back then, and she looked curiously at her vidscreen that was laying on the ground before she laid her hand on Hastin's head. "Food's ready."

Carefully, the younger man pulled himself to his feet, followed much more slowly by Oliver. Ame lingered then for a moment, taking Hastin's hand in hers.

"Baby...are you mad at me?" she asked.

He shook his head, eager to talk now that he had found his words. "No, no, Ame... I was afraid. I don't want anything to happen to you. I was just so scared." He shook his head.

She hugged him. "Nothing's going to happen. We're going to figure this out. All of us. Okay?"

"I...I feel a little better now. I just... I was scared for you. And for Rosa, and Captain."

"We're going to be okay. And—" She pulled back to look at him. "We ain't goin' anywhere. You know how hard I would have cried if we had to leave tonight? Oh, honey..."

"Why?"

Oliver looked over at him, and Ame for a moment did the same thing. They were both surprised by the question.

"Why would you cry?" he asked again, tilting his head.

"Hastin, oh, Hastin…" Ame hugged him again. "I was gonna go and bawl my eyes out because I don't wanna say goodbye, kid. And Oliver's right. We're not gonna. I know we had a scare, but we're gonna be okay."

They hugged for a long moment, and then Ame let go of him. "Food's gonna get cold. We can talk more after we eat. We're going to have a lot of planning to do if we're going to make this bitch's life miserable."

"I'll get Rosa." Oliver ducked out to do exactly that and Ame tugged Hastin into the kitchen. Hastin stuck next to her for the whole meal, and there was a thick silence over the table as they ate. It wasn't uncomfortable. Oliver was an expert at uncomfortable silences and this wasn't the same.

So he finally spoke up. "What's the verdict on those files?" he asked Rosa.

"Details from the first job and what they were after. Xueying apparently thought finishing it was a bad idea. Can't say I disagree, especially with what we know now. There's a bunch of peripheral information about Violet, too."

She paused to eat more before continuing. "Apparently, she was funding an orphanage at one point. A few years later it dissolved, no trace of the kids, and she buried her ties to it. She's got her fingers in the insurance sector, which makes sense. What she wants from us is to get her hands onto the city records so she can extort people, it looks like. According to Xueying's notes, they managed to get the information, but realized what she could do with it and backed out of the job."

"That's fuckin' dirty," Ame said. "People back out of shit all the time. But you blacklist them, you don't kill them."

Rosa nodded. "Apparently, the files were health records, income, all that kind of stuff. So Violet can fleece them as she pleases."

Oliver, already frustrated, slammed his hand down on the table. No one jumped, but Hastin looked at him sharply.

"Sorry, honey. I just… People have so little. So many people are just scraping by. Most families are clinging to their last chances at having legitimate incomes. I couldn't tell you how hard I looked for a 'real' job. I spent years trying to find some kind of legal work. There's nothing out there. She's going to hurt so many people…"

"She already has. She's been doing this for years. That old bag has been running HiTech for a decade now. She's been pulling this shit the whole time, it looks like," Rosa said, frowning.

"So the question then is... How do we get our asses out of this mess?" Ame sighed, toying with the tab on her drink. "What the fuck are we gonna do about this..."

"First things first, we need to get out of this apartment," Rosa said.

"Thought you said it wasn't bugged?" Oliver asked.

She shook her head. "It's not. But staying still gives her plenty of chances to keep an eye on us. I don't want to give her any handouts if we can help it."

"I can find us a place," Ame said. "I'm good at that."

"And what, we're just going to run? If she starts looking for us now, we're fucked," Oliver pointed out.

Hastin shook his head. "Then we make sure she doesn't start looking now."

They looked at him. He seemed to shrink at that, but Ame caught it when Oliver did. She put her arm around his shoulder. "It's okay, honey. Tell us what's on your mind."

"I'm supposed to give her updates on our progress. I've been... slacking," he admitted. His gaze went to the table guiltily, and then back up to them. "So...I should probably vidcall her anyway. I know how to make a public line secure, but, I'm sure Rosa can work around that..."

Rosa nodded. "What are you getting at?"

"I call her and give her an update. Tell her that we're moving base... but you guys haven't told me the location yet. Tell her I'll get it before the next call. Tell her the job is going fine. Rosa can listen in, make sure I stick to the script—"

"Honey—"

"No," Rosa said. "Hastin. You want me to listen?"

Hastin looked to Oliver, who had been the one to start the objection. "Captain, it would make me feel better if she did. I want a chance to prove myself. Please."

"And she'll buy it?" Ame asked.

Hastin nodded. "She doesn't think I'm capable of lying."

"Serves her fucking right," Oliver spat.

They got the call set up that night. The little 24-hour cafe Hastin picked out was scummy as hell and he stood out like mad, but it was a great place to make a call that you didn't want to be shared.

Although, considering that Hastin had popped the casing off the wiring and fed a feeder into it, it wasn't as though he feared being overheard.

243

It was kind of comforting, actually, because he was alone. Knowing that Rosa would be listening helped him to feel more connected to his team, despite the distance now between them. The night felt almost cold despite the jacket he wore. He didn't realize how much his team changed the very atmosphere he surrounded himself with. The same fear he felt earlier tried to claw its way up his chest, but he was a master of dismissing his own emotions and set it aside for now. Yes, he risked losing them. Yes, finally having something to lose was terrifying.

He took a deep breath. He typed in the code for the call, thanked the server who brought him a hot chocolate, and waited for an answer.

He didn't have to wait long.

"You're late." Violet herself. Sometimes it was her. Sometimes it was Donovan. It was all the same to Hastin.

"Yes," he said calmly. "There've been developments. I was hoping to have more answers before I called."

"And?"

He shook his head. "We're changing locations. Apparently there's been some activity in the building that they don't like the sound of." He shrugged. "What do you expect with apartment blocks? But if it's enough to set them off—"

"We haven't seen anything."

He shrugged again. "That may be the case, but I can't use that information to deter them. I have to abide by their whims."

"Where are you moving?"

He shook his head. "Either they haven't worked out a location, or they haven't considered me worthy of knowing. You will know when I know."

"Better be quick."

He nodded.

"Anything else?"

"Progress on the job is moving well. Despite how much they are unnecessarily complicating things, they do otherwise seem to know what they are doing," he said levelly. This part of the job was not difficult. It was much harder to be honest. He had all the patience in the world for lies. They were so much easier.

He sipped his drink. It was hot, and the chocolate was fake. But it was sweet. "There's nothing to worry about yet. We'll relocate and continue on with the job," he said quietly. "Soon, everything will be taken care of."

"See that it is."

"Ma'am."

She ended the call. He pulled out the wire, closed the case, and finished his hot chocolate. Then, he headed back to the safe-house.

No sooner had he stepped in the door than Ame was there, pulling him into a hug. A little confused—but hardly upset—he hugged her back.

"What is it? Is something wrong?" he asked her.

"I can't believe she talks to you like that!" she said, sounding angry. "She's just... I can't believe it!"

He blinked, still a little confused. "You...heard?"

Ame pulled him into Rosa's room, and it was Oliver who answered him. "We all heard. Rosa thought it would be better if we were all on the same page."

"Good call," he said, smiling.

"It wasn't a good call. What the fuck is wrong with that lady," Ame said.

Hastin looked between all of them. "I didn't think it went that badly? She didn't even have to threaten me."

"She talks to you like you're not a person," Rosa pointed out.

Hastin shrugged. "She doesn't think I am. Captain—" Hastin turned to Oliver. "Why do you think she believes me? I'm not a person. I'm a...a tool, probably comes closest. Not the part with the will, just the part that carries it out."

"That's fucked up, honey," Rosa said.

Hastin shrugged, wrapping his arms around himself. "I...well..."

"Hastin." Oliver took his hands. "Do you remember what I told you about how my brain sometimes just didn't behave itself?"

He nodded.

"Part of that was because of where I grew up," Oliver said. "It was pretty terrible, and it screwed me up pretty good. You had it even worse, baby. It's gonna be rough... But I think a good first step is to recognize that how she sees you isn't how you are."

"Captain?"

"You're not a thing. You're a person," he said.

Hastin swallowed, and looked between the three of them. "But...am I your person?"

"What do you mean?"

Hastin shifted uncomfortably. "What if I'm not ready to be a whole person on my own yet? I...I don't know how."

Oliver sighed, and it didn't take much in the way of coaxing to pull Hastin into a hug. "Yes. You're our person. And we're going to take care of you."

Lost Names

29:

Even with the lights on, Yoru and Xueying moved fast. Their expertise was immediately clear in how quickly they cleared areas and how little they needed to talk. Rusty, with less of a background in subtlety, had some trouble keeping up.

"How many were there?" Yoru asked. No time for caution or complicated plans. He shot out the cameras he saw as they made their way into the building. New cameras meant ones they hadn't leached into, so it was better just to take them down. The modest destruction did nothing to alleviate the scowl.

"I only saw two," Xueying said. "But more will be coming."

"More might already be here," Rusty pointed out.

No sooner had she made her very apt statement then was it followed by both the sounds of feet and gunshots. They were having a shootout in what was, arguably, an office building. It simply wasn't made for that kind of violence. Good cover was scarce, and the harsh, white lighting left no place untouched. It had the stuffy, dust-smell of office despite the back door still being open. Rusty didn't know how people could sit in there for ten hours a day.

"Xueying!"

On cue, she shot out all of the lights she could reach. It didn't do much to dim the hallway, but it was a great distraction.

Rusty didn't need to be told that it was her turn. The waiting and the strategy had never suited her. She was much happier to slide up to the pair of guards and deck them both, landing them at her feet in a matter of seconds. She had a gun on her hip and she knew how to shoot, but if Yoru and Xueying were faster on the draw than her, she'd be happy to stick to what she knew.

"Are those the two you saw?" she asked Xueying. The one's face was a little mushed in, but he shouldn't have been unidentifiable.

The other woman glanced down. "Nope, not mine," she said. Clearly, then, they still had more people to worry about.

Xueying and Yoru took the guns from the downed men as they passed. Better to use the enemy's ammunition than their own, at least for as long as they could. They deadened lights and cameras as they went. For what little it helped them, it may have just been an act of intimidation at this point. Rusty didn't bother to ask for clarification.

With the floor clear, they came to the stairs.

"Downstairs," Xueying said. Yoru was scoping out the stairwell and didn't look to her when he answered.

"You're sure?"

"Upstairs is data storage, right? If they're expecting a fight, they'd risk ruining it all," she said. That's what the blueprints had said.

Yoru looked down the stairwell. There was only one floor below them. Made sense. It wasn't as though the data centre had use for a sprawling underground. He went first. Nothing but concrete, the stairs and walls and one metal door. It had a window that was glass poured over wire hatching, or it did until someone on the other side shot at it. Immediately, the glass shattered and the wire warped, and Xueying was thankful that the ricocheting bullet hadn't hit any of them.

She shot out the door knob and kicked the door open, then took out the light. In the enclosed underground space, it plunged the whole room into darkness. Yoru ran passed her into the shadows. Rusty heard him shoot twice, but a moment later someone else barrelled out of the room. They didn't get very far.

She dropped the last of the targets without so much as a flourish. Xueying clicked her flashlight on and the two of them followed Yoru into the dark.

It looked like the room had been for storage, or perhaps maintenance. They found Yoru as he found Dan and was helping him to his feet.

"H-hey..." he said, looking up at them. He wasn't very steady, and Yoru pulled Dan's arm around his shoulder to help him stand. There was blood on the side of his face.

"Exits first, explanations later," Xueying said. The three of them nodded. They'd have to work fast if they meant to get out of there before the cops turned up. They were slower now, with Dan and Yoru lagging behind.

"Think we can make it?" Rusty asked as the waited for Yoru and Dan to make it up the stairs.

"If we can get outside and into the dark, we're set," Xueying said. "We just have to get there."

Dan was trying to apologize. Rusty could hear him as Yoru helped him up the stairs. But walking was taking all of his focus to do, and trying to talk wasn't helping them move. She hopped down the steps and grabbed him by the collar, although she had to yank him down to her height to talk to him.

"Shut up and walk," she said sharply. His eyes were dazed. Probably a concussion from whatever had hit him in the head, but he seemed to hear her and made a weak sound of agreement.

He moved a little faster after that.

Xueying had a point. If they could get out into the dark before they were caught, they were golden. There were too many ways to get around, too many hidden paths and underground routes for them to get caught out there. They pushed out the back door and into the alley they had entered from just when they heard the police.

Yoru pulled Dan into a dark alley that splintered off from the others as a police car, sirens screaming, whipped down the street. Not after them, then? He didn't stop to listen to where they were headed.

They were safe. For now.

"You okay?" Yoru asked. He leaned Dan against the wall and saw him wince. Both Rusty and Xueying were keeping a lookout while he gave his friend a once over.

"Yeah, okay enough to get back..." Dan said. He hurt, but he didn't think he was dying. "I can't see anything, though," he admitted.

"You're concussed, and it's dark," Yoru told him quietly. "Why do you think they're keeping watch? They couldn't see anything here either," he reassured him.

"That does make me feel a little better. My eyes don't hurt but...I was worried for a minute," Dan admitted with a tired smile.

Yoru hooked Dan's arm around him again and the four of them made their way back to the safe-house. When Yoru started getting tired and lagging behind, Rusty switched him jobs and she helped them drag Dan the rest of the way.

"That was a fucking mess." Xueying fell against the door when it had closed and rubbed her eyes. "I don't even want to think about the kind of shit they're going to have built in next time we try that."

Dan was struggling to string together an apology and Rusty talked over him. "There's no point in worrying about that now. We fucked up. We'll figure it out." Regret would get them absolutely nowhere.

Yoru took Dan from her, but took an extra moment to find her hand and give it a squeeze. She met his eyes and he looked at her for a long moment, but she wasn't certain what it was supposed to mean.

Yoru helped Dan limp to their room and laid him down to get a better look at his injuries. He was badly bruised in places, but the wound on his head had stopped bleeding and was only a little sticky.

"They beat the stuffing out of you, honey…" Yoru said, frowning.

Dan, his eyes closed, flashed him an 'okay' sign in agreement instead of nodding. "Yeah… I…I really fucked up, this time…"

"Hey, mistakes happen," Yoru said.

Dan shook his head, and then immediately winced. "No, no, I mean… I really fucked up. I…I froze, I guess. I didn't know where I was."

As he explained, Yoru helped him out of his clothes and started to clean up the cut on his head to get a closer look at it. He had managed to grab his hat before they had dragged him out of there, and it currently laid on the floor, where he had dropped it. The idea of parting with it had been sad enough that he had managed to hold onto it that whole time.

"You didn't know where you were?"

Dan hesitated. "I didn't know when I was," he corrected.

Yoru, who was carefully cleaning blood out of Dan's short hair, looked down at him in concern. "You mean…"

"I thought I was back there. At the camp. I don't know what set it off… I just, I was with Xueying one minute and then bang! I was back there, and I couldn't breathe. I couldn't think."

"And…now?"

Dan sighed. "I'm… I'm here. I don't feel great, but I don't know if that's because of my brain short circuiting or because they kicked the shit out of me." He shrugged.

It was Yoru's turn to sigh. "Come on, we should get you cleaned up for real. The only thing that's going to help your brain right now is sleep, but I'm sure you'll sleep better after."

It wasn't much of a shower. Dan leaned heavily on the wall and let Yoru wash most of the blood and dirt off of him before he helped him into bed. Once there, Dan wouldn't let him go.

"You have to sleep," Yoru said. He was soundly misinterpreting Dan's intentions, but the fact that Dan was kissing him didn't help.

"Stay with me," Dan insisted, sounding so much more than tired.

"You're hurt."

Dan didn't let go of him. "Please. I feel safer when you're close by."

That didn't leave much room for argument. Yoru kicked off his shoes and pulled off his shirt and climbed into bed next to his friend. Dan curled into him immediately.

"I'm sorry for what happened today," Yoru said, kissing Dan's forehead.

"What? You rescued me. What are you apologizing for?"

"I should have been there."

Dan made an unhappy noise low in his throat. "Yoru… I'm gonna be fucked up forever. You can't babysit me."

He felt the other man sigh. "I know. I just…"

Dan moved his head only far enough to kiss the part of Yoru's chest that he was planted against.

"We'll talk about it more in the morning," Yoru said. Dan agreed.

Sleep was blessedly dreamless, and he woke up to the feeling of Yoru breathing, the gentle rise and fall of his chest. It wasn't often he was awake before his friend. Still, he felt like garbage, and wasn't exactly inclined to move until he felt Yoru wake up a short while later.

"Hey," he said.

"Morning," Yoru answered him. He stretched, cat-like, simultaneously graceful and a little weird. Dan smiled.

"How are you feeling?"

"Like I was hit by a car. But I can open my eyes, at least," Dan said.

"Progress."

Moving too fast made his stomach lurch, and that was when Dan remembered. Concussion, right. So he laid back down on his pillow and closed his eyes.

"I don't think I'll be moving much today," he said reluctantly.

"I'll get you something to eat," Yoru said, dragging his fingers through Dan's hair and careful to avoid the cut. It already looked a lot better now that it was cleaned up and starting to heal.

"Hey, will you tell Xueying to come in here? I want to say sorry for fucking up the job," Dan said.

"Nope."

Dan opened his eyes to see Yoru pulling on his shirt. "No?"

"No, I won't tell her to come in here so you can apologize for something that isn't your fault. But I'll tell her to come say hi."

This was not an argument Dan felt he would win.

When Xueying did come in, she had some food for him and a glass of water. Taking a deep breath and bracing himself, he pushed himself up to sit so he could eat and talk to her.

"How are you feeling?"

"Like someone scrambled my brains," Dan said, truthfully. "But I've been worse. Did everyone get out okay?"

"Yeah," she said. She brushed some of her damp hair out of her face.

252

She must have just come from the shower. "No one else is hurt."

"Just the one who deserves it." Dan gestured with his fork. She laughed. It was a little sour, though.

"No, no... It's not like you screwed us on purpose. Sometimes, shit just happens." She shook her head. "This isn't the first job that's gotten complicated on me. Every time I step out of what is strictly 'my field', it always does." Xueying shrugged, and smiled at him. "We'll figure it out. I've been doing this shit a long time. Sometimes, jobs are rough. That's just the nature of the business."

"You're a spy? Or, you used to be?" Dan asked her.

"Still am," Xueying said with a nod. "Just not, you know, right now. But that's what I'm best at. Getting into people, and out of them again."

Dan snickered at her phrasing and Xueying grinned.

"Yoru's right. It's a little harder when there's no one to manipulate." She sighed. "But we'll figure it out. Right now, it's looking like the best course of action, honestly, is to wait until they've done the repairs and then go and fuck them up again." Xueying shrugged.

"Why wait?" Dan asked.

"There will be more people in the building while it's being worked on." She rubbed her eyes with her hand. "They're probably going to have them there in three shifts a day. It isn't really like they can take their time with it."

"On second thought, I don't know how cool I am with shooting up construction people," Dan agreed.

It was Xueying's turn to laugh. "That, too. But we need the time to look at making a real plan anyway, and I wouldn't be surprised if they had cops posted there twenty four-seven until it is done."

Dan scoffed. "And killing cops is bad, right?"

"Killing cops is bad because then they have it out for you, and there is literally nothing more inconvenient to this business than a policeman with a grudge," Xueying said.

"I think I'm learning," Dan mused.

She never brought up what happened. Dan at least thought she would ask, but maybe she knew, Maybe she had asked Yoru. It didn't really bother him that Yoru may have answered for him, but he found that he was somewhat troubled by how little it was being spoken about. He had almost gotten them all killed!

Sure, once the four of them were on-site, everything had been so much easier. But that still didn't mean that his little episode was something that should be allowed to happen again.

While his head healed up, and while he waited on word of what their new plan would be, he decided to do a little reading. Maybe he couldn't be the most useful in the field. He was a damn good shot, but that meant nothing if he couldn't stay in his head long enough to actually do it.

So he snagged Yoru's vidscreen, found a little workaround that would allow him to access more content online than it was supposed to, and started to research. He started with looking up what might be happening to his brain, but with all the time he had to kill, it wasn't long before he was reading about other things, too.

"You know, our client used to fund an orphanage," he said to Yoru one day as he sat at the table in the kitchen.

Yoru looked at him quizzically.

"Is that a 'why would she bother' or a 'why did she stop' look?" Dan asked.

"It's a 'why are you looking up stuff about our client' look," Yoru corrected him, smiling.

Dan shrugged. "I didn't start with that. I just ended up there. Her name shows up a lot."

"She has a lot of money." Yoru sat down across from him. "You won't find anything nice, I can guarantee you that. No one with that kind of money is up to anything good."

Yoru probably had a point, but Dan shrugged. "Maybe it's better to know. I still have a lot to learn about this business, and until Xueying tells me how to be useful again, I might as well do something that might be of value."

He thought Yoru looked a little proud of him. That made the waiting easier to bear.

And he was right. There was lots of stuff to read about their client. Maybe it wasn't as practical as staying on topic and looking at what was going on with him, but it was fascinating to see the kind of person who would hire people like them. Yoru had pointed out that their clients were usually pretty wealthy, but not nearly as well-heeled as Violet.

"Financially stable and morally bankrupt," Yoru had called them, smiling serenely.

The orphanage was just the start of the oddities he found. Who opened an orphanage for a year? Like, what purpose did that serve except as a huge waste of money? Then again, it probably felt like nothing to someone like that.

He talked about it with Xueying, but it was Rusty who spoke up to give him the answer. "Probably money laundering. No one pays attention whether there's more or less kids on the street."

That wasn't just a Spectra City problem. In a sharp flash of clarity, Dan realized that the exact same stunt could have been pulled in his own city and he would have never known. Hell, maybe every major city in the world. People were just so wrapped up in surviving that noticing something like that would draw from energy they just simply didn't have.

He had joined the military because he thought it was right, but he had been kind of hoping one day he'd get to use it to see the world. He was slowly figuring out that maybe it was better if he didn't.

30:

"So, we're scaring up a change in location?" Oliver confirmed, looking over at Ame. "You've got something for us?"

"Yeah, friends of my folks." Ame gave a low whistle. "There's a lot of those, even in a shit city like this. I'm gonna go and chat them up and see what they have in mind."

"Will that work?" Hastin asked her quietly. "I mean...will they really be able to find us somewhere safe?"

Ame spun around on the floor, spinning her butt on the carpet so she moved from facing Oliver to facing Hastin. "Oh, yeah. There's lots to consider. How long are we going to be there? Any length of time eventually gets to be unsafe, right? But we actually don't need to be there that long before we hit the road for real. We just need something to hold us over, and they should be able to get that."

"Not like your folks aren't professionals at being in trouble," Rosa said.

Ame laughed. "I gotta get it from somewhere, bitch. Speaking of, you coming with me to go talk to these people or what?"

Rosa shook her head. "Nah, I'm still pulling apart that file that Oliver found for us. Hastin, you should stay and help me, I think, seeing as you know Violet better than any of us."

"'Kay."

"You're up, then, Captain," Ame said, flashing him a bright grin. "You ready? We're gonna go be dangerous."

She expected him to grimace at her joke, or to otherwise look uncomfortable, but he nodded. "This all makes the most sense, I think. With my knowledge of how to get around the city itself, and your connections, it does make us the best two to scope out a new place."

He was calmer now. It was almost as though having a problem to face made him that way. Ame wasn't sure how that worked, really. She wasn't a brain doctor. And Oliver, being the closest thing they had to one, wasn't exactly going to explain it to her.

"You'll be safe, though, right?" Hastin asked the two of them.

Oliver nodded. "Ame will deck anybody she's gotta, and I've got a lot of experience staying out of trouble. We'll manage. And we'll have you guys on comm."

"You think that's necessary?" Rosa asked.

Oliver shrugged. "Why not? It's not like we got anything to lose by it, right?"

Rosa found she had to agree. "Fair enough. I'll get you guys linked up. Hastin, you'll talk to them while I work? I'm sure you can multitask between us."

"I will do my best!" he said brightly.

Oliver stood up and ran a hand through his unmanageable curls before going to search out where he had left his shoes. They were in a pile at the front door, and he managed to get them on without having to undo them. Ame was considerably slower to get to her feet, but eventually she joined him.

"You gonna put up with me the whole time?" she asked.

"Oh, you're not that bad," Oliver said lightly as they left.

"That's not what you used to say," she pointed out.

He laughed. "Yeah, I know. And you are terrible. That part wasn't a lie."

She mock-bowed, despite the people who might have seen them. At the very least, Ame didn't really care about the impressions she made on other people. Her confidence made her likeable, but not very subtle.

"You seem different today. What's going on?"

Oliver shrugged. "I...I'm not sure. I guess I'm trying to figure that out myself."

"Well, terrible I may be, but I'm usually pretty good at figuring shit out. We might as well walk and talk," she suggested.

It earned another laugh from him. "I mean, sure, I won't say no. But I can't promise that it's very interesting."

She waved him off and they took the elevator down. One day, Ame promised herself, when she retired, she was going to have a nice, ground floor apartment. One that wasn't shit, but also that didn't have a million goddamn stairs. That was the dream.

"So, what's on your mind?"

Oliver took a deep breath and let it out as a sigh. "I guess I just realized something."

"Yeah?"

"I was really lonely," he told her, plainly. "I didn't even know that I was. But there was just...nothing in my life. And then I met Dan, and he was good and cool, and then I lost him. But I met you guys! Like, sure, I knew you and Rosa before, but not like... We weren't friends."

"I get it, I get it." Ame nodded.

"So, yeah. I was...really, genuinely unhappy. And then we became a team! And man, was I ever a lame fuckin' addition to our little group. But, I've been learning...and more than learning, I think I've just gotten more comfortable with it."

"This whole flagrant lawbreaking thing?" she asked him. She wove between the groups of people who walked the street and Oliver had no trouble following her. Then, before he could continue, she sneezed. The dust was bad today. As if the streets could get any dirtier.

"Bless you."

"By god, do I need it." She laughed.

"Anyway, yeah. I'm getting more used to what we do...and then, well, I realized how easy it would be to lose everyone."

"When Hastin pulled that gun, right?"

Oliver sighed again. "Yeah, like... I know I'm not as seasoned as you and Rosa, and I'll admit, he's had me played since day one. But I knew he meant it, too. He wants to be with us. Not just me, either. With you guys, too. And since we're all universally being fucked over by this..."

"You want us to stick together."

"My knowledge of criminality, limited as it might be compared to yours and Rosa's, tells me that it would be smarter for us to split up...but I don't think that's the case. I really do think we'd do better together. We'd at least be happier. And tell me right now that you don't kill people a little better when you have a smile on your face."

"How'd you get to know me so good?" Ame teased, laughing.

Oliver laughed, too. "So...I want us to stick together. And if I want that, I have to work for it. And that means being useful. And I know how to be useful."

"Oh?"

"Yeah," Oliver said, completely unabashed. "I'm organized, I'm a good planner, I communicate well. That's something we don't have, as a team. Someone to figure out our logistics. Someone to make sure we're playing to our best strengths."

"So...the leader. You might even say...the Captain?" Ame grinned.

Oliver blushed.

"If that's going to be my job...I want to give it my all. Even if..."

"Even if this gets us all killed," Ame finished.

Oliver nodded, but didn't look disheartened. "Hey, I'd rather die with you guys than die alone."

"I appreciate the sentiment, but I'd rather just not die," Ame said, with enough sarcasm in her voice to make Oliver smile but not enough to make him think she was disagreeing with him entirely. "That's sort of the point of this whole escapade. Come on, I said I'd meet them in here."

It was a crowded diner. The menu was written in a language Oliver didn't speak, but it smelled amazing. He looked around in a mild state of confusion and wonder.

Were they going to get something to eat?

Ame pulled him out of the front of the restaurant, where people were waiting to pick up their food, into the back. Then she shoved him into a booth, where he sat, still confused.

"What do you want to eat?" she asked him.

He blinked at her. "Dude, I don't even know what they have here."

"What do you like?"

"...Food."

"'Kay. I'll order for us." Ame waved him off, the simple motion letting him know that she'd handle it. She turned to talk to someone who might have been an employee, and Oliver just looked around, content to try and get his bearings while she did.

"My contacts should be here any minute, but since we're not at home to have any of Rosa's manchow soup, well, I figured we'd get something else."

"I'm not gonna argue," Oliver said. He loved food nearly indiscriminately. Being poor did that to a guy.

They weren't kept waiting for long, for food or the contacts. A man and a woman, both older than Ame, slid into their booth out of the crowd. They had seemingly appeared out of nowhere. That was a little disconcerting but probably a good sign.

"Oliver, these are friends of my folks. Ferrol and Matias. Nice to see you," she said, smiling.

"Good to see you, kid," the guy, presumably Ferrol, said. "Been a while. You holding up okay?"

"Oh, yeah. This city's got nothing to scare me," Ame boasted. "How's business?"

"Busy," Matias said. She had a smile like Ame's, Oliver thought. Bright, almost reckless. It made her immediately likeable. He really did try to be skeptical of people, and maybe they would give him reason to be later, but honestly, he trusted Ame. If they were good by her, chances are they were good by him, too.

"Hear you're looking for a place to stay," Matias said.

Ame nodded, and as their food came, she nodded all the more. "Oh, god, yes. Look at this shit," she said excitedly, before looking back to her friends. "Yeah, not long term. We're thinking..." She paused. "How long are we thinking?" she asked Oliver.

"A week, at most. Probably just a few days," he said. Ideally, they'd get moving as fast as they could. There was no reason to take their time, and the sooner it was over with, the sooner they could disappear.

"Somewhere in The Dim. Somewhere that's a pain in the ass to keep an eye on, or to get an ear in," Ame said.

"You up to something bad?"

"Ain't I always?"

They laughed, and Oliver couldn't help but smile. It all came so naturally to Ame.

Eventually, they worked out some information, and they wrote an address down on a napkin that Ame shoved in her jacket. They even paid for their food.

"Gotta make sure you're eating well, or your parents will be pissed," Ferrol said.

Ame squeezed his hand as they were leaving. "Next time it's on me, then, okay?"

"Your parents seem like a big deal," Oliver said as they ate. He was mostly joking, but was unsurprised with Ame nodded completely without embarrassment.

"They are. I mean, they kinda are. Because, like, in the business, you end up a big deal to some people, but most people don't know your name, right? That's the way this shit works."

Oliver nodded along. He supposed that made sense. The same accomplishments didn't carry the same weight in different social circles. And, a little anonymity would make their lives a lot easier, at least most of the time.

"They in the business, too, you said?"

"Yeah. Raised me in it!" she said proudly. "Can you imagine that? My mom running around gunning people down with tiny baby Amethyst strapped to her chest?"

Oliver laughed. "For real?!"

Ame shook her head, also laughing. "Nah, nah, I'm kidding... My dad usually carried me. My mom did a lot of climbing, I guess, so it wasn't as easy for her."

It was a completely practical explanation, of course, but it was no less hilarious for that fact.

"You've always done this?"

She slurped some of her noodles and set her chopsticks aside. "Yeah, since I could walk. You know, the shit parents teach you. Read, write, pick locks, punch a guy in the throat. The usual."

Oliver nodded, his mouth full of food. When he swallowed, he spoke. "Sounds...pretty great, actually. I don't think my anxiety could have handled it, but that sounds like exactly the kind of childhood I'd expect you to have, really."

"I lucked out," Ame said flatly. "My parents are pretty great. They loved me, and still love me, and we even get along. A lot of people don't get to say that."

Oliver paused, and then gave her a long, serious look. "You know, I'm really happy that's the case. Really happy," he told her.

She blinked at him. "Why the sudden change?"

He shrugged. "I just... Like, you know what Hastin's background is, and you know that it's, well..."

"Fuckin' terrible."

"Right. And mine wasn't that cartoonishly horrific but, like... It wasn't a good time. So I'm glad we're not all fucked from the get-go."

"Rosa's parents were rad too," Ame reassured him. "I mean, even if they hadn't been, it's not like it would have stopped her. But they're really nice folks, I've talked to them a few times."

"She's from, like...ways away, right?"

Ame nodded. "Kinda weird to think our computer queen didn't even grow up in the city. That's also why she doesn't visit them much, but they've called before, that's how I've talked to them."

"Did you utterly embarrass her?"

"Kinda," she said proudly.

They finished their food, and once they were back on the street Ame pulled the address out of her pocket. "I...don't know this street," she said, passing the napkin to Oliver.

"Ah, I do, though," he said, looking at it. "I mean...assuming I'm reading that right... Even my handwriting isn't this bad."

Ame laughed, but when Oliver wandered away and motioned for her to follow, she did.

"This is slum town for sure..."

"That'll be better for us, won't it?" Ame asked.

Oliver laughed. "I'm gonna look right at home, but the kid... We're

261

going to have to sneak him in or something. He's going to look really out of place."

Ame was still laughing as they stepped into the subway, but Oliver seemed to realize something. "That's actually not much of a problem," he said, thoughtfully. "Whether or not people realize he's there, we just need to be done fast enough that they can't get ears and eyes on us. Mostly just ears, even. Screw it."

"I think it's kind of funny that the one who is best at being subtle out of all of us is also the least subtle in appearance," Ame joked.

The subway, because of the way the city had been constructed, ran from stops that were pretty mediocre in quality, right into The Dim; the old central hub, and then back out the other side, into where things weren't so bad anymore. Most of the richer areas had access to it, seeing as they were all new.

It did mean that the stop they got off on was pretty terrible, though.

Ame looked around, pulling a face, and then directed that same face to Oliver.

"I mean, yeah. But also, what other choice do people have?" he said. Oliver knew a little too well how inescapable poverty could be. And dirt. Dirt was pretty inescapable, too.

Ame heard him out, and then shrugged in concession. He had a point.

Despite the ear-piece she had on, Ame hadn't heard much from Rosa and Hastin, and she took a moment to tell them where they were headed, but with that done, she turned her attention back to the narrow, crowded streets around them. There were no cars this far into The Dim, not even the occasional taxi. It was just people-movement, and wind blowing dust and garbage through the streets. There was no stillness.

"We could even lose Hastin in a place like this," she said.

"Well, let's try not to." Oliver smiled.

They eventually found the apartment they had been listed. Ame actually greeted it with surprisingly spirited curiosity, and it was Oliver who seemed disappointed.

"If I had a few days to clean this place up, it wouldn't be so bad," he mused. "I've lived in worse places."

"Well, you won't have to live here. Think of it like a bad weekend," Ame reassured him, her hand on his shoulder.

"Will Rosa be able to work here? Is there enough room?"

Ame frowned, looking over the space, and nodded. "Yeah. Won't be able to cook though, so we're probably going to be having take-out for a few days. That kitchen is…yeah." She laughed.

"So the real question is, can we survive without Rosa's cooking?"

Ame sighed. "The things I do for this job, I tell you."

But, it had places to sleep, didn't appear to be actively infested with anything and had both power and water. That was still better than some places Oliver had been. A few days in a dirty apartment living off of take out actually didn't sound that awful.

"Can we get pizza, though?" he asked. Ame laughed, but he just looked at her. "I'm serious, man, I'd kill for a pizza."

It felt good to make real progress. The next step was packing up all of Rosa's equipment and helping her change locales, but hell, her and Ame had done that originally, just the two of them. With four people, it would be simple.

"You guys get to live like me for a few days," Oliver said as they stepped into the subway again.

"And then, when we split, you get to live like us." Ame grinned. "You ready to be hardcore?"

"I'm already hardcore," Oliver answered her back. He didn't even bother being sarcastic; there was no way she was going to take him seriously.

By the time they got back, Rosa had already started packing. That saved them some trouble, Oliver thought, as he looked at the black bags that were already stacked in the kitchen. Still, he felt almost…nostalgic, looking at them. It hadn't been that long ago that they had come to this place.

Once upon a time, he had been hoping to make a buck and maybe share some of that with a few people he knew. Now he was looking at a whole life lived on the run.

It was strange how welcoming the idea was.

31:

Now, they were in limbo. With the building being repaired and security at an all-time high, there just wasn't a lot they could do to make productive use of their time.

It really wasn't a surprise when Xueying threw her hands in the air one night and said, "To hell with it. Let's go to the bar. I know a place."

"That karaoke bar you like?" Yoru asked her.

"Karaoke? Man, I'm not singing..." Dan said defensively.

"Don't worry. We'll get a few drinks into Xueying and she won't let the mic alone," Yoru told him with a grin.

"First of all, screw you, I am very polite with my mic time. Second of all, Dan, hun, you don't have to sing, no one is going to make you," she told him.

"Rusty, you in?" Yoru asked.

"Do I have a choice?" she answered, in a voice that was not nearly harsh enough to tell them that she was truly upset. Yoru had been the fastest of them to understand her very moderate use of inflection, but Xueying had caught on pretty quickly, too.

Dan cheated. When she spoke, he looked to the others for cues on if she was serious or not. He was making progress, it was just slow.

"Let's get cleaned up, then," Yoru said. "And drink like responsible adults."

"You get cleaned up to go to a bar?" Rusty asked him. "What kind of bar is this?"

It seemed like she was kidding, though, as she also decided to throw on a clean shirt. Dan took a look down at himself and shrugged. There wasn't much to be done for it. It wasn't as though he had enough hair to do anything with yet, and he didn't have much in the way of clothes.

Yoru brushed his hair out and tied it back more neatly, but even in his usual all-black attire, he looked too classy to be drinking with them.

"Who is driving?" Dan asked.

"No one, since I'm pretty sure we're all going to wildly disappoint Yoru with the differences in what we consider to be 'responsible' drinking," Xueying said. "We'll take the subway."

It was the first time Dan had stopped to really get a look at the four of them together. They...did not make much of a group, to be honest. Xueying had that sort of polished look to her, bright and sparkling, that was impossible to hide even when she was dressed in something unremarkable. Rusty seemed in a perpetual state of annoyance, though he knew that to not be a true representation of her feelings. He looked...kind of tired, he thought. Bland. Not bad, but not good, either.

Weird friends. But the idea of going out with them still made him smile. It would be nice to get some air.

The bar was called The Tint and it wasn't much. But Xueying had spoken true. They did have karaoke sometimes, and it looked like today was one of those days.

"Plan: Get wrecked, sing my lungs out," she said.

Yoru countered her with, "Plan: Make sure you do."

Dan still didn't intend to do any singing, and he shared a look with Rusty that left him feeling as though she commiserated with that.

It was a pretty lively place. Not crowded enough that he felt panicky, even with the low light. A few people were singing already (and they varied widely in talent) but the sound of it seemed to keep him anchored. Yoru leaning against his arm didn't hurt.

"'Kay, I'm going up," the other man said, a few drinks in.

Rusty snorted. "You're going to sing?"

"Yes. At best, I do fairly well. At worst, I make everyone happier when Xueying takes a turn," he told her with a bright smile.

"Wish me luck!"

"Break a leg," Dan joked.

They sat together at the bar and watched him go up. Most people were clustered around tables, but seeing as their group was small, they managed to get spots that much closer to the drinks. Yoru had a few songs to wait through, but no one seemed in any hurry.

And it turned out...he wasn't bad.

"I mean, he spends enough time talking, so I figure..." Rusty muttered in Dan's ear. He laughed. Yeah, it wasn't as though he didn't have practice. And it was clear he had no problem being the centre of attention.

Being dramatic had its perks, surely.

"He's pretty good," the guy beside Dan spoke up, and Dan, having forgotten there was anyone there, jumped. It earned a sheepish laugh from him. "Sorry, man."

"Nah, it's okay, I'm just...jittery, you know?" Dan said, waving it off.

265

"He your friend?"

Dan nodded. "Yeah. Lunatic," he added, rolling his eyes. The guy laughed.

He had a cloud of dark curly hair, and two horns that twisted out of it to point at the ceiling. His sweater was olive green and way too big for him, but he seemed comfortable enough.

"You ever get up there and do that?"

Dan figured he was just chatty from the drinking, so he played along. What was the harm? Besides, he really should get to talking to people more often. He was going to have to be functional at some point. And as much as he kept saying that as a joke, it really was true. He had to start somewhere.

"God, no. You couldn't pay me enough. But I think she's—" He pointed to Xueying. "—going to go up soon. So I'll just sit here and be entertained."

"That's the way, man," the other guy agreed.

They drank together in silence while Yoru finished up, and true to his plan, Xueying pulled herself from her chair to go put herself on the list. Yoru waved at him, but didn't return to his seat, electing instead to wait with Xueying for her turn.

They didn't have to wait long. To his surprise, soon after the song started up, the man next to him started to laugh.

"What's up?" he asked.

"This song has to be like...I don't know, fifteen years old. And it's...just wait," he said.

This wasn't Dan's first time watching people do this sort of stuff. He was familiar with karaoke. But, the sheer saccharine sweetness of the song that Xueying had picked, and the fact that she seemed to know the dance to it, was on a whole different level.

"What the—"

Beside him, the stranger was still cracking up.

To be fair, Xueying did more than well. She did amazingly. It was just so far out of left field that Dan was having trouble processing it.

Rusty, who seemed to be entirely, intently focused on something about what they had just seen, said nothing.

"Wait... I think I know that song," Dan said, then, to the stranger. "I mean, I know it's in Cinia, but I think I remember hearing it on the radio..."

"Where are you from?" the guy asked.

"Syama."

"Oh, well, probably. It was a huge, world-wide phenomenon. Like, they even played it here. How do you think I know it? Couldn't tell you what it means, but I think I've learned some of the words through pure exposure."

Now it was Dan's turn to laugh.

"What's your name, by the way?" he asked the stranger.

"Oliver." He gestured with his drink, and Dan grinned, knocking his own glass against his.

"I'm Dan."

"Well, Dan from Syama, this is as good a place to drown in pop music as any." Oliver smiled.

They talked. It was that quiet, lean-in-to-speak thing that you had to do in bars to be heard over the music, one eye on whoever was singing and one eye on the other person. The more they talked, the more there seemed to be to talk about.

"My sisters used to listen to that song nonstop," Dan said. "I remember it now. They played it constantly. That's where I know it from."

"Did you feel like killing them?" Oliver asked. "I've never had sisters, but I've been told that's a common side effect."

"Oh, man, did I ever." Dan rolled his eyes. And, for now at least, there was no guilt in those thoughts. No sadness. Here, they made him smile. "I'm pretty sure I threatened to every time they played it. Must have driven my parents crazy."

"See, I only have brothers," Oliver said. "But that song was still in our house, because my mom used to listen to it. Which, you know, when you're a kid, you can't really do much about."

Dan laughed, pressing a hand to his mouth. "That sounds terrible."

"It was terrible!"

"Is having brothers as exciting as everyone says?" Dan asked. "I was the only boy in my family, and I was always, I don't know, pretty well behaved." It wasn't a lie. Besides occasionally fighting with his sisters, he had never really gotten into serious trouble. At least, not until recently.

"'Exciting'. That's one word for it." Oliver rolled his eyes. "Now, don't take what I'm saying as a generalization. There's tons of kids who grow up just fine, right? You turned out pretty okay, and well, I'm…I'm not causing anyone trouble." Oliver laughed. "But those two…wow."

"Older or younger?"

"Both younger," Oliver said. "God, what a nightmare…"

"You don't seem to have turned out too bad," Dan pointed out.

Oliver smiled. "I'm…I'm working on it, you know? We all have to try."

And that seemed meaningful to Dan, who had tried so hard to be good. Who still tried, despite the circumstances he found himself in. So hearing Oliver say that, and seeing the way he smiled as he did, it really meant something to him.

"Oh heck, your friend is back." Oliver pointed to the mic-stand again, where Xueying was now waiting for her second turn.

"If I slip into a diabetic coma, will you call me an ambulance?"

"You really want me to try and send you to a hospital here?" Oliver laughed.

Dan joined him, also laughing. "On second thought, you have a point. Better to just let me die."

"At least the soundtrack will be amazing."

She really was something else. Rusty didn't seem to react much, but that seemed neither here nor there to Dan. She drank, and sometimes spoke to him, but mostly kept to herself. She did seem a little rapt when Xueying was singing, but Dan ascribed that to her being a little bewildered by the woman's actions. Dan had to admit, he was equal parts impressed and confused himself.

The night wore on, and he felt good. Even when Yoru came to check on him, he smiled and told his friend that everything was going well. He cast a brief look at Oliver, but didn't say anything before going back to Xueying.

"Your friends seem...interesting," Oliver noted. "Not that I mean that in a bad way."

Dan shrugged. "Don't see how you could," he said reasonably.

This was nice. And talking to a stranger wasn't so hard.

"I'll buy your next one," Oliver offered as Dan got near the end of his drink.

He couldn't seem to stop smiling and it wasn't the alcohol. Oliver was good company. He bought Dan's next drink, just as he said he would. And then, Dan returned the favour.

"You in town much?" Oliver asked him.

Dan shrugged. "Hard to tell. I don't know how long we'll be in the city for, since we tend to go where the work is. That's how I ended up with these crazy people in the first place, you know."

Oliver shot him an inquisitive look over the top of his drink and Dan continued. "My friend, that guy, he picked me up when he was on a job in Syama. We've travelled together ever since. And, come to think of it..."

"Come to think of what," Oliver prompted him.

Dan frowned, but it was thoughtful, not sad. "I think the other two will probably be joining us. History says otherwise but...I got a feeling."

"So you think you're gonna leave town, then?"

Dan shrugged, and Oliver looked as though he was hesitating to say something.

"Well, come on," Dan said, his turn to prompt Oliver.

"Want my number?" Oliver asked him then.

Dan couldn't help but beam. "Yeah, man. I do. Here, let me get my phone."

He dug his phone out of his pocket and passed it to Oliver. "Just add yourself, and I'll message you so you'll have mine."

"Cool. Here, like this...." Oliver handed him his phone back. It had his number, and his name, followed by several ridiculous faces. Dan laughed.

"Okay, but when you add my name into your phone, I have to get those by mine, too." He sent a text to him that was just a string of random letters, and Oliver's phone in his hand dinged.

So, the other man leaned a little closer. "What ones you want?" he asked, laughing.

It was ridiculous, really. Something so small. But, it brought Dan genuine joy. Actual, real laughter. And that was nice, since he sometimes thought he forgot how to do that.

"There, now we're both set. When do you think you're leaving?" Oliver asked him.

Dan made a seesaw motion with his hand. "Hard to say. We're waiting to finish up a job, so...a few days, a week, maybe more. It's kind of out of our hands right now."

"That sort of not-knowing sounds pretty shitty, actually," Oliver pointed out.

Dan nodded. "I'm okay with it, because I'm not the one doing any of the planning. But this lady, here, my friend—" He gestured to Xueying with his glass. "She's kind of running this whole operation, and it's driving her nuts. That's kind of why we're here. Blow off steam, you know."

"You all going back together when you're done?" Oliver asked. It was so natural-sounding that Dan answered without thinking.

"Oh, probably. I mean, I don't know, it's not a rule or anything," he said with a shrug.

"So...if I asked you if you wanted to come over, that wouldn't, like, strain your professional relationships or whatever?" Oliver looked at him.

Dan blinked at him for a minute. Just long enough for Oliver to start to look nervous.

But then Dan shook his head. "No, no, it wouldn't be a problem at

269

all…"

"So…you wanna go back to my place?" Oliver asked, laughing nervously.

Dan felt himself blush. He wasn't sure it could be seen in the dim light, but he knew it was there. "I…yeah, actually. I'd love to. You mean…like, now?"

Oliver shrugged. "Well…I mean, sure. Yeah. Now. Why not." He laughed again.

So, they were both pretty nervous, and neither of them seemed to have an idea of how to gracefully handle the situation. But they seemed to be on the same page, at least.

Dan smiled. "I'm just going to let them know where I'm headed," he said, nodding to his friends.

Oliver agreed enthusiastically. "Oh, for sure. Here, let me give you my address—" He reached for Dan's phone.

Dan handed it to him. "Really?"

Oliver nodded. "Man, this city is spooky as fuck. I mean, you're not from here, so I get you not knowing…but honestly, I'd rather them have an idea of where we're headed. You know, just in case."

If Dan was unsure he was making the right decision, that solidified it. Still smiling, he hurried over to Yoru.

And it was only then, away from Oliver, that he started to be really nervous.

"Hey—" he said, getting Yoru's attention. The taller man turned and smiled at him.

"Making friends, I see," he teased.

Dan nodded. "I…uh… I think we're going to—"

He couldn't say it. But, Yoru seemed to understand.

"Really?" he asked, blooming suddenly into a smile. "That's wonderful!"

Surprised at his enthusiasm, Dan looked at him in confusion. "I sort of worried that you'd be…you know…upset."

Yoru shook his head and took Dan's hand in his own. "No. Although, I am happy that you still wanted to do something that would make you happy even if I was going to be unreasonable about it," Yoru pointed out.

Before Dan could stammer something of an answer, he continued. "I'm glad you're talking to people. I'm glad you're talking to nice people. Nice enough that you'd feel okay to go home with them. You've got my number, so you can call me if you have any trouble."

"I actually have his address," Dan said, showing Yoru his phone. "He gave it to me. Said it was safer if I told you guys where I'm headed."

Yoru looked impressed. "This man, he knows things. I just hope he continues to be as pleasant when you leave."

"He's not very big. If he's a jerk, I'll just deck him and call a cab," Dan said.

Yoru smiled, copying down the address. "Okay. Go, have fun." And then, he laughed. "I sound like a parent!"

"Okay, but I have a different kind of fun with you than I do with my parents," Dan said. That earned him another laugh.

It reassured him, just like the way Yoru squeezed his hand. This was okay to do. It was, as they had said back in the army, 'living a little'.

He was back to Oliver's side in moments. "Okay, we're good to go!" he said.

They left the bar. It was in the back of a dark taxi that they finally kissed. There was a nervousness here that he didn't feel with Yoru, but it wasn't bad. Dan thought that maybe everyone felt different when you got this close to them. Oliver had an air of fear around him, sure...but also excitement.

Kissing soon progressed to a lot more than that. So much so that he found it hard to keep his hands to himself when they got out of the car. Sure, it wasn't against any kind of rules, but how were they supposed to get up to his apartment if Dan didn't let him walk?

Oliver didn't seem to mind, and, in a pleasant set of events, seemed just as eager as Dan was.

He unlocked his door—several locks, Dan noticed, not that he thought that was a bad idea—pulled Dan inside and closed it behind him. Dan crowded him back against the door, kissing him again, and Oliver looked up at him.

"I didn't realize how tall you were," he said, laughing.

Dan looked down and realized he was right. Compared to Oliver, he was noticeably taller. It was kind of nice to be the tall one for once!

It was hard to laugh and kiss him at the same time, but it was a good problem to have.

32:

They'd be leaving the next morning. No point in trying to make the move at night; if someone tried to rob them, they'd have their hands too full to react. Besides, where they were going wasn't really that important. What that did mean was that most of Rosa's technology was all packed up and ready to go, so she laid on her bed, her fingers gliding over the actual paper pages of a book. It was a little beaten up, the corners ragged and the spine cracked, but it was still readable. It had been one of her favourites for a long time.

It was this quiet that the knock interrupted. It wasn't quite a full-fledged attempt. There was no sharpness to it. The others were probably asleep; it would explain why whoever was there seemed intent on being polite.

She set her book aside and got to her feet. Cracking the door open, she could tell who it was immediately. She didn't have her 'eyes' on, so it wasn't the silhouette that gave them away. It was their perfume.

Hastin.

"Rosa," he said, quietly. "Do you have a minute?"

Even if she hadn't, she would have said yes. She liked to think he didn't hold the same sway over her as he did Oliver, and she was pretty sure she was right. But at the same time, he also wasn't likely to seek her out over something trivial.

"Sure."

She was certain her room looked pretty empty, packed away as everything was. She sat on the side of her bed and when Hastin hesitated, she gestured for him to sit next to her. He did, and she heard the deep breath he took.

"What did you need?" she asked.

"I just wanted to talk to you. You're always, well…"

"Always what?" she asked, smiling faintly.

"The voice of reason," he said.

Her smile widened. "It's not exactly tough competition."

He laughed, but was cautious enough to keep it quiet.

"I actually wanted to talk to you about something," she said. It wasn't the kind of mystery that kept her up at night, but if he was going to make it so

272

easy to ask, she thought she might as well.

"Anything at all," he said, without hesitation.

"It's about Violet," she prefaced, giving him warning for what might have been an uncomfortable topic. "How does she think so little of you? You lied right to her face. Using skills that she probably insisted you have, but she doesn't see that?" It just seemed so short-sighted, to Rosa. She couldn't fathom making such a mistake.

He didn't answer her immediately. He shifted in his seat, seemed to think to himself, and then finally spoke. "Well, you heard what I told the Captain. Violet doesn't see me as a person capable of anything like that. And, I guess... I'm not really a person at all, when she's around."

"Like when we came home from the meeting," Rosa said.

Hastin nodded. "I can shake that, if I try really hard...but it's not very comfortable. And I knew I didn't have to. I knew if I had to be, um, not okay, for a little while, you guys would understand."

"Oliver does have a way with those things," Rosa agreed.

Hastin nodded. She felt it in the way the bed shook. "Yeah! The captain, he..."

Rosa reached over to him and he took her hand when it lingered in the air. His touch was soft, and warm.

"When I saw him, I knew right away. I... You know... No one's ever looked at me that way before," Hastin said, stumbling over his words but finishing with hope in his voice.

"Like what?"

"Like I was a human being," he said. There was no upset in his voice. Instead, he laughed. "And then you and Ame walked in the door, and suddenly it happened again. I've never been so happy in my whole life." He squeezed her hand. "Rosa, I... I think I love you."

This time, Rosa squeezed his hand. "Would you be upset if I wondered if you knew what that meant?"

"No, no..." Hastin brought her hand to his lips and kissed it. "I wondered that, too."

When he sighed, it sounded like breathless adoration. "Even if it's not love, I've never felt so...so much. It's ...wonderful."

Rosa smiled. "What does it feel like?"

But he shook his head. "I don't know. I don't have the words... It feels like...breathing, I think. When I take a deep breath, I can feel it in my whole body. It just feels so...good."

Then, he laughed again. "I'm sorry, that's silly. But it's true. And I love

Ame, too. And the captain…" She could hear the blush in his voice.

"I don't think that's silly," she said calmly. "I think, for someone who doesn't have a lot of the words they need to discuss this, that you're doing very well."

"That's why I like talking to you, Rosa. You know and understand so many things… Which is why I wanted to ask you a favour."

Ah, yes. The reason he came to talk to her. Although, she didn't doubt that coming to confess his love was part of his motivation. It seemed there was more, just as she thought.

"What is that?"

"If something goes wrong…if it looks like they're going to take me back… Will you kill me?" he asked her.

Her hand tightened where it held his. "Do you really think that will be needed?"

"No… I don't intend to give them the chance. I intend to succeed," he said.
"But the captain said a backup plan is never a bad idea."

He sighed. "I can't stand the thought of failing, and what it might mean for you and Ame and the captain. But if it comes to that…I guess I'm selfish in the end."

"That doesn't make you selfish," Rosa said calmly. "Though, I can see why you wouldn't ask Oliver."

"And were I to ask Ame…I think the captain would get upset with her," Hastin said sadly. "But, they respect you and trust you, like I do." He sighed. "I know, it's a pretty lousy favour," he said, as though 'lousy' could ever hope to cover it.

"If it comes to that," Rosa said quietly, "you have my word."

"I don't have anything to pay you back with," Hastin noted, his voice faintly bitter. "You're supposed to repay favours, but I don't have anything to give you."

Rosa smiled. "You're supposed to repay them when the opportunity arrives. There's no deadline, Hastin. I'm sure we'll have plenty of chances in the future."

A sudden intake of breath, and he pulled his hand from hers. "I have an idea!"

"Oh?" she asked, but no sooner had she done so than did he moved closed to her and pressed a kiss to the corner of her mouth.

She grabbed his shoulder. Leaned in close as he was, it wasn't hard to find.

"You don't need to do that," she said.

"Maybe I don't have to..." he said quietly. "But I could. If...if you wanted to."

"Hastin..."

"I've never done it, you know, because I wanted to before..." he said, still leaning against her. "I...Ame says it's fun. I'd be happy to repay the favour like that, if it would make you happy."

"You shouldn't do things like that for other people. They should be something that you enjoy, too. It's supposed to be for everyone's benefit."

"How am I supposed to know if I enjoy it if I never get to do it with anyone nice?" He nuzzled against her shoulder, leaning into her comfortably and without insinuation. "I'm sure you can figure out what it's been like."

"That's what I'm worried about." She reached over and brushed her fingers through his hair. "I don't want you to rush into something in haste if it might hurt you."

"You wouldn't hurt me," he said quietly. "I know that."

"No," she admitted. "I wouldn't."

"If there isn't that to fear, then..."

She turned to him properly, her hands on his shoulders. "Is this really what you want?"

"Well...yes," He said earnestly. "But you just said, it can't just be about that. It has to be about what you want, too."

"You know, for someone who isn't sure if they're a whole person... you are doing a lot better than most people I know," she said. Her hands slid down from his shoulders, letting him lean in closer to her.

"You make me want to try my best," Hastin said. She could feel the silk of his blouse under her fingers, the frailty of him as he pressed close to her. "All of you do. But that doesn't answer my question," he pointed out.

That made her smile, too.

"Yes. I want this too," she said to him. She meant it. Hastin might not have been her usual 'type', if she had one at all, but he felt good in her arms and thinking of him made her smile. When he kissed her, he tasted sweet on her lips.

"You're so beautiful..." he breathed, kissing from her lips down her neck. She tilted her head back, her eyes flickering closed, and she pulled him close. "What were you reading?" he asked, his breath ghosting over her skin.

Rosa had to try not to laugh. "Is this your idea of dirty talk?"

When Hastin laughed, he pressed more kisses against her skin. "I want to know. I'm interested."

275

She fell back onto the bed, giving up any hope of staying upright and falling comfortably onto the threadbare blanket. Hastin giggled and pulled himself up to sit astride her. He weighed nothing. The heat he built in her was slow, lazily coiling under her skin, like sinking down into a well-earned bath. Even Hastin's gentlest kisses made you feel powerful.

"It's...sort of a fairytale, I guess. It's always been one of my favourites," she told him finally.

"That's sweet," he said, no trace of sarcasm in his voice. Knowing him, he meant it. He helped her out of her shirt. Her hair didn't take that too kindly and she had to take a minute to try and push the loose strands away from her eyes, her tail flicking with annoyance. He reached for her hand, pressed it against his chest and hushed her.

"I'll get it, I'll get it..." he said gently. "You relax."

And he did, brushing her hair out of her face and kissing it all over. She smiled, but it was brief.

"Are you...shaking?" she asked him.

He laughed. "Probably."

"... Are you afraid?" Rosa pulled him closer, trying to reassure him.

"Oh, terrified," he said, calmly. "It's so different...and you're so soft..."

"You're not going to hurt me," she told him. As she spoke, her fingers found the buttons of his blouse and started to undo them. She felt him laugh, so faint and quiet she barely heard it.

"I would rather die," he said.

"I'm not going to hurt you," she added.

This time, he hesitated. "... I know."

Rosa used the now-open sides of his shirt to pull him into a kiss. "If you're scared, we don't have to do this. Even now, you never have to," she told him.

"Where better for me to be afraid than in your arms?" he asked her. "Where in the world would I be safer?"

Spirited, if nothing else, Hastin moved down her body. Everywhere his mouth touched her skin bloomed with heat, her pulse quickening, her breath starting to go short. "You smell nice," he said, apropos of nothing, and she laughed. "And I like hearing you laugh."

They managed to get each other undressed with equal parts clumsiness and earnest desire. Rosa did desire him, certainly. Not for the same reasons as her teammates (the aesthetic was mostly lost on her) but it was there all the same. And, certain tell-tale physical indicators let her know that she was not alone in her arousal.

276

Rosa's underclothes were much indicative of her character; they were quality and functional but without adornment. She abandoned them without much of a thought, tossing them onto the floor to find later.

Hastin's were a tad more complicated. "How do you even—" Rosa tried to keep her laughter quiet. There was no need to wake everyone. Oliver, at least, was probably asleep.

"Here, they hold my stockings up. Like this—" He guided her hands so she could feel what he was doing, undoing the garters so he could slip the stockings off. If nothing else, she learned something new.

Under all the satin and lace, Hastin was exactly as Rosa thought he might be. Soft and gentle and sweet. Hands fumbled in the dark, teasing and learning. She could feel him smile when they kissed.

He did not stay so close for long. The mischief on his lips turned out to be true, and he pushed himself lower over her body again.

Soon, his hands were not enough to contain his desire for her. The warmth of his mouth was unexpected and her surprise was half-laugh, half breathy moan. He tasted her, found her skin to be a pleasant delicacy and seemed to find himself insatiable. She tangled her fingers in his hair, her body shifting to allow him better access. Hastin took advantage of it, she felt his nails dig into her skin. Just enough to give it an edge, never enough to hurt. He settled between her legs, apparently just as happy to kiss her there as anywhere else.

She moaned his name, full and wanting, and he actually stopped. It was hilarious and frustrating and she groaned when she felt him lift his head.

"Something wrong?" she asked, short of breath, her cheeks flushed and heated.

"I've never heard someone say my name that way," he said. He nuzzled against her leg. "It's nice. I like it."

She pressed a hand to her mouth, breathlessly laughing. It was a struggle to keep herself quiet when he continued, but it was a struggle she relished.

Her back arched, her hand tightening in his hair as he urged her ever closer to release. Soon, she was shuddering under his attention, the shakes of her body settling into shivers as she finally settled down into the bed.

He raised his head, but she could still feel his breath against her skin.

"I did okay?" he asked.

"Was I not evidence enough?" she teased.

He intended to go back to what he was doing, but instead she pulled him close again, tugging him up to lay against her. He wiped at his mouth haphazardly but when she kissed him she could taste herself on his lips. Rosa met his enthusiasm with her own. His hips moved against hers and it was her turn to hold him tightly when she felt his teeth scrape the pulse-point of her neck.

He could feel the hunger in her touch now, and while his fear was not yet quieted, it didn't eclipse the thrill of it all. She pulled him under her, pressing him into the mattress as she kissed him. He was open to her touch, squirming sweetly at the sensations she wrought. She didn't stop until he was breathless from more than just his previous activities.

She sat up and brushed her hair out of her face, thought better of it, and pulled an elastic from her wrist to tie it back messily. This was easier. Her tail flicked and swished behind her, happy to be freed from where it had been laid on.

"Wow," Hastin breathed, looking up at her.

"What is it?" she asked him.

"You're amazing," he said. He reached up to her and brushed his fingers against her cheek. "Rosa, you're beautiful. You're wonderful"

He spoke in such awe of her. She had heard that warmth in his voice before, like she was the sun and the stars. Like there was nothing else in the world but her. She bent down, he met her halfway and when she kissed him she tried to show him what he showed her. That he was wonderful and beautiful, too. If she told him, she knew he would hear but did not think that it would mean the same. So she showed him, or she tried.

She eased him down again, and her feather-light fingers over his body had him short of breath and shaking. The arrangements were simply made and Rosa found it easy to straddle his hips. She could not see the darkness but she could feel the way it hung around them, comforting and safe. She pressed herself to him, met no resistance and sighed as she felt herself fit snugly against him. His hands smoothed up her thighs, gripping her hips. The longer she sat still, the more impatient he seemed to get.

"Rosa—" And like she had said his name, hearing the arousal in his voice was captivating. It was more than enough motivation to spur her on.

Luscious, slick heat, the darkness dampening the sounds they made together. Rosa knew her body well, knew how to move to meet her satisfaction. He moved with her, met every motion of her body without hesitation, without thought. There was nothing but the noise of their breathing, the sounds of their moving bodies, as though nothing else mattered. However brief it was, it was comforting.

She met her end first but he was not long behind, and when she fell against him she felt him shudder and he cried out against her shoulder. Out of breath, she held him tight until they both stopped shaking. When she moved away from him, it earned her a whimper and the feeling of exhaustion creeping into her. It was late. She had no idea how late it really was.

She lay against him, wrapping her arms around him and he settled in comfortably against her. For a long while, they merely laid there together in the dark.

Hastin moved to kiss her cheek. "I should probably let you sleep. It must be very late now."

"Where are you going?" she asked, making no move to disentangle him from her arms.

He hesitated, nuzzling against her, before he answered. "I don't want to get you in trouble with the others. You know, the captain made Ame promise not to sleep with me..."

Rosa's response was half-laugh and half-sigh and to pull him closer. "Ame can get a little...enthusiastic. I'm sure Oliver just wanted to make sure she didn't pressure you. You are allowed to make your own choices, and so am I."

She could feel the flicker of his eyelashes against her arm where he rested his head. "So... I, um..."

"You could stay here, if you wanted," she offered.

He shifted closer to her in the bed. She rolled onto her side, and behind her, her tail swished contentedly.

"I'd really like that. Are you sure I won't be in the way?"

"I'm sure. We'll get all cleaned up in the morning." She kissed his forehead.

It had been awhile since she had shared her bed with anyone, but she found that she rather enjoyed the sudden change.

33:

Xueying awoke the next morning without any real hangover to speak of. No, what hurt instead was her throat. She had done an awful lot of singing, and had done exactly zero warm ups. Plus, it wasn't like she was drinking water regularly. Whoops. So much for partying hard. She definitely wasn't as young as she used to be. Her mother would have scolded her at length…and then laughed about it, probably.

So, she rolled herself out of bed, pulled a t-shirt on to at least cover the part of her that her underwear didn't, and went to get some tea. She leaned against the counter, on her feet, sure, but barely. While she waited in the kitchen half asleep, Rusty also stuck her head out of their bedroom door.

"It's early," she said simply.

Xueying shrugged. "I'm up. Maybe not for good, I don't know." The idea of a nap sounded amazing already, and she hadn't done anything of value. She winced then, frowning when speaking hurt her, and rubbed her throat.

"You pull a muscle or something?" Rusty asked.

That made her laugh, which also hurt, and she made a rude gesture at the other woman. This was rough. Not being able to keep up with Rusty, of all people, meant her voice really was down the drain "Wait until I've had my tea, alright? Stop it."

So, Rusty went back in their room. When the water was ready, Xueying made two cups. She knocked on the door awkwardly with her knee until Rusty opened it. It took a few times.

"Is this my reward for almost making you throw up?" she asked.

"This is a peace offering so you won't do it again," Xueying joked.

The room was small, but it wasn't terrible. There was a tiny window with metals bars on it that would have been off-putting had Xueying not theorized they were there for stability rather than security. The whole apartment didn't seem put together very well. Nothing had broken on them yet, but she spent a lot of her time side-eyeing things, feeling as though they were waiting for the perfect time to do so.

She tried to sip her tea, found it too hot, and sat down on her bed, facing the other woman. Rusty did nearly exactly the same thing and Xueying smiled.

"You know...those songs you sang last night," she started, suddenly, piquing Xueying's interest. "I think I know them."

"They were pretty popular once," Xueying said, neutrally. Still, she looked at Rusty with curiosity. She hadn't expected her to start a conversation, and especially not about something like that. "And they're pretty old. Where did you hear them?"

Rusty frowned, not answering. Xueying wasn't going to press her, but still glanced over where she was sitting as she waited for her tea to cool. She was curious, but Rusty would speak in her own time if she wanted to at all.

"When I was young...my town was destroyed in a flood. The whole thing was wiped out," Rusty told her suddenly. "I had no family and nowhere to go. Relief workers picked me up. They couldn't send me to an orphanage in my own country. They were too full, they said. So they sent me here, to The Ves."

Xueying winced, this time in sympathy. "You didn't speak the language or anything, did you?" she asked.

Rusty shook her head, not looking at Xueying. "No. I didn't speak any Omni at the time. And I was...upset. So I learned very slow. The other kids did not like me. And, when they were mean, I fought them." She shrugged. "I didn't make any friends."

Xueying smiled. "It must have been terrible. But I'm glad you beat them up. Little jerks."

That made Rusty smile, too, and she finally looked at Xueying. "I beat them up a lot," she said, sounding a little pleased with herself. And then, after a few moments of thoughtful silence, she continued. "That's where I know those songs from. They used to play on the radio, in the orphanage. They were on the radio every day."

"Did they drive you crazy? That's what everyone else tells me," Xueying asked. "I mean, if they get played all the time, they're bound to, right?"

But Rusty shook her head. "No, no...nothing like that. They made me smile," she said, solemnly. "They were something nice to hear. And I didn't know the language. Nobody else around me did, either, so it made me feel like we were finally equal. But they'd be on all the time, and I liked them. Hearing them again, last night..." She paused, thinking. "Can I show you something?" Rusty asked her then.

Xueying didn't hesitate to agree. It was rare that Rusty talked this much, and she would greedily take advantage of it if given half the chance. It

281

was nice to listen to her talk.

Rusty pulled her shirt off then, leaving her in just her undershirt. She didn't toss it away, but left it wrapped around her hand as she spoke. "Here, this scar—" She pointed to a jagged mark on her chest, one that disappeared farther under her shirt. "During the flood, I was dragged away by the water. A piece of scrap lodged itself in my chest."

Xueying winced. "Right through the heart. Someone's got good aim."

Rusty's smile was rough and charming. "I know. Thankfully, I have two of them. The other kids used to make fun of the scar. But then you get into ring fighting and suddenly they make you look cool." She shrugged. "You know, they still played those songs when I was training."

Xueying's smile turned a little concerned. "I didn't mean to make things hard for you. I'm sorry, Rusty."

She shook her head. "No, it's not bad... It was nice. Especially to hear you sing them. It sounded...really familiar." She sighed, but it didn't sound unhappy. "They made me feel just like they used to."

At that, Xueying stood up with her cup of tea and went to sit beside the other woman. "Well... You just told me something really important to you... I..." She sighed. "I can tell you something, too. Fair's fair, right? And it's about those songs," she offered.

Rusty smiled. It was faint, the way they always were. "I'd like that."

Xueying took a deep breath and then nodded. "You said it sounded natural when I sang them, right? Like... I don't know. Like I've had a lot of practice or something." She was trying to find the best way to approach it, and she didn't feel as though she was doing a very good job.

But, Rusty nodded. "It didn't sound like they did on the radio. I think the singer was younger. Much younger. But they sounded... I don't know. They sounded right."

Xueying smiled. "The singer was a lot younger. About fifteen, actually. And very famous, at least where she was from. She also really enjoyed those songs, the ones that got crazy popular. Which might be why she, you know... still sings them."

Rusty blinked at her, her tea halfway raised to her lips for the sip she was going to take before she lowered her glass in shock.

"You mean..." She looked at Xueying closely.

Xueying laughed, and then winced again. "Yeah. I mean. I tried out for a talent company when I was ten. Debuted when I was fourteen. Put out some songs at fifteen that, for whatever reason, got famous world-wide. I'm not sure why. But it was...pretty crazy." She sighed, but she was smiling. It felt kind of nice to say it out loud. Sure, it wasn't a secret, it wasn't something that she deliberately hid, but it wasn't something she talked about. Yoru knew, but he also knew how to keep things quiet.

And then, finally, she took a sip of her tea. Immediately, her throat felt noticeably better.

Rusty was still staring at her in surprise. "I don't believe it. How did that...how are you... What happened?"

Xueying laughed, trying not to cough up the second sip she took. "Well... It's a long story. Being famous got me into a lot of places, and talking to a lot of people. I got good at it. Eventually CD sales dropped off, but my connections didn't. I still had work...just a different kind." She shrugged. "It was just me and my mom growing up, so I already knew I'd do whatever I had to to help her. It was why I even tried out in the first place. We made pretty good money off the music, but you know...you never stop worrying." She shrugged.

Rusty took a long drink of her tea, and this time when she smiled it was immediately obvious. "I can't believe it. I can't. That's..." She shook her head. "You don't know what you've done for me," she said then. "You have no idea. I always..." She shook her head again. "I would think about the girl who sang those songs when I was lonely, you know. I wanted to be friends with her. She sounded so nice."

"We are friends, Rusty," Xueying said. She leaned against the woman's arm. "Why do you think I followed you around until you let me talk to you? And why do you think I went through so much trouble to get you out of that contract? I wanted to be friends with you, too," she said, smiling.

Rusty laughed. It was a deeper sound than Xueying's pained giggling, but just as lovely. "You wanted to be my friend. That's why you did all of that?" she asked.

Xueying shrugged. "Well, you know... I came to watch you fight. Everyone was like, 'she's so small, how the fuck does she do it' and all the stuff I'm sure you've heard a million times —" Rusty rolled her eyes and Xueying waved it off, "—so I was curious, and had nothing to do, so I figured why not. And then I saw you, and..."

"And?"

"I just had this feeling in my heart," she said quietly. "Something came over me. And I wanted to get you out of there. Not that you couldn't do it, the fighting, I mean. You can do it. I've seen it. You're unbelievably good. But the idea that you had to, that they were holding it over your head... That really upset me. I've never felt that way before."

283

Xueying had seen a lot of injustice. Some of it she could help, and some of it she couldn't. The world was too vast, and too dark, for her to take it on by herself. She knew that. But she had never felt so strongly about something as she had about getting Rusty out of there. It was undeniable.

Xueying sighed and looked down. Rusty hooked a finger under her chin and drew her gaze up again. "So you took my place, in order to get me out of there."

"I cheated," Xueying admitted with a small smile. "I did. I poisoned him. There's no way I could go toe-to-toe with someone who hoped to win against you. I should be dead." She shrugged, still smiling. "But getting you out of there was more important than the rules. Hell, everything is more important than their rules," she said quietly.

"You risked a lot for me. And I barely gave you the time of day."

Xueying shook her head and took Rusty's hand in her own. "That's not your way. I know that. I wouldn't change that for the world, Rusty," she said, giving her hand a squeeze. "I'm...well, I'm actually really surprised that you've told me as much as you have."

"I wanted to hope it was you, you know," Rusty said softly. "I wanted to hope that it wasn't a trick of my mind. That maybe it really was you that had been comforting me for years, without even knowing it." Where Xueying held her hand in both of her own, Rusty now added her other hand, laying it over hers.

Xueying smiled. "You know, hearing that... I don't think anything could make me happier. Nothing in the world."

"Nothing?" Rusty asked.

Xueying laughed again and shook her head. "Nope. Nothing."

So Rusty kissed her. It was simple. It felt so right it was almost effortless. And Xueying kissed her back.

"I was wrong," Xueying said, as soon as they parted. "You know what. I was wrong."

Rusty smiled, and kissed her again.

~*~

Dan didn't come home until later that morning, and he seemed no worse for the wear. He waved hello to Yoru, but immediately jumped in the shower before they could talk. When he stumbled out of it, finally, he was much more amenable to a conversation.

"So?" Yoru asked, smiling.

"So...nothing bad happened," Dan said, grinning.

Yoru laughed. "That's what I like to hear. He is nice?"

284

Dan nodded. "He is nice. And I didn't freak out or anything. Everything was cool. And sleeping away was kind of neat but—" He shrugged. "It feels weird to not be home."

Yoru looked at him strangely. "This is home?"

Dan laughed. "No, idiot. Wherever you are is home. I don't care about this place," he said.

He was busy drying himself off in their room, but he kept talking. Yoru, a true gentleman, asked for no details. He just wanted to make sure that everyone had a good time.

"You know, there's a lot of work in Spectra City," he said. "There's a good chance we'll be back here before long."

Dan nodded. "I'm hoping so. Oliver and I even talked about, like, strings and shit. Apparently, his problem is people keep trying to date him, and when he says no, they disappear. I'm very not in any position for that. So, it works out great."

"Glad to hear it," Yoru said, smiling. "Maybe next time we get drinks, I can meet him, too. I'm not trying to steal your boy—" He added. "But he sounds fun."

Dan shook his head. "I was hoping you'd say that. He's very funny, and surprisingly well-read. I think you two would be super annoying together, which is exactly why you should meet."

"You set yourself up for disaster," Yoru noted.

Dan nodded, laughing again.

All cleaned up, he went in search of food, and ended up crashing into his bed to eat. Yoru lay in his own bed, reading, when Dan spoke up again.

"Where are the girls?"

"In their room," Yoru said, looking over his vidscreen at Dan. "I haven't seen them all morning."

"...Then how do you know they're in their room?"

"I heard them talking. And, perhaps...congratulations may be in order," he said.

Dan looked at him blankly. "Congratulations for what? There's... there's a lot of possibilities that come to mind, you know," he said.

Yoru laughed, then, and turned to face him properly. "Our dear Xueying has been pining over Rusty for a years now. How many, I'm not precisely certain, but enough, surely."

Dan snapped his fingers, almost spilling his food. "We talked about this! That's why. That's why we did that."

Yoru nodded. "Yes, exactly. I mean, she's proven her worth to the job

285

as well, Xueying is very clever like that, but that's why it had to be her, surely."

"And Rusty? What did she say?" Dan asked, excited. "Don't keep me hanging, now, I'm really invested in this," he insisted.

Yoru held up his hand to stop him. "I did not eavesdrop. Xueying is my friend, and until she decides to tell me, her privacy is her own. I had only heard what I did when I was going to ask them if they wanted something to eat."

"So, you don't know what happened?" Dan asked.

Yoru shrugged. "I haven't heard any crying and they haven't come out. Whatever happened, I don't think it's bad," he said, shrugging.

Dan seemed pleased. "Man, that's really sweet. That's so sweet. Damn," he said, grinning. "I'm so glad. Xueying's so nice. And Rusty could use someone to care about her. I'm all warm and fuzzy and shit." He was clearly delighted.

"I am just as pleased," Yoru told him. "I think it will be good for them both, and we, as their friends, will be happy for them. It seems everyone is having a good day."

And then Dan frowned. "You haven't had anything special happen. That's kind of sucky."

Yoru shook his head. He got up and then leisurely sat himself down next to his friend, comfortable and relaxed.

"Dan, you idiot," he said, smiling. Dan pretended to be insulted. "You came back from making a new friend. You successfully found someone who, by your own words, is nice to you and you have a common, ah, interest." He laughed lightly. "And, one of my best friends has just decided to bear her heart to someone she loves with positive results. I've had a very special day!"

Dan smiled at him. "You're something else, you know."

"People keep telling me that," Yoru replied smartly.

Dan made a motion as if to swat him away with the chopsticks he held. "I mean it. You really are."

"Can I have some?" Yoru asked, smiling, and Dan rolled his eyes but returned his smile and held some out on his chopsticks for him, which Yoru happily, and not together all that messily, ate.

"It's just... This is really nice," Dan said, when he had swallowed. "I know the job is kind of being an asshole right now, but we'll figure it out. In the meantime, it's great that things are going so well. I'm really happy for them, and hell, I'm really happy for me. And you're just..." He shook his head. "I'm going to have to learn how to write poetry if I'm ever going to do you justice."

"I could teach you," Yoru said offhandedly. "But then you risk sounding pretentious and insufferable, like a certain someone we both know."

"You're not that insufferable," Dan joked. "You know...I grew up with guys who would be pissed if the people around them all got this kind of good news," he added.

"Then they are selfish and short-sighted," Yoru said easily.

Dan shrugged and agreed. "I mean, yeah, but that doesn't stop them."

Yoru gestured around himself, but especially at Dan. "Everyone's happiness does not take away from mine, and, in fact, causes it to grow. Your new friend does not detract from our friendship. Xueying and Rusty's possible relationship does not detract from their relationships with me. I lose nothing, and gain everything."

Dan smiled. "I like the way you look at things. I want to be able to see things like you do," he said.

"You honour me."

"How about you honour me with a poetry lesson when I'm done with this food?" Dan asked him, smiling.

Yoru clapped his hands together excitedly. "Oh, certainly. I'll even try not to sound too pretentious, how does that sound?"

287

34:

They normally woke up around the same time as each other. Oliver and Rosa first, followed by Hastin and then Ame. So when Ame woke up, and there was no sign of the other two, it led to some mild confusion. Ame knocked on Rosa's door before letting herself in.

"Hey, Rosa, have you—" she said, flinging the door open and looking at the bed. "Oh. There he is."

Her tactless entrance woke them both. Hastin sat up straight away, blinking and looking around the room in a brief moment of distress. He saw Ame and his eyes immediately cleared.

Rosa, slower to rise, pushed herself to sit up and wrapped her arm languidly around Hastin's waist. "We overslept?" she asked, her hair hanging heavy around her face.

"Yeah. Up late?" Ame asked, grinning.

"Hey, it sounds like—Oh." Oliver stuck his head in the room and for someone whose complexion was as dark as he was, he did manage to turn remarkably red. "Oh."

"Hi, Captain..." Hastin said. His blush was much lighter, but no less damning.

"I should—" Oliver made an embarrassed motion with his hand, signalling that he was going to leave.

"I'm staying," Ame laughed.

"Are you... Are you upset, Captain?" Hastin asked. His hands twisted in the bedsheets and Ame saw Rosa's hand tighten against his skin.

Oliver, still red, did not run away. Nor did he seem to panic.

"No," he said, taking a deep breath. He forced himself to look over at them, despite his apparent discomfort. "I worry about taking advantage of the situation. You know me." He shrugged. "I'm not upset about...about that. As long as you're both okay."

"Oliver, if I wasn't comfortable with you seeing me topless, I would have covered up," Rosa pointed out.

He laughed, although it did sound a little strained. "Having never seen you without a shirt before, uh, it's a nice view."

"I mean, having never seen myself topless, I'll take your word for it," she remarked wryly.

"It's very true, Rosa." Hastin leaned back against her happily. "You're so pretty."

"I actually think it's you making him so red, Hastin," Ame pointed out.

"Don't be embarrassed, Captain. Everyone's seen me naked before," he said, matter-of-factly.

"I'm just shy," Oliver said. "It's got nothing to do with you, honest."

"If I was going to voluntarily be naked in front of anyone in the world, it's the people in this room," Hastin said. "But...I'm kind of gross, and should probably go shower. You might want to cover your eyes, okay, Captain?"

"On it," Oliver said. This time, his laugh sounded a little more natural. Hastin got out of bed and kissed Rosa on the cheek. "I'll be quick," he promised her. "Then you can get in."

Shamelessly unclothed, he kissed Ame on the cheek, too as he passed her, and kissed Oliver's hand where it covered his eyes. "Sorry, Captain," he apologized.

"You don't have to be sorry for me," Oliver said reasonably. "Why should you being comfortably undressed bother me?"

"Because you have all the morals the rest of us lack," Ame joked. "And you worry you're going to make someone uncomfortable."

"Yeah, but when informed otherwise...I should be able to chill. Unfortunately, that's not something I've ever been good at."

"Morals suit you, Captain." Hastin kissed his other hand and Oliver heard him wander away.

"I think all my blood is returning to places it is supposed to be in," Oliver said when he heard him leave.

"Pretty sure it rushed to more than your face," Rosa joked. "Are you going to be okay when I get out of bed?"

"I'm going back to the kitchen is what I'm doing," Oliver said. And when everyone is done being naked, we can start talking plans."

It was back in the kitchen, where he was sipping his coffee, that Ame found him a few moments later. "Well, I mean...I feel more awake now," she said amiably.

"That's one way to get the morning started," Oliver agreed.

"You're really okay?" she asked him then, looking at him without pretense over her own mug of coffee.

"Despite my dramatics, I'm totally okay with naked people," Oliver told her with a smile. "I have been laid before, as hard as that is to believe."

"Not at all, now that you have a sense of humour, I'd get on that,"

Ame told him.

"Thank you," he said with a laugh. "It was just the context. I hadn't meant to walk in on them. I'm just glad I didn't make anyone uncomfortable."

"Her ass is as great as her tits are," Ame told him.

Oliver coughed, nearly choking on his coffee. "I don't doubt it, honestly. I was mostly worried about Hastin. I get the feeling he hasn't been allowed a lot of privacy."

"He'll be okay," Ame said. "You have to trust him to talk to us if he isn't. He's told you before when he's unhappy. Give him some credit."

Oliver had to admit she had a point.

Soon, the four of them were clothed and collected in the living room. "You guys have seen where we're going, so you lead the way," Rosa told them.

They divided what they had to carry between them, and on their way out the door Oliver cast a look back at the kitchen.

"Something wrong, Captain?" Hastin asked him. He was holding the door with his foot and waiting for Oliver to join up with them.

"There's still dishes in the sink," he said, frowning. Their breakfast dishes, true to his word, still sat there together.

"You're so responsible." Hastin smiled at him and held out his free hand, the other one holding a bag of Rosa's equipment.

"No one is going to be mad at you for not doing the dishes," he said gently. "Come on."

Following Hastin was so easy.

He took Hastin's hand and let him tug him out the door. He didn't even look back to see if it had been locked behind them.

It was an extra hot day outside, of course. Just their luck. Weather oscillated madly in the city between wickedly cold and terribly hot. When it was overcast, the city got colder than anywhere else because the sun hit so little of it, blocked as it was by all the skyscrapers. When the sun returned, every surface was dark or reflective and it seemed to suck the heat of the sun right out of the sky. The press of people and the ever-present smog and dust did little to make the problem better. Once upon a time, there had been a system of seasons, but any rationale in that area seemed to have been lost. It was either a metallic, icy frost or, like today, hot and dirty and heavy.

"You said this place had running water, right? Because I'm gonna need another shower," Rosa said. Of all of them, she had the lightest hair and so had spent the least time feeling like she was being cooked, but she was still well smudged in dirt by the time they got there.

"This time, you get to shower first," Hastin said. His cheeks were flushed with heat but he seemed the less wilted of all of them. Unnatural, to be sure, but so was he.

They got in, and got washed up, and Ame laid on the floor in the living area. It looked like such a good idea that the others joined her soon after. None of them had bothered turning on the lights.

"It's cooler down here," Rosa noted.

"We can plan from the floor," Oliver agreed. He had his hair wrapped in a t-shirt and it provided a useful pillow for him. Also, the carpet was stained, but thankfully not actually that dirty. He had been pretty reluctant to lay down on it.

"So...what is the plan?" Rosa asked.

"Kill Violet," Oliver said. There was silence for a moment as it sunk in, not only that it was the simplest option, but that it was he who said it. Was it that easy? The idea of violence used to set him on edge. And he knew it would, again, when it came down to it.

But he knew it was the only way out.

"'Kay. How do we do it?" Ame asked eventually.

"I know the layout of the HiTech building and all of the door passcodes," Hastin offered.

"You fucking what," Ame said incredulously.

Hastin sat up and looked between them. "Yeah. I know the whole building, inside and out."

"Why didn't you leave?!" Ame sat up, too, looking at him in shock.

Oliver made a strangled noise and hurriedly looked to Hastin, worried he would be upset. Rosa sighed.

"Well... I mean...it was terrible there. But what did I have to leave for? Every time they let me out, it was terrible out here, too," he said, thoughtfully. "And most of the time, well..." Hastin shrugged. "I really wasn't in any state to get out."

"You know the whole building?" Rosa asked him, redirecting their focus to the task at hand. "How did you manage that? And the door codes?"

Hastin nodded. "Yeah. It's like... You remember how I told you, Rosa, that I knew Oliver was different as soon as I saw him?"

"You said it was the way he looked at you," she said offhandedly. Ame was the only one who caught Oliver looking surprised.

"It was. But also I...I heard it. I hear all kinds of stuff."

Rosa snapped her fingers, remembering. "Like how you heard Oliver tell Ame not to sleep with you, even though I could not hear it."

"Yeah!"

"You heard that?" Oliver asked.

"Extrasensory hearing? Like really strong? Like Rosa's laser eyes?"

"I don't have laser eyes," Rosa corrected Ame. Fruitlessly, of course, as Ame was not worried about being correct.

But Hastin shook his head. "You don't hear what kind of person someone is with sensitive hearing. But it kind of feels like that," he said, and then shrugged. "I've never been wrong," he said proudly.

"It wouldn't be the weirdest thing I've heard," Ame admitted.

"Okay, but how do we get the map out of your head and into our eyes?" Oliver asked.

"I can probably figure that out," Rosa suggested. "Hastin, if I were to give you a tablet to draw the layout on, do you think you could?"

"Mmhm," he said, as he laid back down on the carpet. "I'm sure I could."

"If he does that, I can make my computer show you guys what he's drawn. And I can program the door keys into this thing—" She pointed at her headset. "So we can have them on hand."

"Do you know how many people are in the building on a given night?" Oliver asked him.

He made a thinking noise. "I could puzzle it out. The top floors all have security guards that patrol. It's the basement we have to worry about. That's where the actual security force is based, and also where, like, the lab and stuff is. Violet's apartment is on that level as well."

"They have an on-site security force? That's handy," Oliver said.

"I fail to see what's handy about that shit," Ame disagreed.

"They won't bother calling the cops if they're sure they can handle it on their own, and once they're not sure, they won't be in any state to call the cops," Oliver pointed out.

Ame laughed. "Okay, yeah. It'll save us some heat if we don't have to worry about that when we're done. An on-site force means more trouble upfront, but...I'm kind of itching to kill somebody, so..."

"We should see if we can't keep the upstairs people upstairs, and stop them from coming down behind us," Oliver said. "Any hope we could, like...lock out the elevators or something?"

"Probably. I'm sure we can make them useless. And then we just have to lock or block the stairs," Rosa said thoughtfully.

"The doors that lead to the stairs don't have electronic locks, just key locks."

"I can pick them to get us in," Ame told them. "But that begs the question, how do we make sure the people with the keys don't get in after us?"

"Could we make those locks unusable, somehow?" Oliver asked.

"We could melt them," Rosa said. "Melting them the right amount should make them unopenable, at least with the key."

"And with the majority of their people underground, they will probably figure we're walking to our deaths, if they even realize what we've done," Ame reasoned.

"But if we do that, how the heck do we get out?" Oliver rolled over onto his stomach so he could look at them. "We do still have to get out."

"There's an exit in Violet's apartment. That one has a key code," Hastin said.

"Of course there is. Bitch." Ame rolled her eyes.

"Surely they don't spend all their time around you thinking classified information?" Rosa joked.

Hastin laughed. "Well, no. But I've had a long, long time to collect it all. A very long time," he said. Oliver tried not to think too hard on his words.

"We should figure out what kind of gear we're working with and get started on that map," Oliver said next. "Sound like a plan?"

"Give me a minute to get Hastin set up with my computer and then we'll get all of our shit together." Rosa reluctantly pulled herself up to sitting.

"Oh, this place only has two rooms. Which room should I get set up in? And who is bunking with me?"

"Not me. You snore," Ame said.

"Liar."

"Twice, actually. I'll room with you, we've done it before." She waved it off. "But we're going to need his gear for this, too. Can you at least get him started in here?"

"I'll get my stuff first. I don't have much of it," Hastin volunteered, hopping lightly to his feet.

He was true to his word, and he set up his stash in the middle of the room before following Rosa to where she was setting up her computer.

"Ame, this is where I need you, because I don't know what a lot of this is any good for. But, I think looking at what we're working with should give us a better idea of what tools we have at our disposal."

"It can't hurt. It will also let us check what kind of ammunition we have hanging around. Nothing worse than running out of bullets," she said. As she talked, she was unloading her own bag next to Hastin's stuff.

"You can see that the kid usually carries smaller things. Not just because they fit under his dress better, but because of what he's trained for."

Oliver frowned. "Which is different than...what you are trained for?"

Ame laughed. "He's more of an assassin-type. Get in, kill somebody, get out. He's not a room-clearer. And that's cool, because we have Rosa."

"Rosa is that," Oliver assumed.

"Just wait, you'll love it." Ame laughed.

With Hastin set up, Rosa had re-joined them and started contributing her own equipment. "Luckily, I don't use a lot of ammo. That will mostly be Ame and Hastin who take care of that."

"Judging from the fuckin' knives that kid carries, we won't exactly be in trouble if we run out, either," Ame said.

Rosa was constructing something in her lap, and Oliver watched her in both interest and confusion. "That looks...complicated."

"Well, I mean, I can do it with my eyes off, so it's not that hard once you know it," Rosa told him.

"What are you making?" Oliver asked. And then he frowned. "You were wearing this at the other job, right?"

Ame clapped her hands together excitedly and Rosa held the finished product in her hands.

"That looks terrifying. I mean, it was terrifying before but I didn't have the chance to ask about it. What is it?" Oliver looked at her equipment with his eyebrows raised.

"It's just a gauntlet," Rosa said. "But it's a very useful gauntlet. The ammunition for it is pretty limited, but even if they're wearing the usual bulletproof get-up, it won't help much. Plus, it's heavy and good to throw around, and pointy where it counts. It also has a built in grappling hook, although since we are going down and not up, I don't expect we'll need it."

Oliver looked at her, his expression nonplussed. "You built this. Didn't you? Tell me you built this."

Rosa laughed. "I did, I built it."

"It's art!" Ame announced. "Art, I tell you. Remember how I said Hastin wasn't a room-clearer? This bitch is. Just wait and see. It's so good."

"Remember how I was feeling better about being out of my league? I'm second guessing that again." Oliver was only half joking, looking at the array of weaponry that they had collected.

"I'm going to show you how to shoot all of these, everything short of pulling the trigger," Ame said to him, firmly. "And that way if they get dropped and you pick it up, you won't be so startled."

"What good am I if I can't hit anyone?"

But Ame shook her head. "It's called 'suppressive fire', and it's when you fire near somebody to keep them out of your way. So what if you don't have a body count? You'll still be useful. And you're our idea guy, you basically planned this whole thing."

Oliver took a deep breath. "Last time we did something like this, I got exploded. And I was useless. I won't let that happen again."

"Being exploded sucks," Ame agreed.

Oliver reached out, picking up the nearest gun. He had been holding a gun, then, too. He didn't even think he had fired it. He couldn't remember everything that had happened. They were going into this one more well prepared. They would have the element of surprise, and they knew they were looking for a fight.

He wasn't going to let them down again.

35:

"You found this?" Xueying asked Yoru as he started to climb his way up the outside of the building. His grin was so bright that it could be seen even in the low light. The four of them were there, three of them waiting in the dark for him as he worked. They hadn't ever discussed it fully, but it seemed that the idea of splitting up had been unanimously discarded. It hadn't gone so well for them before and they universally seemed to loathe trying it again.

He worked his way up to where a rusted old fire escape still clung tenuously to the building, his fingers finding purchase in impossible cracks, spots that Dan could not even see in the dark. Once he was up there, he tied a rope to it and they worked their way up to join him.

"It's a lucky find, hm?" he said thoughtfully, when he pulled Xueying up onto the platform. She started climbing the steps to the next landing, but he stayed there to help both Dan and Rusty up before untying the rope again and winding it around his arm. Dan took the longest to get up, but he did it without needing help.

"This is brilliant," Dan told him excitedly.

"Oh, it's nothing," Yoru demurred. Still, Rusty agreed with him once they got up there.

"It really is nothing." She noticed, looking around. They had come in through a broken window on that floor, only to find the whole area empty. The entire floor was without any sign that it had ever been occupied.

"Apparently it's for rent...but has been for as long back as I can find documentation of it," Yoru explained. It was certainly dusty enough that Dan would buy that as true. "Everything we set up in the target before the remodel will be of no use to us, so we're back to step one."

"What we do have is a clear view of the repairs being done across the road." He gestured as he spoke, and Dan's eyes followed his motion.

Xueying rubbed her hands together. "This is awesome. We can easily keep an eye on them from here. And, since the entrance is on the far side of the building, there's no reason they'd ever see us."

"How do you want to do this?" Dan asked. He peered out through the darkened glass. It was hard to see, but not impossible. And the tint meant that they would be invisible even in the daylight.

296

The pink-haired woman breathed out heavily, less of a sigh than a noise of her thinking. "I don't know that it needs twenty-four seven surveillance. We're probably best coming by here at night. We don't plan on hitting the place during the day, anyway. What we want to see is how busy this place is in the dark."

She gestured to all the lights that were currently strung up outside of their target, across the road and one building down. "A lot of those lights aren't permanent. They'll come down when the repairs are done. After that, we'll want to keep an eye on how the security looks, because it is undoubtedly going to be more."

"We can't see into there from here," Rusty said, frowning.

"Not from this side. From that far corner, we can probably get more details," Yoru said. They had the whole floor to themselves, so they might as well use it. "My binoculars will make an easy job of it, and they can untint the view, too," he said, reaching out to tap their side of the windows. The glass stretched the height of the room and all the way down the wall.

The idea seemed sensible enough to Dan. And, it seemed, to Rusty. She nodded at his words.

"That solves that problem."

"So we'll swing by here every night until we notice the lights go down, and then we'll collect some information," Dan said. "Once we get a good idea of what we're looking at as far as the new parameters go, we can bust in there and get what we need."

"You have those things?" Rusty asked, sticking her hand out to Yoru.

"Those...things," he said. Then it clicked in. "Ah, yes. Those things. I have them." He dug around in the bag strapped to his hip and held the binoculars out to her.

She took them, and the three others followed her to the far corner that was nearest their target. Once there, she unfolded them and took a look.

"Hm," she said, and then handed them back.

"Works like a charm, no?" Yoru asked, grinning. She gave him a look that was short of scathing, just enough to make him laugh. Still, she didn't make any complaints about the technology.

"Well, that's one step done. Good find." Xueying squeezed Yoru's shoulder.

"Remind me when we come back here to bring a mask or my sneezing is going to get us arrested," Dan added, pulling a face.

They cleared out. It was pretty obvious, what with the lights and all, that the place was still being worked on. They could see people going in and out of it. It was more than repairs, surely. They were going to fix all the bullet holes and mop up all the blood, and then beef up their security. It was going to be a few more days, at least.

But, that meant a lot of time to get other things organized, like supplies.

"Who's that?" Yoru asked, glancing over to see Dan tapping away at his phone.

"Oh, just Oliver," Dan said.

Yoru brightened. "So he didn't disappear on you. Handy."

They were walking together, heading to a little, nondescript shop that Yoru knew. A place that would sell them a few things that they intended to make good use of. And, of course, they weren't alone. Behind them, Rusty and Xueying walked. Xueying's arm was hooked through Rusty's, but no one commented on it.

"Is that your new friend?" she asked, though, at Dan's comment.

"Yeah, I met him when you were reliving your glory days," Dan joked.

"Oh, Yoru told you all about that, did he?"

Dan laughed again. "I mean, he did, but he almost didn't have to. I can't believe I didn't figure it out."

"Hey." She shrugged. "No one else figures it out, either. It's a good set up."

He had to admit, he agreed with that one. Besides, she really was killer at it. It must have been a great way to get rid of some stress.

The stairs to the store went lower than street level, and if it had ever had a sign, it was long burnt-out and sun-bleached into being unreadable. Now, there were papers taped to the window glass and lights that flickered badly inside. It looked, at first glance, like any other hollowed-out store that might have struggled to survive in the age of neon and plasteel.

Yoru, being Yoru, waltzed into it without any apparent concern.

"Hello, my friends," he said, resting his hands on the glass countertop. As if on cue, both Xueying and Dan reacted; the former rolled her eyes and the latter shot him a look. Did he know everyone in the city? Some days it certainly seemed like he did.

The men working there had an accent that Dan couldn't place, but at least two of the three smiled when Yoru spoke.

"Hey, been a long time," one of them said. "What can I get for you?"

"We've got a shopping list, actually," he said, motioning to Xueying. He followed it with a, "Don't mind them, they're mine."

"Even the little one?" the frowning man asked, nodding to Rusty.

"Especially the little one." Yoru smiled, but Dan thought there was something in his tone that made the statement beyond questioning.

It was a sketchy place. Not as dirty as it looked from the outside, but crowded with stock, half of it broken. Dan felt a little more comfortable here than he did on the job; weapons he knew, and weapon quality wasn't beyond him. He had paid attention in training and in the field. He knew a decent amount about what he saw, and what they were looking for.

As Yoru and Xueying talked to the shop owners, Dan and Rusty browsed what they had on display. "We'll leave the haggling to them, huh?" Dan muttered to her. She smirked, but didn't answer. Yeah, leave it to the ones with charisma.

They amused themselves with what they found around to look at, and Dan kept up a running commentary under his breath about what they were examining. Rusty nodded along, but he didn't seem to be boring her. He supposed she had probably seen a fair number of guns, but seeing as she didn't usually work with them, that probably didn't mean she knew a lot about them in general. Her preferred method, and undoubtedly what she was the most impressive at, was punching people right to death. It worked for her.

But a little learning never hurt.

"That one's shit," Dan muttered, pointing at one of the guns. "I mean, normally it's okay, but that's broken. I don't know why they're selling it."

"Waiting for someone who knows less than you," she pointed out.

He laughed under his breath, a reaction more felt than heard. With her leaning against his arm, he knew she got it.

Yoru was boxing up what they had come for, and Xueying was taking care of paying the man. Dan frowned a little. He would have liked to see what they were getting. Still, common sense told him not to crowd the front. There was hardly a chance they'd be able to steal anything that was under the glass without making it noticeable, but the four of them up close to the three people in the shop...it seemed like it could be seen as unnecessary pressure. Dan wasn't here to scare anyone. As far as he knew, they weren't getting paid for that.

Once they got back, though, Yoru unloaded their score and Dan was able to see that he wasn't disappointed. Yoru was as sensible as ever. Either that, or Xueying hadn't let him get anything ridiculous. He supposed it could have gone either way.

"Nothing exciting." Rusty noticed.

"Why would I buy anything exciting? We're all right here," Yoru noted. It was her turn to roll her eyes. Dan grinned.

They spent most of the afternoon going over what their supplies were, and that night they went back to the empty floor to take a look at their target again. While Yoru sat and watched the building for anything interesting, the other three used the dust to re-draw what they remembered of the layout.

"Do you think they'll do a whole redesign?" Xueying asked.

Dan frowned. "I mean, I'd like to say they would, since this layout is pretty terrible...but chances are they won't. I can't imagine them putting more work into it than they need to."

"I've had less trouble robbing gang strongholds." Xueying cursed.

"You also weren't after anything tangible," Yoru reminded her. "It's different when you can walk in and out and have nothing missing when you've stolen something."

She sighed, frowning, but didn't argue.

"If we split here, we can cover each other better." Rusty pointed out on their makeshift map.

"Yeah, that's true. It would be a lot easier to watch each other's backs like that," Dan agreed with her.

"And then we're headed upstairs," he said, marking where the stairwell was. "We can't use the lower terminals?"

Xueying shook her head. "No. The box I have, it—" She hesitated, looking for the words. "—It just drains data in sections. The less of a user-oriented operating system it has to work around, the more work it can get done. It's basically going to just cut out a big chunk of the information and copy it over."

"So you don't want it getting shit it doesn't need in favour of shit it does need, okay," he said, understanding.

"We have no idea what the upstairs looks like," Rusty pointed out.

"Probably doesn't look like much," Yoru said.

"Yeah? How can you be sure?" Xueying looked over to him.

"There's no reason for them to change it from the blueprints, and there aren't any windows on any floors that aren't the main one. Just vents going up the building, probably to keep the lot of it from overheating. It's probably going to be fairly crowded and largely neglected, judging from the rest of the building."

"Mm. No windows is kind of a bitch..." Dan said. "I'd like for us to have another exit that wasn't the way we came in, or the goddamn front door. A window usually makes a good emergency door."

"How big are those vents, Yoru?" Xueying called.

Catching her drift, his answer was succinct. "Enough for Rusty, and maybe for you. Not much hope for Dan and I. Even then, that's pretty heavy on the 'maybe'."

It was Xueying's turn to frown. "I don't like that much, either. Still, it might just be the way it is."

"Shitty." Rusty certainly summed it up well enough.

It looked as though the plan was fairly simple. Bust in through the backdoor, shoot up whatever was in their way, and do a preliminary clearing of the floor. Now that they knew about the basement, and that it seemed to be where the security guys hung out, they'd know where to expect more trouble from. They'd work from the door, to the stairs, and then work up to the next floor so they could get into the data area itself. Once there, they'd cover Xueying until her little box did its cut and paste job, and then they'd fight their way out the way they came in.

Ideally, the security team would be out of guys by the time they made their way up the stairs, but if not, they'd pick them off on their way down again. Then it was back into the darkness and off into the night.

Simple. A little more head-on dangerous than they'd like, but nothing that seemed out of their reach.

"How long does that thing take?" Rusty asked, looking at the hand-held case that Xueying was inspecting.

"A minute, at most," she said. "That's what I was promised. It'll give me the green light when we're cleared to go."

"And if they lied?"

"Well, then I'll save a few bullets for them," Xueying said. That seemed to make Rusty amenable enough to the idea.

It was a solid plan. Simple, and with as little moving pieces as possible.

"Unneeded complexity is a recipe for disaster," Yoru said, when Dan remarked on how straight-forward everything seemed. "The goal is not that they don't know the plan, but that they are unable to stop it. As strange as it is, we're not actually dealing in secrets here."

Because, naturally, he usually did exactly that.

They'd end up back in that dusty room a few more times, until their surveillance showed them that the lights were down. That night they made an impromptu camp, sitting together up there for a few hours.

Again, it was Yoru who looked out. It seemed easiest to have him do it.

"I can see them pass by the windows when they are on their rounds.

301

Every fifteen minutes," he said, glancing at his watch.

"Fifteen? That's not a lot of time for them to get lazy," Xueying remarked.

"If we had six months time, I'd say we should wait." Yoru set the binoculars on his knee and looked over his shoulder at them. "They're more likely to get lazy as time goes on, and I'm sure we'd have more leeway to take advantage of their complacency. But we don't have that kind of time. They're going to be fairly awake and alert, even if we aim to do it late at night."

"I'm getting pretty good at these late nights," Dan said agreeably. "I don't see why we wouldn't. Even if it only helps us a little, it still helps."

"We're still going to surprise them," Rusty pointed out.

Xueying nodded. "Maybe their alertness would be to our advantage. They're going to be more predictable for the first little while."

"That is true," Yoru said.

They'd go the next night, it was decided. Two nights after the repairs had been done. It was hardly worth repairing the place at all, Dan thought, seeing as they were just going to shoot it up again.

He brought up the idea to Yoru, who laughed. "Well, aim to put your bullets into the people and not the new walls, if you feel so terrible about it."

That made Dan laugh, too. "Well, I mean...what if the paint is a really awful colour?"

Yoru shrugged. "I don't know much about interior design. Although, I did once stay in this place where the walls were this awful yellow..."

"Did it bother you that much?" Dan leaned back in his chair, stretching his arms above his head. His bowl, long bereft of food, still sat on the table as he had been in no hurry to vacate the space.

"It bothered me enough that I wrote a poem about it and left that book there for someone to find." Yoru shrugged. "Maybe it will bring someone joy when they are similarly trapped within that yellow hell."

"Yellow Hell sounds...like some kind of hot sauce, actually," Dan noted.

Yoru looked at him in surprise, and then laughed. "I bet you that it is, now that you mention it," he said, amused.

"Speaking of other safe houses, though, do we know where we're headed after this?" Dan asked him.

He received a shrug in response. "We'll probably hang around the city a little while, although not here, as that's going to be a little close to the fire, even for my taste. But Spectra is big and nonsensical enough that it seems unlikely we'll have to run very far. I have a few places in mind."

"Are we going...alone?" Dan asked.

Catching on immediately, as Dan thought he might, Yoru smiled. "Well...that's not a question I can answer, is it?" he asked. "But, I'll have you know, some of these places are suitable for more than two people."

Dan nodded, and found himself smiling too.

36:

"So on a scale of one to ten, how sketchy are these people?" Rosa asked Ame.

"Eleven," she answered calmly. "But not really. Here's the deal. I haven't worked with them myself, but I know people who have. They're going to think we're nobodies who don't know the score. Once we prove them wrong, we shouldn't have any problem."

"So, they're fake tough guys, basically," Rosa surmised.

Ame clapped her hands together. "You got it. We just have to show them that we're harder than they are."

"And how are you going to do that?" Oliver asked.

"Easy. Hastin, honey, how do you feel about being spooky?"

"I'll be spooky!" he said, excitedly.

Oliver looked at Ame expectantly, and the woman sighed. "Okay, okay...here's the plan. Rosa and I are going to go talk to them, face to face, no shenanigans. Hastin, darling, you're going to follow us."

"Low-key, I assume."

"That's right, babe. And then when they inevitably pull something, you'll be there so we can pull something right back."

"...Do you want me to kill them?" he asked, and Ame laughed.

"No, no, we need them. I just want you to scare them," she told him.

"I can do that." He rocked back and forth where he sat, looking pleased.

"You're sure that's going to work? And that they can get us out of the city?" Oliver crossed his arms. Like their last discussion, they had defaulted to sitting on the floor together and talking.

"I'm sure. Like I said, I got their contact from a friend. Someone I trust, and who has nothing to gain by fucking me over. They're solid. We just gotta...apply a little force."

"So, what am I doing, then?" Oliver asked.

Ame laughed. "Well, you're the leader. What do you think you'll be doing?"

He stuck his tongue out at her. "I will be...looking at maps and figuring out alternative routes to the exit point. Once you get one, that is. Until then I'll be...worrying about you guys."

"That's the biggest part of your job, Captain," Hastin said, looking at him. "No one else worries about us." No one else worries about me. He didn't say that. Oliver wasn't even sure he meant that. It would have been uncharacteristic of him to think of himself before the others. But, it was what Oliver heard when he spoke, nonetheless.

Maybe he was pretty good at this reading between the lines thing after all.

"Take it easy for now. We'll be in touch." Rosa lightly tapped the side of Hastin's head and pressed an ear piece into his hand. She held the other one out to Oliver. "Hastin can let you know where we are, where we're going, and where the meetup will be. Then you can get started right away."

"Be careful," Oliver said to them.

"We will," Ame told him. "These guys don't know who they're dealing with."

Her and Rosa ducked out the front door. Hastin waited, and once a few moments had passed he took Oliver's hand in his own and kissed it.

"You know, we worry about you, too, Captain," he said, smiling. Then he left, too.

"Been awhile since it was just us," Rosa noted as she walked with Ame. "And I suspect it will be again."

"Oh, it's not so bad. The boys are alright." Ame laughed. "And they wince at my jokes just like you do."

"The last thing you need is a captive audience." Rosa sighed.

But, it was nice to be together again.

Rosa was unarmed, or at least she carried no firearms on her. Ame wasn't anywhere near the definition of unarmed. Still, if someone were to get the drop on them, as these people were certainly going to try and do, there was no telling if it would truly be enough. Rosa couldn't bring herself to be very worried about it. Worry did not solve the problem.

It took them a while to get to the meeting spot. More than once Ame glanced around, looking for Hastin, but was unable to find him. She did worry a little that perhaps they had lost him, but it wasn't as though they were trying. It seemed like a pretty baseless fear. She'd just have to trust him.

They met up with two men. A small one and a big one. It was always a small one and a big one, Ame thought. She wasn't sure why that was. Then, she took a look at herself and Rosa and noticed the similarity.

A small one and a big one. Ha ha. Very funny. Still, at least the realization led to her keeping her mouth shut.

305

"You Amethyst Orchid?" one of the guys asked her.

"You my pa?" she shot back. "Why you using my full name? Call me Ame." That was a trick of theirs, and an easy one to spot. She hadn't given him her full name. He had to go find it. But, of course, that was a name that was meant to be found. That's why she used it. There was no point in being in the business if people, the right people, couldn't find you. So, she met his words with a grin, and her handshake was a tad enthusiastic. You know, to make a point.

"You brought a friend," he noted.

"So did you."

"Yeah." He shot a look over at his partner, the bigger guy. "This is Luciano."

"Let me guess. Shortening it to Lucy didn't seem worth it?" Ame laughed. The shorter guy's name was Noah. He was the one her friend had recommended. Luciano must have been his muscle.

"This is Rosa. Rosa, Noah and Luciano. They're going to help us get the fuck out of dodge."

"I certainly hope they will," Rosa said, as level as ever.

Noah laughed. "Don't you worry. We've got more ways out of town than you've got curly hairs on your head, kid." He elbowed Ame lightly.

"Better hope I ain't. Didn't know Luciano had an eye for that sort of thing." Shamelessly, Ame pointed at the man in question, the same man who had been unabashedly checking her out only a second beforehand.

It earned her a laugh.

"Come on. We're going someplace a little quieter. Talk some details. You know the drill," Noah said. He waved them along to follow him, and they did.

The Dim was largely homogeneous. There were probably neighbourhood differences to those who lived there, Ame thought, looking around while they walked, but a lot of that nuance was lost on her. She had been in The Dim many times, more than she could count, but so often it was just for work that she had never really learned the ins and outs of the area. Here, at least, they had Noah and Luciano to guide them. She wasn't worried about that part. Killing Ame and Rosa wouldn't get them paid, after all.

The buildings in The Dim were shorter than those on the edge of town. They were older, so they were less advanced in both height and breadth. To make up for it, they were squished in together as closely as they had been able to. It was kind of claustrophobic, really. Ame took a deep breath and shook it off. They'd be out of town soon enough, and she'd be finding things to complain about in a new city. There was always something.

Noah led them through a maze of alleyways and crumbling roads, finally stopping at one building that seemed indistinguishable from the rest. He ducked inside, and the others followed. The twisting path that led them there would have led to confusion for anyone who might have been on their tail, especially anyone who wasn't used to The Dim.

Someone like Hastin, for example, who was more used to the richer areas of town.

Ame's frown barely changed at the thought. All they could do now was see this through as best they could.

"So... You have to get four people out of town two nights from now," Noah said.

"Yeah. Us two, and two more." Ame nodded. The room looked like the living room of an apartment. It wasn't too crowded or dirty, and she wondered then if the place was even lived in at all, or if they just left it like that specifically for meetings like these.

"And what kind of heat are you expecting to pull?"

"All of it," she told him flatly. "I mean, ideally, we'll get out before the word does and things won't be that rough, but what's the point of hoping. It could be all of it."

He nodded, his hands in his pockets. That was sort of funny, too. Neither of them had sat, and Rosa and Ame knew instinctively not to. This wasn't a place to get too comfortable in, despite the amount of seating available.

"So we pay you half now, and we'll give you the other half to your contact when we safely cross the border," Rosa said.

"I mean, that's how it usually happens. But things have been getting a little more hectic, lately," Noah said, dismissively. "We're going to need it upfront. And we're going to need more than the current offer."

There it was. They had been waiting for the catch, and Noah had been so kind as to give them two. Of course. Nothing was ever that easy.

Ame laughed.

"You're kidding me, right? Look, I came here because Mia told me you were legit and knew what you were doing. I didn't come here to get fucked. I'm not paying you those prices." She waved him off.

"Then Mia must have told you we were the only guys in town who can get you across the border in one night. You'll pay whatever we ask."

"Will we?" Rosa asked.

"Yeah, you will." From inside his baggy jacket, Noah pulled a gun on them. Needless posturing. He might have been able to talk them into a higher price if he had been reasonable about it, but he wasn't a negotiator. Ame wondered then why his boss didn't stick someone else in his spot, but then again, clever negotiators weren't really the hallmark of the underworld, were they?

Of course, now that weapons were an option, Luciano pulled his, too. Better that than the alternative. At least now they knew he was packing, and had an idea what with. Not that they'd be dealing with it themselves.

Ame sighed. "Look. You can't just spring this shit on me, you know I ain't the—"

It was very quick. The feeling that you got when you guessed wrong on the number of stairs at the top, and you went to place your foot on a step that didn't exist. That second of shock and the feeling of falling.

Luciano was on the ground, and Hastin was behind Noah. He had a wire around Noah's throat and the man dropped his gun to claw at it, to try and free himself.

"Whoa, kid! Hastin, you okay?" Ame exclaimed, a little needlessly.

He didn't look up at her, his gaze fixed on the man who was struggling against him. Making sure he didn't accidentally kill him, probably.

"I'm fine."

"You didn't kill him, did you?" Rosa jutted a thumb out at the other man on the ground.

"Nope. Just unconscious."

"Good boy," Ame said. He looked up then, the brightness in his eyes probably mildly unhealthy, but he wasn't distracted for long.

"Okay, okay. I think we got the point across. Let him go, and we'll try this again," Ame instructed him.

So he did.

Noah, coughing and gasping, rubbed at the marks on his throat. They'd last a while, surely. He'd have some explaining to do.

"Noah. Man, why're you screwing with me?" Ame asked him. "Why you gotta do that?"

"You don't have to fuckin' kill me for it." He cursed.

"You ain't dead."

He was grumbling, sitting on the floor and trying to collect himself. Ame got down on one knee to talk to him at his level, but she didn't look particularly sympathetic.

"Come on. You were trying to screw us. I know it and you know it. Now you know you can't! No harm done. You're fine."

He scowled at her. "Yeah, yeah, whatever. Who the fuck is that?" He pointed at Hastin.

"One of mine," Ame said with a laugh. "He's something else, isn't he? And that's what you'll be dealing with if you try to pull something like that again. Come on, now. What's the real breaks? Level with me."

Grudgingly, he nodded. "3 am. We'll have a guy posted at the Samhain metro station. You have to get there on the minute. He ain't gonna wait for you."

"That's cool," Ame said, nodding. "I'm not here to waste anyone's time. What then?"

"Then, they get you and your crew onto a train that crosses into Syama territory. From there, you're home free. Whatever law is after you here can't get you. But I can't do shit about people who ain't the law."

"Oh, honey," Ame said, pushing herself to stand again. The word made Hastin tilt his head at her. It didn't sound at all like when she called him 'honey'. "Don't you worry about those bad, bad folks. We're in good hands there. All we need is to keep the law off our backs, and we'll be just fine."

"Once you hit Syama, you pay the rest of what you owe to your contact," Noah said, dragging himself to his feet much less gracefully than she had. "That's the deal."

"That's no problem. I'm not about to cheap out on your guys," Ame said amicably. "After all, I wasn't the one who tried."

He glared at her, but wisely said nothing.

"Tell your boss it's all cool with me, and we'll see your friend at 3am. Bye-bye now, honey." She looked then to Hastin. "We'll meet you back at the house, babe. No point in you getting attention by going the long way." By that, of course, she meant going with them.

"See you soon." He gave them a little wave and, strangely enough, disappeared into another room of the apartment. It must have been the same way he came from.

With that done, Ame and Rosa left. Once their feet hit the street again, and they were confident they weren't being followed, they both let out a sigh of relief.

"I don't have patience for those kinds of dramatics," Rosa said, rolling her eyes. "I don't know how you do it."

"Oh, don't be like that. It's kinda fun," Ame said. "Besides, Noah ain't so bad. Just a little skeezy. He won't screw us over now. Not when he knows that Hastin could show up like the boogeyman and take his head right off his shoulders."

309

"Well, would you screw around if you knew that?" Rosa teased her. Ame laughed.

By the time they got back to the apartment, Hastin was already there. Ame wasn't sure what means he had used to traverse the city, and she didn't ask. Moving solo, she knew, was much faster than moving even in a pair. Especially when that pair was doing their best to specifically not look like they were suspicious or in a hurry.

"Wel-come back~" he singsonged, hopping to his feet to hug Ame as soon as she stepped into the room. She hugged him tightly.

"You were brilliant, honey. Such a good job," she said.

He hugged Rosa next, who chuckled a little but indulged him.

"Yo, Oliver. You heard where the meet-up is?" Ame sat down on the floor again, looking up at him.

"Samhain metro station. So we have to get from HiTech to there, which is totally doable," Oliver said. "I can think of three ways from one to the other right now."

"How do you know this city so well?" Rosa asked him.

He shrugged. "Lived here too long. And they weren't really inventive when they built most of it. A lot of the neighbourhoods look the same. You can tell that Spectra got really big really fast from how they copy and pasted different areas of it together."

"So what are you going to do when we leave town?" Ame teased him.

He blinked at her. "What?"

"When we leave Spectra. When we leave The Ves. What are you going to do then?" she elaborated. "You know Spectra inside out, but what about other cities?"

He frowned for a moment, thinking, and then shrugged. "I guess I'll have to learn."

That made her laugh.

"Speaking of after," Hastin spoke up inquisitively. "Do we have work contacts in Syama? How are we going to do business there?"

"I know some people," Ame said.

"Ame knows people everywhere." Rosa shook her head. "But she's not lying."

"Hey, I'm no liar. Unless it's, like, in bed, and the guy is like, 'baby, how do you like that?' and I tell them it's so good." She snorted.

"No, you don't." Hastin's grin was sharp, but not dangerous.

"You're right, babe. I don't. I ain't lyin' for anybody."

"So, we have tonight and tomorrow night," Oliver said. "And then we're on. That's plenty of time to get those building blueprints finished and studied, and for me to teach you guys the routes we'll be taking."

"Why do you have to teach us the routes?" Hastin asked him, tilting his head.

"Well, if something happens to me, you guys still have to be able to get out," Oliver said. He was quick to add, "Not that I expect something to happen, but if a piano falls out of the sky and crushes me, that's no reason why that should stop you all from getting out."

"Nothing is going to happen to you, Captain," Hastin said, looking at him with a sudden expression that Oliver couldn't place. "Nothing is going to happen to any of you."

37:

Dan was leaning against the alley wall, his head back and his eyes closed. Alone, it would have been a bad idea. Even armed as he was, it was sort of asking to get robbed or shot. He had no worry about that here, where he was just taking a moment to quietly collect himself before the fun started.

He felt ready. But then again, he thought he had felt ready before.

He wasn't going to let them down again. He wouldn't let that happen. This time, he was going to stay when, and where, he was needed. They were going to finish this together.

Yoru waited, his binoculars around his neck, scanning the window that could be seen from their current vantage point. He had one hand up, telling them to wait. When he dropped his hand, Rusty nudged Dan and he opened his eyes.

Time to get to work.

They crept through the dark and every time he stepped on some unseen rubbish or the hard plastic of his gun casing tapped against the exterior of his body armour, Dan winced. Too much noise. Quieter than the cars speeding past on the street, but still. Any noise felt like too much. He'd have to ask Yoru or Xueying how they did it, as they seemed to pass noiselessly in front of him.

They reached the back door, the same one they had broken into originally, and Xueying wasted neither time nor subtlety. She shot out the handle, kicked the door in, and tossed a flashbang in after it. The door frame protected them from the brief but overwhelming light, and their covered ears left them in a better position than their targets. Quick and easy. They snaked their way inside, where Xueying and Yoru took out cameras and lights alike as they came to them. Dan saw someone flailing on the ground, having been stunned by the grenade, and Rusty was quick to swoop in and kick them in the head. They dropped, unconscious.

It was a little more than just impressive when your body was more effective than bullets, he thought fleetingly as they kept moving.

They hadn't redesigned the first floor. It was still laid out in crowded hallways, full-height walls making it hard to see or hear what was going on anywhere else. They had to manually work their way through the whole area, and the grenade had only been useful for a very small part of it. They moved as quickly as they could without letting themselves be surprised. It was more tedious than they had hoped.

It didn't take long for the other guards who had heard the noises to come running, and for the shooting to start in earnest.

Dan felt surprisingly solid. Whole. He could feel the ends of his fingers, and could feel the grip of his toes in his boots. He could do this.

He ducked behind a desk, watched Yoru do the same, and they peeked out in order to try and get the security at the other end to shoot at them so they could guess how many there were.

Neither side moved at first, doing nothing more than scattering bullets when they stuck their heads out to see what was going on. When Yoru covered for him, Dan rolled across the hallway to join him where he was.

Once there, he could look down the side hallway and see what it was that Yoru was waiting for. Almost imperceptible in the dark, at least to Dan, he recognized the figures who ran down that side of the hallway. Well, he recognized that they were smaller than he was, and at this point, that was basically a dead give-away.

In moments, with the occasional continued distraction by Yoru, the shooting stopped. He stuck his head out experimentally, but no bullets came flying their way. They ran down to the end of the hall and, just like they had thought, both Xueying and Rusty were waiting there with their targets at their feet. It was impossible for the guards to have numbered them in the dark. Now, if they could keep pressing their luck, they might just get this over with.

They kept going. Clearing that floor would be the most complicated part, and until they could get their backs to the second floor, they couldn't be sure that there wasn't going to be anyone breathing down their necks. Dan wasn't sure how anyone got any work done in this place. It all looked like a disaster to him, and that was before they shot it up.

But they kept going. They cleared the floor and headed to the stairs and he found that breathing came a little more easily now. He wasn't scared, not really. He was just tense. He could feel it when he moved. It felt like being ready.

And when the shots started coming from the basement, he proved he was ready. He took out two of the shooters before the other three could even pinpoint their location.

Yoru shot him a look and Dan met it with a grin. Hey, he had to be good for something.

That wasn't the end of it, though. Even with them gone, there were still more people below them. They could tell from all the shouting they heard. Dan estimated probably about four more people. That would put them up to a team of...eight? That would make sense, wouldn't it? No, nine. That was still a possibility though.

They went backwards up the stairs to the door of the second floor and Xueying picked the lock like magic. Poof, and it was done. Dan pulled a face, although briefly. He'd have to practice if he was going to be that fast, too. He wondered if Yoru was any faster.

They ducked inside. They being Xueying and Rusty, leaving the two others to cover the stairway. It made sense. Dan was the better shot, and Yoru was the one who could see everything that was going on even after they shot out the emergency lights. Unless the men coming after them had infra, they had a distinct advantage.

Although, judging from how close one of the bullets had gotten to Dan, he thought it was not out of the question that they might.

They were being more cautious now, not coming out of cover for long enough for Dan to pick them off. He frowned. They'd have to get back down those stairs, but moving put them at a serious disadvantage and he wasn't really in a hurry for anyone to get shot again.

"How are we coming on that?" Yoru called back over his shoulder.

"Working on it!" Xueying answered him. Whatever her and Rusty were doing with the computer, they were undoubtedly hurrying. That wasn't much of an answer, but at least it let them know that something was happening. It was kind of anxiety-inducing, waiting there under the occasional hail of gunfire while Xueying and Rusty worked to complete a process that he couldn't see. That worried him more than the danger below. It gave him zero gauge for how long it would take them to finish, and thus, he had no idea how long he had to hold his position for.

As long as they didn't let the people under them gain any ground they should be fine, and so far they were good in that department. Unless they tried to rush them and managed to pull themselves up to the next floor all in one go, it would have been very hard for them to break out of where Dan and Yoru had them pinned down. But that was an idea that went both ways. They weren't going to get down there very easily, either.

"Got it!" Rusty that time, sounding triumphant. There was some scrambling behind him and then all at once, they were together again. Rusty and Xueying abandoned the computer they had been pulling information from to rejoin their group. Still, they couldn't move.

"We can't get down there, can we?"

"Doesn't look like a good idea to try," Yoru agreed.

"We're going to need another way out," Xueying said. Dan could have swore. Wasn't he the one who was cursing about windows? Hadn't that been a thing they had discussed?

Rusty thought faster than he did, though. She grabbed another grenade from his vest, hollered at them to cover up and dropped it down the stairs. He almost wasn't fast enough to be ready.

The explosion was close enough to violate several safety regulations, surely. He could feel it ripple through the air, feel the building shake around them.

That sure as hell solved the problem, though.

The shooting froze up and the four of them poured down the stairs, wildly scanning for any sign of trouble. They found two men ducked behind a doorway. Rusty took out one and Yoru the other. But it was a third man, from down the hall, that let off the shot that hit Xueying.

She let out something that was less of a scream of pain and more a sound of frustration, but she immediately dropped behind cover. Surprised, Rusty followed suit. Yoru did not, and Dan watched him bolt down the hall and bodily take out the man who had shot her and the one beside him.

He turned his attention to Xueying. "Where'd you get hit?" he asked.

She showed him where she was bleeding. It was just a graze. It had hit her over her ribs, right between the straps of the armour she wore. Of course!

They didn't have much in the way of first-aid kits handy. Instead, Dan went to one of the unconscious men and yanked off his shirt, balling it up in his hands. Xueying held her arms out of the way as he worked the fabric in-between the straps of her vest, using the pressure to hold it there and to keep it pressed against the cut. It wasn't a great fix, but it would certainly help to stop her from bleeding everywhere.

Yoru was back at their side in a heartbeat. They kept Xueying behind them and worked their way backwards out of the building just like how they had come in. Rusty took the other side, the very back of their little group, not wanting to give anyone the chance to sneak up on them.

And then it was done. They stuck close together as they hurried out into the dark. There was a quick, breathless scramble to holster weapons and check for damages before they were disappearing off into the night, using the winding, narrow alleyways to their advantage. They hadn't heard any police, and any footage the cameras had gotten of them would have been unusable for the lack of light. It looked like they had gotten off scot-free, as long as they

315

could make it back to the safe-house. Hanging up their weapons had purely been to allow them to move faster, and they removed themselves from the scene of the crime with the same amount of noise they had arrived with.

Dan must have breathed sometime before they crossed the threshold. It felt like they had crossed half the city, although he did know that they hadn't gone nearly that far. It felt like the first real breath he took was the one that filled his lungs when he felt the awful, carpeted entryway of the apartment under his boots. That was it! They had done it!

They heaved a collective sigh of relief.

It was short-lived, at least for now.

"You're hurt." Yoru turned to Xueying immediately.

"Yeah, yeah... " She was already pulling her clothes off. The armour first, then the long sleeved shirt and the tank top. She tossed them all haphazardly on the floor, and then thought better of it and scooped one of her shirts up again to press it to where she had been cut.

"I'll get the first-aid stuff," Yoru said, disappearing do exactly that. Xueying hopped up to sit on the kitchen table with a wince, keeping the shirt pressed against her side. Rusty leaned against the countertop with her arms crossed, scowling.

She was worried. Dan knew that much without having to ask.

Yoru was back in moments. It clearly wasn't the first time he had done this, and he worked quickly to clean her up.

"You're going to have a scar there unless you really want me to stitch this up," he said, wrinkling his nose at the idea. "I don't even know that it would help, really. The wound isn't that bad, it's just wide."

"I'm totally not feeling like having a line of stitches in my side," Xueying agreed, sounding just as sour about it. "I'm not that vain. It isn't my face." She wrinkled her nose as if to drive the point home.

And then she looked to Rusty. "It's not going to bother you, is it?" she asked. Her tone didn't sound like she was joking, but she did smile at the end of it.

Rusty snorted and shook her head. "You think I care?"

Yoru bandaged Xueying up. "As gross as I am sure you feel, no showering until tomorrow. Give it some time to stop bleeding," he told her.

"Yeah, yeah... " She sighed, waving him off. Her usual pleasant demeanour was dampened slightly but Dan couldn't really blame her. In the same hand she gestured with, she still held the computer, which she then held out in front of her.

"We did it. We finally did it. After all that, after all of my attempts to avoid going in guns blazing, that was what finally worked." She groaned. "What a headache."

"Hey, we're done now." Dan reached out and put a hand on her shoulder. "Relax. We did it. Who cares how we got here. You don't have to worry about it anymore."

"Remind me not to take jobs in infrastructure again," she joked.

Dan thought he wouldn't mind if the jobs they took in the future were a little simpler, either, and judging from how Rusty's expression hadn't changed, he had to think she agreed.

They were all exhausted. The high of completing the job was watered-down by how long it had taken them to be successful, but Dan could feel the relief deep in his bones. Unlike Xueying, who had been banned from doing so, he took a shower.

And, for the first time in a long time, he took a good look at himself in the mirror.

He looked...better than he had thought he would, honestly.

His hair had come back an appreciable amount, finally. He almost had enough to have an actual hairstyle. His eyes looked a lot better. More alive. And he thought the scar where his arm ended prematurely was more faded than it once was.

Taking a breath to brace himself, he turned his back to the mirror and looked over his shoulder.

His back didn't look as bad as he feared. It wasn't red and angry anymore, it wasn't swollen or dirty. The metal plates that were embedded in his skin seemed nearly to be a part of him now.

They were on each side of his spine, cut right into the flesh of him. Flat metal faceplates with a long slot down the middle of each, for whatever he had been hooked up to. They didn't hurt anymore. Looking at them made him feel strangely empty, but he managed a bit of a smile.

He'd looked worse. He'd certainly felt worse.

He tied the towel around his waist, grabbed his phone and shot off a text to Oliver. When he saw Yoru in their bedroom, he kissed him. No real reason. He wasn't looking to get laid, it just seemed like a good idea. It felt like a good idea.

And it made Yoru smile.

"Writing again? Already?" Dan asked him, sitting down on the bed. Yoru was leaned back in a chair, his notebook on his lap. He looked like he had been there forever, as though his perpetual state of being was that of someone who created calmly and at their leisure.

Of course, an hour or two ago, he had seemed just as comfortably in his element as well.

"Why not?" Yoru smiled at him. "I want to have enough poems to leave here, after all, for whoever ends up in this...charming establishment once we've vacated it."

"What are you writing about now?"

Yoru held the book out at arm's length, regarding it critically. "Rusty, actually. Our own Nguyen Han."

"Does she know?" Dan asked.

Yoru laughed. "I've never said as much, not explicitly...but neither is she explicitly mentioned. I mean, it's poetry. That would kind of defeat the purpose."

"What are you writing?"

"About a sparrow, something small and quick and sharp."

"I don't think that is deadly enough," Dan remarked.

"There is more to her than her body count," Yoru pointed out. "There is more to all of us than that."

Dan made a thinking noise and Yoru looked over to him curiously.

"Back in Syama, in the army...they used to make a big deal out of that." He was lying back on the bed, staring at the ceiling. "It was all this... macho posturing bullshit. I was always kind of worried I'd end up like that."

"One wayward comment does not a stereotype make," Yoru reassured him.

"I guess," he said thoughtfully. "It's not so bad being reminded that there's more to the world than that."

"I am here to remind you that things are not so simple," Yoru said, and then laughed. "And you are here to remind me that not everything needs to be esoteric."

At that, Dan sat up and looked at him. "What the fuck is that word?"

Yoru laughed. "Esoteric. That just means something that's specifically designed not to be widely understood."

"Oh, god, it's you." Dan groaned, falling back down to lying again.

Yoru laughed again. He rocked his chair back to four legs and stood up, moving to sit near where Dan lay. "You want to hear what I've been working on?"

Dan took a deep breath, but the sigh that followed was contented and he closed his eyes. "Yeah. Tell me."

He propped up his leg on the bed and Yoru leaned against it, reading aloud from his little notebook. Dan lay there, damp and cool and happy just to

318

hear him talk.

38:

Hastin never hurried. While that wasn't universally true to all who knew him, it was very true to those who would lay claim to him. He never hurried because he never had to hurry. He was never supposed to. Being enough steps ahead should have made that kind of panic obsolete.

It wasn't panic that quickened his steps. It was impatience.

He flicked his hair over his shoulder, waiting for the vidscreen to stop ringing at him. It would, he knew. His phone calls didn't get ignored. It was kind of funny, really. He was worth so little, but they wouldn't dare ignore him. The dichotomy was amusing, although he wasn't sure what it meant, if anything, to the bigger picture.

Violet would answer. One way or another, she always did.

The others were back at the house. As before, he had left on his own to make the call, but made sure they'd be allowed to listen in. Just knowing that they would hear it made him feel less alone.

Being alone hadn't ever bothered him before. He had been alone forever. He thought it might have felt like dying. Idly, he wondered if it was possible to be dying without ever knowing you were. Surely it was. People dropped dead of all kinds of things every day, right? Why would his situation be any different?

The phone call picked up.

"You sure took your time," she spat. Immediately, she took in where he was calling from. Somewhere dirty. They were well-entrenched in The Dim, as it was, so unless he wanted to needlessly go out of his way, that was where he would call from. The little tech cafe was quiet, no one there had even given Hastin a second glance. Considering what he was, what he looked like, that gave it away as a good place to call from.

The person at the desk was obviously strung out on something, and the only other patron was asleep, or perhaps not so much asleep as unconscious. It wasn't his concern. They didn't care about him. That was enough.

"I did," Hastin answered her calmly. "I wanted to make sure that we were staying put, as there was talk of moving again. It seems that we are not. We will be there until we finish the job."

"And where is that?"

He rattled off the address to her casually, followed by, "Which I'm certain you already knew, but yes. That's where we are. The transportation is more central to this area. It will help us get around better. That's what was decided."

"And what did you have to say to that?"

Trick question. She'd have to be faster than that if she wanted him to screw up. "Nothing. My opinion wasn't asked for."

Lying was as easy as breathing. It was nearly synonymous with it. The idea would have stricken Oliver, but Hastin felt nothing for it. Not excitement, not guilt. Nothing.

"It's taking an awful long time if everything is going according to plan," Violet said.

"Yes," Hastin agreed. "They're cautious. While the deaths of Xueying's team weren't related to the job itself, it still puts them on edge. They are twice as careful."

He thought that would be the end of it. Their new location, and her complaining about the time it took. But, to his mild and distant surprise, she kept talking.

"If this keeps up, I'll have to call you out again. No reason we can't have you doing both."

"Wherever I am needed," he said. The hollow in his voice was so deep that he half expected to hear it echo. Still, the tone meant nothing to Violet. He always sounded that way. Why would this be any different?

"We've decided where we're going to do the hand-off," she said then, wrinkling her nose as she thought of the last attempt they had made at it. It wasn't until the hand-off that she had learned of Xueying's betrayal, as she saw it.

"Not the warehouse?" Hastin asked. There was the barest lilt of inquisitiveness in his voice.

Violet shook her head. "No. We were lucky not to damage too much product last time. You would have thought they were trying to destroy my stock." She sighed. "Did they really have to let them struggle for so long? Goodness. If you can't manage to do any better, it will be incredibly disappointing."

She rolled her eyes.

Distantly, under miles of ice, Hastin was angry. His Captain had loved those people. He wasn't sure in what ways, when the feeling itself seemed to have so many faces. But some kind of love. Something nice.

321

Maybe he should have been angry about something else. Maybe there were more worthy causes. It did seem a little impotent to be angry about people who were already dead.

He didn't know. He just felt. Like the ebb and flow of a very distant tide.

And none of it showed.

"We have some office space rented out that we'll use. It'll give them less room to get in the way. And then when I'm clear with the data, you'll be free to clean everything up."

"Yes, ma'am," he said.

Clean up the mess. Of course he could. It was three on one, but only two of them had enough experience to even come close, and zero of the three of them would expect it.

If they followed that plan, Hastin could wipe them out. Easy as breathing. Easy as lying.

The idea was so absurd, so impossible, that it didn't even earn a flicker of emotion in response. There were a lot of things he would do. A lot of bad things. A whisper from the right person, and sure, he was exactly as dangerous as she needed him to be.

But that wasn't what was going to happen. Even if he had to die to stop it.

"I'll message you with the address."

He nodded.

"It shouldn't be too much to ask. I mean, one of them's blind, aren't they? If you screw this up, you really are worthless." She sighed. "What a waste."

Hastin waited, and said nothing. Sometimes, that was best.

"Well, I suppose that's it, then. Update me if anything relevant happens. I'll contact you if you have another job."

He nodded. She hung up. He sighed.

He could taste something awful in his mouth and feel it on his skin. Something vile. But his disgust was just as far away as everything else.

He unhooked the cord from the base of the vidscreen and twisted it between his fingers as he slipped his hand in his pocket and stepped out the door.

The Dim. Not a place he knew well. It should have been eye-opening, maybe, to see the economic ruin that had been wrought on the city. Hastin had no real scale for it, and certainly no personal connection to the suffering that he saw.

Some of the people he passed looked more alive than he felt, so maybe it wasn't so simple. He had learned that things rarely were.

But he'd learn. It might be a while, but he would. Oliver would help. He didn't smile, but even just thinking his name lit a match somewhere in a dark corner of his mind. Oliver. Ame. Rosa.

Hastin had never prayed before and had no idea what faith felt like. But, if people who loved god felt like that when they prayed, he could see why they kept coming back to it.

His next breath was deeper. Their names, a litany in his head despite the chill that wrapped itself around his shoulders. Sometimes, he forgot where he was. Not where in the city. Spectra was pervasive, it got its talons in you.

But he forgot where he was in his body, like he did when he was thinking of them. When that happened, it felt less like the void was around him and more like it was in him.

Maybe it was. Maybe he was all empty on the inside. Usually, that's how it felt. Not bad. Not good. Just nothing.

He took the next turn in the street. Someone in the alleyway grabbed his wrist, thinking he was an easy target. He looked it. Vacant-eyed and pretty, that sense of nothing wrapped around his head, wrapped around all of him.

The hand around his wrist was tight enough to hurt, but that was distant, too.

Hastin punched them in the throat, using where they held him to pull them into the blow.

They let him go.

He kept walking.

He didn't have a comm on. For a minute, he wished he did. There was something distinctly uncomfortable about not having their voices in his ear.

That was dependency, right? Normal people didn't do that, didn't feel like that.

But what was statistically average was virtually meaningless. Even your most average person wasn't average in every aspect. That, itself, would have been exceptional.

And, of course, the team was nothing if not exceptional.

Hastin had never thought of the future. There hadn't been any future to think about. There was no time. There was nothing but his concrete room, the steel of the lab, the brief moments of chained freedom when he was let out to work. Where he could breathe the outside air, move through crowds who had never seen him before and who would never see him again.

That was all the future held. More nights in the dark. More days under the lights. Stolen moments of real oxygen.

But that wasn't true anymore, was it? Now there was More. Now there was Beyond.

There was After.

And what would that be? What could it be? He had nothing to compare it to. The idea should have scared him. Weren't people afraid of the unknown?

But it didn't bother him. That's sort of why he felt like maybe he wasn't a whole person. He didn't have to worry. They would be there. Ame and Rosa and Oliver. The captain. Hastin didn't need anything else.

Could the future be worse than the past? Well, it was possible...but he didn't fear that, either.

They had long run out of ways to hurt him. Even their most inventive torture became banal after a while. If the future was to be worse, someone would have to try very hard, and would have to be very clever.

Hastin didn't give anyone that kind of credit. Not right now, not when they still moved through the world like shadows. Anonymity. He was nothing but a passing novelty in the street. A shiny penny left on the sidewalk. A bit of wrapper flickering out of the drain. Nothing important. Not here.

He kept walking. His feet knew where to go. They always did.

And if they got lost, his heart wouldn't. The force that pulled him back seemed every bit as tangible to him as the cord he still twisted between his fingers.

Dependence. Right. Something that was wrong with him.

Oh, but it was a long, long list, and he didn't half care enough to worry about it. He was useful. He was more than useful where it mattered. He didn't need anything else.

The money that passed over him was more than he could comprehend. He knew it was important. He knew he was expensive. But that had no meaning for him.

Hastin derived meaning from other things. Like kisses.

He didn't bother trying to shake the person following him. For now, they knew where he was going. There was no point wasting his energy. Eventually, he'd disappear off their radar entirely.

He meandered, taking his time, knowing he was being followed. He would be, at least, until he went too far to follow. Syama, they said. They were going to Syama. He had never been there. He'd only ever read about the place. He knew the train had an ID scanner that they'd have to bypass, but Rosa just laughed when they talked about it.

She was so smart.

Maybe he was easily impressed, but he thought that was better than not being impressed. It was better to hold more of an opinion than less. It was better to have more feeling, and less emptiness.

And, maybe, for others, it meant he wouldn't underestimate them. But that wasn't something he had ever had a problem with in the past.

When he stepped into the safe-house, the chill was swept from his shoulders by Oliver wrapping his arms around them. Hastin breathed out, sinking down against him, burying his face against the man's sweater. He always smelled the same. Maybe home wasn't a place. Maybe home was people.

Hastin had never had one of those before.

He hugged him tight, and Oliver brushed Hastin's long hair back from his face. "Hey, kid. How did it go?"

Hastin shrugged. "You heard."

"Doesn't think too highly of us, does she?" he said with a chuckle.

Hastin's smile had an edge to it. He wasn't always sure what he was feeling, but he knew this wasn't a good one. He'd learn the name for it one day.

Well, he knew most of the names, but had trouble matching them together.

"Thankfully, she doesn't have to," he said, to answer Oliver.

Oliver pulled him into the living room where the others were waiting. Rosa spotted him and grinned.

He knew why.

"So you heard that?" he asked.

"Yeah. Man, you think she'd be a little more aware." Rosa shook her head. "I mean, I guess we don't go out of our way to spell it out, but..."

"It's so weird. She thinks we're capable enough to get the job done, but then expects us to just waltz into the grave without a fight. Like, which is it, lady? Are we capable or not?" Ame snorted. "It's bullshit, I tell you. And she's gonna learn herself a thing."

"She will," Hastin said quietly. "Although...I don't know that it will help."

He doubted she would be walking away from that in order to put her knowledge to good use. One of them was going to die in there. Either she was, or he was. Rosa had promised him. He trusted her.

"How are you feeling?" Oliver asked him. They sat down together, his arm around the younger man, and Hastin sighed as he slouched against him.

"I taste bad," he said. "I feel bad. Like...I feel gross." He sighed again.

"You are not gross," Oliver told him. "But a shower might help. Or what about a bath? I scrubbed the bathtub."

There was hardly enough room in there for them to all pack in, but instead of just a standing shower they did indeed have a bathtub. Oliver had no idea who designed this place or where their priorities where.

"A bath?" Hastin pulled a face. "The only time I take baths is when the lab people think I am dirty but I can't stand up to do it myself. They aren't any fun."

He caught it, the split second where Oliver was going to say or do something else before he stopped himself. He wondered what it was, briefly, but didn't ask. Oliver was allowed to change his mind about things. Not everything had to be Hastin's business.

"I think this is a little different," he said, giving his shoulders a squeeze.

"Actually... Hey, Ame?"

"Yeah?"

"Do you have smelly shit in your bag?" he asked, and then laughed when she looked offended. "No, I mean, like, shower stuff."

"You feeling girly?"

"I mean, always. But, do you have some?"

Ame had been scrolling through something on her vidscreen, and she set it down then and got to her feet. It was pretty clear she was out of the loop of their conversation, but she nodded anyway. "Yeah, actually, gimme a sec..."

She disappeared into the room she shared with Rosa and came back a minute later carrying a fist-sized bottle. It was bright pink, and the cap was moulded plastic in the shape of a flower. Oliver stood up to meet her when she returned.

"Something like this?"

"Yeah. Mind if he borrows some?" Oliver asked, jutting his finger at Hastin. Hastin, who remained sitting at his feet, blinking up at them with calm interest.

"Oh, sure, babe," Ame said amicably. "I'll share. Go to town."

"C'mon." Oliver offered him a hand up. "I want to teach you something."

Hastin followed, obedient as ever. Oliver perched him in the bathroom, sitting him on the edge of the bath while he started to fill it with water.

"Stick your hand under there and tell me if it's too hot," Oliver said.

Hastin did and shook his head. "No, it's warm," he said. He twisted his hand back and forth under the flow of water. "It's nice. I, um... I always turn the water to really warm when I have a shower here, because the water in the building was always so cold..." He pulled a face. "And all the metal was always cold, and there was always blood everywhere. It's a mess."

Oliver laughed gently. Maybe he shouldn't have been laughing, but Hastin's tone made it all too easy. "It's warm enough, then?" he asked, and Hastin nodded.

He took a sniff of Ame's body wash and found that it was appropriately flowery, but he was pleased when Hastin did the same and smiled sweetly.

"It smells so nice!"

So he poured some in and set it aside, and Hastin watched, amused, as bubbles rolled and popped and foamed as the water churned.

"Go on, get in," Oliver said. "Take as much time as you want. We're not doing a whole hell of a lot tonight. It might make you feel better."

"You think it will?" Hastin asked him earnestly.

Oliver shrugged. "I find that doing something nice for myself, like taking some time to enjoy a bubble bath, can help me when I'm feeling gross."

"Okay." Hastin smiled sunnily, and started pulling his clothes off without much concern.

Oliver sighed, smiled, and brushed his fingers through Hastin's hair. "I'm going. Yell if you need something, kid."

"I will!" he said, though Oliver knew he wouldn't. He didn't think he was lying. Hastin meant he would call if he needed something. 'Need' being the keyword, of course.

Oliver couldn't be too upset with him, not when he would be much the same way.

39:

Xueying told Violet that the job was done, and they set up a meeting time. Dan didn't know the specifics, but he didn't really have to. This little operation wasn't really under his control. He knew they had a day or two to kill in between. Apparently, Violet wasn't going to be able to meet them until then, so they had some time to waste. That wasn't terrible news. Even the data centre getting robbed wasn't interesting enough to snap people out of their apathy. There was so much more to worry about.

Yoru made them all breakfast the morning after. Xueying sat at the table in her bra, bandages around her middle, sipping tea out of a chipped cup.

"No coffee this morning?" Dan asked. "We out?"

"Nah, there's still some," she said, and smiled at him. She wore no makeup and no jewellery, and was still as pretty as the day they had met. "But we're not working today. Tea is for days off."

"That's a good system." He nodded, but snagged himself a cup of coffee anyways. He was just so used to it by now.

"So, what's the plan? Now that, you know, we don't need one," Yoru asked aloud to the room, though he didn't turn to look at anyone from where he was cooking.

"I don't know. I figured we could just lay around. I'm definitely having a shower," Xueying answered. "But I didn't have anything specific planned."

"Mind if I have a look at the information we snagged?" Dan asked. This time, Yoru did look over his shoulder at him, but Dan shrugged. "Hey, we weren't told not to, that wasn't part of the contract, at least not that you've told me. I'm just curious. I want to understand our client a little better."

"It's not against the rules," Rusty said simply.

He shot her a quick smile as a 'thank you'.

Xueying sighed. "You're right. She didn't swear us to secrecy. And, in all honesty, they usually do make it very clear when it isn't for our eyes, so I can't see the harm in it," she said.

"I just want to do some peeking, I'm not going to fuck with anything," Dan told her.

She shrugged. "Go to town. If that's what you want to use your day off for."

"I was thinking I might...make a phone call," Yoru mused.

It was Dan's turn to look sharply at him. Something in the tone of his voice caught his attention.

"A phone call?"

"Yes," Yoru said, bringing some plates to the table. "You know, it's been a little while, and since there's good news and everything..." He looked at Dan with no immediately identifiable expression, but it was a long, long look that Dan understood.

"Yeah. That sounds like a good idea," he agreed, nodding. "A phone call. Yeah."

"You two." Rusty shook her head, clicking her chopsticks together before she started to eat. Dan let it go. Some things were just not meant to be explained.

"We should go out to dinner tonight, the four of us," Xueying said then. "We'll spend today laying around, and then tonight we'll go out and eat. Give Yoru a break from the cooking."

"Then we better go some place that can cook better than I can," he said lightly, sliding into his seat next to Dan. He too had a plate of his own.

"I think that sounds fun."

If he did make another phone call, Dan wasn't sure what kind of head space he would be in for that kind of adventure. But maybe getting out would be good for him no matter how he felt. Moving forwards sometimes took a lot of effort. He still had some energy left for that, right?

"Wait, you mean, not the bar?" Rusty asked. "So Xueying isn't going to get drunk and serenade us again?"

"I will serenade you, sober, right now," the other woman threatened.

Yoru and Dan laughed, Rusty just smiled. Even her smaller reactions were good to see.

When breakfast was finished up, Dan volunteered to do dishes and waved Yoru off when he offered to help. He was still getting the hang of how to do certain things with one hand, and weirdly, it was a lot easier to kill a man one-handed than it was to wash breakfast dishes. They were both things he could do on his own, but he figured he could use the practice.

When that was done, he snagged the little memory box from Xueying —'Lose it and you're a dead man', she warned him casually—and headed back to his room. When the door closed, he looked to Yoru, who was waiting for him.

"What was this about a phone call?"

"Nothing exciting," Yoru said. "But I thought you might want to, so when I got up this morning, I talked to my sneaky friends and they mentioned they could buy us a few minutes again, if you were interested."

Dan smiled. "Yeah. Yeah, I'm interested. I'd like that a lot."

Yoru tossed him the vidscreen, since he'd be using it to look at the data lode when they were done anyway, and Dan keyed in the number.

"Wait...are you going to stay with me?" he asked Yoru.

The taller man shrugged. "Am I?"

Dan hesitated. Did he need him to? Then again, even if he didn't need it, did he want him to? That was much easier to answer.

"Yeah." Dan nodded, moving over on his bed to make room for his friend. "Yeah, you are. Plus, you can tell my mom that you kept your word, and that I'm not dead."

"It was a very serious promise, and I don't consider it completed yet," Yoru pointed out.

Dan laughed. "I mean, really, she probably agrees with you," he said.

He hit the call button, and this time when he was answered, there was no screaming. He even managed to get through the whole phone call without crying, even if he felt a little teary-eyed when he hung up. It still hurt to say goodbye.

But it hurt a lot less knowing that it wasn't goodbye forever.

~*~

Rusty was sitting on the edge of her bed, rubbing at her hands when Xueying came in. She didn't look up at first, intent on what she was doing, but eventually realized she was being stared at and stopped pulling at her fingers to look at the other woman.

"What?"

"What you," Xueying shot back, giggling. "What were you doing?"

"My hands are all stiff. I'm trying to make them...not stiff." Rusty couldn't think of a better word to explain it, and she frowned.

Her words, and her expression, earned another giggle from Xueying. She came and sat next to her on the bed. They had both been sharing it, recently, while the other one had sat, unmade and unoccupied.

"They're really bothering you?" Xueying asked her. There was no joking in her voice then, and it was the sincerity of it that Rusty found hard to take. It was easier to brush that sort of stuff off than to deal with someone worrying about her.

But Xueying seemed pretty dead-set on caring about her, and it wasn't as though Rusty could claim she didn't like that.

330

So she shrugged and tossed her braid over her shoulder. "They're not bad," she said noncommittally.

Xueying clicked her tongue at her, not buying it for even a second. "Here, give me one of your hands," she said.

Not quick enough to think of a good excuse not to, Rusty did exactly that. Xueying held her hand in both of hers, which were surprisingly warm. The heat felt, admittedly, rather good.

"I guess it wears on them after a while, huh?" Xueying asked. "You can't spend your whole life using them to beat the hell out of people and not have them be a little roughed up."

"It's not bad," Rusty said again, but sounded even less convinced. "You don't have to do...this." Whatever this was, she still wasn't wholly sure.

But, as usual, Xueying would not be swayed. She reached over and pressed her finger to Rusty's nose, telling her to stay put, while she dug something out of her bag. She was back in seconds.

When she pressed her hands to Rusty's again, they were sticky, and Rusty almost pulled her hand away. "Hey! What is that?"

Xueying laughed. "It's just hand cream. Here, maybe it will help. If it doesn't, it will at least feel nice," she said. With that, she started rubbing Rusty's hand. It was much what Rusty had been doing moments before, but much better. Xueying had two hands to do it with, after all.

And she was right, as always. It did feel nice. Rusty wasn't sure that it would fix the problem, but by the time she was done she could wiggle her fingers a little more comfortably than before.

Xueying repeated the process with her other hand, and this time Rusty complained notably less.

"There. How do they feel?" she asked when she was done.

Rusty flexed her fingers. "More...movable," she said. "That was strange. But...it was really nice," she admitted.

"Glad to help," Xueying said with a smile. "You use them for a lot. It's no wonder they need a little care now and again."

Rusty laughed quietly. "You make me sound like I'm some sort of machine."

"No more than the rest of us," Xueying told her, leaning in to kiss her gently.

"Now, what am I going to do with sticky hands?" Rusty looked at her fingers, frowning but not really unhappy. It was not a serious problem.

"Be entirely defenceless to my whims," Xueying said smartly.

"Ah. That was your plan the whole time." Rusty's lips quirked into a smile.

"That's it. You've got me," Xueying admitted. "I wanted to make your hands useless, so I could have you all to myself."

"You've done that," Rusty pointed out.

"Pretty sure I was just hoping to kiss you without being stopped."

"Pretty sure I did not need to be...made sticky, for that." Again, she frowned, not being able to come up with a clearer phrase. Xueying laughed and kissed her.

"It can't be that bad," she said.

Rusty said nothing, but felt that she had to agree.

~*~

They got together for dinner that night, although Yoru had to pry Dan away from digging through the memory box.

"There's all kinds of stuff in there. I can't imagine what it would be useful for," he said as they were leaving. "She really paid us for that?"

"Sometimes, there is no understanding it," Yoru told him with a shrug. "It is not always easy to understand the value that other people place in things, or to imagine the applications that they might be put towards. This is the reason why we are the ones who take the jobs, and not the ones who give the jobs."

Dan didn't think he'd ever be in the position to hire, rather than the position of being a hiree. Wasn't it nerve-wracking to sit around and hope that someone wasn't screwing up your job? Being involved was so much easier.

Plus, he didn't think he'd ever have that kind of cash to blow. It wasn't like they came cheap or anything.

Xueying, using her powers of being in charge of the team, had figured out where they were going to eat. They all seemed happy enough to defer to her on things, anyway, despite Yoru's joking as they made their way to the restaurant.

"I've never been here. If the food is terrible, I'm going to blame you personally," he said, pointing his finger at Xueying.

"Watch where you stick your fingers, thief, or you might lose them," she said back to him, laughing.

Quickly, he snatched his hand back and pretended to be deeply offended. "How dare you imply that someone could steal from me that which I've already stolen."

Rusty looked at him. "Whose fingers did you steal?"

He laughed and shook his head. "It is a secret."

It was nice to go out and eat together without the stress of the job hanging over their heads. It was just a relief for it to be done.

Most of the other jobs that Dan and Yoru had taken together were one-and-done types. Easy, off-the-cuff work. Simple. Doing a job like this, well, it wore you down after a while. Dan couldn't imagine how much pressure had been on Xueying.

"Do most of your jobs take this long?" he asked her as they sat down.

Xueying shrugged. "It's hard to say. When I'm doing my stuff, it's usually a lot smaller scale. As Yoru likes to remind me, a lot of what I'm used to stealing are things that you can't touch." She see-sawed her hand in the air. "So, usually, I have a few days of research, and then one night where I go in and get what I need. Sometimes it's a more lengthy affair because I have to take the time to get into someone's good books. But usually, it's a lot less direct."

"Is that better or worse that what we were doing?" He grinned.

She laughed, too, and shrugged again. "It's all the same in the end, I think. But it is nice to work with people. All this spy shit is...kind of lonely, after a while. I work alone a lot. It's nice having you guys around."

"Well, you have our numbers. We're not going that far," Dan said.

She nodded. "This is true. Yoru and I have been friends for years, and we work together when we can. He's also pretty good at that kind of nonsense. And...Rusty said she was going to stick around, too."

Dan looked over to the woman who sat next to her, but only received a nod as confirmation. She didn't elaborate. Dan didn't ask her to.

"To us," Yoru said, when their drinks came.

"To new employment opportunities," Dan joked.

Xueying thought for a minute before she raised her glass with theirs. "To more practice." She winked at Dan.

"To friends," Rusty added, simply.

They could all agree to that.

It wasn't as much of a party as it had been when they went to The Tint, but they also didn't have the same kind of stress to work off. They ate together, drank together, and enjoyed their time out.

When they returned home, Yoru went back to his writing and Dan went back to his reading. There was a sizable amount to get through, really. The download was huge! And most of it, he didn't understand. It was a lot of numbers, but also a lot of names.

It took him a while to realize that what he was scrolling through were names and ID numbers. A whole slew of them. Well, that didn't bode well. What did Violet want with all these IDs? Surely, as a tech corporation, they already had access to a great deal of most people's personal information.

Well, unless they were too poor to shop there, surely.

It took a little puzzling; every time the information output changed, he had to try and figure out again what he was looking at. After the names and ID numbers came a different set of names and a different set of numbers, these ones dollars and cents. Some of them were in the thousands. But thousands of dollars for what?

It looked like bills of some kind. Amounts owed. He realized they were divided into sections by codes and a cursory search revealed the codes to be debt companies associated with major hospitals. Man, if he thought that the situation in Syama was bad, it was nothing compared to this.

His heart sank as he kept reading. None of this seemed good. Names and addresses followed that. The IDs were probably tied to addresses, too, he thought, but these lists seemed pretty varied in who they contained. The box had just taken a big chunk of data and spit it out in plain text, leaving it for him to decode. What part of this had Violet been after?

This was a whole slew of blackmail material, targeting people who really, dearly did not need or deserve to be blackmailed.

Dan didn't know what to think about that. This wasn't looking at a kill count at the end of the night and wishing it had been a few less. This was city-wide. The list might have had a million names on it, maybe more. He had just been jumping to points on it and scrolling, but it seemed nearly endless.

How many people would be impacted if they handed this over to her? He didn't need to be a genius to know what it was for. It would be really easy to exploit people who already had nothing.

And what about the people who actually had something to lose? Giving her power over anyone with any standing didn't seem like a good idea, either.

There was no way this was going to end well for anyone.

He thought about telling Yoru, and it would have been easy, he was right there. But Yoru wouldn't have the answers he needed.

Dan pulled himself out of bed and crossed the apartment to the only other bedroom door, which he then knocked on.

Xueying opened it and looked at him curiously. In his hands he still held the memory box and the vidscreen that showed the data it had pulled, and though he showed her the screen he knew it meant nothing to her without context.

"Do you have a minute?" he asked her. "I think you need to see this."

Lost Names

40:

Hastin had been curled up on the floor with a tablet and a stylus, and had been hand drawing the map to HiTech for what seemed like ages. Oliver watched him with a sense of curiosity and mild worry. It couldn't have been very comfortable to be folded up like that, but he never looked up and he never complained. The only break he had was to go and talk to Violet, which was hardly a break at all. Late that night, after Hastin had shaken it off, he finished the maps and had given them to Rosa to compile.

The next day, they all collected together to start going over them.

It had been quite a process, but once Oliver had the map in front of him, he immediately felt a little better. It was nice just to know where they were going.

"So, like, honestly...we don't even need most of these floors," Ame said, flicking through the plans on her vidscreen. "We're not planning to go up, just down, right?"

"A lot of the floors in between are offices and have very similar layouts," Hastin said to her. "It would be good to know, just in case, but you're right in that I don't think we intend to go up that way."

"This basement area is...obnoxious." Oliver sighed.

Hastin nodded, but said nothing.

"We have codes for these doors?" Rosa was flicking her hand in front of her eyes, manually scrolling through the images as they appeared to her.

Hastin nodded again. "Yes. If we go through it together I can give them to you. Most of them are four digits entered via punch-pad. That means every time someone forgets their keys, they don't have to override it."

"There's a lot of employees so that seems like it would make sense. How many people work in the underground area?" Oliver asked.

Hastin frowned. "Hard to say. Overnight? Not many. A lot of them commute in just like the office workers. There's a doctor who stays overnight, maybe one or two technicians, and the security people. There would be more staff if I was there and training, but seeing as that isn't on the schedule, everyone else will have likely gone home. Also, most of those people aren't combatants, anyway."

"If wiping out a bunch of scientists is what it takes, I think my morals can handle it," Oliver said.

"What, you got something against academics?" Ame laughed.

Oliver shrugged. "Just the ones that hurt people."

He didn't have much experience with doctors. A lot of what he had learned about taking care of himself, his brain included, had been gleaned from books. But he'd heard stories. Good ones and bad ones. And, occasionally, ones like Hastin's. Horrific ones.

So, needless to say, he wasn't feeling too morally burdened by the upcoming challenge.

"Here, walk through this with me and tell me all the codes." Rosa gestured for Hastin to come closer to her. She sat in one of the chairs and Hastin curled up at her feet, leaning his head on her knee. As she went through the rooms in her visor, he went through them on the screen he held in his hands.

"Yeah, so it's just like we discussed. We stop the elevator and take the stairs," Ame was saying.

"I was second guessing our lock idea, though," Oliver pointed out. "We don't have the time to go and get something that could do that for us in a way that wouldn't be suspicious."

Rosa raised her hand. "I was thinking about that, too, but I think I have a solution."

"Mm?"

"I can build us something," she said, and then shrugged. "I should be able to build something that's electric powered and hot enough to melt most stuff. Now, because we don't know what the doors are made out of, we're probably going to have to hope that it had a lower melting point than whatever I make this thing out of."

"And if it doesn't?"

"Wouldn't hurt to have a backup plan," Rosa said.

Oliver thought quietly for a moment, closing his eyes. Without hard-copy keys, locking the doors wasn't an option, and even then the people trying to get in would have their own, same keys. That wouldn't work either.

His eyes flashed open. "Hey, could we trap the door?" he asked.

Rosa snapped her fingers. "You mean build a bomb that goes off when the door opens? You bet your ass I can. That's easier, in fact. And I can count ahead of time how many we'll need."

"Make one more than we need, just in case," Oliver said, cautiously.

Rosa laughed, but nodded. "Yeah, we can make that happen. That's no problem at all. There's enough scrap in the back alley alone to make a handful of them. Ame can help me, she's good with explosives."

"I want to learn," Hastin said, an eager a student as ever. "I mean, if you can show me. If we have the time."

At that, Ame laughed. "Are we really going to turn bomb making into a communal activity? Please tell me we are."

"Well, I'm not going to tell you that you can't," Oliver pointed out.

"You wanna learn too?" Ame offered. "We can show you!"

This wasn't the conversation that Oliver had been expecting to have... but it couldn't hurt to know, surely? He'd only be more useful to know how to do it.

"You know what, maybe I will learn," Oliver said.

Hastin clapped. "Yay! We're going to build bombs!"

"That should not sound so endearing," Rosa joked.

With that, it was another several minutes taken to go through the maps and see where bombs could be placed.

"Wait, if we arm that one, should we really do the door after it?" Oliver asked, looking over at Ame's vidscreen to see what she was marking down.

"I mean, the worst case is that it doesn't go off because they never get that far," Ame said. "Aren't you supposed to be the cautious one?"

"Well, yeah," Oliver admitted. "I just don't want to press us for time too badly. Are we sure we can make all these?"

"It will be fine," Rosa reassured him. "Especially with the four of us working on it. Have some faith."

"It's not really us that I don't have faith in," Oliver said. He smiled, but it wasn't necessarily a happy one.

"Okay. So we have the doors marked for codes, and for bombs. What else do we need?"

"There's an alarm system here—" Hastin pointed it out on his tablet, which highlighted it for Rosa.

"I don't want to get dinged at," Ame said, frowning. "Do not ding at me, please."

Hastin laughed. "I'm going to mark down all the things that ding. There will be no ding-ing."

"Good."

"How do we get that alarm system not to scream at us?" Oliver asked. "Or does that fall to you, too, Rosa?"

"Look how fancy and indispensable I am," the woman noted. "But, yeah. To be honest, I probably have something already built in my bag that I

338

can just click into and fry the whole damn thing. They'll know something's up, but not what."

"I think that's better than you taking the time to try and turn it off quietly," Oliver said. "The basement is big, but not that big. I think moving faster will be more advantageous to us. And after that they won't know where we are, so..."

"I've marked the cameras down, too, just in case," Hastin pointed out.

"What is that room?" Ame asked. He leaned over to look at what she was pointing at on her screen.

"That's my room," he said.

"There's two cameras in it."

"Mhm."

Ame saw Oliver wince, but, to his credit, he didn't say anything.

"That's fucked up, babe."

She wasn't as tactful as he was. Hastin laughed and leaned into her shoulder.

"We shouldn't have to go in there, anyway. It's like, a five foot concrete square, and then a little bathroom corner. It doesn't lead to anything, and there's cameras in it, like you said. I mean, we'll kill the cameras as we go, but even then, there's nothing in there we'd need," he said easily.

"Yeah, we already got you, so there's no reason to bother," Oliver said. He sounded a little tense, but Hastin seemed all too pleased at his words.

"So far so good. I mean, there have been plans I've felt worse about," Ame admitted, looking over their map.

"You're not usually one for plans much, anyway" Rosa told her.

"I mean, this is true. I'm one for motivation. But you best believe I have that shit in spades for this job."

Of all of them, Ame certainly seemed the most eager for bloodshed. Oliver figured that no matter what jobs they took in the future, she'd probably always be the one that was the most eager for it.

"Where's this backdoor we're using to get the fuck out when we're done at this party?" Oliver asked, looking at the map again.

"Here." Hastin took the screen from his hands and flicked over to the diagram he needed. "That's the door, that one right there."

"And we have the code for that one?"

Hastin nodded. "Normally, when she's doing an inspection, it's in the back of her mind. She never really has to think about using the escape route, so it took me a long time to get it, but I did."

"So, what." Ame tilted her head. "She'd just fuckin' wander in and stick her nose into everyone's work?"

Hastin nodded. "Yes. She didn't oversee most of my training personally. It was on her dime, and done according to her schedule, but the actual activities were left up to Mr. Helman."

"Donovan, right?" Rosa remembered.

"Man, I knew he was a sick sonofabitch," Ame said, wrinkling her nose. "I knew it as soon as I saw the fucker."

"He..." Hastin started. Two of the three looked at him, and Rosa tilted her head.

But Hastin closed his mouth and shook his head. "It's nothing."

Oliver leaned into his shoulder and Hastin sank down against him.

"If all goes well, they'll both burn by the time we're done," Rosa said calmly. "And we intend for everything to go well."

"It's a simple plan," Oliver said, and sighed. "And I like that, actually. Less of a chance for us to fuck up. We already have enough to worry about, I think."

"Think it's kind of funny that we used the money Violet paid us upfront to put the down payment on our escape." Ame snorted.

"And there's no chance of her knowing that?" Oliver asked.

"There's a whole bunch of questions she'd need to be able to answer if she was going to try and track us down ahead of time," Ame said. "There's no chance of it. If we can get out that door and to the rendezvous, we're home free. That's where her power ends, that doorstep."

"That's still too much power for my taste," Oliver said sourly. "But I guess it won't be for long."

"One thing at a time, Captain," Hastin reassured him. "We have to do it all together, step by step. That's the only way it will work."

"I know, honey." Oliver leaned over and kissed the side of his head.

"So...what about those bombs?" he asked, brightening. "We should get started."

This is where Oliver thought he truly shone. Sifting through the trash in the alley, looking for materials. Hastin had gotten a little better at dressing down, but he still seemed so out of place among the dirt.

The other two were out there with them, but Oliver was hands down the fastest between them. He was more than a little proud of that. They worked together to gather materials, and Oliver kept Hastin close, teaching him about the things they were digging up.

"You're burying me in garbage," Rosa noted when Oliver brought her back more materials.

"R.I.P. to the garbage queen," Oliver joked.

"You called?" Ame grinned.

"Yeah, you would be the garbage queen." Rosa waved her off.

With the four of them, it went fast. And with the four of them sitting together in the living room again, building them went just as quickly.

"I can't remember the last day I had that was this productive," Ame said.

"What, you don't routinely build shrapnel bombs out of garbage?" Oliver looked at his handiwork and tilted his head. "Honestly...I'm kind of surprised that I didn't. You'd think I would have figured out how to do this ages ago."

"Don't feel bad, Captain," Hastin said quietly. "We all learn things differently. You wouldn't have used them, anyway, even if you knew how to build them," he pointed out.

He was right there, Oliver knew. There was little point in arguing that.

"Look at us. We're some regular revolutionaries." Rosa put her hands on her hips, surveying their collection at the end of the day. "That's a bang-up job if I've ever seen one."

"Better be a fucking bang up job." Ame laughed.

"So, what is there left to do?" Oliver wondered aloud. "We have the maps. We've seen them, and at least two of us have them on file, basically." Hastin and Rosa, then, who had access to them, although in two very different ways.

"We have our supplies, we have our way in and ways out..." He counted them off on his fingers as he thought of them.

"What else do we need?"

"I have to pack a few things, but not until it gets later into tomorrow," Rosa said. "I think that goes for all of us."

Oliver nodded. "Yeah... But I think that's it. I think that's everything."

"All that's left is to eat something, and to get a good night's sleep," Ame said. "Let me tell you, there's nothing worse than trying to go into a job where you aren't at the top of your game. It's needlessly frustrating."

And we can't afford that here, Oliver thought. Not the frustration, but the chance of any of them being at less than their best. They'd need everything they had to make this work. And they'd have to do it together.

They ordered more take-out. After a brief walk, the four of them sat on the floor in the living room, eating out of paper boxes and plastic containers together. It was a little messy, but Oliver wasn't exactly worried about impressions at this point.

"I guess...we should probably go to bed, at some point," Ame said, but her frown told them that, strangely, she didn't seem very enthused about the idea.

"What's wrong?" Hastin asked, leaning against her and nuzzling his head against her shoulder.

"I dunno. I don't really feel like going to bed. I mean, I know Rosa's in there, but not like, close. And you guys are all the way on the other side of the apartment."

"It's not a very big apartment," Oliver pointed out, confused.

But Hastin seemed to understand. He wrapped his arms around her waist and rubbed his cheek against her again. "It's okay, Ame... I don't like thinking about it, either. I could go to bed with you?" he offered innocently.

She smiled and kissed his cheek. "You're sweet, baby. But how about we do one better. Go get the stuff from your bed and bring it out here," she said. Then she looked at Oliver. "You too, Captain, if you're not too much of an adult."

"I feel vaguely insulted and I don't really know why..." he said as he stood.

"It's fine. You're fine," Ame said in reply, waving him off.

They went back to their room, and just as Ame had said, both he and Hastin pulled the blankets and pillows from their beds and dragged them into the living room. When they returned, Ame and Rosa had done the exact same thing.

"There. Come on down here with me, honey," Ame said, beckoning Hastin near her. "Put your stuff on the floor. We'll all sleep here together."

"You really going to sleep well enough on the floor?" Oliver asked.

Rosa laughed quietly. "Is it that much better than the beds in this place?"

Oliver chuckled, too. And, when it came down to it, he didn't really want to argue. He wanted to be close to them, too.

So they piled the pillows together and threw the blankets down. They put all their heads in the middle, an idea of Oliver's.

"Sleeping in a line still defeats the purpose," he pointed out. "Someone is going to be too far from you no matter what."

So, like spokes of a wheel, they laid there together. He hadn't realized how much he had been dreading laying alone in the dark. And, like Ame had said, they shared a room, but that didn't really solve the problem in the end.

Hastin laid on his stomach, kicking his feet back and forth with his head resting happily in his hands. "This was a really nice idea. I...wasn't sure how much sleep I was going to get."

"Don't worry. If it takes you awhile to get to bed, that's okay. We can sleep late tomorrow. We're going to be up late anyway" Rosa reassured him.

"Yeah, but I didn't want to keep the Captain up." Hastin's eyes flicked his way and Oliver brushed it off.

"You don't have to worry about that, honey," Oliver said. "You're allowed."

Hastin dropped his arms, face planted into his pillow, and rolled over to be next to Ame, who laughed to see the whole thing and then shifted to fling her arm around him and pull him close.

Oliver smiled.

This was so much better than sleeping alone.

41:

Dan and Xueying ended up in the kitchen for some time. Long enough that the other two came looking for them.

"We're just figuring something out," Xueying said, waving Rusty off. "I'll be back in a little while."

It took longer for Yoru to come asking, but he received something of the same response. It was a little unusual, but as of yet it didn't seem like it was anything to panic about. Time crawled slowly onwards, and though it got later and later, Xueying and Dan still discussed in quiet voices. Eventually, it seemed they got too tired to continue and both of them went to bed.

Dan fell onto his cot and slept uneasily, discomfort and uncertainty twisting in his stomach. Xueying slept no better. And their friends, concerned for what was distressing them, did not seem to get much rest themselves.

In the morning, no one seemed to want to talk. The tension was clear, palpable in the air. Yoru could taste it when he breathed. And still, there were no answers.

Until Xueying put her hands on the table and looked around at all of them. "Okay...we need to talk," she said finally.

And that in itself was almost a relief, for the waiting had been nearly unbearable.

"Something is clearly on your minds," Yoru said. He sat down at the table as well. "Surely we can figure it out as a team, if you tell us what it is."

Xueying looked to Dan, his cue to explain, and he took a deep breath before he did.

"I looked at what Violet asked us to get. I didn't think it'd be anything good. I'm not that naive." He managed a bitter smile. "I figured it was some sort of underhanded bullshit that she'd use for, I don't know, getting a bigger share of the market, wiping out debt or getting some of her opponents killed or whatever. You know. The usually shit."

"But?" Rusty asked.

"But it's not," Dan said simply. "That's not it at all. It's just swaths of information about everyday people. Specifically, identification and medical information. Just, like, buckets of it. Names and addresses and medical histories and government ID numbers and loan accounts. Everyone who has

344

ever been in the hole for hospital costs, or even anyone who has checked into one of the big hospitals in the past... I don't know. I found stuff dating from more than a year ago. In a city this size, I can't even imagine how many people that is."

"What would she want that for?" Rusty frowned. "I mean...some of that she can get access to legally, I think."

"Yeah, but not altogether. And god knows why the fuckin' city has it all lined up so nice or how she even found out about it. But you can guess what she's after. There's only one option," Xueying pointed out.

Dan only needed to look at Yoru to know he understood. There was something in his eyes that he couldn't immediately name. Some time later, playing the scene over in his head, he would recognize the emotion as wrath.

But for now, he was quiet.

"She's going to use this information to go after people," Rusty said. Her frown deepened. "Large scale. Anyone she can get."

Xueying sighed. "It's not the first time I've been unhappy with an employer's choices. But, I'll admit, it's never been something on this scale," she told them quietly. "I've been involved in stealing business secrets from people who seemed like they were decent folks. I've planted adultery evidence so heirs could take each other to court and prove that one or the other was morally unfit to take over whatever they had been left... And I don't always agree with who wins. But..." She frowned. "That's not the same. This is..." She shook her head.

"What do you think we should do?" Rusty asked her, but Dan answered before she could.

"What can we do? Violet already knows we have it. And on top of that, should we really do anything? What are our options, really?"

Panic had edged its way into his voice and quietly, Yoru reached over to take Dan's hand in his own. Visibly, he started to calm down.

Then Xueying spoke up. "She doesn't know we have it exactly... I just told her we had to meet up. I assume she thinks we have it, but I never told her that, not explicitly..." There was leeway in non-specifics, Xueying knew that. She hadn't imagined something like this happening, though. Usually the purpose behind vague messages was something as simple as plausible deniability. As a spy, that was something she had gotten used to.

The use seemed quite different here, though.

"I still don't see how that leaves us much choice... Or should we even be considering this as a choice?" Dan looked between them. "I don't know... I don't know anything about this kind of work. Should I even be this confused?"

He sighed.

He looked tired. And though he seemed the most animated in his worry out of all of them, he was not the only one to feel that way.

"Xueying, I defer to your judgment with complete trust, as I always will," Yoru said quietly. "But…my heart is not in this. This is not a job that I feel successful in. There's no reward here."

"So what, we don't do it and you ruin your reputation?" Rusty asked.

"My reputation isn't your worry," Yoru said, but there was nothing but kindness in both his voice and his eyes when he looked to her.

"Even knowing what we do, I could probably name ten people who would hand this in without a second thought," Xueying said. She smiled just a little at that. "I mean…I guess it's nice to know that my friends aren't completely heartless, but I feel that I'll have failed you no matter what we decide."

"You failed no one," Rusty said sharply. While normally she could be intense, the way she was looking at Xueying now was even beyond that. "You were a perfectly capable leader and did your job successfully. Our employer should be ashamed." There was a heatedness to her voice that Dan hadn't expected to hear. Of all of them, he thought she would care the least.

When Rusty realized they were all looking at her, she crossed her arms, still frowning, and continued. "You thought I would be okay with this? How many years did I suffer in the system? How many people will live like I did?" she demanded. "How many names are on that list?"

"I don't know," Dan admitted. Yoru let go of his hand and reached across the table to Rusty. It took some coaxing, but eventually she uncrossed her arms and gave her hands to him. He kissed them both.

"Rusty. Don't be like that. You speak to my heart with your anger," he told her softly. "You are not alone in these feelings."

That seemed to help, at least a little. His thumbs rubbed soothing circles on the back of her hands until she sighed and shook her head.

"I am not angry with you. And maybe I am taking this too personally… But, like you said—" She looked at Yoru. "This doesn't seem like we won."

Xueying ran a hand through her short hair. "Are we really considering turning this job down now?" she asked, finally saying it out loud. "Is that what we want to talk about?"

Dan leaned his head in his hand. "I'm a little lost here, I guess. I don't know what I'm supposed to think is okay or not okay. So, you're right, Yoru, I don't like this…but I'm never sure if that's how I should feel or just because, you know…"

"Who cares if it is because you are new to the scene?" Yoru asked him. "I did not drag you into this to turn you into someone else."

That reassured him a little. More than a little, even, as it gave him the strength to nod. "In that case, then yes. I'm with you. I don't like this." He looked then to Xueying, the only one of them who hadn't yet agreed.

"I just want to do what is best for you guys," she said, looking at them. "I'd hand this thing in, even if I hated it, if you guys thought it was best. You and I have something in common, Dan."

He looked at her curiously and she smiled. "I worry about being soft all the time. I'm not really in the killing business. Bodies leave trails, and it is better for me if there is nothing to show where I have been. I worry, a lot, that I'm not adapted to this work because of the way I feel about things...but I've never had to take a job before where I really, truly felt so much against it."

"You hate this, too?" Rusty asked.

"Yeah," Xueying said. She sighed. "My mind was made up the minute Dan showed it to me, but I'm not just responsible for myself. I'm responsible for you lot." She looked around at them again. "I didn't want to decide anything that was going to hurt you."

"So, what are we looking at, as far as damages go?" Yoru asked.

"Financially, nothing," Xueying said. "I've played that game enough times to know. I didn't touch her deposit. We can return it without it hurting us, except for time lost. It's rough, but I'm not going to starve."

Rusty said nothing until Xueying put her arm around her shoulders. "You're not going to starve, either."

"I could fight again." And there was no anger in her voice now. It was a sincere offer. Xueying leaned in and kissed her cheek.

"No, no...we don't have to do that. We'll find something. We'll find more work."

"Will people want to hire you after they hear about this?" Dan asked. He didn't want to be skeptical, but he couldn't help it. He wanted to know they would be okay, and that meant confronting his own uncomfortable questions.

"No one big," Xueying admitted. "It'll be a while before we can shake it. But we're pretty adaptable. We'll find work. What about you guys?"

"Everyone's failed a job at one point or another," Yoru said. "This won't be the first hit I've come back from." He seemed to feel fairly calm about it. There was no nervousness or unhappiness in his voice. "If the decision is between the paycheck and prestige and my being able to sleep, I'll take the good nights sleep every time, you know that."

"What about me?" Dan asked quietly.

"Need you even ask?" Yoru said, but his smile was as gentle. "You'll be with me. I'll take care of you. I did promise, didn't I?"

"Which ones of us are actually dating again?" Rusty joked quietly.

Yoru's smile strengthened just a little. "All that aside, though… perhaps we can stay as we are."

"What do you mean?" Rusty asked.

But Dan caught on well enough. He knew how Yoru thought. "The four of us. We'll have a better chance of making ends meet if we work together, I think. Even after all this shit. We're no strangers to having very little space, we all get along, and if it will help us stay on our feet, well…why not?"

Xueying looked to Rusty. "What do you think?"

Rusty frowned. "I mean, on the one hand, Yoru's poetry—" she said, which drew a perfectly stricken face from the man, "—on the other, his cooking."

"What, am I not even a part of the equation?" Dan laughed. He had reached over and pulled Yoru against him, to comfort him against the woman's stinging words.

"You're fine," Rusty said simply, the faintest smile on her lips.

Dan found himself smiling, too.

"It's going to be rough. But I think sticking together might at least keep our sense of humours alive," Xueying agreed. "And we won't be entirely out of work. We're adaptable, and there's lots of people out there who don't give a shit about Violet. It'll be rougher jobs but, I mean, apparently we're good at that," she mused.

"So we agreed, then?" Yoru asked, sitting up again. He was looking at them with earnest eyes, no pretense in his voice now. "We're going to return the deposit and turn down the job?"

"I want to hear everyone say it," Xueying said. "Each of you. And I need to know that you're being honest. I'm not going to drag you into this shit unless you're really committed to it."

"I'll go first then," Rusty said. "I love you, but I would not do this, even if you did."

That was all she said, and it left Xueying in a stunned silence.

"I…" she started, and then found the words to stick in her throat. With a resolute expression, she leaned forward and kissed the other woman. "I love you, too. And good."

"Well, I don't have anything that dramatic to say," Dan said dryly. "But yes, I agree. Let's give the deposit back and find work that we can live with. I mean, it's worked for you guys, right? And...I still kind of want to be able to look my mom in the eye when this is all done."

"What, killing people is not that line?" Rusty asked him. It was blunt enough that even Xueying looked shocked but, surprisingly, Dan laughed.

"Not when your boy was in the army. But I think she'd want me to make the best choices I could. This is one of them. I don't want any part in this."

"Yoru?"

Xueying looked at him, where he had been sitting quietly.

"I loathe nothing more than to give someone with so much the means to take even more from those who have nothing," he said. "It's rare in this work that you get to make those kinds of choices. We are all trapped within the rules of the society that provides us with employment. But, this is a chance I will not let pass me by."

"That's a surprisingly eloquent way of telling Violet to go fuck herself," Xueying noted.

Yoru smiled and said nothing.

"Okay. We return the deposit, admit to the failed job, and face the consequences together," she announced. "It's not going to be a good day tomorrow, but we'll come back here together and move on."

"What are we doing to do with the drive?" Dan asked.

"Destroy it," Rusty said. "Just, smash the thing. Don't let anyone else get it."

"She has a point," Yoru agreed.

Xueying nodded. "I'll make sure it's unsalvageable. Nothing to fear there. Now...I really need to eat." She let out a noise that was half-laugh, half-sigh. Like all of them, her stomach had been so twisted she hadn't even thought about food until then.

"I'll make us something." Yoru got to his feet. As he circled the table, each person got a kiss on the head, even Rusty.

"Now that you mention it—" Dan agreed, looking over to Xueying. Food sounded like a good idea. He met her smile with one of his own.

"Give me the drive," Rusty said, holding her hand out to Xueying. "I'll go and break it up before the food is even done."

Xueying handed it over with a smile. It would have been hard to argue with her about it. Of all of them, she certainly seemed the most capable.

She was true to her word,and brought the scraps of the memory drive back before Yoru had even finished. The mood in the apartment was subdued, but not unhappy. If anything...Dan was feeling a lot better. It had been really weighing on him, and he had felt so lost and alone. Xueying had been playing her cards close to her chest throughout their whole discussion, and while it had been hard at the time, he totally understood why.

She was looking out for them. Now that it was over with, he could appreciate that.

If anything, he felt closer with them for it. And he was kind of glad that they wouldn't be splitting up, at least for awhile.

This sucked. They had almost died for nothing. But they'd move on from it together.

He thought it was all dealt with, until he and Yoru ended up in their room again and he noticed that the other man seemed noticeably quieter than normal. What really gave away that something was wrong was that he wasn't writing, although he held his notebook in his hand.

"Why the gloom, mushroom?" he asked, sitting next to him.

It earned him a laugh, at least. It was short lived, and probably mostly a product of surprise, but Dan still counted it as a victory.

"I am happy for our decision earlier," Yoru said. "But..."

There was always one of those. "But?"

"But something still weighs heavy on my mind," he admitted quietly.

"Tell me," Dan said. When Yoru was still reluctant, Dan tugged his notebook out of his hand and replaced it with his own fingers. "We're friends. You can tell me what's wrong."

Yoru squeezed his hand and sighed. "It's a matter of...the phone calls, actually."

Dan's heart immediately froze up. "My phone calls?" he asked. "Were we...I mean..."

Were we caught? He couldn't bring himself to ask it.

Yoru caught on immediately. "Oh! No! No. Not that. My goodness, I didn't mean to scare you," he apologized quickly. "I'm so sorry. No, you're safe. They're safe. I'm sorry."

Dan managed a weak laugh. "Well, if it's not that, I'm sure I can stand whatever it is." He took a deep breath. "What's on your mind?"

It was Yoru's turn to steady himself. "Well, if we are regaled to taking smaller jobs, I... I don't know when I'll be able to pay those connections of mine for a phone call for you. The answer isn't never, but...it may be a while."

That was something that Dan had never thought about. Yoru hadn't mentioned the phone calls coming out of his pocket, but it certainly made sense that they did. And the idea that he would have to wait before he could talk to his family again was hard to bear.

But he had thought, once, that he would never see them again. He could be patient. And with enough work, he could pay the toll himself.

"Don't be sad for me," Dan told him. "You've already done so much. I'm incredibly thankful. They know that I'm alive. I told them I would call when I could, and I meant it. You haven't wronged me," he reassured him. "Besides, maybe next time I can pay for it myself." He smiled. "It was kind of you to have already done so."

"We are friends," Yoru told him, looking much more at ease now than he had. "That's what friends do."

42:

Oliver was the first to wake up. It was afternoon already, which was weird for him, but they had been up much later than usual. At the very least, he knew that he wasn't the only one affected by nerves.

Raising his head and brushing his hair from his eyes, he saw what a mess they had made. There was little sense to how the bedding had ended up. Rosa, her hair similarly undone, was still asleep, haloed by the spilling of white around her head. Their two other spokes were no longer separate. Hastin and Ame were tangled together and Oliver didn't have it in him to be jealous. He was just happy they hadn't had to sleep alone.

Now, dozy morning-time Oliver had to figure out how to make coffee, and he was glad that the rest of his team weren't awake to watch him struggle. Usually, Rosa was the one who dealt with new and unusual coffee makers, but she was still asleep.

He was leaning back against the countertop, his head lolling back against the cupboards, when the sound of feet lulled him awake again.

Rosa, of course. A few minutes too late.

"Morning," Oliver said.

"Good morning," Rosa replied, and then she stretched. Her hands tapped the ceiling and she jerked them back reflexively.

"Sucks being tall."

"I mean, you wouldn't know or anything," Rosa answered. Oliver's answer was less words and more noise, a hum of assent or disagreement that he wasn't awake enough to elaborate on.

He was thankful for the help, though, when Rosa grabbed the other two cups and brought them out to the living room.

"Hey—" She nudged Ame's shoulder gently with her foot. "Rise and shine."

Ame groaned, lifting her head up off of Hastin's chest. Oliver watched as Hastin's eyes flicked open and his hands tightened around his teammate before he realized where he was and relaxed again.

"Brought some for you too, honey," Oliver told him.

"Yay," he said sleepily, and he smiled.

They disentangled themselves, and the four of them sat on the floor, sipping their coffee, until Ame finally spoke up.

"So...we ready to go fuck something up?" she asked.

Oliver chuckled and held out his cup of coffee. "To our future endeavours of...fucking something up."

They all touched their glasses to his, but talking came a little easier after that.

"Ah, shit," Rosa cursed.

"What's wrong?"

"Realized I have to leave most of my tech here. I can't carry it and personally escort some asshole to the gates of hell, now can I?"

"Oh, babe—" Ame pulled a face and waved her words off. "What's the worry? There's always more. You act like you haven't had it all broken before, and I know you have."

Rosa laughed. "Okay, that's fair. Sometimes, you forget that things are replaceable."

"Not people," Oliver said. Hastin looked at him over the rim of his coffee and Oliver quickly added. "And not you, either, despite what you've been told."

"I didn't say anything," Hastin said with a giggle.

Oliver laughed, too. "I know what you were thinking, kid."

The waiting was the worst of it, but at least they had something to do with the time. Rosa went through her equipment and decided what was to stay and what was to go, and they used one of the empty bags to pack the bombs into.

"I'm carrying those," Oliver said.

"What, so you can explode yourself again?" Ame laughed.

"Because all you guys are going to be covering me anyway, because you know I suck at this shit," he pointed out. "Even if I wasn't carrying it, you'd be keeping half an eye on me. Better to make that job easier for you."

"Smart boy."

"Try telling that to my parents," he joked.

"Too bad for that. Now you are parents." She jutted her finger over to where Hastin was winding a wire around his hand and attaching it to his rigging.

"You make things weird," Oliver told her then, laughing in a mixture of surprise and feigned disgust. "Has anyone told you that?"

"Pretty sure I have a shirt that says that."

By the time they were ready to go, the only thing left to do was eat. Take-out again, and they were careful not to let the delivery guy see anything too suspicious. Not that he'd probably care. That was the thing about working to make ends meet, right? You just didn't have the energy.

They ate. Hastin braided Rosa's long hair and Ame scrubbed a part of the bathroom mirror clean so she could put her makeup on.

"Really?" Oliver asked, watching her.

"Yeah," Ame said. "Either I'm going in to kill or I'm going in to die. I gotta look my best."

Though he didn't use a mirror, Hastin seemed to agree, as when they gathered at the door, Oliver noticed that he had done the same thing.

"Ready?" Oliver asked, straightening the bag on his shoulders. The gun in his hand still felt strange, but at least it brought him no discomfort.

"As we'll ever be," Rosa answered. Her tail flicked behind her, and whether it was in agitation or excitement, Oliver couldn't even hazard a guess. Instead, he just nodded and opened the door.

This was it. The next few hours would decide everything.

They crept through the streets of town. Oliver knew the way. He didn't need a map, and the others didn't need to ask him. They followed, and they trusted. The darkest corners gave them plenty of room to press in to, to disguise themselves in the shadows.

Even in the light, there was little to be suspicious of. Oliver, in his same ugly sweater that he had left his apartment in some weeks ago, a duffle bag hanging from his shoulder, was much more likely to be transporting weapons or stolen tech or even drugs rather than bombs, but that was impossible to tell by looking at him. If it weren't for the fact that Ame was wearing running shoes and not heels, Oliver would have thought she was going out.

Rosa looked a little out of place with the massive piece of equipment she wore on her arm, but Hastin seemed to acknowledge that. Whenever they had to pass through the light, or cross a place where more people could be found, he pressed himself to her side, hiding the suspicious gauntlet from view. Getting stopped by the police was really not on their to-do list.

HiTech loomed, a dark tower in the distance.

"Man, am I ever glad we don't have to go up that," Ame said.

Oliver blinked at her in surprise. He had been so busy thinking about how overwhelming it looked before he promptly realized that it didn't matter. What it looked like had zero bearing on what they were there to do.

It could have been twice the size. So what?

He smiled. "Kinda handy that we're going down, eh?" he said.

The doorways weren't lit. It was an office building, and everyone had long clocked out for the day. The windows, though they seemed to stretch endlessly upwards, held no light. It glistened a little in the yellow-blue tones that were reflected off the glass, streetlights and neon signs, but largely it stood still and quiet.

Of course, they didn't go for the front door, the one that clients or visiting professionals used.

"It's going to be a race as soon as that camera sees us," Oliver said, pointing to the one over the doorway. "We're going to have to bust our asses to get in there and mop everything up as fast as we humanly can."

"Then don't fall on your face this time," Ame said.

"First of all, fuck you. Second of all, also fuck you. Lastly, you're right," he said, deadpan.

"Don't be afraid," Hastin said, to no one in particular.

"Either we'll make it happen or we won't, but the answer isn't out here, it's in there," Rosa pointed out.

Collectively, they took a deep breath. Then they moved.

Ame took out the camera in a single shot. It wasn't a hard target. Hastin immediately punched in the code to open the back door and that was it: they were inside.

There was no turning back now.

Ame took out every camera she could reach. Anything she could do to open up their blind spots would make their life easier. Walking through the layout in the dark was very different than merely memorizing a map and Oliver panicked for several seconds, disoriented.

Eventually, his instincts kicked in and he regained a sense of place. He knew where they were, or at least he knew enough.

They hadn't counted on having to wait to call the damn elevator, but although they were ready for a fight when the doors open, none came.

Rosa tossed him a chair, literally tossed, and he used it to jam the doors open. It wouldn't be going anywhere like that.

And Oliver stuck a bomb to it anyway, just in case. They did the other doors on the main level, going around the floor to tag all the entrances.. Anyone trying to get in that way wasn't going to get very far.

Then, they headed for the stairs.

"And another one—" Oliver said, sticking the bomb in the doorway once they had stepped through it. Opening the door again would pull it apart and set it off. It really was a very simple design.

The bag was getting lighter, and Oliver was feeling faster on his feet. That's good, because the shooting was going to start any second and when it did, that was the only thing that would save him.

Hastin keyed in the code for the last door, the one at the bottom of the stairs, but hesitated before he entered it.

"Ready?" Oliver asked. That was his job, after all.

Even in the dim of the stairwell's safety lights, he saw all three of them nod.

"Okay. Punch it."

Hastin did. The door slid open. The lights on the other side were on. The shooting started immediately.

"Not even gonna let us in the door," Ame said, swearing under her breath, both hands on her gun.

"Hey, Oliver, you got anything in the bag?" Rosa asked.

Oh. "Yeah, actually... So what do I do, just whip it in there?"

"Yeah. Ame will shoot it. That will buy us the chance to get in there. You will shoot it, right, Ame?"

"Girl, you picked a hell of a time to doubt me."

Their bickering seemed so strangely mundane, even in the circumstances that surrounded them. Oliver wasn't nearly afraid now that they were in the thick of it. It was the waiting that had been the worst.

He pulled another one out of his bag and when there was a break in the shooting he winged it into the room as hard as he could. A wayward shot put a hole in his hoodie, but not in him.

Ame shot the bomb, and they heard the aftermath; a bang, and then screaming. There was something viscerally satisfying about that, Oliver felt. He had always been so careful about that. In a violent world, it was so easy not to care, too easy. He never wanted to do one worse, to become someone who actually enjoyed hurting others.

But, if there was ever going to be an exception, he supposed now was the time

They ducked into the room. Oliver held the gun in his hand but didn't raise it, didn't see anyone to take aim at. The others were faster. Next to him, Ame shot down two of them, Hastin a third.

"That can't be everyone," Oliver said.

"Nope," Hastin agreed. "They're trying to group up, but we got here too fast. There will be more coming."

"Good," Rosa said calmly.

They crossed the first room. It was some kind of entryway. There was low furniture, and thank god it was empty as there was nothing that would have made good cover for them in it. The walls were all concrete and windowless, which made sense since they were underground, but at least they were brightly painted. Whoever had to stay down there on overnights at least wasn't in entirely dismal straights. Well, unless they were dead, that was. The basement would have been an unholy maze to navigate if they hadn't been given the maps beforehand.

Ame took out every camera as it came up, and Oliver knew every twist and turn of the halls his feet led them down. They passed bunks, file rooms, a goddamn armoury...which Oliver stopped to stick another device to. It was a little obvious, seeing as he couldn't get it on the inside of the door like the others, but anything to make their lives more difficult.

Then, the hallway opened up, spilling them into what was unmistakably a lab area. Oliver remembered it from the maps. Looking at it in person, he realized how little of it he understood.

But when he heard the shouting across the room, he sure as hell understood that.

At least in here there were desks, the metal kind. He hefted one over, Ame at his side. One aisle over, he watched Rosa do the same thing. The next few gunshots told him that it had been a damn good idea. The bullets dented the shit out of the table, but hadn't punched right through yet.

"We gotta clear them out, this isn't gonna hold," Oliver said. The noise drowned him out and his words never reached Rosa or Hastin. It was only Ame who heard him, and she was the one that answered.

"Don't worry, Rosa's got it." She cast a glance over to the other table and snickered.

Oliver watched as Rosa vaulted over the side of the table, hailing down on their targets like so much heavenly fire. It was a slight miracle that he wasn't shot, sitting where he was, peeking over the table, but the people who would have shot him were more than adequately distracted.

Her gauntlet cut through them like like a hot knife through butter. It shredded the people who had stood there, and she dropped the four of them long before they could tighten up their aim on the new target.

"Oliver!" she called.

"It's my last one," he said, rushing over to her side. That would have to do. Whoever else was trapped down there with them would be their problem to deal with.

He didn't make it to the door. Another hail of bullets left him skidding to a stop and stumbling back behind cover. Too far from her own, Rosa jumped back and bodily dragged another table in front of herself.

It was a lone man in the doorway. Very tall, impossibly broad at the shoulder. Oliver was struck by a flash of recognition, but he couldn't pull up the man's name.

He was pulled from his thoughts when he heard a loud, piercing laugh.

Hastin's.

Watching him stand up from behind cover was a moment of pure, unadulterated horror and Ame must have realized this because she grabbed Oliver immediately, to stop him from running after him.

"Donovan," he said, laughter still bubbling in his voice. "Hi."

"Should have known it was you, goddamn psychotic bitch." The name rung a bell to Oliver and he remembered. Violet's right hand guy. Hastin's handler.

Why were no bullets flying around?

"Stay still so I can shoot you," he said.

"Really?" Hastin asked, sweetly. "You've spent the last twenty years dreaming about strangling me with your own two hands and now that you're finally allowed...you're going to shoot me?"

"Before your stupid friends get a chance to shoot me, yes."

"They won't," Hastin said. On reflex, Oliver turned to look at Ame, looking alarmed. She yanked his arm where she was still holding it.

"Stop. He's got it. It's fine," she whispered harshly.

They couldn't see Rosa where she was waiting, but she hadn't moved yet either.

"Come on." Hastin held his arms out, openly, to the other man. "She can't even fire you for this. You might as well try~"

Oliver couldn't understand why he was laughing. Nothing about this was hilarious, and it didn't sound like he was afraid.

He heard Donovan drop his gun. He went to ready his own and Ame shook her head.

"We'll cheat if we got to, but just...hold on a minute."

What was Hastin doing? He wasn't trying to protect them, surely. They were four to one, and if he meant for it to be a distraction he didn't even look back at them.

And then his words finally seemed to register. 'You've spent the last twenty years dreaming about strangling me,' he had said.

What if Donovan wasn't the only one who had been waiting?

Oliver took a deep breath.

"We'll intervene if it gets too hairy," he said. Ame nodded.

He was resolved to do that until he heard the first punch being thrown and quickly looked over the table to see Hastin sprawled on the ground, picking himself up off the tiled floor with blood dripping from his lips.

"Oh, come on. You've hit me harder than that in practice," Hastin said, pulling himself to his feet.

Ame popped up next to Oliver, peeking over the edge of the table, and watched as Hastin took a running start to regain the ground he had lost.

"Holy shit—"

Hastin fought like a man possessed and Oliver thought that maybe he was. The size difference seemed like nothing. Donovan's only recourse was throwing Hastin away from him, but catching him and holding him seemed a trial in itself. He managed it once more, but Hastin still picked himself up off the floor. When he brushed his bangs out of his face, red streaked the blue.

But Donovan was bleeding and winded, too. Hastin didn't seem tired yet, or at least, not too tired to laugh. Nor did he seem tired enough to stop goading the man who was trying to kill him.

"Feels kind of different when you take the training wheels off, doesn't it?" Hastin asked. "Don't tell me, I already know. You're just jealous you didn't get to be a part of the other training I had to do."

"You worthless little—" Donovan managed through his ragged breaths. "You disgust me."

"Is that so?" Hastin said. Oliver saw his hand slip under his skirt and Ame nudged him hard in the side. He didn't look away to tell her that he saw it, too. They weren't the only ones planning on playing dirty.

This time, Donovan was the one to make the move, stepping forward to try and grab at him. Hastin ducked him easily, sliding behind him and kicking out the man's knee with a sound that made Oliver think he was going to be sick.

When Donovan went down, Hastin revealed what he had taken from under his skirt; a garrote wire that was, in a flash, wound tight around the man's neck.

"I disgust you, is that right?" Hastin asked breathlessly. "Good. Choke on it."

43:

It looked like it was going to be an uncomfortable day. Dan could feel it when he got out of bed, like a strange air that hung over them. But, shared suffering was half, his mother had said, so this was a mere fragment of it in the end. Everyone else had the same disposition; mildly hopeful and a little resigned to a pretty terrible time. They'd get through it together.

It didn't really help that they were lying about being failures. The fact that they had succeeded didn't mean very much in the end. It still kind of felt like they were failures. But it was better than the alternative. One day of discomfort was much better than a lifetime of regret. That was what Yoru had told him.

They got themselves ready, and he was only a little surprised when he saw the others slip various armaments into their clothing.

"Do we really think it's going to go that badly?" he asked, despite also having a handgun in his jacket.

"No, no," Xueying said. "Like we've said, it would be a really stupid choice for her to retaliate. She'd never be able to hire another person. It would be a disaster." She waved it off. "This, really, is just a habit. And you know, in case shit pops up on the way there."

"And I see you are not alone in feeling this way." Yoru tapped the exact spot of Dan's coat where his gun rested, despite not being able to see it through the bulky jacket. Dan rolled his eyes.

"Next you're going to tell me that those eyes of yours can see through clothing."

"But why would I ever tell you," Yoru joked.

It got a laugh out of Rusty, who had been listening to them bicker. She was the only one who he didn't see pack a gun, but then again, she was probably just as useful without one.

"All set? Ready to face the music?" Xueying asked.

"I've never faced the music with such capable dance partners," Dan noted.

This time, Yoru laughed. "You sound like me."

"Oh, someone save me." Rusty rolled her eyes.

They left together. The familiar press of the city was around them instantly, and today, it did not seem to bother Dan too much. He could feel it, picking at the sides of his sensitivities, prickling there, waiting for the chance to upset him...but it didn't seem enough. It just waited, on the edge of his mind.

"Doing alright?" Xueying asked him, nudging him with her arm. The harsh yellow of the sunlight that bounced its way down on them from the skyscrapers made her glow, like some sort of common goddess or something.

"Yeah, yeah. Today isn't bad," he said, referring more to his own mind than their current situation. "I'm doing okay."

"I was just worried, the added stress and all."

He shook his head. "I'm hanging in there."

She smiled at him then, and let it go. He didn't mind that she had asked. It was nice of her to. Maybe with more people, with more connections, it could have been overwhelming. It could have been downright annoying, even. But all he had were the three of them.

Yoru seemed to know how he felt in a look, and Dan didn't mind. It was nice to be understood.

But, it was nice to be able to talk about it, too.

They had a stop to make on the way to the meeting. Xueying announced it as they walked, declaring that their first goal did not involve Violet at all. They were heading for the same bar they had gone drinking at.

"What, we are running errands, too?" Rusty asked.

"I'll just be a second," Xueying said, shaking her head. "I just have to drop something off to a friend. What, are you in a hurry?"

Rusty rolled her eyes, but no one else bothered her when she ducked into the darkened building. True to her word, she was back within minutes.

"Was that fast enough?" she asked Rusty sarcastically. The shorter woman answered her with a scowling kiss, but it certainly shut her up.

They weren't headed for HiTech itself. Dan remembered the towering building, so tall it looked like it leaned over the smaller skyscrapers around it. No, they were headed to a warehouse. All the quieter for something like this to go down. It was much easier to do a trade in an out of the way place than to have the four of them drawing attention at her HQ. He was surprised they had been allowed to meet there to begin with.

"Is she really going to come herself?" Rusty wondered aloud.

"No idea," Xueying said. "As long as it's her, or one of her people I've dealt with, it doesn't really matter."

"I guess not," Rusty agreed.

The walk was nice. It gave them something to do. So much of the discomfort was from sitting around and waiting for the inevitable bad news to drop. The air was chilly despite the bright sun, and Dan spotted Yoru making heavy breaths just to watch the condensation.

"You're a child," he told his friend.

"And well aware of it," Yoru agreed.

Where was the harm? Today was going to suck. At least they were smiling.

The warehouse was in a fairly crowded part of town. It must have been expensive to get such a wide real-estate area for something that wasn't a skyscraper. At least then, you made your money back with all the levels. And this building was tall, certainly, but not even close to that height. It couldn't have been more than a few floors. After all, it was just made for keeping stock, not people.

There didn't seem to be much staff around, which struck Dan as a little odd. Then again, if Violet gave everyone the day off, who would see her being suspicious? No one, surely. So maybe it wasn't so strange in the end. He was learning more about the business every day.

They stepped in the side door and someone met them there. A woman, dressed in tactical blacks and armed. Well, at least Dan didn't feel so out of place, then.

As she led them to where they were supposed to meet Violet, he cast his eyes around them. Shelves and shelves of things, all in boxes or crates. This must have been some kind of receiving centre. There were empty pallets stacked up, too. He certainly couldn't see anything suspicious.

He also wasn't sure why he was looking for it. This wasn't supposed to be one of those jobs, after all. Maybe it was just habit. Maybe you broke into enough places and did enough jobs that it was just the way you looked at things after a while. It seemed a bit early for him to be adapting like that, though. The idea made him chuckle quietly to himself.

It was Violet, in the flesh, who they were then taken to meet. She wore a skirt and a blazer and looked tidy and normal and a little out of place in a building like this one. She smiled to see them, and reached to shake Xueying's hand.

"Good to see you, Miss Violet," Xueying said.

"And you, Xueying. I hope you have some good news for me."

There was nowhere to sit here, between the aisles. They weren't going to be there that long, then. That was a good sign. Better to get it over with and get out. Lingering in it would do them no favours, Dan thought.

"Unfortunately, I have bad news," Xueying said. In that moment, Dan was sold completely. Her tone was completely believable. "We've worked hard these past few weeks to try and complete our contract to you...but there have been a lot of problems."

"You weren't out of time yet," Violet said to her cautiously. "So why call me here?"

"We didn't want to waste your time any further," Xueying said. "We felt it was best that we returned your deposit to you as quickly as we could. As soon as we realized what the job entailed, we realized it was out of our reach to complete it."

Dan, even knowing the story as he did, felt that Xueying made a compelling statement. She sounded like she was telling the truth. The fact that her words could have a different interpretation didn't occur to him.

It had occurred to Xueying how closely her words mirrored the truth, but that was deliberate. She would sound more convincing if she had to fake as little as possible. It was an old tactic, but it held up.

Maybe that was what ruined them. Maybe it was something else. They'd never know.

"You can take your deposit out of the account you put it in," she said to Violet. "You will find that the total amount is there, according to our agreement."

This was clearly not what Violet had thought she would hear, and definitely not what she hoped to hear. For a moment, she only looked at Xueying in shock. It was muted, but the expression was unmistakable.

Dan could understand. It had been out of the blue, even for them. Her being surprised was the least of their worries.

Eventually, she sighed, and nodded. "Yes, yes, I understand," she said. "I'm sorry that it turned out this way."

"Me too," Xueying agreed.

They turned to leave. Out of the corner of his eye, Dan saw Violet raise her hand, gesturing to someone above them. It was too conspicuous a motion to have been unintentional. He glanced up, and saw more people, openly armed, step out from around the shipping containers and wooden crates on the shelves above them.

He barely had time to consider what that meant before the gunfire started.

They were trapped in the aisles, and these people had the advantage of height. He didn't even have time to scream a warning to the others before the sound of gunfire drowned out any noise he could have hoped to make.

He ran, throwing himself against a shelf, trying to find any kind of cover he could against the death that hailed down on them from above. He whirled around in time to see the others do the same.

Except for Rusty, who had started to run before being pelted with bullets. She fell to her knees and even then still struggled to pull herself to where Xueying waited.

Xueying was sheltered from the bullets but was reaching for Rusty anyways. A bullet split open her arm but she wouldn't pull it back. She was frozen in place, shouting and crying.

"Rusty!" Xueying screamed. "Rusty, you have to-!" She didn't make it. Dan wasn't sure how many shots it took, but they had more than enough to spare.

She was finally still when they stopped shooting her.

"Clean this up!" He heard Violet yell. "I have work to do."

This wasn't supposed to happen. This was supposed to be impossible. It was so openly malicious and needless that Dan couldn't understand why. And though he knew it was useless to try and understand here, his heart attempted it anyway.

Why was this happening? Why was Rusty dead?

Why them? After making what was supposed to be the good choice, the better choice.

This wasn't the price he had wanted to pay.

Yoru grabbed his hand and yanked, hard, pulling him away from where he hid, trying to make for the exit. At least outside their attackers would lose their advantage. They'd have to come down to leave through the door. It'd be as fair a fight as they could make it.

Xueying found them, her gun already in her hand. She was crying and out of breath, but when she looked at him Dan saw anger in her eyes. Her grief could wait. It would have to.

Yoru turned to look at her just as their attackers repelled to ground level, the first of them filling her back with bullets. Like Rusty, she fell slowly. Her anger, her stubbornness kept her on her feet longer than she had any right to be.

Dan saw the light fade from her eyes before she fell. He wasn't crying, not yet. He hadn't processed any of it. He could feel grief around his heart like a vice, making every breath harder and harder to draw.

But he wasn't sad yet. It would settle eventually, and when it did he knew the tears would come. And they would be endless.

"Go, go—" Yoru, as always, urging him on. He seemed to be able to look everywhere at once. It was he who pushed Dan into places to hide, pulled him to make him run. Dan followed, wildly, loyally, anything Yoru directed. He had no time to think. He had no room for it. There was just too much of everything. He felt like he was drowning.

When the pain erupted in his leg, he screamed. It couldn't carry his weight suddenly, and he toppled into Yoru, falling on him and pulling him down. The scream was short-lived, replaced with harsh, pained breaths. Pain brought clarity, at least. He was used to pain. He could think now, he could breathe, even if it was hard. He had to get up. If nothing else, he had to get away from Yoru. The heartbreak was instant and sharp and Dan swallowed it, accepted it, leaned in to where it hurt him. Anything that would make him let go of his friend.

Yoru hadn't been hit. He could still run if Dan could get off him and let him go.

The next one hit him on the lower back, and he didn't scream then, either. It knocked the wind from him, the flare of agony resulting in nothing more than a groan. Another shot hit him in the shoulder. Yoru was firing back over him, having pulled his gun on the people who were advancing.

He ran out of bullets and plunged his hand into Dan's coat, slicking his fingers with blood when he pulled out the weapon, still firing even then.

"I've got you," he murmured, his other arm around Dan's shoulders, pulling him close. "I've—"

He ran out of bullets and threw the gun aside, looking for something, for anything he could use. It was only then that he looked down and realized that Dan, his friend, had bled out in his very arms.

I was supposed to protect you, Yoru thought. The grief was too deep for words. Too deep for tears. He pulled his friend's body close to him, burying his face against his jacket.

I promised them I would protect—

And then, there was nothing.

365

44:

"Babe...has anyone told you that you're real pretty when you're doing your thing?" Ame said, finally stepping out from behind the downed table.

Hastin was out of breath and bleeding, but didn't seem seriously hurt. When he laughed, it had the same wild feeling to it...but his smile softened when he looked at her. "That's very sweet, Ame," he said, winding the garrote wire around his hand again, looking pleased. He tucked it under his skirt where it had been before.

"Two things," Oliver said, joining them. "One, Rosa. Don't let this make you think that I didn't see what you did, because holy shit. Two, baby, are you okay?"

"I'm okay, Captain." Even now, his voice seemed more himself, like he was coming down from whatever had possessed him. He laid his hand on Oliver's arm. "I'm more than well enough to fight. We're not done yet," he reassured him. That wasn't what Oliver had been worried about, not at all... but maybe he should have been, a little. They needed Hastin, and for more than just their hearts.

The knuckles on his hand had been split open, just like his lip. Some of the broken glass that had been thrown to the floor when they commandeered the tables must have been what gave him the cut over his eye. Every once in awhile, he would reach to where it was dripping and brush it back, streaking it into his hair.

But he was smiling, and his words were soft.

"I believe you," Oliver said, managing to smile back.

Rosa joined them, and she held out her un-gloved hand for a high-five that Hastin enthusiastically indulged in. "Good job. Who's next?"

"There should be more ahead. I don't think that's everyone," Ame said, looking around. "I haven't killed nearly enough people to feel satisfied yet."

"Me neither," Rosa said easily. "So let's go."

Regrouped as they were, Oliver felt lightness in his heart again. Watching Hastin had been stressful, to say the least, but that much was done now. And, one of the most imposing targets they had been focused on was now entirely out of the way.　　　They hadn't planned for Donovan...or at least, they hadn't planned for him out loud. Oliver wouldn't have been surprised if Hastin had brought the wire for exactly that purpose.

They cleared another room, but didn't make it farther than that before they were pinned down again.

"Motherfucker. I'm out," Ame growled, tucking her gun back under her skirt.

"Me too," Hastin said.

"Should we go back and loot the dead guys?" Oliver suggested. He still had his gun, but it wasn't going to make much of a difference if they were both out. They had taken out a few of the guys on the other side of the room, but it wasn't nearly enough when they kept firing back.

"Nah." Ame pulled a knife from under her belt and grinned at the other three. "What's say we go around the back way and bring the fight to them?"

"I'll take a couple of shots to make them think you're still with me," Oliver said. Splitting up worried him, but it seemed the only way. He'd just have to convince himself that it wouldn't be for long. And, you know, that just because he couldn't see them didn't mean they were dead.

He was careful. Knowing that he held the last of their bullets made him more cautious than he otherwise might have been. And shooting felt... weird. It was oddly satisfying in a way that kind of made him nervous. If just shooting felt like that...how would hitting something feel? He didn't want to find that out, and had no shame in admitting that he was afraid of the results. There was no chance of that here, as they were too well defended. Oliver was just a decoy. He was kind of thankful for that.

Eventually, the bullets stopped coming across the gap and he heard the sounds of a struggle. That was his cue. Figuring it was as good a time as any, he ran the same way they had, and stepped behind the cover there in time to see them finishing up.

Ame might have gotten hit once or twice, she was looking a little ruffled, but the blood that was soaked into her shirt clearly wasn't hers. She had gotten blood soaked into the hair on her tail, too. Her lipstick was smudged, but it suited her, Oliver thought. It had almost looked too clean before, which wasn't very Ame at all. Out of breath, and a little rough around the edges, seemed so much more true to her style.

Hastin and Rosa looked no worse for the wear, and for that he was glad.

"We just gotta keep this up," Ame said, grinning. "We keep this up, and there's fuck all they can do to stop us."

Another lab. The lights in this one were still bright. Nauseatingly so, Oliver felt, the harsh fluorescent glare of them causing him to scrunch up his face in unhappiness. What were they doing on? Who needed that much light? He saw more of those metal tables. A long metal trough along the wall, with taps and hoses presumably used, Oliver thought, for cleaning equipment. It was the one thing he felt he could make an accurate guess at the purpose of, as the rest of it seemed so out of context to him as to be the stuff of sci-fi movies or obscure text books. It all looked sciencey, but that did so little to tell him what he was looking at.

They found a scientist. Or, rather, he found them and tried to run.

Rosa caught him. Even with the added weight she was incredibly fast, running up behind him and knocking him roughly into the wall. He fell and spent several seconds twitching on the floor before he even tried to get to his feet. He had hit the wall hard, and with a sound that had made Oliver flinch. He was surprised the guy tried to get up at all.

"You shouldn't be here," Ame said, stepping up to him. She still held her knife in her hand, and grabbed the man by the collar. She then proceeded to shake him a little, trying to rattle his brain back into working. Oliver wasn't too sure about her logic on that one. "Didn't they sound some kind of alarm? What's the deal?"

He was an older man, and was stammering, trying to answer and trying to pull himself out of Ame's hand and away from her knife. "N-no, they didn't. I heard the gunshots, but I thought—"

"Don't be silly, that's not what training sounds like," Hastin scoffed. "You were just too lost in your work. You're always doing that. That's why you're here so late."

The man jerked to look at Hastin, his eyes wide with shock. "Y-you!"

"Hi, Doctor." Hastin gave him a little wave. "It's like a dream, isn't it? You think of me and...here I am." He gave a little flourish with his hands, and it would have been cute had he not been so bloody. Really, Oliver thought, it was kind of cute anyway.

Ame looked at him. "Wait, am I not supposed to kill this guy?"

Hastin waved her off carelessly. "No, you should. It's fine." Then he looked to Oliver. "Don't look, okay?"

For a moment, Oliver thought his worry was sweet. But he did hide his eyes when Ame gutted him. That was not something he was eager to see up close. Even the sound of it made him feel a little sick.

"Let me guess...that guy was a whole bunch of mad science." Rosa nudged the body with her foot.

"Whatever he was working on, it's over now," Hastin said. "The world will be better for it."

Oliver believed him.

More concrete hallways. If there were more people waiting for them, they wouldn't be hiding here. There was no cover. It was enough to make them antsy. All of them, even Oliver, tried to look everywhere at once. Ahead of them, and behind, despite all the precaution they had taken.

One of the doors was open and Ame stuck her head inside before she could stop herself and realign with the map in her head. Better to know what it was than to walk by something useful, she thought.

It was a concrete square with no windows. It clicked, then, which room it was.

"These were your digs?" she asked, looking back at Hastin. He blinked at her, big dark eyes all confused, before he realized what she meant.

"Oh. Yes. My room," he said. "Don't go in. Remember, there's two cameras, and we're out of bullets." They hadn't grabbed guns from the men they had killed. It might have been a stupid decision. The cameras were sort of a lost cause now anyway, to be fair, but there wasn't anything in there that they needed.

That seemed to be all he had to say about it. She looked around it again, casting her eyes over the cheap mattress on the floor and the blanket that was with it, the small bathroom area, its utter lack of, well, anything.

And then she saw how thick the door was and she laughed.

"Oh, look at this. They were fuckin' terrified of you getting out, weren't they?" she said. Hastin's smile might have been a little bit proud and she laughed again. "Good. They should be scared." There was a viciousness in her voice that Oliver could appreciate.

Rosa took ahold of Oliver's arm before he could follow Ame's lead and look inside. For a moment, he resented being stopped...but it was brief. He didn't need to see it for himself. His sympathy would help no one, not right now. He needed to focus.

Any fights from then on out were hardly noticeable. They ran into a person here or there; some kind of scientist who had been taking cover, a pair of security guards that they quickly dispatched. Whatever major form of resistance Violet had against them, they had cut through. They had blown in like a bad storm, and they weren't finished yet.

"This is it," Hastin said, pointing to the door in front of them. Violet's room. And, on the other side of it, their escape. There was one more obstacle to go.

"And she's in there, right? We didn't do all this for nothing?" Oliver asked. He knew. It was almost like he could feel it. But he didn't want to trust himself to hope.

Hastin tilted his head, staring at the door. Oliver wondered for a moment if he could see through it, but his eyes didn't seem focused on that, or on anything in particular. "Oh, yes. She's there." Was all he said.

"It's time for her to pay the band," Ame said. "Open it up, let's get this done."

Hastin keyed in the code, and when the others were ready, he hit the button and the door opened for them, like all the rest. They ran in, three of them at the ready, Oliver at the back.

Violet was waiting for them.

It was not an ornate room. It was very clean, and very well-lit. None of the cheap, harsh lighting of the lab, Oliver noticed. It was much softer, more natural. It didn't hurt his eyes the way the other rooms had. Everything was simply decorated, quietly classy.

He had always liked that kind of design. Something that wasn't too overwhelming. But the sight of it was quickly and heavily soured by the woman who stood in front of them.

"Hello, Oliver," she said.

"Hi," he answered. He wished he was wittier.

"What, nothing for us?" Ame said, sounding offended. "Look, lady, we worked real hard to get in here—"

"Not half as hard as we should have," Rosa cut her off. No need for any expletives; the insult was as quiet and sharp as Rosa herself. Damn, Oliver wished he had been smart enough to say that.

"So...you're here to kill me, then," Violet said. She had been sitting behind her desk and stood up as she spoke.

"You want to tell us that you weren't going to murder us when this was all done?" Ame laughed.

"Or try and tell me that you didn't kill Xueying and her team?" Oliver said. He thought saying it would be harder, or that he might cry, but the words came easily. He didn't even really feel sad. It was just a strange, hollow feeling. Maybe that was how grief and adrenaline interacted.

But, he had to admit that for once, he didn't feel tired.

"Your friend—"

"Is innocent," Oliver cut her off. "Dan didn't do fuck all to hurt them and you know it. But if you didn't slander his name, nobody was going to fuckin' work for you, now were they?"

"He was a nobody," she said easily. "The ideal person. Had I picked one of the others, say, Xueying herself, they would have been knocking down my door in disbelief. But he was—"

"Disposable." Ame was the one who cut her off this time. "Yeah. I know your type, lady. You're a stain on the whole business. I mean, you should be pretty happy that we're just here to kill you. I know some folks who'd take this shit pretty personal."

"I dunno," Rosa said. "I'm feeling kind of personally slighted myself."

"We don't have time for this, and she's not worth it anyway" Oliver said. The words had formed before he had thought them through, and he surprised himself by how right he was. They didn't have the kind of time to stand there and talk to he, and that sudden revelation was immensely relieving.

She wasn't...anything, actually. She didn't have to be. Just another terrible person in a sea of terrible people. There was nothing special about her. She was a mundane horror in a world full of the same.

Suddenly, Violet seemed very small to him. An old woman, alone in the world, with all the power she could want and none of the sense to back it up. Someone who was needlessly malicious, like so many other people. Why? Why did it matter? Who cared?

Usually, that would be where Oliver stopped. He cared, would be the answer. And he did! He cared about a lot. Too much, even.

But he found, very acutely, that he didn't care about her at all.

Of course, all of this occurred very fast, the thoughts falling into place as though they had always been there and had always made sense.

"Let's get this cleaned up and go eat something," he said.

That was when Violet pulled a gun from under the desk. Oliver thought she'd aim for him immediately, seeing as he was the one calling the shots, but she didn't. Instead, she did the first smart thing she may have ever done and aimed the gun at Hastin.

"Move, and your little toy is dead. I made him a lot of things, but he sure as hell isn't bulletproof," she said.

A quick glance over to Hastin showed him frozen, dark-eyed and silent. Was he dissociating again, or was he waiting? It was impossible to tell.

"What are you going to do? Shoot us?" Ame asked, sounding offended.

"No." Violet shook her head. "If I shoot you, then you'll just die. I want to see you rot. I am going to make an example out of you. When the cops come, and they have already been called, they're going to drag you away.

You won't even get a trial. You'll just be lost in the system until you finally give up and die and you—" She looked back to where her gun was aimed. "You will learn to behave yourself, come hell or high water, because I have wasted too much time and too much money for you to keep pretending that you're anything more than a tool."

The emptiness that Oliver had felt, the hollowness, didn't last. Anger took its place. Oliver's hands tightened into fists, feeling the heat rise up his chest and that was when he realized something that she didn't.

Actually, he didn't think the rest of his team realized it, either.

While Violet was busy spewing some god-awful filth at his poor, dear Hastin, Oliver raised his arm and emptied what little was left in his clip. Two shots was all he had. He hit her once in the chest, once in the shoulder.

And she dropped without ever firing a bullet.

"Holy shit," Ame said, her voice deadpan. "What the fuck was that?"

Rosa rushed over to Violet, not trusting her to be down for good. She wasn't going to risk it. Oliver saw these things happen, watched as Ame jumped up and down, hollering in happiness. But, he felt strangely detached from that. He had been so worried that he'd be too satisfied, but he just felt angry.

"Captain…" Not disassociated, then. Hastin came to him, wrapping his arms around Oliver's shoulders. Oliver felt stiff and sluggish, and the warmth from Hastin's body was slow to sink into his.

And then Hastin kissed him. He was sweet and soft and tasted like copper. Oliver could feel where his lip was cut, but he could also feel where Hastin pressed his body close to his. The gun slipped from his fingers, clattering on the ground.

Killing Violet may not have been satisfying, but this was. Oliver kissed him back for everything he was worth.

"Do you feel better, Captain?" Hastin asked, breaking the kiss but not pulling away.

He was bloody and tired and beautiful, and Oliver smiled.

"Yeah," he said, and then chuckled. "Yeah, I am. How are we holding up?"

"I'm okay, too," Hastin said, kissing his cheek and pulling away from his arms.

"We're good. Just making sure this bitch doesn't raise herself from the dead or some shit." Ame scoffed. She ran her fingers through her curls, brushing them out of her face. "But you heard what she said, police are on the way."

"Let's get moving, then." Rosa nodded. "And look what she had on her desk."

Rosa held out a notebook to Oliver. He gave it a weird look as he took it from her. It didn't look like it belonged there. It was cheap and worn and seemed incredibly out of place. It made sense then, why Rosa had picked it up.

Oliver flicked open the front page, and written in neat script were four clear letters.

YORU.

Oliver pocketed the book.

"There's a shower in Syama that's calling my name," Rosa said, heading to the door. Hastin followed her and punched in the code, making the door snap open. They passed through it to the sound of Ame laughing. "You can hear it from here? I gotta get me some of that fancy technology."

"Captain—" Hastin waited on the other side of the door, holding his hand out to Oliver. Smiling, Oliver twined their fingers together. "Have you ever been to Syama?"

"Never. Have you?"

"Oh, no. But I'm excited for us to go together." He leaned his head against Oliver's shoulder. It wouldn't be long until they reached the pick up point, and the sound of sirens was far, far in the distance. Oliver smiled, and turned his head to place a kiss into Hastin's hair.

"Me too."

A.N. Mouse

Want to see more of Oliver, Ame, Rosa and Hastin?
There's still another story to tell...

Lost Names

The death of Selene Violet was a quiet affair. What should have been a lavish public ceremony was instead underpopulated and private. In a statement to the press, her only son Malise had said that Her death was very sudden, and it will take me some time to make peace with it. He asked the press to respect his needs, pleading with them for some empathy. In reality, he just wasn't sure how to hide the bullet wounds that killed her. How was he supposed to grieve a woman he barely knew? It put him in an unusual spot emotionally, but setting that conundrum aside for a moment he also had a job to do. Selene was a very powerful woman, and Malise had a lot of work to do now that she was gone.

He stayed out of the public eye and made sure that her work would resume uninterrupted. There was much to do and while he did it, he discovered that there was a lot more to her work than he had realized.

And that is how he found out about the boy.

The folder had just been marked SECURITY AUGMENTATION AND OUTREACH. It wasn't very easy to get into, but with a little patience he managed to figure out what was inside. It was an enormous file. It had medical records of every sort, training and diet regimens, completed and yet to be completed jobs. There were language and technology lesson plans. Looking at the jobs themselves, the work was staggering. Espionage, thievery, blackmail, murder. Every last second of it was intimately detailed and meticulously planned. Whatever his mother had made, it was a wild, riotous success.

Until it killed her, that was. The notes didn't say that, but it was easy enough to figure. The blueprints in front of him were not...empathetic. There was no emotional basis for the lot of it. Whatever she built, whoever she built, could not have been doing very well. The latter few pages were notes on the last assignation, unfinished. Certainly it could have been one of the other team members, but reading the notes in front of him...

Malise would not have blamed the boy if he had done it himself.

In neat, typed letters, the notes told him the boy's name. Not the project, the person. Hastin. No surname, of course, because why would he ever need it? It wasn't as though they considered him human. Or maybe he took a different name now that he was free. Malise wouldn't have blamed him

376

for that either.

But there was another job for him, if he would take it.

Malise did what he could to track him down. In the end, it turned out that what he could do was very little. Someone very professional was responsible for the ways in which they had dropped off the grid. He could always find someone else to take the work and that would clearly be easier. Yet, it seemed better to do this. Logically, it made more sense to extend the olive branch sooner rather than later, lest his mother's pet project decide that he, too, was following in her footsteps and needed to be quieted. There was very little in the file about any actual personality Hastin was supposed to have, just the traits they desired him to possess and whether or not he was making gains in them.

Maybe he wasn't the vengeful type. Maybe he was just happy for everything to be over. Of course, maybe he wasn't.

And maybe Malise felt a little bad for the kid that his mother had yanked off the street and turned into a weapon. The medical records alone were enough to turn his stomach.

Still, that pity wasn't going to save his life. Better bank on the pragmatism. That was more likely to help.

In order to gain the upper hand, he turned to something underhanded. While digging through his files, he had discovered something about the boy; he could be tracked. Now, he was going to have to be careful not to abuse this feature. If he made it too obvious in the way he contacted them, they would be suspicious. Ideally, he could use this information to get a discussion going, and then quietly shut down the tracker before anyone was ever the wiser. It was the only option he had, and for the moment he set aside his moral qualms in pursuit of his larger goal. Perhaps it was good practice. Morality was not going to make running his mother's company any easier.

A little more digging provided him some useful information. The boy he was looking for, and the team he seemed to work with, were for hire. They were looking for work. He used a third party and planted the seed of a possible job, hoping to catch their interest. When they inquired as to the work, that seemed to be a good sign. He sent an emissary of sorts, someone more versed in these things. Somehow, when someone put so much effort into hiding, it seemed unwise to just knock on their door and hope for the best.

He hoped that they were not suspicious even though he asked to meet with Hastin, specifically. It seemed only right. For all his worry, he really felt that he could not be the only one who asked for such a thing. He had read the other files, and two of them at least had their own connections, but Hastin had, arguably, been made for precisely that kind of work. He wouldn't have been surprised if most of their clientele asked to meet with him. Hopefully, it would fly under the radar. If not, he would have to be honest with them, but that was not so bad an alternative.

It was a careful, elaborate set up. He thought that maybe these things always were. He didn't exactly have a history of these kinds of dealings, but he supposed he would have to start making one. The usual conditions were in place, as were the usual ideas that they would probably be broken. Malise brought no visible backup but they were there. Just as he assumed Hastin's would be.

The meeting place was chosen by them. He let them have it. When you were trying to make amends, you did not make too many demands. They were still in Siama, where they had run after the attack. Finding them in The Ves would have been enough of a headache so of course crossing an international border only made it that much worse. They picked the back room of a bar, one noted for both it's karaoke and its shady clientele. He wasn't sure what he thought of that combination.

And, trying to put his best foot forward, Malise made sure he was on time.

What he came to discover was that Hastin was everything his dossier said he was and more.

Beautiful did not even begin to describe him. He sat across from Malise with his legs crossed, his elbows resting on the table. He looked relaxed, with long-lashed eyes flitting around the room casually. Looking for cameras or microphones or other surveillance equipment, certainly. He wouldn't find any. The room was not mic'ed. Malise, on the other hand, was.

He was also armed, despite asking Hastin to show up empty-handed. The boy didn't need a gun to kill him and they both knew that. It seemed only fair, all things considered. He wasn't sure that Hastin would have agreed, but he also didn't intend to bring it up in open conversation.

"I appreciate you meeting with me. I understand that the choice couldn't have been easy," he said.

Hastin smiled. Daydream-pretty. Docile, his record had stated. A lie, proven by his rebellion. Malise had scratched it out and wrote Careful next to it instead.

"I don't think there ever was a choice, was there?" he answered. Cotton candy in his voice. It would be too easy to believe him. And, his words were specifically picked to give Malise the false belief of having the upper hand. Already at work. Malise took a breath and tried not to let it affect him.

"Well, I appreciate the effort nonetheless," he said.

"What should I call you?" Hastin asked the question with sweet, open-eyed sincerity. Of course he knew who Malise was. He had probably known about Malise longer than Malise had known about him. It was just a question of formality. "Mister Violet doesn't seem...apt."

To his credit, he said the name without any visible distaste. It was rather impressive.

"Not for you, I'm sure," Malise said. He couldn't help but smile. Even warned as he had been, there was something irresistibly charming about the boy. What defence did he possibly have? "How about just Malise. Or, if you're feeling comfortable, Mal is fine," he answered.

He expected Hastin to merely use his first name, an indication that Malise hadn't yet won his trust. But to his surprise, Hastin smiled warmly.

"Mal, then," he said, and the emphasis in his voice twisted something in Malise's stomach. He didn't even like men, honestly, but he supposed that Hastin saw orientation as nothing more than a minor inconvenience. It certainly wasn't making him any less appealing. That was what he was designed for, of course.

"And you are...Hastin," he attempted.

"That's me," Hastin answered brightly. He brushed his bangs from his eyes, the former blue and the latter black. The rest of his hair was braided simply and hanging over his shoulder.

"I understand there was a...falling out of sorts, between your team and the last time you were employed by my company." Tactful. Bordering on incorrect. But Hastin did not reprimand or correct him.

"It was a disappointment to everyone," he said instead. Careful was right.

Malise swallowed a smile. It was not a good sign that he was enjoying this as much as he was. Still, it was about time he got to enjoy something. Downgrading the company to modest, corporate evil from the heinous things it had been doing was not easy or enjoyable. The education he had been away to receive before that also fit neither of those categories. This was...almost fun.

"I'd like to offer your team another job. My way of making amends. The company's previous owner—"

"Your mother," Hastin interjected quietly. And there it was, finally, the trace of something in his eyes, or maybe in his tone. Malise couldn't place it, but there was something.

"Yes," Malise said without hesitation. "My mother. Her company was certainly much more than it advertised itself as. I'm sure you are well aware of that."

"I am," he said amicably.

"I've been trying to…consolidate things, so to speak. I don't have her enthusiasm for picking fights. Running the company within fairly flexible moral parameters is enough. Everything else seems a little excessive."

"Like hiring mercenaries?" Hastin rested his head in his hands, looking at Malise with mild amusement. There was no way to tell for real, but Malise hoped that Hastin was having fun, too.

"I consider that to be a reasonable choice in these circumstances. I'd actually like to hire your team to help clean up the mess my mother has created. You will, of course, be paid, and you get the added emotional bonus of undoing more of her work, if that appeals to you. Meanwhile, I receive additional help with what has been a monumental task and the chance to make a better impression on both you and your associates," he explained. It was a tenuous offer at best, and the more he spoke, the more unsure he felt. He tried not to make that obvious.

"Is that important?" Hastin asked him in response.

"Considering her eventual fate, yes."

Hastin's smile widened almost imperceptibly. "You're hoping to avoid that."

"I should like to give people less reasons to want to," he answered.

"My Captain will like the idea. I think he'd be glad to get paid to do something nice, for once." Hastin sighed, but he didn't seem unhappy. Wistful, almost. Affectionate. Everything he did, everything he felt, was put on display. If Malise wasn't forewarned, he would have merely assumed that he was emotive. Of course, he knew now that he was being actively played with.

"Well, I can't guarantee that it will be nice," Malise pointed out. "But it will at least be for a good cause. Your captain… That's Oliver Muriel, correct? There was a file on him, albeit, not a very big one…"

"A file?" Hastin asked.

Malise nodded. "She had a file on all of you. And many others, but those aren't really important right now. Needless to say, she liked to keep track of people."

"May I ask another question?" Hastin leaned back from the table and got to his feet in a quiet, fluid motion. Malise watched him with unguarded interest. He moved as lightly and gracefully as smoke. Even just this, watching him walk to the other side of the table, was enchanting. Malise did not mind when he came closer.

"Of course. I am at your service," Malise offered.

"May I ask how you kept track of us, exactly? I'm personally familiar with those who manufactured our disappearance, and for you to have found us with such ease..." Hastin leaned against his side of the table and Malise looked up at him. It wasn't a bad view.

"I assure you, you are very well hidden. It was not an easy task, and all of the usual means lead to nothing. I'm afraid I had to resort to more... uncomfortable, underhanded means." He frowned.

"Oh, it's the business," Hastin said airily. "But I'd love to know what they missed, if you're able to tell me." He traced his fingers over the table, close enough that Malise could see every rise and fall of his breath. Was it perfume or cologne he wore? The scent was faint and pleasant.

Still, Malise's frown deepened faintly. He could lie. He wasn't sure if it would take, or if it would break his chance at this. He settled for the truth. "I'm afraid it was my mother's doing. You see, she implanted a tracking chip in you. It was in the medical records. It wasn't easy to get into her files, and I hesitated to use something so...invasive," he explained.

"A tracking chip," Hastin said thoughtfully. "Accessed from her computer? I guess I shouldn't be surprised..."

And then, before he even knew what was happening, Hastin slipped the gun from inside Malise's coat, whirling to slam the other man's head against the table and coming to a stop only with the weapon's muzzle pressed sharply, painfully against the side of his head.

Malise, dazed and now injured, was stuck. Pinned to the table by the gun, and the man holding it.

"Are you mic'ed?" He leaned in close, his breath on Malise's cheek. "Can they hear me?" he asked.

Malise tried to nod and was both uncomfortable and unsuccessful. "Yes!" he answered instead.

"Good. I'm going to kill you. And when I'm sure you're dead, I'm going to kill myself. No one will be able to use that tracking chip ever again. They will be impossible to find."

Then the door banged open. Not his back up, too fast for that. Malise's heart was hammering. He had considered Hastin fleeing, or even threatening him. This just seemed so sudden and direct. His head was still spinning.

"Hastin! We heard—" A female voice, cut off quickly.

"I'm...I'm okay." Hastin's voice was shaking.

"Here, gimme the gun, babe. Come on. Whatever this guy did, we'll take care of it." A man's voice. Hastin removed the gun from Malise's head and backed away slowly. Malise gingerly raised his head, and his hands to show he was not visibly armed. He moved in the smallest increments, wary that any wrong motion might end up with him thrown against the table a second time.

"Okay, Mister Violet. What's the deal?" The woman had dark purple curls and was pulling Hastin into her arms. He was quick enough to see the young man wiping at his face with his sleeve. Had he been crying? The boy buried his face against her, and Malise received no answer to that question.

The gun was now held by the other man. Oliver. Two dark, twisted horns and a cloud of black curls framed an unimpressed expression. Unlike Hastin, his clothes were simple and comfortable. Though he now held the gun, his hand was incredibly steady.

"I'm actually not sure," Malise admitted. He was still putting the pieces together. He took a moment to try and catch his breath, looking between the four of them.

"They found us because...I..." Hastin was stuttering, but he shook his head as he pulled away from the woman. Then, he took a shaking breath and composed himself. The tallest of them, presumably the woman who was Rosa Sylvia, put her hand on his shoulder to reassure him.

"Miss Violet put a tracking chip in me. I had no idea. I'm so sorry—" His breath hitched and the woman pulled him close again. Amethyst, if Malise remembered right. Her records started very suddenly in her adulthood, presumably when she took up the name.

"Shhh, honey, it's not your fault." Amethyst consoled Hastin, so quiet that Malise was unsure if he had even heard them.

"That's not cool, man," Oliver said, not having taken his eyes off of the man across the table. Calmer now, a little more clear-headed, Malise looked back to him.

"I needed to get in contact. I wanted to offer you a job, to try and make amends. I am trying to do things differently than my...my biological progenitor." He stumbled over the words.

"You're off to a hell of a start," Rosa noted. Frowning, she continued. "If she had a tracking chip, what was the deal with her being on your ass to keep in touch?" She asked Hastin.

He stepped away from Ame again, and brushed his long bangs out of his eyes with a sigh. He looked a little more composed now. "Knowing where I am is different than knowing what I was doing. I was probably never meant to know about the chip."

"I know the news is unpleasant. I can't imagine having that kept from you... There's probably even more in the files." Malise tried to explain hurriedly, while he had a chance, and the idea came to him suddenly. That was it! As he said it, he saw their interest pique as well.

"Yes, the files! I'd be glad to give them to you. Whether or not you take the job, I won't have need of them anyway. I'd be glad to get rid of them," he said quickly.

"Of course she had files on us. She was the type," Rosa noted. "I'd like to see what she dug up. At the very least, it would give us an idea of what people have been finding out about us. It would only be accurate until they were last updated, probably before she died, but still..."

"It'd be useful for us," Amethyst said. She still had her arm around Hastin's waist.

"I want Hastin's file," Oliver said. "The whole thing."

Simple as that. Malise thought that Hastin himself would have asked for it, or may have protested it going to someone else, but he did neither. He looked up from where he had gone back to Amethyst's shoulder and nodded at Oliver.

Oliver set the gun down on the table and took the seat that Hastin had previously occupied. "Okay, then, Mister Businessman. Let's talk trade."

Malise pressed his hand to the bruise that was forming on his head and nodded.

Adrian Noventa Mouse is a Canadian currently living in Milwaukee, Wisconsin, and he finds that just as hard to believe as you do. He drinks altogether too much tea and spends a lot of time petting his cat. Mouse's professional time is spent writing, editing, and networking with Words After Dark, enjoying his work with both Ace Layton and Alexa Windsor. He appreciates both of them immensely: Ace for his ability to stop Mouse from doing stupid things, and Alexa for her ability to encourage him to do those same, stupid things. One day he will learn to be less compulsive, but it probably won't be any time soon.

Made in the USA
Columbia, SC
23 February 2018